WHERE THE BA

by Sha

"The

By Rudyard Kipling

They bear, in place of classic names,
Letters and numbers on their skin.
They play their grisly blindfold games
In little boxes made of tin.
Sometimes they stalk the Zeppelin,
Sometimes they learn where mines are laid,
Or where the Baltic ice is thin.
That is the custom of "The Trade."

To Tony,

Thank you for your support.

Shaun.

Dedicated to Moira Eileen Lewis, 1936 – 2019

GAZETTEER

I have tended to use the names of places that were commonly in use at the time of my story. Since then, the countries of Finland, Estonia, Latvia and Lithuania have become independent of Russia. Moreover, following the Russian Revolutions, several of the street names have changed, too. For the purposes of clarification, the following list gives the modern names for some of the places named in my novel.

Old name	*Current name*
Catherine Canal	Griboyedov Canal
Dago	Hiiumaa
Danzig	Gdansk
Hango	Hanko
Helsingfors	Helsinski
Irben Strait	Irbe Strait
Lake Bieloe	Lake Beloye
Libau	Lipaja
Memel	Klaipeda
Moon Sound	Muhu Vain
Nicholaevsky Bridge	Annunciation Bridge
Nicholaevsky Station	Moskovsky Station
Osel	Saaremaa
Petrograd	St Petersburg
Pernau	Parnu
Reval	Tallinn
Rogekul	Rohukula
Tsarsko Selo	Pushkin
Vaist Bay	Vaiste Laht

CHAPTER ONE
January 1916

Commander Richard Miller, VC, the newly appointed Commanding Officer of HMS *E19*, was beside himself with rage as he watched the dockyard foreman and his men down tools, walk away down the jetty and leave the work on the submarine unfinished. For the past three weeks, the submarine had been temporarily berthed away from her depot ship, just visible across the water. The loud noises of hammering and machinery of the Elswick shipyard enveloped him and the shorter officer standing next to him, much as the fog creeping up the Tyne threated to do. However, that was not the reason his second-in-command, *E19*'s first lieutenant, Lieutenant 'Dai' Evans, stood nervously in silence. Evans had only known the new CO for two weeks, but he had soon learned when it was best to leave him to his own thoughts. Already Miller had proved capable of a quick temper when frustrated, as well as being a hard task master, and the ship's company had already christened him 'Menty' as an abbreviated form of 'Demented'.

The sailors knew that 'Menty' had sealed orders for a secret mission… and it wasn't for the Mediterranean where they knew the CO had operated his previous submarine, *E9*, with distinction to earn him the VC and instant promotion for his patrols in the Dardanelles and the Sea of Marmara. It was not usual for the Royal Navy to appoint such a high-ranking officer in command of an *E*-class submarine, so that meant he was taking command of a squadron somewhere in company with their sister submarine, HMS *E13*, at this moment berthed nearby alongside the depot ship, HMS *Maidstone*. Like the sailors, Evans deduced they must be headed for the Baltic.

A year earlier, other *E*-boats had been despatched to the Baltic in support of the Russian Navy with orders to stop Germany's imports by sea of iron ore from Sweden. Evans did not relish the prospect of such a deployment. Just to enter the Baltic, the submarines would first have to pass through the shallow and narrow waters of the Skagerrak and Kattegat between Scandinavia and Denmark. These represented not just a massive navigational challenge to a submerged submarine, but were the home waters of the Imperial German Navy and heavily patrolled. Even if the submarines made it to Russia, the crew would then face the hardships and danger of the cold and ice. Evans shivered at the thought of it.

'You think, perhaps, I was too hard on the dockyard mateys, First Lieutenant?'

'I think, sir, that it might have been prudent not to have mentioned the fact your wife owned and ran a shipyard. The increasing role of women in the workplace is a bit of an issue round here.'

'Quite, but there's a war on and needs must. Hello, what's this then?' A small, tabby kitten had appeared from behind some oil drums, but cautiously, was not venturing closer than a few yards from the two officers.

'It's a stray that seems to have adopted us or been adopted by the men. I'm not sure which, sir. Either way, some of the men have taken to leaving it some food and have become attached to the little thing.'

'It seems very timid. Does it let the men approach it?'

'Only after it's eaten, sir. It always shows its gratitude and then disappears off again. I think the ship's company would like to adopt it as a mascot, sir, but, naturally, that's your decision.'

'Quite right.'

Evans noted that the CO seemed a little distracted, so he left him to his thoughts again. Whilst Evans's attention was on the kitten, Miller was staring intently at *E13*, alongside the depot ship. Suddenly, he roused himself and turned back to his first lieutenant.

'Very good, Number One. Kindly inform the CERA and Coxswain I wish to see them in my cabin on board the depot ship in thirty minutes. I require you at this meeting, too, First Lieutenant.'

Evans saluted his superior and watched him head over to *Maidstone*. He's a cold fish, he thought. Evans wore the gold, double-intertwined stripes of the Royal Naval Reserve on his uniform sleeves. Prior to the war, he had been a merchant navy officer and had entered the submarine service as a navigating officer. A friend of his, or *oppo* in naval parlance, 'Paddy' O'Connell, was still serving in Miller's former submarine, HMS *E9*. Paddy had warned him by letter that Miller was a devout Catholic and not a loveable character, but that his former ship's company had worshipped him. Clearly, they had seen something yet to be revealed to the ship's company of *E19*, Evans thought. So far, his impression of the new CO was that he was a martinet. He could not help but think that Miller had brought the current breakdown in dockyard relations on himself.

Before Christmas, the previous CO had taken the submarine out to a buoy to 'swing the compasses'. Although the *E*-boats were fitted with gyro compasses, they still relied on magnetic compasses as a back-up. It was navy practice to check the magnetic deviation by manoeuvring ships and submarines around a buoy to record and compensate for magnetic variations on different headings. During this evolution, the starboard electric motor had burnt out. Although Vickers, the Barrow builder of the submarine, had sent out a new armature promptly, over the previous two weeks the Tyneside shipyard workers had worked at their own pace to fit it. This had infuriated the new CO, under Admiralty orders to sail in company with *E13* within three weeks. Unfortunately, in Evans's opinion, Miller had chosen to tackle the dockyard foreman about the lack of progress. The foreman, the electricians' union's shop steward and a Clydebanker known as 'Lenny the Red' for his Marxist views, had regarded Miller's intervention as unwarranted interference and not been afraid to voice his opinion.

'If ye dinnae mind me askin', sah, what the fook do ye ken aboot it?'

Evans had witnessed Miller wince at the foul language. The CO had already made it clear to the ship's company that he did not approve of swearing and blasphemy. It was just another facet of Miller's character that didn't endear him to the ship's company.

'Enough to know that you've been on this job now for two weeks and I have to be at sea within the week. There is a war on, after all,' Miller had implored.

'Aye, well it's not my fookin' war.'

'Of course, it's your war.' Miller had clearly been bemused by the reply.

'Nay, it's you *Sassenachs's* war. My war's that of the proletariat against the fookin' roolin' class. Besides, pal. I say this is a three-week job and there's none'll persuade me differently.' Thinking he had had the final word on the subject, Lenny had then resumed his work, but Miller had not been satisfied.

'You could have had this job done inside a week.'

Lenny stopped working again and wiped his forehead with his bright-red scarf. 'Oh, really? And what makes you such a fookin' expert on the subject, pal?'

'My wife is the expert. She runs a shipyard that builds these submarines, so she knows about the subject.'

'A wench runnin' a shipyard? Haud on a wee minute. That's no' the yard in Liverpool by chance?'

'Well, Birkenhead actually.'

'Aye, I've heard o' it. The yard that's takin' on women to take over men's jobs when they should rightly be at hame with the bairns. Well, that fookin' does it. Lads pack up yer tools. We're outta here.'

'But where are you going?' Miller had seemed stunned by the action.

'I dinnae ken right noo, but I'll tell ye this, pal. Ye'll no' get another member of the union workin' on this boat. So you an' yer wee wifie can fuck yersels.'

At that point, just as Lenny had made to leave the motor room, one of the Petty Officer Stokers, Hamon, a huge Irishman, had taken a firm hold of Lenny from behind. 'No, Jock. You're goin' nowhere 'til you've apologised to the Captain. Un'erstond?' Another stoker picked up a huge wrench and began to tap it in the palm of one hand menacingly. Lenny watched him warily.

'Aye, fair enof. Mebbe I shouldna said the last bit, but it meks no difference. There'll be nae more work on this boat.'

Hamon had looked at Evans questioningly and Evans had nodded. As apologies went, it had lacked something, but Evans had worried that any physical violence might bring the whole yard out on strike. He now wondered what Miller had in mind and went back on board the submarine to seek out the Chief Engine Room Artificer, the senior engineering rating of the submarine, and the Coxswain, the submarine's senior rating.

'Senior officers, hey?' he muttered aloud. 'What would we do without them?'

*****

For the next four days, all leave was cancelled. The new CO informed his senior ratings and first lieutenant that if the dockyard would not finish the task of fitting the new armature to the starboard motor, the task must fall to the ship's company as he intended sailing on the fourth day as planned. He ordered all members of the crew, without exception, to work in twelve-hour shifts either to store ship, load torpedoes or to support the engineering department in reassembling the damaged motor. This was not universally popular. On the evening of the third day, *E19*'s ship's company was still storing ship when 'Hands to Dinner' was called in the depot ship. Leading Telegraphist Dawes was near the end of the line, on a ladder, stowing the incoming gear wherever he could find space.

'Do ye hear that, Shiner? Hands to scran, but not for us. Not for the poor fucking bastards of His Majesty's Submarine *E19.*'

Dawes was so preoccupied by what sailors call 'dripping' that he failed to see the CO enter the compartment.

'And I'll tell you what, Shiner. I'm pissed off with those fucking Cheshire Cats of *E13*… smirking whilst they go off to the pubs and we're still working. It ain't fair, I tells you. Right, pass me that next hose.' Dawes took the proffered long piece of flexible piping and sought to find a way of cramming it underneath the deckhead. He didn't hear Richard Miller's instruction to Able Seaman 'Shiner' Wright.

'Wright, I'll take over here. You nip and organise a fanny of tea for down here. The Cox'n reckons we'll be finished in half an hour and *Maidstone* will hold your dinner until then.' Meanwhile, Dawes continued his monologue.

'I mean, what's the fucking hurry? I ain't in no hurry to freeze my fucking bollocks off. In any case, it was the new CO what upset the dockyard mateys. But for 'im, I could 've been ashore last night, getting my end away with that barmaid of *The Marquis of Montagu.* Get in there, you bastard.' This last remark was addressed to the flexible hose as he forced it into its new stowage.

'Got 'im. All right, Shiner. Room for just one more, I think.' Richard passed him another hose.

'I calls it insensitive. That's the word. Insensitive. The CO's not just demented, he's insensitive. Just cos he's a fucking war hero already, he seems to want to finish the war on his own. Fuck me! I don't think I'm going to be able to fit this one in here. What you reckon, Shiner?'

'I'm probably everything you say I am, Dawes, but for goodness sake get on with stowing that hose or we'll all go hungry.' Had Richard not steadied the ladder quickly, Dawes would certainly have come down to Earth with a great crash.

*****

The following day, the twenty-sixth of January, Richard was satisfied his submarine was ready for sea. He had sent a signal to the Admiralty reporting this fact and, accordingly, he 'cleared lower deck' to address the whole ship's company of two other officers and twenty-eight ratings.

'Men, thanks to you and your hard work these past few days, HMS *E19* is once again ready for war. I have signalled our readiness for sea to the Admiralty and fully expect to be ordered to sail this evening in company with *E13* for a secret rendezvous. Until we are well underway, I cannot divulge our destination, but I can tell you we are being sent to a spot where we can put maximum pressure on the enemy's war effort. I appreciate that all of you have worked immensely hard to prepare for this deployment and it was made especially hard by the industrial unrest ashore.' Richard spotted a couple of the senior rates exchanging wry grins, but he continued unabashed.

'In recognition of that fact, I have given the Cox'n my permission for all hands to take it in turn to visit the depot ship's canteen this afternoon. There you will each be entitled to partake of two pints of beer at my expense.' A cheer erupted aft and through to the control room.

'Leave will expire at 17.00 and the submarine is under sailing orders. I trust that every man will be back on board by that time and in a fit state to sail as ordered.' Richard was pleased to see the men's mood lighten, but he had one last surprise for them.

'Finally, gentlemen, the Cox'n has informed me that some of you have taken a shine to a little stray on the dockside. We may be in need of some light relief where we're going, so I have given permission for the kitten to be adopted as our mascot.'

The news was met with a chorus of approval. 'There is, however, one condition.' Richard held up a hand for silence. 'I will name the cat. I expect every single member of my ship's company to pull his weight over the coming months and that applies equally to the cat. I have seen his ability to make one laugh. Given that I expect him to continue to provide light relief, I am naming him after a Roman playwright, Publius Terentius Afer.' A groan seemed to pass around the submarine, but Richard could not detect its source. Even so, he was not surprised to see the quizzical looks on the men's faces and his first lieutenant's look of disapproval.

'As many of you will no doubt already be aware, Publius Terentius Afer was a great writer of comedies.' Richard paused for effect. 'He is better known in English as 'Terence' and to that end, I think the name 'Terry' might be a suitable diminutive.'

Slowly, the ship's company cottoned on that the CO had just made a joke. After the tension of the past four days, any relief was welcome and, after a long pause, ripples of merriment passed throughout the whole ship's company. Even so, Richard decided he was a better submarine CO than comedian. He resolved it be a long while before he cracked another joke.

CHAPTER 2
February 1916

Richard Miller and the lookouts ducked beneath the flimsy canvas screen as yet another wave swamped the bridge of HMS *E19*. It was a cold night, but mercifully dry. The lack of rain did not keep the men any drier, but it did offer better visibility for the passage through the
high waves of the North Sea. The wind had shifted to blow from the north-east and that meant *E19* was heading into the waves as she carved her course for the northern Danish coastline in company with *E13*. Once the water had finished dripping from his oilskin hat and he could see again, Richard judged the wind strength to be about force six, perhaps twenty-five knots in speed, but as the boat ploughed through the waves into the wind, the speed across the bridge was nearly forty knots. He had ordered the lookouts to be relieved every hour, to keep them alert, but his own watch would last two hours.

Above, the sky was overcast, but there was a glimmer of moonlight to reflect off the white spumes of the waves as they crashed over the bows of the submarine. Despite the good visibility, Richard could see no sign of his charge, *E13*. Earlier, she had been about four miles ahead, but Richard had recently been forced to dive to avoid detection by an approaching merchant vessel. Both commanding officers were under orders to avoid neutral shipping for fear of alerting the Germans that two British submarines were *en route* to the Kattegat. The success of the British *E*-class submarines in the Baltic the year before had determined the Imperial German Navy to prevent any further submarines from entering the narrow entrance to the sea. Richard knew there would be patrols and it would be difficult for both submarines to avoid them. But neither that nor the present uncomfortable conditions were worrying him at that moment. He knew that the cold would be far worse in the Gulf of Finland, of course.

Richard's main concern was ice. The burnt-out motor and the ensuing problems with the Tyneside dockyard workers had delayed the departure of both submarines by two weeks. January was already uncomfortably late to be sending the submarines into the Baltic. Now they would be attempting to penetrate the northern parts of the Baltic just as it froze over. Even if the sea was not completely frozen over, he worried about the damage floating slabs of ice might pose to the delicate hydroplanes of the boat. If he had to dive to avoid the enemy, would his main vents open to allow the air to escape his ballast tanks and the water to enter? What if they were frozen open so that he couldn't surface again?

He shook off such fears and tried to think about something more pleasant as he scanned the horizon for signs of either *E13* or surface ships. A glow of warmth coursed through his body as he thought of his cousin and new wife, Elizabeth. There had been little time to arrange their wedding and honeymoon since his return from the Dardanelles, and he valued each precious day they had spent together. Of one thing he had no fear. There was no prospect of her pining her time away worrying for his return. Lizzy was unusual in many ways and he loved her for it. A committed suffragette, she had a fiercely independent spirit. Moreover, since her brother had left to join first the RN's Armoured Car Division and then the Royal Naval Division, she had taken over the running of the family shipyard. Richard was enormously proud that under Lizzy's stewardship, Miller's Yard in Birkenhead was now building other *E*-boats… and at a faster rate than those previously built by Vickers in Barrow. Notwithstanding the many problems ahead, just short of his thirty-third birthday, a commander in rank and soon to command the Baltic submarine flotilla, a holder of both the coveted Victoria Cross and the Distinguished Service Order, and very happily married to a woman who he not only loved dearly, but of whom he was immensely proud, Richard knew that he was an extremely lucky man.

*****

'Captain, sir.' The Navigating Officer, Sub Lieutenant Owen Gilbert, like his first lieutenant, a Royal Naval Reserve officer, shook Richard gently. 'Skaw Light's now on the starboard beam, sir.'

Richard had been taking a nap after lunch on his bunk in the wardroom. The officers' mess was actually a part of the control room that had been curtained off, but it offered the three submarine officers a modicum of privacy and comfort nobody else in the boat enjoyed. Its two bunks were the only beds on board. The ship's company had to make do with hammocks or mattresses positioned in any spare space in the submarine, including the deck plates.

Instantly awake, Richard leapt to his feet and followed Gilbert to the control room. The first lieutenant had the watch on the bridge. Richard looked through the search periscope and observed the view to starboard. He could see clearly the white octagonal tower of the White Light House and its successor, the grey tower now used to warn mariners of the long, sandy spit marking the northern tip of Jutland. To the left, he could see the red rooves of the fishing port. He and *E19* were too far offshore to be visible from the land, but Richard had ordered the submarine to be trimmed down as it entered the Skaggerak, the stretch of water between the southern coast of Norway and the northern coast of Denmark. By partially flooding the ballast tanks, only the fin of the submarine was above water, but it allowed the bridge to be used by the Officer of the Watch and lookouts where the enhanced height afforded better visibility of the surrounding sea area. Richard noted some rain clouds ahead and the absence of any shipping in the vicinity before joining Gilbert at the chart table.

'Very well, Navigator. We'll remain on the surface unless we're forced to dive again and we'll continue south on the course you've plotted through the Kattegat. What time's Nautical Twilight in The Sound this evening?'

'Er – I'm not sure, sir,' Gilbert blustered. 'Sunset's about 15.45, but I've not worked out the time of twilight, sir.'

'Very well, Gilbert. I shall want to know when I return from the bridge. I'm going to see the first lieutenant.'

'Bridge, Control Room. Captain coming to the bridge.' The helmsman passed the information up to the bridge, via the voice pipe, so that the first lieutenant didn't allow anybody to come down the conning tower to impede the captain's ascent. The tower was too narrow to allow passage in both directions at once.

Richard was annoyed. He knew the time of Nautical Twilight already and felt sure his second-in-command would, too. Knowing not just the time of sunset, but the time it would actually start to be dark was second nature to a submarine commander and should be to all navigators. It was another example of Gilbert failing to impress. Richard was worried that his former merchant navy navigating officer might not be up to the mark for the difficult and hazardous penetration of The Sound into the Baltic.

*****

Gilbert thought these twelve, interminable hours must be the longest he had ever experienced. Never before had he spent such a lengthy period in a submarine sitting on the bottom of the sea. After entering the Kattegat the day before, the CO and first lieutenant had come across many more merchant vessels than they had anticipated. Forced to dive to avoid detection, the submarine's progress on its battery-powered motors had been much slower than might have been achieved on the surface using the diesels. As a result, they had not reached the entrance to The Sound in time to pass through in darkness and the skipper had bottomed the boat to await darkness this evening.

Gilbert checked his chart again. This narrow section of water, between Helsingborg and Malmo on the Swedish coast, and Helsingor and Copenhagen on the Danish coast, was the most challenging of the approaches to the Baltic. It was only two and a half miles wide at its narrowest point, with a surface current running between the gap of over three knots. However, that wasn't the major navigational challenge. At its deepest, the channel was about 120 feet deep, enough for the submarine to pass through dived to avoid the prying eyes of neutral shipping or the more hostile forces of the German Navy. But much of the channel was shallower than that, shelving to twenty-three feet. At that depth, even with the best trim, a dived submarine risked showing its periscope standards, the sections of the periscopes that cannot be retracted inside the submarine, or leaving barely three feet beneath the keel.

It was the silence that Gilbert found more difficult to endure than the boredom. He did at least have his charts to correct as a form of occupation. With all the machinery stopped, the only sounds were man-made. Initially, some of the men had borrowed the wardroom gramophone to play a few records, but interest had soon palled after the limited selection of records had been played several times. Any conversation was carried out in a murmur or whisper, but even that was limited. The ominous silence was only interrupted occasionally by the swishing of the propeller of a large merchantman passing by above. The silence reminded Gilbert unsettlingly of a grave and that brought to mind thoughts that he could now be lying in his tomb.

Like every man on board, Gilbert had volunteered for service in submarines. The flotilla had been pleased to receive him for his navigational skills, gained from twelve years at sea as a cadet and then second mate of a shipping line plying between Southampton and Capetown. His motivation in volunteering had been to be somebody different. The idea of the 'silent service' had appealed to him and it had marked him out from his peers, but now the realities of submarine life were beginning to pall. In the Merchant Navy he had been used to order. Things were done *properly* in a merchant ship, even if the discipline was less rigid than that of the Royal Navy. As far as he could judge, submariners seemed to relish chaos.

Moreover, he could not understand how they could live in such conditions. His uncle's pigs fared better. What passed for air stank of diesel, oil, sweat, body odour and expelled stomach gases. It could only be replenished on the surface when the boat's diesel engines sucked it through the conning tower hatch. Now that the boat had been dived for so long, it was fetid. With each breath of the thirty-one men trapped inside the steel hull the concentration of carbon dioxide increased and as well as having a splitting headache, Gilbert could feel his breathing becoming shallower. Worse, the build-up of carbon dioxide and reduction in the oxygen levels had caused some of the men to be sick in the buckets provided for the purpose. These buckets would not be emptied until after surfacing. As if that was not bad enough, somebody had accidentally kicked over that in the control room and the acidic smell was beginning to cause Gilbert to wish to vomit, too.

He shook his head to try to clear it so that he could concentrate on updating his chart folio to reflect the latest variations in magnetic deviation, tidal streams and the rising of the moon and sun. It was not something he had ever thought to do previously, but this martinet of a CO seemed obsessed by such details and was riding him hard. Gilbert didn't like Miller. There was something of the zealot in him. It wasn't just that he spent much of his time studying the Bible or never drank alcohol. Gilbert had come across several Bible-crunching masters in his time, but few teetotallers in submarines. As a non-smoker, Gilbert didn't mind the unusual ban on smoking inside the submarine either. It not only made the air even worse than normal, but the CO had a point that lighted cigarettes and the hydrogen gas leaking from the battery cells were a potentially explosive combination. It was his obsession with the minutiae of everything that irked Gilbert and Miller expected all his officers and senior rates to be equally zealous. As an example, he had ordered silhouettes of every German, Russian, Danish and Swedish warship they might by even the slightest chance encounter in the Baltic to be posted around the control room with the heights of their masts listed. The task had taken Gilbert hours to complete, as if he didn't already have enough to do.

'Navigator, have you the times of twilight handy for tomorrow?' Gilbert had not noticed the captain's approach and he jumped in surprise, banging his head on an overhead pipe. 'Sorry, I didn't mean to startle you,' Richard added.

'Yes, sir. Astronomical Twilight is at 04.52,' Gilbert replied, referring to the notes in his notebook. 'Nautical Twilight is at 05.35, Civil Twilight at 06.19 and sunrise at 07.00. All times GMT, sir.' Gilbert was pleased not to be caught out this time. The data related to the time the sun rose beyond eighteen degrees below the horizon and offered the CO the information that *E19* might be silhouetted against the horizon to the east anytime from 90 minutes before sunrise.

'Thank you, Gilbert. The sun should have set by now, so if we surface in an hour, that will give us about twelve hours to cover the seventy-odd miles. Let's hope that's enough. I don't fancy going through the Flint Channel dived.'

*****

The weather on the surface was unusually calm. Ideally, there was no moon either. As a result, *E19* made good progress through The Sound. To port, the lights of neutral Sweden burned brightly. Similarly, ahead and to starboard, the city of Copenhagen was equally well illuminated, but in addition, powerful searchlights were continually sweeping back and forth over the channel. Their attention seemed to be focused on the island of Saltholm, off which the anchor lights of a number of ships were plainly visible. Richard ordered the submarine to be trimmed down as he feared the searchlights would illuminate the dark outline of *E19*'s casing. He, also, reduced speed to six knots to reduce the wash and an engine to be shut down to lessen the noise levels. With him on the bridge were Gilbert and the lookouts whilst Evans manned the trim board down below.

A few minutes later, Gilbert advised him that it was time to alter course to starboard to begin the entry into the northern end of the Flint Channel. The city of Malmo was plainly visible to port, blotting out the approaching dawn. Without any warning, just as the submarine settled on her new course, a star shell burst in the dark sky on the starboard beam, rendering the submarine naked in its bright light. Richard's hand hovered over the klaxon, ready to order the submarine to dive in emergency, but he hesitated due to the shallow depth below. The bright illumination of the star shell had ruined his night-sight, but he could see enough to cause feelings of horror and relief to pass through him simultaneously. Clearly stranded off the island of Saltholm, like a great beached whale, the shape of another *E*-boat was plainly visible. It could only be *E13* and to augment Richard's alarm, she was surrounded not just by Danish patrol vessels, but a German destroyer, too.

'Clear the bridge,' he ordered. 'I'm going to dive the submarine.'

'But, sir?' Gilbert responded. 'The water's less than forty feet deep here.'

'I know that, Navigator, but don't argue. We're sitting ducks in this light,' Richard replied tersely. He shaded his eyes from the bright light in the sky and opened the cover from the voice pipe to the control room. 'First Lieutenant, Captain,' he called. 'I'm not going to use the klaxon, but as soon as I order you to dive the submarine, I want you to take her down gently to periscope depth. Don't use too much angle or we'll hit the bottom.'

'Aye, sir. Take her down *gently* to PD and avoid too much of an angle. Ready and waiting, sir.'

The light of the star shell fizzled out and Richard, by now alone on the bridge, cast one last circular look around him as he wondered what could have happened to *E13*. With his night-sight slowly returning, something caught his eye off the starboard bow. He stopped and allowed his eyes to focus on the smudge that broke up the horizon.

‘By George!’ he shouted before reaching over to the voice pipe. ‘First Lieutenant, Captain. Take her down… and quickly.’ Drifting fewer than 200 yards off the starboard bow was a German destroyer not burning any navigation lights.

CHAPTER 3

Premierløjtnant Svend Hansen, Commanding Officer of the Danish torpedo boat *Søulven*, had been astonished to discover a foreign submarine grounded on a sandbar 400 yards off the south coast of the island of Saltholm. It wasn't just that she was lying on Danish territory that surprised him, it was that a submarine should attempt to pass through the confined waters of The Sound in the first place. As the submarine's predicament proved, these were tricky waters for navigation.

Hansen manoeuvred his command into a position between two other Danish vessels attending the plight of the Royal Navy's ship's company. He was aware that the submarine had been discovered aground at 05.00 and, in accordance with international law, her captain advised that he had twenty-four hours to re-float his submarine or else he and his ship's company would be interned until the end of the war with Germany. Unlike many of his fellow Danish officers, Hansen hoped the captain would be able to float off his submarine at the next high tide.

Although Hansen still smarted from the memory of Nelson's success in bombarding Copenhagen over a hundred years earlier, his sense of fair play bridled at the way Denmark's declared neutrality in the war between Britain and Germany was actually biased in Germany's favour. Denmark had caved in to German demands that it mined its territorial waters to deny access to them by the Royal Navy and Germany was now openly calling the shots too much in Danish politics. Of course, he understood the difficulties for his country's politicians. Germany was too powerful a neighbour to upset and in Schleswig-Holstein there still lived a large enclave of citizens of Danish ethnicity. Moreover, at the beginning of the war, there had been a fear that the Royal Navy might mount an invasion of Danish territory to attack Germany's northern flank, but such doubts had passed since the fiasco of the Dardanelles adventure and the demise of Churchill and Fisher. To Hansen, neutrality was a sensible policy for Denmark, but it had to be enforced even-handedly. The sudden arrival on scene of a German destroyer was, thus, of huge concern to him.

Hansen's orders were to remain passive. He was to observe proceedings and, if the British submarine failed to leave Danish waters by 05.00 the next day, he and his fellow Danes were to assist the British sailors off the submarine and to escort them ashore for internment. It was now just after 09.00 local time, 08.00 GMT, and he watched the activities of the submarine's sailors jettisoning equipment and stores over the side to lighten the boat. One of the officers was returning by boat from a meeting with the senior Danish officer on board the Danish destroyer on *Søulven*'s port bow. With a cry, Hansen's attention was drawn by a lookout to something further to the south. A German destroyer and a torpedo boat were approaching at high speed, their battle ensigns taut at the mast heads. Hansen immediately gave orders for his own torpedo boat to weigh anchor.

He glanced across at the Danish destroyer for any signals from his senior officer, but the only activity on board was connected with recovering its boat. The two Germans were now at a range of only a thousand yards and did not seem to be slowing in preparation for anchoring. Some sixth sense warned Hansen of sinister activity afoot. He urged his small fo'c's'l party to hurry in raising the anchor. Looking back to the fast-approaching destroyer, he saw it raise a flag signal from its rippling halyard and seconds later the torpedo boat launched one of its torpedoes. Events were unfolding very quickly. By now the anchor was reported clear of the waterline and Hansen ordered astern revolutions as he swung the bow to port in the direction of the oncoming German force. Still he could see no signals from the Danish destroyer, but a large number of men were now manning the sides to watch the action. On board the British submarine, men were climbing from below up on to the casing and Hansen could see much gesticulation from the captain on the bridge.

Simultaneously, the torpedo hit the sandbar and exploded with a cascade of water, but it had missed its target. With huge relief and no longer waiting for orders, Hansen set a course to pass between the two German ships and the stricken submarine. In his peripheral vision he could see another Danish torpedo boat making preparations to weigh anchor, too. Still the two Germans screamed in towards their quarry, thick black smoke billowing from their stacks, their bows slicing through the water behind huge waves either side. Now only 200 yards off *Søulven*'s bow, under the international rules of the road, they should have been altering course to starboard to give way to him, Hansen thought, but whilst the torpedo boat veered away, the destroyer stood on and he feared his small ship would be sliced in two. Almost immediately, both the approaching German destroyer and that at anchor opened fire with their eight-point-eight-centimetre guns.

It only took a few minutes before the British submarine was ablaze and Hansen could see men lying wounded on the casing, writhing in agony. Surely, the submarine's captain will fire one of his beam tubes, Hansen thought, but then he realised that the angle of the submarine, heeled on the sandbank, prevented this. The submariners began to jump overboard, some heading for the anchored Danish destroyer, others towards the island. The blaze in the submarine was spreading and had taken hold fore and aft. Hansen watched the captain climb down from the bridge to the casing and, before jumping into the water, shake his fist defiantly at the anchored destroyer, now making its own preparations to get underway.

Meanwhile, the other destroyer had avoided a collision with *Søulven* by turning to port and reducing speed. Whilst this was a relief to Hansen, it allowed the destroyer to bring all its guns to bear on its enemy. In a sickening moment, Hansen realised that the Germans were no longer firing high-explosive shells, but shrapnel to kill or maim the fleeing British sailors. The nearest destroyer had also opened up with her heavy machine guns on the unarmed men in the water who were fleeing for their lives. It was too much to bear for Hansen. He exploded in anger and ordered his men to man the small deck gun and the torpedo launchers. This wasn't war, this was murder… and in Danish waters, too, he thought. Still with the benefit of two eyes, he was unable to emulate Denmark's old foe and instead, simply chose not to look to his senior officer for orders.

With a surge of speed, he manoeuvred his vessel to a position for a short-range attack on the starboard beam of the nearby destroyer and ordered his own battle ensign to be hoisted. With a feeling of pride, he noticed that the other Danish torpedo boat had copied his actions and was now positioned off the German's port quarter. The significance of the manoeuvres was not lost on the captain of the German warship, clearly visible on his open bridge. Within seconds, the destroyer ceased firing and a further flag signal was unfurled at the yardarm. Even so, firing continued from the second destroyer for a further thirty or forty seconds. Finally, all firing stopped and the only sounds in the air were those of the wind, warship engines and the screams of the dying men on board the submarine. Whether as an act of German arrogance or a tribute to his courage, Hansen could not tell, but the German commander saluted him smartly, before ordering his destroyer to accelerate away from the scene back to Germany.

*****

E19 hit the bottom with a great thump, knocking members of the ship's company to their feet and sending some of the breakfast preparations to the deck. Richard immediately ordered the engines to be stopped.

'Sorry, sir,' Evans said sheepishly. 'You did say to get down quickly. What's the problem, sir?'

'Don't worry, Number One. I think we'll just catch our breath for a few minutes whilst I work out what to do next. There's a German destroyer up there, drifting with no lights, right in our path.'

'Do you plan on sinking her, sir?' Gilbert asked. 'She might be lying in wait for *E13* to float off.'

'What's this about *E13*, sir?' Evans interjected.

'She seems to have run aground off Saltholm and now has an audience not just of the Danes, but two German destroyers. One of them is firing star shell to keep an eye on things.' Richard turned to Gilbert.

'As for sinking the destroyer above, Navigator, I think not. I have no intention of bringing the full might of the Imperial German Navy on us before we've exited The Sound. *E13* is as good as lost, so we'll use the distraction to edge past our friend up top and clear the area whilst all the attention is all on poor Layton and his boat.'

'But, sir! Isn't that like leaving a lamb to the slaughter?' Gilbert unwisely retorted.

'Don't question my orders, Navigator,' Richard said quietly in an icy tone. 'I've warned you about that before. I have the welfare of the thirty men under my command, including yours, and I will not have my authority questioned. Do you understand me, Gilbert?'

'Perfectly, sir.' Gilbert blushed and his mouth opened and closed repeatedly like that of a fish out of water.

'Good. Then check the chart and tell me how much water we have ahead of us.' Richard met Evans's eyes and received a look of understanding. 'Number One, take in a bit of water to hold us on the bottom for a short while. When I return to PD, I hope we'll have no further company.'

Twenty minutes later, Evans manoeuvred *E19* six feet off the bottom to a depth of twenty feet. Even before reaching periscope depth, Richard was on his haunches looking through the periscope as it rose to two feet off the deck. Just two seconds later, even before Evans had announced the depth, Richard immediately ordered, 'Down. Keep twenty-four feet.'

As the periscope hissed back down its well, he rushed over to the chart table. 'Revolutions for two knots, First Lieutenant, and come to port two degrees.' Once Evans had given the necessary orders, Richard added, 'Our fat German friend's still up there, but this time he's only fifty to eighty yards off our starboard beam. I don't know what he's playing at.'

Richard's expressions of his thoughts were interrupted by a soft rumble through the boat as it struck bottom again. 'Stop engines,' he ordered. 'Come back onto your original course, Number One. Adjust revolutions to maintain steerage way.'

For the next three hours, the captain and his second-in-command continued to bump the submarine along the bottom, never daring to return to periscope depth to check their position or that of the enemy. Finally, Richard ordered the boat to be bottomed again, with the depth at a safe forty-eight feet, and for the hands to be sent to breakfast. By now it was fully light up top and Richard announced his intention to remain on the bottom until dark, when he would make his final run into the Baltic.

CHAPTER 4

'God, it's bloody freezing up here, Betty,' Gertrude 'Gerty' Woods announced to her friend on the staging below.

'Mind your language, pet, or you'll give poor Bert an 'art attack,' Betty replied, gesturing with her thumb to their 'minder' shuffling along the bottom of the submarine's dock below. Bert had been appointed to ensure that this team of women painters didn't suffer unwanted attention from the overwhelming majority of men working in Miller's Shipyard. As was his usual custom, he began hanging signs up around the staging warning other workers, *'Women – No bad language'*.

'Ee, it's as well 'es not round my place when my brother Norman's back 'ome from France. Then 'e'd 'ear some right choice language. It's, also, just as well I'm not a man or else my bollocks 'd be freezin'.

'You should mebbe have stayed in that munitions factory, then Gerty. You'd 'a bin tucked up right cosy in a warm factory now, rather than trampin' through two inches o' snow to start your work. Come on now. Go chuck us a line and I'll pass up the paint.'

'Stay in munitions! No fear. I was sick of those vile fumes and you couldn't guess what it did to my complexion, Betty. It'd make your hairs stand on end. I looked like a chink. No, I'll stick to the fresh air, even if it is brass monkeys.'

'Why aye, and the pay's not bad either, is it? I've bought a new bed for when my Wes is back home. And not on tick either. Next pay packet I'm goin' to use the overtime to buy the bairns some new clogs. Right, haul away. There's two cans tied on. I'll just light us a fag each.'

'Jim,' Gerty called up to one of the men on the bridge of the submarine. 'Betty and I are just havin' a fag. Give us a shout if you see Marjorie about.' Marjorie was the women's supervisor employed for their welfare and, as such, would have not approved of her women smoking in the vicinity of opened and flammable paint cans.

'Overtime! I'm sick of bloody overtime,' Gerty resumed her conversation with Betty. 'I had three half shifts on top of my hours last week, including Sunday. That's fifty-nine and a half hours. By the time my ma had taken her cut, I was still only left with thirteen shillin'. And out of that I 'ave to buy my own clothes. As soon as I can, I'm going to find my own place. Quick, Betty. Shift your arse up here. Gaffer's coming.'

*****

Elizabeth Miller stared out from her office overlooking the Mersey with a view of the city of Liverpool in the distance. The amber colours of the setting sun enhanced the golden hues of her long auburn hair. She was finding the discussion tedious. Every month it was the same old story from the unions. Shipbuilding was a *man*'s industry. Whilst her managers and the shop stewards argued interminably, going over the same ground, she tried to recall her lessons at her old school on Engels, Marx and political economy. Something came back to her and she decided to interrupt the discussion.

'Mister Wavertree,' she addressed the delegate from the Confederation of Shipbuilding and Engineering Unions. She knew that if she could persuade this Marxist, the shop stewards of the trades unions working in the yard might be persuaded to follow.

'I believe Karl Marx suggested the existence of a source of labour supply that could be called upon in the event of a crisis in production.'

'That's true, ma'am,' Wavertree responded cautiously. 'He called it "*the reserve army*".

'Is that not what we are discussing here?' Wavertree looked puzzled, but Elizabeth enlightened him. 'As I see it, I have two alternatives before me if I am to meet the Admiralty's quotas for the production of ships and submarines. My choice of *reserve army*. If I recall what Marx said correctly, he had in mind for his reserve army individuals who could be set to expanding sectors of production without affecting the levels of production in other sectors. I believe he had in mind migrants or the under-employed.' Elizabeth let her words hang before continuing and noted with glee the look of consternation on Wavertree's face as he began to see her point.

'I could bring in migrant labour, such as the Irish for instance… or I could bring in women.'

Some of the shop stewards burst into heated conversation indicating they would be unhappy with '*paddy labour*'. Elizabeth let them whitter on for a short while before raising a hand to silence them.

'Gentlemen, I can see that migrant labour might well present a problem for you all. Who is to say that such migrants might not become... er... long term?' Elizabeth deliberately adopted a serene and conciliatory tone. 'Now surely, women might offer a more flexible and *disposable* labour force.'

Again, a conversation ensued between the union members, but this time Wavertree cut them short.

'What do you take the meaning of *disposable* to be, ma'am?'

'Oh, I was just thinking that many of the married women on Merseyside have men away at the Front or at sea, several of them from this very yard. Were we to employ them, they would more than likely return to their homes once their men came back at the end of the war.'

'Would you be prepared to offer a guarantee on that, ma'am?'

'Not entirely, Mister Wavertree. I'm not going to turn away women who may end up widows. But in the main, I can promise you a return to "*normal practice*" when the needs of production are sated.'

Wavertree turned to his colleagues and although some muttering was going on, several of the delegates were nodding cautiously.

'And what about wages, ma'am? Women earn less than their men. How do we know you're not going to keep on the women afterwards to save on wages?'

'Because I've just given you my word that *normal practice* will be resumed. However, I am not a profiteer. I cannot see women taking on the most skilled work where the rates are the highest, but in the less skilled trades... I will donate any difference between the rates of men and women to a fund that the unions may manage for the benefit of the widows and orphans of your members.'

The shop stewards received that news very favourably and enthusiastically, but Wavertree wasn't finished yet.'

'I was coming to that. What about *dilution* of skilled work? We won't have less skilled women taking on skilled work.'

'I'm with you there, gentlemen' Elizabeth replied emphatically. 'My husband commands a submarine similar to the ones we're building and I don't want any diminution of standards in workmanship. But some dilution will be necessary to accelerate the timeframes for completion of the Admiralty orders.'

'Oh, aye?' several men murmured in unison.

'Changes in mechanisation can make some skilled work less demanding. Take riveting for example.'

'I knew it,' one of the shop stewards called out. 'My members pride themselves on their skill as riveters and now you're planning to replace them with women.'

'That is not what I was about to say,' Elizabeth retorted sharply. 'Nobody will be replaced,' she said more quietly, but still emphatically and her pale skin flushed slightly. 'We'll just get through more work if we upskilled some of the men to become bashers and holders up. We could then train women to become catchers and heaters. Catching's deft work and some of the women might be good at it. In any case, whilst we will always need riveters for the hulls, some of the work on the ships' superstructures could be done by arc welding. We're not exactly awash with men who've embraced the technology.'

'I suppose that could be feasible,' the shop steward replied.

'Thinking on it, ma'am,' the electricians' union's shop steward chipped in, 'With all this extra demand for electrics, my men are struggling to keep up with the production schedule. I reckon women with their smaller hands might be better at running the cables through the bulkheads. I'd have to have proper electricians in charge right enough.'

'There you are then, gentlemen. Women do have their uses, but provided they recognise they'll be the drudges whilst the men are their superiors.' Elizabeth's normally deep-blue eyes seemed to pale to reflect the iciness of her tone. 'But why shouldn't women learn electrics in time? After all, it doesn't require physical strength.'

'That's something on which I will remain to be convinced, ma'am, but if you stick to the promises you've made this afternoon, I think I can persuade my members to accept it.'

'What about you, Mister Wavertree? Do you think the CSEU might accept my proposition?'

'I think they might, ma'am, but any agreement would have to be *conditional.*'

'Go on, Mister Wavertree,' Elizabeth asked suspiciously.

'Any contract would have to state that the employment of women would be a *temporary relaxation of existing customs.*'

'I'm happy to shake hands on that, gentlemen,' Elizabeth's eyes sparkled like sapphires.

CHAPTER 5

An hour after sunset, Evans brought *E19* up to periscope depth whilst Richard manned the attack periscope. As soon as the tip of the periscope broke through the surface, Richard began a rapid 360-degree sweep of the horizon, what submariners called an 'all round look'. Following his initial, rapid sweep, he commenced a slower sweep, occasionally stopping on certain bearings and changing the lens on the periscope from low power to high power. After a further minute, he seemed satisfied. He raised the periscope handles, ordered the periscope to be lowered and ordered, 'Surface'.

Immediately, Evans operated the levers controlling the high-pressure air tanks that noisily blew compressed air into the main ballast tanks to expel the seawater therein. Simultaneously, Gilbert, as the surfacing officer of the watch, and two lookouts, climbed the inner ladder of the conning tower and crouched beneath the upper hatch. One of the lookouts grabbed Gilbert by the thighs as he eased off first one and then the second clip on the hatch and cracked it open. Had the lookout not done so, the high air pressure within the submarine might have caused Gilbert to be sucked out of the hatch into the lower pressure atmosphere above. One submarine officer was reputed to have been lost overboard in this way. As the men passed through the hatch, a blast of icy, but welcome, fresh air was drawn into the entire submarine by the diesel engines being cranked into life. The mighty 800-horse-power engines were greedy for air, but in return provided propulsion for the submarine on the surface and, more importantly, re-charged the thirsty batteries after another day sitting on the bottom. Almost as an afterthought, within minutes the rank and fetid air with its life-threatening concentrations of carbon dioxide was exchanged for the sweet, salt air from above.

Richard again scanned the horizon for any sign of the enemy. Now the submarine was in the Baltic, he was no longer worried by neutral vessels, but until they rounded the island of Bornholm, the men of *E19* would be only fifty miles off the Pomeranian coast of Germany. These waters were the exercise and training areas of the German High Seas Fleet. With that in mind, instead of taking the safer route to the north of Bornholm, Richard planned to have a look into the port of Danzig before heading north for his rendezvous with the Russians. Although the Royal Navy submarine flotilla had been sent to the Baltic with the primary objective of cutting off Germany's iron-ore shipments from Sweden, Richard saw no reason for a little aggression towards Germany's warships, too.

Richard's wish was granted the following morning when the sound of the klaxon was followed by the first lieutenant falling down the conning tower ladder on top of the lookouts below.

'There's a cruiser approaching quickly from right astern, sir,' he reported in response to Richard's questioning look. 'She's about 6,000 yards astern, sir.'

'Any idea which one she might be, Number One?' Richard asked, indicating the silhouettes pasted on the control room bulkhead.

Evans scanned the pictures and shook his head. 'I'm not sure, sir. It might be the *Fürst Bismarck.* It was difficult to tell from her angle on the bow, but she has two masts and three funnels.'

'Very well. We'll stay at this depth and see if she passes over us. If she hasn't spotted us, I might have a shot at her. Bring the submarine to diving stations and load the bow tubes.'

Richard's last order spread like wildfire through the tiny confines of the submarine. After several months the year before of fruitless patrols off the German coast in the North Sea, the ship's company, to a man, relished the prospect of some action. The excitement in the torpedo compartment - called the fore-ends by the ship's company - was especially marked. Each bow tube was already loaded with an eighteen-inch in diameter Whitehead torpedo, or 'mouldy' as they were nicknamed. However, to limit the ill effects of sea water on their workings the tubes were not flooded until just prior to action. The senior torpedo operator, Petty Officer Stockman, known by tradition as the TI, short for torpedo instructor, instructed his men to flood each tube from the internal water round torpedo, or WRT, tank. This action meant that once the bow caps - the sea-water-side hatches to the torpedo tubes - were opened prior to firing, the submarine would not suddenly make a nose dive from the weight of an inrush of sea water. When Stockman was satisfied that the torpedoes were ready for firing, he reported the information back to the control room.

Meanwhile, from their depth of sixty feet, Richard and his men listened to the noises of a twin-screwed ship approaching them. Privately, he doubted Evans' identification of the ship as the *Fürst*

Bismarck, a former ocean liner, and wondered if she might instead be the *Victoria Louise*, an armoured cruiser named after the Kaiser's daughter. If so, she would be armed with torpedoes and would be a more formidable opponent. In either case, she was unlikely to be fitted with the new hydrophones and, thus, incapable of detecting the submarine except on the surface.

The minutes ticked by as the noise of the ship grew louder. Condensation trickled down the bulkheads and ran along a pipe before dripping down onto Richard's back. He barely noticed the inconvenience as he concentrated on the manoeuvre he had planned. Firing at the stern of a fast-moving target would be tricky. Although the forty-knot speed of his torpedoes would outrun the disappearing ship, the longer the range at which he fired the more inaccurate they would be, the more chance there would be for their tracks to be spotted by a keen-eyed stern lookout and there would be a higher chance of the target having the time to alter course away from the direction of the tracks. However, if he showed his periscope too near the ship, there would be a higher probability of being spotted, again giving the ship's captain time to take avoiding action. It was a tricky balance, but he made up his mind.

'First Lieutenant, as soon as the ship passes overhead and I give you the nod, I want you to take the boat to PD… that is unless we hear another vessel in her wake. That should give me time to fire from a range of 500 or 600 yards. Tell the fore-ends to set zero DA.'

The torpedoes could be set at a pre-angle or 'Deflection Angle' since the submarine had to be pointing at the target's future position on firing. For salvoes of more than one torpedo, this DA put the torpedo on the required hitting track after discharge.

Within a minute, the target's propeller noise reached a crescendo. It was suspiciously as if the ship had seen the submarine on the surface and had made a bee-line for them, but Richard thought this unlikely. He already had faith Evans would have been alert enough to dive well before the boat could be spotted. The target passed a little to port and Richard could not hear any sound of another ship being masked by the wake of the cruiser. He looked across to Evans who shook his head to suggest he agreed that the stern was clear. Immediately, Richard nodded to confirm his order for the boat to return to PD and he moved over to the attack periscope.

The first lieutenant ordered the hydroplanes' operators to put ten degrees of rise on the boat and he set the engine telegraph to half ahead. Simultaneously, he began to pump out water to make the boat lighter. As the boat passed fifty feet, Richard ordered the attack periscope to be raised and turned it onto the angle on which he expected to see the cruiser's departing stern.

The coxswain called out the depth regularly, 'Forty feet… thirty-five feet… thirty feet …' Both 'planes operators had now taken off the rise of their hydroplanes to arrest the rate of ascent of the submarine and Evans had ordered 'slow ahead' in anticipation of settling on a depth of twenty-six feet. Nevertheless, the boat continued to rise whilst Richard peered through the periscope at his intended target.

'Bearing that,' he shouted.

'Red zero-seven,' the periscope assistant called back after checking the azimuth above the periscope.

'Port five. Steer zero-seven-eight. Open bow caps. First Lieutenant, you're broaching!' he shouted in reproval.

To Richard's dread, the boat was surfacing, exposing the fin and casing to any onlooker.

'I'm sorry, sir,' replied the harassed Evans. 'I can't hold her.'

Simultaneously, the helmsman reported the submarine was on the new course and the fore-ends reported both bow caps open.'

Richard knew the first lieutenant's problem, but it was too late now. Already he could see a sailor on the stern of the *Victoria Louise*, her name clearly visible on the transom, gesticulating wildly and pointing at the broached submarine.

'Fire one… Fire two,' Richard ordered. The noise of both torpedoes being fired could be heard throughout the submarine and Richard saw their tell-tale surface tracks as they bore down on the target.

'Get her down, First Lieutenant. Keep eighty feet. Take on water if you need to. All hands for'ard, now!'

The submarine ship's company was well-versed in this evolution and everyone not manning an essential position rushed forward to the fore-ends. The shift of weight from aft to forward was significant and enabled the boat to take on a steeper bow-down attitude. In Richard's last view of the cruiser, he saw one of the cruiser's after guns open fire. The sound of the shell's plop in the water just yards to starboard was clearly audible through the hull. Richard was impressed that the gun's crew had been able to fire so quickly and accurately. He knew his rapidly sinking boat was now deep enough to be safe from torpedoes, but he feared the cruiser might be carrying some of the newly-developed depth charges. Just in case, he ordered a course change to deeper water and a depth of 120 feet. As he did so, he and all the ship's company heard the sound of one explosion. The men cheered. They had just achieved their first hit and they all listened anxiously for a second explosion, but it never came.

A few minutes later, Able Seaman Drake, the hydrophone operator, reported no breaking up noises. *E19* had evidently wounded her prey, but not sunk her. Now *E19* would be the hunted.

With the boat now at 120 feet and heading quietly north, calm returned. Evans approached his CO and addressed him quietly. 'Sir, I really am very sorry about that return to PD. It was unforgiveable and I don't understand it, sir. It's never happened to me before like that.'

'Don't worry, First Lieutenant. It wasn't your fault,' Richard replied in a louder voice, audible to all in the control room. 'It's the salinity that did for you. I saw the same effect in the Dardanelles. The upper layer of the Baltic is mainly fresh water and that's less dense than the deeper sea water. It plays havoc with the trim. It's my fault for not warning you, but I forgot. All in all, that wasn't my best attack, I'm afraid, men.'

'Well, at least you hit the bloody thing. Right up the arse,' Evans retorted and several sailors chuckled in response.

*****

Richard and the lookouts were grateful to have the light, southerly wind to their backs as they headed north of the Gulf of Riga. It was ten degrees below freezing. Richard had expected it to be cold, but this was energy sapping. It was grey overhead and Richard forecast snow very soon. Already the spray from the moderate sea was freezing as it struck the submarine, forming a hazardous, shiny sheet of ice. The bridge telegraphs to the engine room had frozen some time before and could not be used. Richard was grateful that he had seen no signs of German ships since the previous day as he feared diving. It wasn't just concern over the operation of the main vents, but it was proving difficult to keep the conning tower upper hatch free of ice. Without a good seal, water would quickly cascade through it to flood the control room below. All around *E19* slabs of ice floated, some as thick as six inches. It caused Richard to rue that the port of Libau, to the south, had fallen to the Germans the previous summer. It meant that the enemy was free to operate in ice-free waters for more of the year. He silently thanked God that the submarine had not been delayed further in Tyneside, even for a few days.

'Permission for Seaman Dyer to come to the bridge, sir?' The muffled voice came through the control room voice pipe. 'Goin' to clean the periscopes, sir.' The helmsman added helpfully.

'Yes, please,' Richard answered. Keeping the periscopes clean and free from ice was another of Richard's concerns. He had authorised the release of a small quantity of the wardroom stock of gin for the purpose. The alcohol wouldn't freeze as readily as water and was good for clearing smears. He wondered if it would all be used for the purpose intended, though. He didn't like alcohol and had only once ever drunk spirits. That had been years ago, in the company of his former CO, Lieutenant Mullan, in Haslar Hospital. He had not enjoyed the experience.

'Smoke, bearing green three-zero, sir!' one of the lookouts suddenly shouted.

Richard swung his binoculars onto the bearing, but they had misted up and he could see nothing. He began cleaning the lenses with a piece of towel. That far north it was surely Russian, he hoped, but it made little difference. All Royal Navy ships had orders to sink submarines on sight unless possessing an escort. Since nobody could predict their date of arrival, the Russians would likely be just as highly energised at the sight of a submarine in their home waters. Richard had taken the precaution of flying the White Ensign from the boat's short masthead. It was currently frozen as stiff as a board, but the Germans had already operated under false colours as a *ruse de guerre*, so Richard had little faith it would make much difference.

'It's at about 8,000 yards, sir,' another lookout added. Submariners spoke in terms of yards instead of cables or miles.

'She's just coming hull-up, sir. Twin funnels. Reckons she's a Russian destroyer, sir. Oates, 'and me that scrap book o' yours.' The signalman carried a scrapbook containing photographs and silhouettes of every Russian and German warship Richard had thought they might encounter.

By now Richard could see through his binoculars and saw for himself the two funnels and the gun, mounted high before them. She did look Russian.

'She's definitely Russian, sir,' the lookout called. 'Reckons she's one of the *Burakov* destroyers.'

'I think you're right. Well done, Wren. Oates, call her up on the aldis.' Richard removed the cap from the voice pipe. 'Control room, Captain. Ask the first lieutenant to come to the control room.'

Within thirty seconds, Evans was at the voice pipe. 'First Lieutenant, there's a Russian destroyer 8,000 yards off the starboard bow. I'm hailing her, but if she responds the wrong way, I'll have to dive. I don't trust the Ruskies' recognition skills.'

'Aye, sir. Understood. I'll be ready, but Lord, I hope she recognises our signal.'

Richard immediately began making preparations to dive. 'Dyer, hurry up with cleaning those periscopes. I may have to dive very soon. The rest of you, start clearing the bridge and go below. I just want Signalman Oates on the bridge. Leave the screen. You'll never unship it.' The only shelter afforded the men on the bridge was that offered by a canvas screen. Normally, it would be stowed away on diving, except in an emergency, but it was now frozen stiff with three inches of ice.

Anxiously, Richard returned his attention to the destroyer, now 7,000 yards away and clearly visible. Half a minute later, she began to alter course to port and Richard recognised the danger. The destroyer captain was obviously preparing to open fire and then ram *E19.*

'Dyer, Oates. Get below, now!' he ordered, but just as Oates was unplugging the signal lamp, a bright light began to wink at them from the bridge of the destroyer.

'She's answering, sir,' Dyer shouted excitedly. 'She's recognised our challenge.'

The Russian signal lamp continued to flash. 'She's the *Metkiy*,' Oates explained. 'There's more, sir. "Stop immediately. You are in a mine field." Oh my God, sir!'

For once, Richard did not issue his customary reprimand for blasphemy in his presence. He bent over the voice pipe. 'Stop engines. Diving Stations, First Lieutenant. We're in the middle of a mine field!'

'Stop engines. Both engines stopped, sir. Christ! Diving Stations it is, sir,' Evans replied, forgetting his captain's devout religious feelings.

CHAPTER 6

The safe arrival of *E19* in Reval, the Russian base at the western end of the Gulf of Finland, now brought the Royal Naval strength up to seven *E*-boats to supplement the twelve submarines of the Russians. After the incident in The Sound, Richard was confident that no more *E*-boats would be sent into the Baltic. The Germans were too alert.

Richard and the side party stood on the casing and looked with awe at their new base port until further notice. The sky was leaden and small flakes of snow were already being blown into their eyes by the east wind. The Russian imperial town to the south reminded Richard of towns he had visited in his mother's native Switzerland. On arrival alongside, Richard had been disappointed to learn that Commander Noel Laurence, his predecessor in command of the flotilla, had already begun the journey back to Britain to take command of the first of the new *J*-class submarines and, accordingly, it was his deputy they were now awaiting.

A car drew up on the jetty and out stepped a Royal Navy lieutenant commander. As he began to cross the brow linking *E19* and the jetty, the side party piped him on board, the courtesy extended to all commanding officers of RN vessels when paying official calls. Lieutenant Commander Goodhart was the CO of *E8*.

'Welcome to Reval, sir.' Goodhart saluted his new CO. 'Francis Goodhart, *E8*. I'm afraid it's a bit brass monkeys up here.'

'I am delighted to be here… and mighty relieved, too, Goodhart. I gather we have you to thank for the reception.' Goodhart had been on the bridge of the *Metkiy* when she had met *E19*.

'I thought it best, sir. Communications between London and the Ruskies are not great at the best of times and, although we knew you were coming, we obviously didn't know when you would arrive… or, indeed, *if* you would arrive,' Goodhart added sadly. 'You won't have heard about Layton and *E13*?'

'I know something of it, but let's repair to the wardroom. It's too cold to be chatting up here.'

A few minutes later, the two officers sat in the wardroom, cradling steaming-hot mugs of tea with Evans present. Gilbert was the Officer of the Day and on the casing.

Richard resumed the conversation. 'By chance, we came through The Sound at about the same time as Layton. I saw that he had run aground. What's the news of him?'

'Not good, I'm afraid, sir. The bastard Huns opened fire on them in neutral waters, right under the very eyes of the Danes. The word is that several of the ship's company, including Layton, made it ashore and have been interned by the Danes. Fifteen are either missing or dead. The bloody Huns even used heavy machine guns on the men in water.' Goodhart's voice cracked with emotion and he paused to collect himself before continuing. 'At least the Danes are offering full military honours to the dead and arranging to return the bodies to England.'

Richard, too, was sickened by the news and silently determined that the Germans would pay for the atrocity. He knew that although there had been some ill feeling from his own ship's company towards that of *E13* in Elswick, his men would feel the same way. No doubt the news was already spreading through the boat. There was no such thing as privacy in a submarine and the curtain separating the wardroom from the control room was hardly sound-proof. Richard had spotted the odd twitch of the curtain and was certain that there were several ears straining just the other side. He thought it best to change the subject.

'My first lieutenant here nearly had heart failure when we discovered we were in a minefield. Was it laid by the Germans or the Russians?'

'Not the calmest moment of my life, I admit,' Evans added.

'It was Russian and fortunately, recently laid, so they had some certainty the mines would be in the same places they were laid. One of us has been out with the Russians every day for the last three days, watching out for you. After all the trouble you have been through to get here, being rammed or shelled would not have been the most appropriate welcome.'

'Quite,' Richard responded, 'And we're very grateful.'

'At least we knew you were coming, sir. The first chaps out were sent to Libau, but nobody told the Russians they were coming. The boats arrived to find the Russians were abandoning the base and had mined the harbour for good measure.'

'Oh dear. So, what's the set up here. Are the Russians friendly?'

'In the main they have tried to make us feel welcome, but life isn't easy here. It's terribly bureaucratic and nothing gets done without chivvying. The sailors are friendly enough, but the officers are often very sniffy. The way they treat their men! Worse than dogs.' Goodhart slammed his mug on the wardroom table and coloured slightly.

'I beg your pardon, sir, for being candid, but Commander Laurence didn't get along with the Russian Naval Staff too well. He was losing patience with them at the end, so you might need to mend a few fences to start.'

'I'd rather know the true lie of the land, thank you.' Richard signalled to Evans to top up Goodhart's mug. 'What's the command like?'

'You'll soon find out, sir, as I'll take you on a few calls. The Baltic C-in-C, Admiral Kanin, is competent enough, but not inspiring. His main preoccupation seems to be with laying mines. Commander Laurence didn't think he liked the British, but he's been happy enough for the *E*-boats to roam about looking for targets of opportunity. The submarine flotillas come under Commodore Podgursky. He's a complete waste of rations.'

'Oh dear. It looks like life will be fraught with interest.'

Evans, the dutiful host as was the custom of the position of First Lieutenant, interjected. 'May I offer you a drop of rum in your tea, sir?'

'Rum! What a treat. I'd love some,' Goodhart responded enthusiastically. 'But I'd guard your stocks if I were you. We can't get the stuff anymore. We've had to replace the daily tot with vodka out here.'

'Really?' Richard replied non-committedly, trying hard to hide his disapproval.

Whilst savouring his tea mixed with rum, Goodhart carried on his brief. 'I must warn you, sir, that vodka is a bone of contention between us and the Russians. The Ruskies like nothing better than to drink themselves silly on the stuff, but it's in short supply. Commander Laurence had to push hard for it and it's said the request had to go up all the way to the Tsar. He wasn't keen apparently, but even so, our lads receive their daily tot of vodka whereas the Russian sailors don't.'

'Another example of the ill effects of the demon alcohol, First Lieutenant.' Richard caught the quizzical look Goodhart gave Evans.

'It does have one advantage, sir,' Goodhart cut in. 'Each boat carries an English-speaking Russian liaison officer and a telegraphist to deal with communications to and from the Naval Staff. It's become the custom out here that the Russians eat and sleep with us, and enjoy the same privileges, including the vodka and prize money. It means we have the pick of the telegraphists. They're all very good, sir.'

'I see. Thank you, Goodhart. I look forward to working with you closely and would be grateful if you would teach me the ropes out here. However, I think we had better not delay my calls on the Naval Staff. I presume an interpreter will be available?'

'Indeed, sir. I've arranged that my own liaison officer will accompany us.'

*****

'No, Gerty. Not like that. You might have hurt poor Bert if he hadn't been more careful. Those rivets are red-hot and weigh a pound now. Move over and I'll show you.'

Miss Miller took the tongs and wooden bowl off her trainee and called down to Tom, the heater boy. 'Right, Tom. We'll try again. As soon as you're ready.'

Tom thrust his long tongs into the coke brazier to heat another rivet. Meanwhile, Bert, in the dock below, bawled at a couple of idlers who had been watching the training session for the two women painters.

'What you two gawpin' at? Ain't you fitters no work to be at? Get along with you.'

High above, two of Tom's male colleagues in the team of riveters gazed on laconically. One was the holder up, whose job was to place a hammer over the head of the rivet, and the other was the basher. He normally worked from inside the ship to hammer the end of the rivet flat and in this way, bind two steel plates tightly together. The trouble was that the two women painters, Betty and Gerty, were struggling to learn the deft job of the fourth member of the team, the catcher, and so the men had had little to do in the last ten minutes.

When Tom threw the rivet up to the catcher, he, or in this case she, was meant to catch it and place it into the pre-drilled hole overlapping the two sheets of steel. It was as well Miss Miller had guaranteed the team their usual rate for this morning's half-shift, Tom thought. The riveters were normally paid piece work and expected to hammer home up to 2,000 rivets in their twelve-hour shift. At this rate, they'd be bloody lucky to manage a hundred, he thought ruefully.

With the rivet now glowing red, he called up, 'Ready, ma'am.'

The mistress nodded and he flicked the tongs in an easy movement that seemed to require no energy and it sailed through the air to land in the bowl outstretched for the purpose. Within two seconds, the Managing Director had placed the rivet in the hole ready and called out, 'Carry on, boys.'

Tom smiled to see the lack of readiness of his colleagues above, but they still flattened it into place before the rivet had cooled. Tom had seen the mistress do this before, but even so he was impressed. She could turn her hand to most things in the yard and even the most misogynist of men could see she worked harder than any of them. 'The Beauty with Brains' they called her. Now she seemed determined to take the lead in training women to take on men's jobs. Some had a problem with that, notwithstanding the shop stewards' promises that the women would go back to their homes once the men came back after the war. However, there was less resentment than one might have thought. Tom had a daughter working in the yard and he thought it better she was here than in some factory. The wives of his younger colleagues in the team worked in the print shop and were glad of the extra money it brought. Miss Miller had made a point of taking on the relatives of the existing work force and, as a result, the yard had a nice, family feel about it. He just wasn't sure that this latest project to form more teams of badly-needed riveters was going to work by upskilling some of these ham-fisted women, though. However, it was Betty's turn now as the catch boy and he flicked another hot rivet in her direction.

'Bravo,' he and others called. This time, Betty caught the rivet cleanly and she swiftly transferred it to the next hole, ready for the holder up and basher to do their work. The dock rang out to their sharp blows and a round of applause.

'What ye gawpin' at yer great daft galumph?' she called down. 'Send us up another rivet. We've a ship to build.'

So, it can be done, Tom thought whilst heating the next rivet. As another of his rivets arched through the air, straight into Betty's bowl, he was dismayed to notice the mistress grab another bowl and vomit into it before rushing away.

'What's wrong with the mistress, Betty?' he called up.

'Plain as day, pet,' Betty replied chuckling. 'There's a bairn on the way, that's what.'

CHAPTER 7
April 1916

'Port ten,' Evans ordered. The submarine was on the surface, under helm from the bridge. 'Steady. Steer 262.'

E19 was now in an ice-free lead, immediately astern of the Russian ice breaker clearing a path for the two submarines through the Gulf of Finland. Richard, also on the bridge, looked astern to check that *E18* had altered course to maintain formation. Despite the spring thaw and it being late in the month, the ice remained several feet thick in parts.

'I'll be honest, sir, I'm awfully glad to be back at sea again. I think it easier waging war against the Germans than fighting Russian officialdom.'

'I'm with you there, Number One. And the Admiralty aren't much better either. I wonder if Laurence had the same issue with stores.'

The Russians did not see themselves as responsible for supporting the British submarines and all the submarines were still classed as being part of the Eighth Submarine Flotilla at Harwich. Unfortunately, the older Baltic *E*-boats were in a poor state as the earliest to arrive had now been without proper base facilities for over a year. All requests for support had to be sent to the depot ship, *Maidstone*, in Britain by post or telegram. The stores then had to be shipped to the ice-free port of Murmansk, shipped over land by sledge to the railhead. then by train to Saint Petersburg and finally, on to Reval.

'I gather Simpson is threatening to blow up a few stores depots when he returns to Britain, sir. He tells me that some of the stores have even been sent to Archangel and are sitting there until the port re-opens in the summer following the thaw. It's shameful inefficiency.'

Fortunately, small parties of men could be sent overland through neutral Norway and Sweden with much less trouble, and Engineer Lieutenant Simpson and his team had been sent to provide much needed engineering support. *E1* needed a new propeller and, just days before, *E8* had suffered a collision with a Russian submarine and needed to be docked to effect the essential repairs.

‘That man was sent to us by providence, Number One. But for him, we’d barely have two boats operational. It’s amazing what he can get done with a few judicious gifts of cigarettes and vodka. You know, he’s even persuaded the Russians to cast a new bronze propeller and nut for *E1*. I wish I could achieve the same results with the Naval Staff.’

‘Some of the other first lieutenants tell me it wasn’t this bad last year, sir,’ Evans chipped in.

‘So you think it’s my fault then do you?’ Richard could see Evans’s discomfort and quickly added, ‘I jest, Number One. I suspect it’s all down to national pride.’

‘In what way, sir?’

‘We’ve seen how inefficient the Russian boats are and it must gall that our boys have done so well. Especially when you consider how badly the war is going for them. They’ve suffered one and a half million casualties and lost one million men as prisoners of war...’

‘Streuth! That makes Gallipoli look like a picnic, sir.’

‘Indeed, Number One. But that’s not the worst of it. A nation as populous as Russian can afford such losses in men. It’s the loss of territory that will hurt most.’ Richard turned forward to watch the ice breaker ahead. Although a grey day, a scintilla of sunshine reflected off the superstructure to suggest that the weather might improve.

‘But surely, sir, Russia’s huge enough to cope with the loss of a few thousand square miles of territory. Even Napoleon couldn’t beat them and he made it all the way to the outskirts of Moscow.’

‘True, Number One, but we’re now in a post-industrial world. With the loss of the industrial regions of Poland, Russia has lost the capacity to produce more railway rolling stock, as well as large chunks of its mining and chemical industries. All essential for the successful conduct of war.’

Evans pondered this information for a while before responding. ‘I hadn’t thought about it that way before, sir. And the relatives of two and a half million men aren’t going to be too happy either.’

‘Not with rampant inflation and so many shortages, too. No. Is it any wonder there are more strikes every day and the occasional mutiny, too?’

‘When you put it that way, sir, I feel sorry for the people and more determined to do my bit to help them.’

‘You’re a good man, First Lieutenant.’

Richard meant what he had said. In their four months together, Richard had begun to like the short Welshman from Carmarthenshire. He had yet to see him in action, but he had proved competent so far and had a deft, human touch with the ship’s company that Richard envied, acutely aware that he found it difficult to be at ease with his men. He was, also, intensely loyal. Even so, Richard did not feel able to share all his concerns with his first lieutenant.

In truth, he felt relieved to have left Goodhart in charge of the flotilla’s administrative affairs whilst *E8* underwent her docking. Over the past two months, Richard had come to realise how difficult it was to command a flotilla of submarines, where every CO’s problems were his, too. Where it was down to him to organise the maintenance, storing and manning of each boat. Where it was down to him to spend interminable hours in meetings with the Russian Naval Staff, squabbling about trivia when they were not talking through their hats about grand offensive strategy that they had no means to achieve. Commanding a submarine was comparatively simple. He had been trained for it all his career and all his men knew their jobs inside out.

The convoy approached the island of Dago and the Moon Sound, leading to the Gulf of Riga and blue sky started to appear above. The ice-breaker and *E18* would now peel off for their run to Riga whilst Richard dived *E19* and continued into the Baltic to commence their patrol. He waved farewell to Halahan on the bridge of *E18* and felt a pang of guilt at the sight of the broad pennant of a Russian commodore flying from her ensign staff. Following the meeting the day before with Admiral Kanin and Commodore Podgursky, he had foisted Podgursky on Halahan for the passage to Riga. The memory of that meeting was yet another reason why he was glad to be back at sea and the sunshine cheered him.

*****

‘I have decided to change the tasking of the British submarines this year, Commander.’ Kanin waited for his words to be translated by

E19's new liaison officer before continuing. 'From now on, your priority is the destruction of German merchant shipping trading between Germany and Sweden. That is, after all, why you were sent here. Of course, you are free to attack any German warships you encounter, but be in no doubt that German commerce is your new priority.'

Kanin fixed Richard with a stare that suggested he would brook no argument. Meanwhile, Richard listened to Kanin's translated words impassively and without saying a word.

'Come, Commander. You seem unhappy with your orders. I would have thought the prospect of sinking unarmed ships appealing to you. If nothing else, think of the prize money.'

'No, sir. I am not unhappy with the orders. Merely surprised, that's all.'

'Surprised? How so? You were sent here to support my country's fight against the Germans and I have just told you how I want you to do it. Where is the surprise in that?' The vice-admiral's normally pale, Slav face flushed slightly with anger and his dark eyes bored into those of Richard.

'My surprise, sir, stems from the fact that you think this the best use of our submarines,' Richard replied calmly. 'You are no doubt aware that under international law it is not permitted to sink a merchant ship without warning. First, I must surface, order the vessel to heave to, and then send a party on board to inspect her papers and cargo. For the latter evolution I must rely on the ship sending across one of its own boats as I cannot risk sending an armed party in my inflatable. Only if I can find proof that the ship is carrying contraband may I lawfully sink an enemy ship, having first allowed the crew to escape to safety by boat. If the ship is neutral and carrying contraband, I must put a prize crew on board her and take her to a neutral port. I have no men for prize crews, no space on board to take prisoners and it all takes time. Time in which my submarine is completely defenceless. I am sure Commodore Podgursky will bear me out on this.'

Podgursky began to speak in Russian to his Commander-in-Chief, but Kanin cut him off by slamming the desk. His gimlet eyes fixed on Richard menacingly. 'Were you a Russian officer, Commander, I would have you shot for such insubordination. You British are trying my patience with your demands. You insist you have better rations for your men. Better accommodation. Access to Russian stores that are in short supply. You are like spoiled children I must indulge whilst millions of Russians spill their blood for the mother country. I have news for you, Commander. This summer, I am expecting a consignment of new submarines from Canada. Podgursky tells me they are the match of your submarines. Perhaps this winter you and your men can be sitting cosily around your hearths in your cottages or tending your gardens whilst real men fight.'

Richard was stung by the oral attack once it had been translated. The successes of the *E*-boats in sinking German warships the year before were well known. Indeed, he suspected that the reason the Germans had not pressed their offensive on Riga was a reluctance to bring their ships so far north in the way of harm from these submarines. The news of the new submarines did take him surprise, but for now he knew he had to remain calm and cause no offence to the volatile commander of the Russian Baltic Fleet. He merely acknowledged his orders, saluted the admiral and returned to his command in a rage.

*****

'Dawes, how is it that your officer is able to tell the range and speed of the ship with such certainty?' *Starshi leytenant* Aleksander Pavlyuchenko, *E19*'s Russian liaison officer asked of the boat's Leading Telegraphist. The Russian lieutenant was not a submariner, but Richard had agreed to take him on board as a favour to his father, an admiral, in the hope it might improve relations with the Russian Naval Staff. Evans was conducting a dummy attack on a passing merchantman.

'It's bloody witchcraft as far as I can tell, sir.'

Richard overheard the conversation and came over to join the two men.

'Witchcraft is putting it too strongly, Dawes. It's more like guesswork. The first lieutenant is guessing the speed by the length of the bow wave as a proportion of the length of the ship. The range is a little more scientific. We know the masthead height for most ships. There are various marks on the periscope that tell us the angle of the masthead above the horizon. Knowing that angle and the height, we can calculate the range by trigonometry. It's simple really.'

'You mean the lieutenant has worked that all out in his head? You submariners must be mathematical geniuses, captain,' Pavlyuchenko asked in wonderment.

'It might look that way, Sasha, but it all comes with experience and it isn't as accurate as it looks. Come over to the chart table and I'll show you both.'

Richard had taken a shine to the short, fair-haired Russian. Pavlyuchenko had previously served as the navigator of a destroyer and was interested in volunteering for service in Russian submarines. The ship's company liked his affability and good humour, but were beginning to tire of his never-ending questions.

Richard waited for Gilbert to plot the latest bearing and estimate of range on the plot before continuing. 'You see, Sasha, the only accurate information we have is the bearing. The rest is guesswork. But by plotting these bearings, provided the target remains on a steady course, we can interpolate its course, range and speed. We gain an idea of the course by measuring our ATB.'

'Excuse me, Captain. What is ATB?'

'Sorry, Sasha. Angle on the Bow. What angle we are on the target's bow. Again, by using mental trigonometry and having a reasonable guess at the range, we can estimate how close it will approach us. Look here. By assuming that merchantman is doing ten knots the navigator has plotted a course through the bearings. If she was going faster, she would have to be further away… like this. But we know she can't be that far off from looking at her and we know her rough course from the ATB. All the navigator has to do now is predict the next bearing when the periscope is raised again. If that matches, we have a firing solution for range, course and speed.'

'But, Captain, what if the target alters course or changes speed?' Richard could see that Pavlyuchenko was fascinated by the subject.

'We can usually pick up the noise from a change in speed, but for an alteration of course - a zig as we call it - we would have to start interpolating a possible course all over again. It makes life more difficult and can be confusing, but we can still work out a firing solution. However, you would be amazed by how few ships bother.'

'Believe me, Captain, I shall advise my father of this as soon as we return to port.'

Richard continued to observe the dummy attack. It was the third time he had given Evans the practice on *E19*'s run down the Baltic to a position between Pomerania and Sweden. He was pleased with the performance of all the attack team and especially Evans. He had a good periscope eye and would make a fine commanding officer with just a little more experience. Gilbert was shaping up well, too. Without a doubt he was competent, although inclined to take short cuts and to be quite glum at times.

Evans raised the attack periscope once more, pre-set on the angle at which he expected to see the prospective target. The bearing matched that predicted and, satisfied that the team had correctly calculated the merchant vessel's course, range and speed, Richard called off the drill.

*****

The following dawn, Gilbert called Richard to the control room. The submarine had dived just an hour earlier after a night on the surface charging her batteries and was now patrolling between the German peninsular of Sassnitz and the Danish island of Bornholm, lying in wait for Swedish iron ore traffic.

'The first lieutenant's spotted a potential target, sir. Red 120.'

'Raise Search,' Richard ordered and, as the search periscope was rising, he asked, 'What do you have, Number One?'

'Not sure, sir. It could be an armed merchantman or a transport. Either way, a legitimate target. It's a bit dark and too far away to say.'

Richard quickly swivelled onto the bearing and agreed that it was too dark to make out the target or her course.

'Down. Starboard fifteen. Group up. Half ahead. Ten down, keep sixty feet,' he ordered. 'Let's see if we can head her off to the south-west, First Lieutenant. We'll have better light soon and if she zigs to port, we might have a chance at a shot at her.'

Time passed slowly as *E19* sped towards the German coast in the hunt for her prey. However, each time the boat slowed down to return to periscope depth, the target, although better illuminated and now clearly a patrol ship, was no nearer. Everyone prayed she would turn to port, to come within range, but she seemed obdurately headed for Stettin and all Evans could do was to watch her gain the safety of the port entrance. Glumly, Evans ordered the periscope down and the boat to a depth of forty feet. There would be no attack.

Suddenly, as the boat was at a depth of thirty feet, she shuddered to a halt with the banshee sound of metal scraping against metal. Evans immediately ordered both engines to be stopped and Richard's heart sank. Unlike his officers, he recognised the signs from his days in the Dardanelles.

CHAPTER 8

'First Lieutenant, we're stuck in an anti-submarine net,' Richard announced.

'What? This far offshore, sir?'

'It would appear so. I just hope we haven't hit it too hard at the speed we were at. I have the submarine. Slow astern.'

The movement had little effect other than to cause teeth-tingling noises as the submarine's hull scraped against the steel mesh of the net. Richard tried going ahead and changes in depth, but after an hour, the boat was still stuck fast. Worse, as he tried more violent manoeuvres, the nerve-shattering sounds of small explosions were plain for the whole ship's company to hear.

'Blummy. What the 'ell's that?' Stoker Burridge asked from his corner of the control room.

'The nets are mined, Burridge,' Evans replied for the benefit of everyone in earshot. 'Which means we'll have company very shortly. And the hunter will become the hunted.'

Within minutes, Evans's prophetic words came true as the propeller sounds of an approaching warship were heard. Instinctively, the sailors looked up at the deck head anxiously.

'Very well, Number One. I think more extreme measures are now in order. Brace yourselves,' Richard cut in. 'Both engines half ahead. Stop engines. Full astern both engines. Blow Six, Seven and Eight main ballast.'

In response to the last order, the stern of the boat popped up like a cork, but the bows were still held fast, giving the boat such a steep angle several of the ship's company fell forward. Richard ordered the search periscope to be raised and immediately identified the problem. The starboard fore-plane was held fast in the net. Moreover, to his horror, they had just surfaced directly in view of the patrol ship above. The startled gun's crew immediately opened fire.

'Open Six, Seven and Eight main vents,' Richard quickly ordered. The boat settled back on an even keel at a safe depth of thirty feet.

'There's a patrol vessel up there, but thankfully, it's not a destroyer with the new depth charges.' The men around him heaved a sigh of relief, but Richard continued, 'Tell the TI I want to see him immediately.'

As soon as Stockman appeared, Richard summoned him, Evans and the Coxswain, Petty Officer Connolly, into the wardroom. The thickness of the wardroom curtain did little to prevent several ears listening in to the council of war.

'Men, I'll be straight with you. We're in a pickle. The starboard fore-plane's snagged on the wire. I can make another attempt to free us, but after that, we won't have enough compressed air to surface again, so it really is the last chance. If we wait too long before taking that chance, the Hun will have called up a warship with depth charges.' Richard's manner was decisive and suggested he was not to be interrupted.

'So, TI, I want you to rig demolition charges to scuttle the submarine. 'Swain, I want you to have the men ready to evacuate the submarine as soon as I take her to the surface. If we're still snagged, First Lieutenant, you lead the men to safety and I'll stay behind to light the fuses. Is that understood?'

'But, sir!' the three men answered in unison. 'Let me light the fuses, sir,' Evans pleaded.

'No, Dai. I caused this pickle and it's my responsibility to get us out of it. I'll brook no dissension. Just follow my orders.' As Richard ripped back the wardroom curtain, he almost bumped into Leading Telegraphist Dawes with his ear to the space where the curtain had just been.

'What do you want, Dawes?' he asked impatiently.

'Nuffink, sir. I was just showin' the Russian officer 'round, like. Just whilst it were quiet.'

Richard spotted Pavlyuchenko behind Dawes. The sombre look on the faces of the control room crew confirmed that some ear-wigging had been taking place.

'I have no doubt you heard every word just said, so start packing up the confidential books in case we have to abandon ship. I shall want them over the side when you leave. Sacha, you'd better brief your telegraphist on the drill.'

Thirty-five minutes later, the TI reported the charges as set and showed Richard the octopus-like splicing of the main fuses.

'All set, Number One?' Richard asked. Evans just nodded in return. 'Very well. If this doesn't work, we won't have time for goodbyes, so take this.' Richard handed Evans a sealed envelope containing a rapidly-scribbled note addressed to Captain (S) Eighth Submarine Flotilla. Richard caught the doubt in Evans's eye.

'Some years ago, I missed out on an early command because my captain died before he could pass on his recommendation to our Captain (S). I wouldn't want history to repeat itself.' Richard gripped Evan's right hand, shook it briskly and turned away.

'Right men,' he announced whilst Evans looked at the envelope in disbelief, 'One last push. Let's get on with it. Half ahead. Starboard thirty. Stand by to blow Five, Six, Seven and Eight main ballast tanks.'

The boat surged ahead and again the movement was accompanied by the screeching of gnashing metal. As soon as Richard detected that forward momentum was lost, he cried out, 'Port thirty, half astern. Blow Five, Six, Seven and Eight main ballast tanks.'

Once more *E19* stern section shot to the surface like a cork, but this time, with a noisy judder throughout the submarine, the bows freed themselves from the net and the whole boat burst through to the surface. Richard didn't even bother looking through the periscope. He could hear the gunfire. 'Open all main vents. Everybody aft. Take her down to sixty feet, First Lieutenant. Stern first.'

Within minutes, the submarine was at sixty feet, running slow ahead and all was calm again.

'First Lieutenant, I'll have that letter back if you don't mind. No point in tempting fate is there?' Evans still held it in his hand and handed it back.

'Certainly, sir.' He seemed in a dream. 'And thank you, sir.'

'Forget it, Number One. Now get the TI to unrig the charges. I'm sure none of us relishes the idea of sitting on a time-bomb. Navigator, give me a course to return to our patrol area.'

'Three-three-zero, sir.'

'Very good. Steer that and make your speed six knots. Once we're clear of here, we'll surface to re-charge the batteries. What was that?' Two loud explosions thudded outside the hull. Richard ignored them and let Gilbert make the change in course and speed. However, a few minutes later, two more explosions rocked the boat, closer this time.

Patently puzzled, Richard ordered the boat deeper to eighty feet. This time it was several minutes before similar explosions were heard. Something was obviously tracking them, but how? He ordered both engines to be stopped and silence throughout the boat.

'Number One, I can only think somebody's sitting up there with a hydrophone in the water, listening to us, but it doesn't make sense.'

'I agree, sir. They'd have had to be following us and we'd have heard their engine noise. It's been too quiet for that, sir.'

'It's a mystery and not one I am enjoying... I'll go to the foot of our stairs!' Richard exclaimed. Two more explosions sounded above, but not close enough to do any harm to the boat. Richard lifted his cap and mopped his brow.

'Most perplexing, but I wonder,' Richard thought aloud. 'What's the depth of water here, Navigator?'

'Twenty fathoms, sir.'

'Very well, Number One. We'll bottom her and see what transpires.'

'What do you have in mind, sir?' Evans asked.

'We might have been spotted by an airship and she's been bombing us.'

'But not once we went deep, sir? We'd have been invisible.'

'Not necessarily, Number One. Last year, in the Dardanelles, I was taken up in an aeroplane and I was surprised by how visible the Turks' underwater mines were from the air. The Baltic water's quite clear, but even so, I would be surprised if we could be seen at eighty feet. So we'll sit on the bottom for a while and hope the problem goes away.'

'Very good, sir. As soon as we're bottomed, I'd better go and check the battery cell readings. I fear they'll be quite low after all that manoeuvring to clear the net, sir.'

'Good thinking, Number One.'

*****

Gilbert now realised that he had made a mistake in volunteering for service in submarines. Yet again, he felt the claustrophobic boredom of sitting on the sea bed as people above were trying to kill him. Whilst the boat lay safely on the bottom, several propeller noises could be heard above, criss-crossing their position. Somehow, the Germans knew they were there, but like dogs at the earth of a fox, they just couldn't reach *E19* whilst she remained deep. However, time was not on the side of the ship's company of the submarine. Nobody voiced the fear, but Gilbert knew it was only a matter of such time before the Germans brought up depth charges to the scene and, in the meantime, the precious batteries were running low. *E19*'s best hope lay in slipping away in the darkness, but sunset was still some hours off.

From his position at the chart table, he looked around him in the dimness of the weakening lights. On the far side of the control room, four sailors were playing Uckers, the navy's form of Ludo. He felt like screaming with frustration that their main preoccupation seemed to be with some apparent 'timber shifting' or cheating. Did they not have the imagination to recognise the fix in which they were now placed? Evans was drawing something in his beloved, coloured pencils. Gilbert knew he only did this when under stress, so clearly, he was feeling on edge. Gilbert warmed to him for it. The captain, on the other hand, seemed completely at home with the situation, quietly reading some letters from home. Gilbert was surprised that the cold-hearted bastard had managed to attract a wife, and a real beauty from the photograph Gilbert had seen. Then again, with his tall, slim figure and dark, handsome looks, Gilbert had to admit the captain would be attractive to women. But what drove him? With a beautiful wife at home and a private income, surely, he wanted to survive the war. Yet despite his VC and the DSO, Miller seemed to want more. Perhaps he yearned to meet the God to whom he was so fervently devoted. That disturbed Gilbert. The skipper's suicidal tendencies would take them all with him.

Gilbert drank from his mug of cold water. His head was splitting from the high levels of carbon dioxide in the air and he knew he was becoming dehydrated, but he only took a few sips. He was anxious to avoid urinating into the control room bucket in front of everyone. At least he could no longer smell the rancid stench of urine. The air was too fetid for that. He saw Evans lay down his sketch book and crayons. Something was evidently troubling him. That was hardly a surprise. After some hesitation, Evans spoke to the captain.

'Sir, have you noticed that it's gone quieter up top?'

Richard looked up at the deck head and cocked his head to one side. 'Now you mention it, Number One, yes. But I doubt our friends have gone. No doubt somebody's up there dangling a hydrophone in the water.'

'I've been thinking about how the Huns found us, sir. It can't be an airship. We're too deep. I know what you said, sir, but I've looked through the periscope and it's as dark as Llanfihangel Uwch-Gwili on a Sunday night out there.'

'So what have you come up with then, after all this thought?' Gilbert observed the CO put his letter away and sit up to listen to the first lieutenant with more concentration.

'Well, I know it might be far-fetched, sir, but I wonder if we're showing something up top. Perhaps, we're spilling oil after the fracas in the net, or maybe we've dragged a fishing float with us. I venture we might have a quick peep from PD, whilst it's quiet, like. If the Hun sees us, it makes no difference. They know we're here anyway. It's just an idea, sir.'

The CO pondered the first lieutenant's suggestion for a short while before responding, 'That's not a bad thought, Number One. Let's do it. Make it so.'

Gilbert felt a sense of relief. Anything was better than sitting doing nothing and even if it meant surrendering, it might persuade the CO to surface.

Gently, Evans took the boat to PD and the CO let him man the periscope. Gilbert watched him pirouette around the control room for his rapid, first all-round look.

'Bearing that. Patrol vessel, 1,000 yards. That, 500 yards. Another patrol vessel,' he called out. He began a slower circular sweep and stopped as he pointed aft.

'There we have it. Mystery explained. Down. I've identified the problem, sir.' Evans laughed before going over to the trim board. He turned one of the handles operating the main ballast tank blowing valves. It moved slightly and he turned back to Miller.

'Bubbles, sir. Number Five ballast tank valve wasn't shut all the way, sir. We've been blowing a thin trickle of bubbles to the surface. Now might I suggest we get out of here whilst we can, sir?'

The captain smiled at the news and looked relieved, but not half as much as Gilbert felt. 'Very definitely, Number One. Well done. Slow ahead. Ten down, keep sixty feet. Steer zero-five-zero,' Miller ordered before turning to Gilbert. 'We'll run on this course until sunset, when we'll surface. Overnight, we'll make our way back to our original patrol area.'

Gilbert was only too pleased to obey his captain's orders.

CHAPTER 9

The following day, after a good night's sleep, fresh air and a hearty breakfast, even Gilbert felt better. The batteries had, also, had a good charge overnight and he was now leading a boarding party onto the German freighter, *Antilla*. There had only been a need to fire one shot across her bows. The German master had immediately stopped his vessel and allowed *E19* to manoeuvre and drift down along her weather side. The CO had decided that as it was a calm day, this would save time. He had also ordered Gilbert to scuttle the ship, but first to collect any fresh meat available and to send it across to the submarine.

Gilbert met the master on the bridge. '*Sprechen sie Englisch*?' he asked in his very imperfect German.

'*Nein. Nein,*' the master replied, but gestured to another officer instead.

'I speak some English, Lieutenant. I am Nordheim and this is Captain Weber.' The German clicked his heels together.

'I need to check your manifest, please.'

'Certainly. I have it here.'

Gilbert spent a few minutes checking the cargo manifest whilst the Germans chatted between themselves. He was relieved to see it was written in English. To his delight, the manifest revealed the ship was carrying a full load of iron ore. The skipper would be pleased. He nodded to the torpedo operator to begin the preparations for scuttling the ship and turned back to the two Germans.

'Captain, I am ordered to sink your ship. But first, I would like your ship's papers, chronometer and any fresh meat you may have,' Gilbert said peremptorily. 'In return, you have fifteen minutes to leave your ship. You may take any personal belongings you wish, but no arms. Understood?'

Nordheim interpreted the message for the master and some exchange took place between them. The master seemed agitated. Nordheim turned back to Gilbert.

'We have women. Boats not safe,' he remonstrated.

'Sorry, skipper. No dice. Look over the port quarter.' Gilbert gestured for the two officers to look over the opposite side, to an overtaking freighter. 'She's Swedish. She'll pick up your crew. Now your papers, please. We have little enough time.'

Grudgingly, the master handed over the ship's papers and his best chronometer. Meanwhile, the torpedo men set gun cotton charges in the after hold and began to open the sea cocks. Seaman Dyer, one of the boarding party, approached Gilbert.

'We found half a flitch of bacon and a side of beef, sir. We're sendin' 'em across now. We also found a load o' this, sir. Tastes not 'alf bad. Fancy some?' The seaman cut off a slice of sausage and handed it over to Gilbert.

Gilbert found it a little spicy for his taste, but had to agree it was pleasant. 'Fine. Take that, too.'

Twenty minutes later, the charges on board the *Antilla* went off with a deep rumble and, after another four minutes, there was no sign of the ship. Gilbert thought that fortunate because just as the freighter disappeared beneath the waves, one of *E19*'s lookouts spotted smoke to the north-west.

*****

As *E19* surfaced 3,000 yards off the German merchantman's bows, it was Richard's first chance to exercise the gun's crew. Barely had the boat broached the surface than the crew filed quickly out from the bottom of the fin to prepare the gun for the first shot. Thirty seconds later, the fore-hatch was opened and a chain of men, under the supervision of Gilbert, began to pass up the shells to the casing, just as the first shot was fired across the bows of the oncoming vessel, her German flag flapping in the wind from her topmost halyard. The master's immediate response was to alter course to starboard and increase speed.

'Put a hole in her hull,' Richard shouted down to the gun layer below. The two-man crew prepared another round, lined up the gun and fired again, but the shell went wide of the retreating vessel. Her name, *Antarus*, was plainly visible in white paintwork against the rusted transom.

Richard considered firing a torpedo, but decided against it as the range was beginning to open. Instead, he ordered the fore-hatch shut and the gun crew into the fin, before ordering maximum speed from the boat's diesel engines. Quickly, the boat reached her maximum speed of fifteen knots and her sharp bows cleaved through the sea, causing huge washes of white water to cascade over the fore-casing. Before long, the submarine was overhauling the *Antarus*, who was, perhaps, two or three knots slower. On the horizon, Richard could see the Danish island of Bornholm six miles off and he realised that the German master was attempting to reach neutral waters. By now he had been joined on the bridge by Evans.

'Would you like me to organise the flooding of the bow tubes, sir? She should be an easy shot.'

'I've thought about that, Number One, but it wouldn't give the crew time to take to the boats. Moreover, why waste precious mouldies on a merchantman when bricks or gun cotton should suffice?'

'So what's the plan, sir? If we don't act soon, she'll be in neutral waters.'

'I'm well aware of that, First Lieutenant. In a minute I'll slow down to eight knots. That should keep the fore-hatch clear of the bow wave. The gun's crew can then pound away at her to their hearts' content. If that doesn't work, we'll speed up and try again. Sprint and drift as it were.'

'Very well, sir. I'll brief them and the ammunition party to be ready.'

Two minutes later, Richard gave the order for the submarine to slow down and for the gun's crew to return to their station. As ordered, they pounded away at the ship, but the fire was inaccurate. The gun had undoubtedly not been rifled properly from the way the shells tumbled in the air. Richard decided there was little point wasting further ammunition.

'Check, check, check,' he ordered. 'Gun's crew to remain closed up, but cease firing until I give further orders. First Lieutenant, nip down to the control room and tell me how much water we have left on this course. We look to be only four miles off the island. You might as well ask the navigator to stand down from ammunition resupply and to take a fix.'

It took Evans a few minutes to respond. 'Sir, we've probably three miles yet on this course before we run out of water, but the German has less than that. She's deeper in the water than us. You should be aware, too, sir, that the navigator reckons we're about to enter Danish territorial waters.'

'Thank you, Number One. We'll remain on this course for now, but I'd appreciate your presence back on the bridge, please,' Richard replied down the voice pipe.

Evans had barely caught his breath after climbing back to the bridge when he observed the German freighter shudder, rise slightly out of the water and then stop as her foremast toppled over and a great wash appeared from her raised screw.

'Stop engines,' Richard ordered. The *Antarus* had run aground. 'See, First Lieutenant, we've not yet lost her. Now I'm going to park alongside her so that you and your men can board her. You'll have no trouble from the Germans. Look.'

Already, the Germans had lowered a boat and were queuing up to embark in it.

'Do you want me to scuttle her, sir?'

'Not yet, Number One, or else I'd send Gilbert. No, we're in neutral waters. I want you to organise a tow. We'll take her off by the stern into deeper and neutral waters… and then scuttle her. Make sure you grab her papers, though, if the master hasn't already taken them.'

'Judging by the speed in which he and his crew have abandoned ship, I suspect that thought was not in his mind, sir. Not unless he was looking for an instant supply of arse paper.'

*****

Lunch for the officers of *E19* that day comprised only a hastily-eaten spam sandwich on the bridge or in the control room. After an hour of frustration, Evans and his towing team had been forced to abandon the evolution. The *Antarus* was too firmly stuck on the bottom. This was a bitter blow to Richard as the hastily-abandoned ship's papers showed her to be carrying a large consignment of iron ore bound for Stettin. However, he and *E19* could not believe their luck over the remainder of the day. With his ship's company shattered after a busy day, Richard reverted to a trick he had learned in the Sea of Marmara and bottomed the submarine overnight to rest everyone.

'Gilbert, pass me the papers of the *Gertrude*, will you, please,' Richard asked. He and Evans were together in the wardroom, writing up the submarine's log and patrol report. 'Oh, yes. She was 3,000 tons. For some reason I had in mind 1,700 tons.'

'No, sir. That was the third ship, the, er… *Wilhelmina.*'

That afternoon *E19* had successfully intercepted two further German merchantmen and then, just as the light was failing, a third. All had been carrying Swedish iron ore. On all three occasions, the German masters had stopped when ordered and *E19* had sunk them through a combination of gun fire at near point-blank range, opening the sea cocks and the use of explosive.

'Capital, Number One. That just leaves the *Klaus Nikolas*. What was she, 4,400 tons?'

'Aye, sir. Four ships in a day. More than a satisfactory day's work, although a pity about the *Antarus*. She was the biggest of the lot at 9,000 tons.'

'I think we might move our hunting ground further north tomorrow, Number One. Perhaps, between Öland and Gotland.'

'Sounds good to me, sir. I think this area might be a little hot tomorrow, once that last crew make their report. A pity about the gun, though, sir.'

'Quite. I think I'll ask our Russian hosts for the loan of one of their forty-seven-millimetre guns when we return to Reval. Anyway, we've had enough excitement for the day and it's an early start tomorrow, so I propose we follow our Russian friend's example and turn in.' Richard pointed to the recumbent figure of Pavlyuchenko lying fast asleep at the base of the attack periscope.

'That man could sleep on a washing line. Diving Stations at 04.00, Number One.'

*****

Soon after breakfast the following morning, Richard was summoned to the control room in response to the sighting of a merchant ship. However, she was Swedish and heading north of Gotland, so Richard decided to leave her unmolested. The next sighting, however, looked more promising. Again, the ship was Swedish, but she was heading south, as if for Stettin. Richard dived and let the ship approach him, before surfacing on her quarter.

'Surface. Gun action.' As the fin broached the surface, Richard scrambled through the upper hatch, followed on this occasion by Pavlyuchenko as the lookout. The gun layer and his assistant rushed out onto the casing and quickly fired off a warning round. As the gun barrel was flooded with water, the first shell was only a clearing round, but it was enough to gain the attention of the Swede who immediately hove to. As had been Richard's practice in his former command, he always dived with the ensign staff rigged and the White Ensign flying. The signalman had plenty of spares to replace what soon became tattered rags underwater.

This time, there was no need to lay the submarine alongside the drifting Swede. The master had immediately ordered a boat to be lowered and then crossed in it himself. The casing party prepared a ladder for him to climb onto the casing where he was met by Evans and escorted to the bridge.

'Good morning, Captain,' the blonde and bearded Swede boomed. 'I have brought my papers and in the boat you will find freshly-baked bread. Help yourselves.' He climbed up to the bridge and shook Richard's hand warmly as he introduced himself as Sven Bjorg.

'Are you the captain that sank the iron ore ships yesterday?'

Richard was taken aback by the question. 'I'm sorry, Captain, but I cannot discuss submarine operations. But why do you ask?'

'It is a little cool to be discussing such topics in the open air, is it not, Captain?' Bjorg replied.

Richard took the hint and invited the Swedish master to the wardroom after arranging for Gilbert to relieve Evans on watch. Whilst Richard drank tea, Bjorg accepted Evans's invitation to a second glass of pink gin, before coming to the subject.

'I come as a friend, gentlemen. I rather hoped I might run into you or one of your colleagues, so came fully prepared. As you will see from my papers, I am carrying timber to England. I have nothing to fear from your submarines, but the Germans now... They fear you greatly.'

'How is that so, Captain?' Richard asked.

'Call me Sven and I shall call you what, Captain?'

'Richard… and this is Dai, my second-in-command.'

'You are not English, then Dai? I have been to Cardiff and Swansea many times.'

'No, Captain, I mean Sven, but I am still British.'

'Me, I like the Scottish best. They are so generous with their whisky.'

Richard nodded to Evans's questioning look. 'I think we could lay our hands on a bottle of Scotch somewhere in return for the bread and any information you have, Sven,' Evans responded quickly and began hunting for such a bottle.

'Yesterday, I understand a British submarine, or perhaps, many submarines, were responsible for the sinking of four German ships carrying iron ore and driving one ashore. The news is all over the telegraph this morning.'

'That's interesting, Sven, but something we already knew,' Richard stated a little guardedly.

'Yes, but my friend, Richard, what you might not know is that the Germans have ordered all further shipments of iron ore to cease with immediate effect, including our own ships.'

'I'm delighted to hear it, Sven. First Lieutenant, might you break open that bottle of Scotch you've now found? Would you like a glass, Sven?'

'Thank you, Richard. I prefer it to our own *brännwin.* So, if you are lying in wait for more ore shipments, you will have to wait a few days. The Germans intend providing armed escorts for their ships to travel in convoy, but I cannot see my countrymen agreeing to sail under the protection of German guns. It poses an interesting dilemma for our government, does it not, Richard?' Bjorg placed his glass down on the wardroom table with a bang and stood up, rather too quickly, banging his head on a locker above. Evans rushed across to his aid and sat him back on the bunk seat.

'Now my head really does hurt, gentlemen. Richard, how can tall men such as you live in so confined a space? I could fit your whole submarine in one of my holds.'

'One tends to learn from experience when to duck, Sven. Are you all right?'

'I will be fine, but if I am seen to sway on my return to my ship, I will say it is due to the bang on my head. Ha. A good ruse, what? Now I must go. Thank you for your hospitality.'

'Just one more thing, sir,' Evans asked. 'Since you're bound for England, could you take the mail for us? There's not much as we weren't expecting to have the opportunity.'

Bjorg waved away the bank notes being proffered by Evans. 'Of course, of course. But I will gladly exchange the postage for one more bottle of that excellent Scotch. Then I can drink the health of the brave British submarine crews and wish them a safe return.'

Richard and Evans escorted the Swede to the casing and safely back into his boat. He seemed to suffer no ill effects from his two gins and a whisky. As his men rowed him back to his ship, he called farewell and waved with one of the bottles of Scotch.

'Interesting news, Number One. What do you make of it?'

'It sounds like we may enjoy lean pickings for the rest of the patrol, sir.'

'Not necessarily, Number One. It gives me an idea.'

CHAPTER 10
May 1916

Richard had ordered the submarine further north and she now lay in wait, trimmed down, off the coast of Oxelösund, south of Stockholm. It was a bright, sunny morning with only a light, southerly breeze to ruffle the small waves on the slight swell. Richard felt home-sick. It was May Day and always the day for the first public display of the clog dances by his father's mill workers in preparation for the summer competitions. Before the war, it had been an event to captivate *Mutti* as nothing of the sort took place in her native Switzerland. Richard wondered if the shipyard workers had a clog dancing team. It was something he would have to ask Lizzy in his next letter home. He had been too busy to write home for a while, but would pen something on the way back from patrol shortly.

Oddly, now he was a married man, he had started to feel the loneliness of command. Some would think that stupid. How could one feel lonely in a submarine, living cheek by jowl with his two officers and twenty-eight men? But they could never be friends. He had to bear the absolute responsibility for their lives and efficiency, leaving no place for emotional attachments. The closest he had come to friendship amongst his men had been with Algernon Steele, his first lieutenant in *E9*. They had corresponded since Richard's wedding, but mail was so slow out here, he had heard nothing from him for months. It was the same of Lizzy. He yearned to hear from her again. Only with her could he open his heart, but even then, he was careful to spare her the details of the strain he felt. Why worry her? In any case, she had enough problems of her own running a shipyard in a time of war. If only he could be home, helping her to share that burden.

'Smoke, bearing green one-two-zero,' a lookout disturbed his thoughts. He swung onto the bearing and saw the thin column on the horizon for himself. He lowered his glasses and assessed the visibility. There was little haze and, with the submarine trimmed down, his height of eye was relatively low. He estimated that the horizon was at a range of ten thousand yards. If so, the ship would be, perhaps, two thousand yards further out. He decided to take no action for the moment and hoped that his plan had worked.

*****

Lieutenant Pavlyuchenko was roused from his slumbers by the sound of the klaxon and much rushing around as the submarine went to Diving Stations. He felt the movement of the submarine's steep bow-down angle and heard the relative silence as the diesel engines were shut down and the submarine became reliant on the electric power of her batteries. In quick succession, four lookouts collapsed on the deck below the conning tower and only two managed to evade before Commander Miller fell on top of the last two. Within a minute, the frantic action inside the submarine was replaced by an atmosphere of calmness, but total concentration. Pavlyuchenko made to ask his Welsh friend what was going on, but Evans shook his head and held a finger to his lips. However, as soon as the submarine settled on an even keel, the captain called him over to the periscopes where he now stood with two stop watches around his neck. The captain spoke loudly enough for all the control room crew to hear him.

'Now, Sasha, I hope you will witness your first attack on a German warship. There are three up there - a three-funnelled cruiser and two destroyers, approaching from the east. I suspect they're on their way to escort an iron ore convoy from Sweden. Let's see what we can do to deny our fat German friends an escort shall we? I suggest you stand with the navigator whilst we go about our business.'

Pavlyuchenko squeezed himself into the corner by the chart table where Gilbert was poised to draw the bearings of the three enemy ships. He felt a thrill pulsate through his body. He was about to see his first underwater action, or to be more correct, hear it as only the captain would ever see the enemy. Looking around him, he felt embarrassed that only he seemed excited by the prospect. The ship's company appeared to share their officers' nonchalance that this was all in a day's work. Even the cat seemed unfazed by it all. Pavlyuchenko made to tickle Terry's stomach, but he refused to turn over and merely raised one eyelid to offer a look of indignance at the interruption to his sleep.

'Stand by target set up,' the CO called. 'Starboard thirty. Steer one-zero-five. Periscope Depth, First Lieutenant.'

Pavlyuchenko could feel the heel of the submarine as it altered course and the deck rising slightly beneath him as the boat came shallow again. The only sounds were those of the hydroplanes and the calling of the depth and course by the coxswain, now positioned at the helm. He had heard more noise from the audience during a performance of the *Bolshoi*. How calm these men are, he thought.

A hiss came from the periscope well as the attack periscope was raised.

'Bearing that. 3,700 yards. ATB red five. Destroyer.' Richard began calling out the positions of the targets and the Periscope Assistant relayed the information to Gilbert in response.

'Red one-eight.'

'Bearing that. 4,200 yards. ATB red two-five. Heavy.'

'Red two-five.'

'Bearing that. 3,700… no, make that 3,800 yards. Another destroyer. Red seven-zero. Down.'

'Red three-five.'

Pavlyuchenko had no idea what was being said in the staccato exchange, but watched Gilbert draw three lines on the chart and, using his dividers, measure off various distances to mark the estimated position of each ship. He then applied a course to each of them. Evans moved from the trim board to the chart table and waited for Gilbert to finish his work before explaining its meaning to the bemused Russian. Evans spoke quietly.

'That, Sasha, was the captain's initial target set up. He's been calling off the relative bearings of each ship from the ship's head. By choosing a course of one-zero-five, it looks to me as if we are on a reciprocal course to the cruiser, the heavy. By plotting each angle on the bow, Pilot's marked a rough course for them. It looks to me like they're following a very sloppy formation. They're all over the place.'

'Could they not be doing your famous zigging?' Pavlyuchenko asked.

'I suppose they might, Sasha. Well done for remembering. In about a minute or so, the captain will take another look. Once Pilot's plotted everything, he can start refining the courses and judge the speed from the difference in positions.'

Evans returned to his attack station, but was replaced at the plot by the captain. He checked the positions marked of each target. 'I'm not so worried by the starboard escort, Navigator, but we need to watch the port one. I don't want to waste a mouldy on her, but she's a bit close to the cruiser for me to duck under for a clear shot. I'd say the cruiser's the *Prinz Adalbert.* Your silhouettes have their uses, after all.' The CO smiled knowingly, but Pavlyuchenko did not understand the significance.

Again, the attack periscope went up and the exchange of information on the surface plot continued.

'Bearing that. Range 2,000 yards. ATB red three-five. Port escort.'

'Red three-two.'

'Bearing that. Range 2,500 yards. ATB red four-zero. *Prinz Adalbert.*'

'Red four-zero.'

'Bearing that. Range 3,500 yards. ATB red one-two-zero. Starboard escort.'

'Red six-zero.'

The English captain conducted an all-round sweep of the horizon and suddenly called out, 'The cruiser's altering course to starboard. I'm now red one-two-zero. And the port escort's zigged to port. ATB red zero-five. Down. Port fifteen. Steer zero-six-zero. Flood One and Two bow tubes.'

Pavlyuchenko noted the mask of nonchalance of the men around him slip momentarily at the last order and a tremor of excitement pass through the submarine. The captain seemed unmoved, though.

'First Lieutenant, increase speed as necessary to maintain the trim and make her heavy if necessary. I don't want any risk of broaching once we fire.'

'I understand, sir. It won't happen again,' Evans replied sheepishly.

'Very good. Open One and Two tube bow caps.' The captain checked his stopwatch and then cocked his head to one side. Then Pavlyuchenko heard it, too. It was the noise of the twin propellers of an approaching destroyer. Had some sharp-eyed lookout spotted the periscope on that last look? And had that accounted for the change in course towards them, he wondered. Again, the CO glanced quickly at the chart.

'What speed do you make the cruiser?' he asked the navigator.

'Just shy of ten knots, sir.'

'As I thought. If I'm right, I should get a lovely beam-on shot on the next look. Her port escort is opening abaft us nicely. Ready, Number One?'

'Aye, sir. Both bow caps open. Ready to fire.'

'Very good. Order the stern tube flooded, too. We may have to dispose of an unwanted escort shortly.'

'Owen,' Pavlyuchenko asked Gilbert. How does the captain know when to fire?'

'He just does, Sasha. It's something all captains learn, but he seems an expert on the subject. It's all about calculating angles and ranges. I couldn't do it myself. Hush. The periscope's going up.'

'Fire One! Fire Two.' Everyone heard and felt the whoosh of high-pressure air as each torpedo exited the tube.

'Both mouldies running true,' the CO called and immediately swung round to starboard and fixed on the destroyer astern. 'Bearing that. 500 yards.'

He had barely swivelled back onto his target when the whole ship's company heard two loud explosions and almost simultaneously, a massive clap of thunder.

'Oh, my Lord,' the captain muttered. 'The magazine must have gone. Down. Keep forty feet. Port fifteen. Steer two-seven-zero. Revolutions for nine knots.'

Pavlyuchenko watched the CO slump against the bulkhead forward of the periscopes. He seemed in anguish.

'Are you all right, sir?' Evans called quietly.

'I'm fine. It was just a bit of a shock to witness. There was debris raining down even around the periscope. We hit her beam-on at about 1,300 yards. I doubt there'll be any survivors.'

Ah, so that's it, thought Pavlyuchenko. Our illustrious captain has feelings, after all. However, seconds later, the sound of high-speed propellers seemed to shake him out of any potential lethargy. Instantly, Miller ordered the bow caps to be shut and for the submarine to go deep to eighty feet and reduce speed to three knots. Moments later, the destroyer passed astern and Pavlyuchenko relaxed. He knew from his experience in his Russian destroyer, that once a submarine was deep, it could not be attacked by ramming or shell fire. All a destroyer captain could do was to keep the submarine deep so that it was unable charge its batteries. Then the captain would have the choice of suffocation once his battery power was too low to evade the hunters above, or to surface.

He was hugely surprised, therefore, when seconds later the boat was rocked by two great explosions underwater. He was safely wedged in the corner behind the chart table, but two sailors were thrown across the control room and the cat's hammock swung wildly. His eyes lost focus just as the lights went out. Instantly, the emergency lighting kicked in and Pavlyuchenko's sight returned to see pieces of cork rain down on the control room crew and suddenly his ears were hurting. The percussion effect from the shock of the explosion had initially deafened him, but now he could hear the roar of high-pressure air leaking into the boat. Yet within only a few seconds, he saw Frenchy turn a valve to shut off the leaking high-pressure air and the normal order of calm was resumed.

'What for the mother of God was that, Owen?' he whispered.

'Depth charges. Can't say I like them. Our destroyers have them, too. They hadn't been invented when I signed up for submarines or I might not have bothered. Hang on, Sasha. He's coming back.'

Sure enough, Pavlyuchenko could hear the destroyer coming closer. It seemed to pass further astern and he strained his ears for the coming explosions. He just had time to hear a clicking sound before the boat was again rocked by the explosions, but more savagely this time.

'Bloody Hell!' Pavlyuchenko heard somebody exclaim. 'I don't fancy that again for a game of conkers.'

'Fucking sissy,' one of the 'plane operators said in a loud voice. 'I reckon my granny could fart louder than that.'

CHAPTER 11

'The jetties seem rather busy, sir,' Gilbert reported as he lined up *E19* to pass through the breakwater into the harbour of Reval.

'They must have come to look at our prize, Pilot.'

'They probably think their own chaps captured it more like, sir,' Evans added. He cast his eye astern to where the Jolly Roger flew lazily in the light winds and warm sunshine. The flag had been updated to include the red bar to denote the sinking of the *Prinz Adalbert* and the white stars marking the sinking of the merchant ships.

Astern, the Russian torpedo boat, *Dostoini*, was escorting a Swedish freighter into the harbour. The *Caledonia* had been intercepted two days earlier, leaving the Gulf of Bothnia with a full cargo of iron ore bound for Stettin. As a neutral ship, she was not a legitimate target for sinking, so Richard had instead declared her cargo as contraband and put Gilbert and two armed sailors on board her as a prize crew. They had then handed her over to the Russians before returning on board *E19*.

'The Russians are indicating that we should berth alongside the *Gepard*, sir,' Gilbert reported and pointed to the flag hoisted inboard of the Russian submarine. 'That means we'll be berthing port-side-to, sir.'

'Odd,' Richard replied. 'It's not our usual berth, but it will at least mean no manoeuvring inside the harbour.'

'Look, sir,' Evans cut in. 'The Ruskies are manning the sides of their ships. Something's up, I fancy.'

'Permission for Lieutenant Pav to come to the bridge, sir?' The muffled voice emanated from the control room through the voice pipe.

'Negative,' Richard responded. 'We're just lining up for coming alongside. Tell the Liaison Officer he'll have to wait.'

'But sir?' Pavlyuchenko himself piped up. 'I have an extremely urgent signal that you must see before you berth.'

Pavlyuchenko sounded excited to Richard and the message intrigued him. 'Very well, Sacha, but make it up here quickly.' He turned to Gilbert. 'Revolutions to maintain steerage way. We'll wait to see what Sacha has to say before we go alongside. It might be that we've been ordered to go back on patrol.'

Within a minute, the breathless Russian appeared on the bridge clutching a signal pad. In his haste, he had forgotten to don his cap, but Richard chose to overlook the lack of protocol for entering harbour.

'So, what's the urgency, Sacha?'

Pavlyuchenko could barely speak through excitement and the exertion to climb the tower to the bridge. 'It's a personal message, sir… from Admiral Kanin himself.' The Russian gasped for more breath before continuing. 'The Tsar, sir! The Tsar has awarded you the Order of Saint George. That's the highest decoration for bravery, sir.' Pavlyuchenko beamed as he searched Richard's face for a reaction, but Richard had his emotions in check.

'And there's more, sir. He has summoned you to Petrograd to bestow the order on you personally next week. Imagine that, sir. You are to meet the Tsar in person.' Pavlyuchenko's cheeks, already red through physical exertion, now flushed deeper with pride.

'Well, that's very gratifying, Sacha, but it was hardly call to interrupt our berthing plans. Since you are improperly dressed, I suggest you go down below.' Richard felt no pride in the honour, but annoyance at the interference with a delicate seamanship manoeuvre.

'But that's not all, sir.' The Russian tarried on the bridge. 'Admiral Kanin is on the jetty, sir, to meet you. The Tsar has decreed that five of your men are to be awarded the Silver Cross of the Order for their part in the recent patrol. You are to give the admiral the names on arrival. That is why I felt it necessary to disturb you, sir.'

'I see.' Richard thought about the matter for a few seconds. 'Thank you, Sacha. I will certainly discuss it with the admiral. Now, let's get ourselves alongside before somebody starts thinking we've had a propulsion failure. First Lieutenant, you have the submarine. You can take us alongside. I'm going below to change into my harbour uniform. If I am to meet the C-in-C, I need to look less of the pirate.'

'You want me to take us alongside, sir? On my own?' Evans seemed stupefied.

'Naturally, Number One. It'll be good experience for you. For when you have your own command. And Gilbert will help you.'

'But I've never done it before, sir.'

'There's always a first time for everything. Look, it's straight forward. We're on an ebb tide, so take her in slowly on the port shaft, put the fore spring across and kick the stern in with a burst of astern on the starboard shaft. You'll be fine.' Richard didn't wait for an answer, but quickly followed Pavlyuchenko through the upper hatch and down to the wardroom.

*****

Richard's meeting with Kanin was more cordial than the last one. The admiral even offered him a glass of vodka, but Richard opted for tea instead.

'Let us raise a toast to our glorious Tsar, Captain. I, in true Russian vodka and you in your English tea, although, naturally, it is Russian Caravan tea.' The Russians raised their glasses of vodka to the portrait of the Tsar behind Kanin's desk and Richard in turn raised his glass of sweet Russian tea.

'Now to business, Captain.' Kanin resumed his seat and gestured to Richard to do the same. 'Commodore Podgursky and I have considered carefully the complaints you made before leaving on patrol about your men's living conditions and we have made a few changes. The Commodore will explain.'

The news surprised Richard as he had not been aware that he had made any such complaints.

'Yes, Captain. Your arrival with the men of your submarine has caused too much overcrowding in the depot ships *Ruinda* and *Voyne*, so in your absence, we have replaced both ships with an old cruiser, the *Dvina*. This has the merit that all your sailors will be living in the same ship.'

'Even better,' Kanin interrupted, 'I have instructed the victualling yard that from now on, as our honoured guests, your men will draw rations from our stores and on the same scale to which you are accustomed. Of course, these are more generous than those afforded to Podgursky's men, but it is only right after your men have done so much virtually to put an end to the traffic in iron ore from Sweden to Germany.'

Richard's face must have betrayed his surprise at the news as Kanin continued, 'Ah, so you have not heard, Captain. Our intelligence sources report that Prince Henry, my German counterpart, is unwilling to give way to the pressure from the German shipping companies to introduce convoys to protect their ships. He feels that not only would a convoy offer the submarines a concentrated choice of targets, but that protected ships might be torpedoed without warning. I suspect he is not keen to offer up his warships as potential targets again either. The *Prinz Adelbert* was lost with virtually all hands.'

Richard silently digested the news with satisfaction as well as a little suspicion and sadness at the loss of the sailors' lives. He wondered at the apparent efficiency of the Russian intelligence service compared with that of its navy and army. He didn't think this sudden affability on Kanin's part suited the admiral, but the news was welcome and he was not in a position to look a gift horse in the mouth.

'Sir, I am most gratified by the news, but can assure you that all the men under my command have only one aim. That is to help Russia defeat our common enemy.'

'Let us drink to that.' Kanin indicated to a steward to refill Richard's tea glass and to another to pass around a fresh tray of vodka glasses.

After toasting the health of both their countries and their future co-operation in the war with Germany, Podgursky asked if there was more that the Russian Navy could do for the British submarine flotilla.

'As a matter of fact, there is, sir. I wonder if I might swap my gun for one of your forty-seven-millimetre versions. Mine's absolutely useless.'

Once the request was translated, Kanin nodded to Podgursky who answered, 'Why, of course, Captain. It all aids the war effort.'

Kanin leaned forward. 'One other thing before we go on to discuss your visit to the capital next week. It is no longer fitting for an officer of your importance and stature to share the wardroom of the depot ship with your fellow Royal Navy and Russian officers. I have arranged for your dunnage to be moved to the house of a Mrs Henderson in the town. She is an English widow who makes a living teaching English to my officers. You will, also, be provided with a sleigh, groom and a valet from my own household staff.'

Pavlyuchenko was bursting with pride at the admiral's largesse as he translated the news, but Richard rebuffed the offer.

'Sir, that is awfully generous of you, but I would rather continue to be accommodated with my officers.'

'Sir, you can't reject the admiral's arrangements,' Pavlyuchenko protested. 'It is a signal honour he pays you.'

'Just confine yourself to interpreting duties, Sacha, and keep your opinions to yourself.' Richard could see that Kanin was confused by the conversation with Sacha and then his face clouded over as Pavlyuchenko translated the polite refusal.

'No, Captain. It is not your position to refuse. You may only be a commander in rank, but your Russian equivalents are captains and are not messed with their subordinates. It is a matter of discipline. I demand your compliance.'

Richard feared that he may have overstepped the mark and dissolved the new spirit of friendship so recently fostered, but Kanin's face softened as he added, 'Besides, Captain, it is time you learnt Russian and Mrs Henderson will be a good tutor. I am told she has lived here for many years and speaks Russian very well. You could do worse than exchanging a few pleasantries with the Tsar in Russian and there is to be a dinner in your honour after the medal presentation. Besides…' Kanin winked conspiratorially, 'I'm reliably informed that Mrs Henderson is a… a comely woman and I am sure a little female company would not come amiss.'

Richard blushed at the potential imputation, but confined himself to the main points of the admiral's offer. 'Very well, sir. I accept your arrangements most graciously. Thank you.'

'Good. Now do you have the names of the five men to receive the Silver Star? I must pass them to the Palace.'

'Ah, there I really must disappoint you, sir. It's the nature of our work in submarines that I cannot single out any officer or man as being more deserving than another. We all face the same risks and it is a team effort as I am sure Captain Podgursky will affirm.' Richard looked appealingly to Podgursky for support.

'But surely you would wish to recognise the status of your officers and most senior rates, Captain?' Podgursky was not as helpful as Richard had hoped.

'I'm sorry, sir, but it's not that simple. How do I place a value on the work of the torpedo men, without whom I could not have sunk the cruiser, over that of the gun's crew who fired the shots to stop the merchantmen? What about the boarding parties who laid the explosive charges or the hydroplanes operators who kept me at an accurate depth to attack the cruiser? And that's before one considers the efforts of the engine room staff to keep the boat running.'

Kanin and Podgursky began a discussion that took many minutes and one which Richard told Pavlyuchenko not to translate. He could see that Kanin was not pleased with his response, but eventually the two senior Russian officers seemed to form some sense of agreement. It was Kanin that responded.

'Very well. I have listened to the Commodore's representation and made my decision. I shall report to the Palace that your two officers will receive the Silver Cross. I will then explain that it is not possible to differentiate between the bravery of the rest of your crew and to seek the Tsar's permission to bestow on *every* other member of your ship's company the lowest class of the Cross of Saint George. I will offer to honour your men by making the awards myself. That is my final decision, Captain. I think you have tried my patience enough already for the present.'

Kanin stood and shook Richard's hand to signify that the meeting was at an end. Pavlyuchenko almost fled the C-in-C's office.

CHAPTER 12

'Good afternoon, ma'am. I'm Richard Miller. Mrs Henderson, I presume?'

'Really, Commander. This is hardly Ujiji. I've been expecting you.' Rachel Henderson stretched out her right hand and shook that of Richard firmly.

Richard was surprised at Rachel's appearance. She was barely five feet in height and very slight in build. Moreover, unlike any other woman of his acquaintance, she wore her dark hair short, curled just below the ear in the style of a mediaeval page boy. Indeed, despite her plain. bottle-green, crinoline dress, her boyish figure reminded him of the character, Buttons, in a pantomime of *Cinderella* he had once watched.

'And this ma'am, is my assistant, Leading Telegraphist Dawes. I've brought him along so that he knows how to find this place. I hope you don't mind?' Richard asked.

'Not at all. But I can't follow all these naval ranks. What's your first name?' She was addressing Dawes.

'Just call me Frenchy. That's what most people do.' Dawes took off his cap and lowered his eyes shyly.

Rachel smiled and ushered both men into the spacious hall of her home on the outskirts of Reval. Richard guessed that she was in her late thirties and her smile improved her otherwise plain appearance.

'I'm sorry to intrude, ma'am. This was not an arrangement of my own making. I was more than happy…'

'Nonsense,' Rachel interrupted. 'You're most welcome, but you must stop calling me, "ma'am". It makes me feel quite old. You must call me Rachel and I will call you Richard… and you, Frenchy, of course,' she added as an afterthought. 'Why is it that you're known as Frenchy?'

'I'm half French… On my mother's side, so I speak fluent French. It's a name that kind of stuck, ma'am.'

The news surprised Richard and he felt embarrassed that he had never thought to enquire. It was an obvious example of how he knew too little of the personal lives of his men. The thoughts threw his train of thinking momentarily.

'Er, very well, Mrs… Richard, I mean, Rachel.' Richard was taken aback, too, at this tiny lady's boldness. He detected a trace of a Lancashire accent in her voice.

'May I ask? Are you by chance from the North of England?'

''Tis true and proud of it. I'm from Rossendale. D'you know it?'

'I do, although not well. My family are from a bit further north. Closer to Lancaster.'

'Well, that's grand. We'll rub along famously. You can tell me all about it once we've got you settled. But I daresay you'd like a bath before then.'

Richard smiled inwardly to hear the northern shorter vowel sound of the word 'bath' before he thought he detected a slight wrinkling of his landlady's nose. Suddenly, he became conscious that after nearly three weeks on patrol, and even in his harbour uniform, he would have brought with him various unwelcome aromas from his submarine. A Russian sailor suddenly appeared in the hall, stood to attention and saluted. Rachel addressed him in Russian before turning back to Richard.

'This is Vasily, your valet. He doesn't speak much English, I'm afraid, but he'll take your valise and run you a bath. There's no shortage of hot water. I'll show you to your quarters and when you're done, I'll have a brew ready. Perhaps, Frenchy would like to give him a hand?' She gestured for Dawes to take Richard's case upstairs, but Richard cut in quickly.

'No, Rachel. Dawes isn't that sort of assistant. He acts more as a secretary to me.' He turned to Dawes. 'Perhaps, now you know where I'm billeted, you'd better head back to the depot ship, Dawes. On your return, you may dismiss the groom, but tell him to meet me back here at 07.00 sharp tomorrow.'

Dawes replaced his cap on his head before saluting first Richard and then Rachel, turning about smartly and returning to the *troika*.

*****

As Richard knotted his tie in front of the looking glass, he had to admit that his present accommodation was much more comfortable than that in the old *Ruinda*, or even *Maidstone* for that matter. The wooden-walled house was very spacious and grand for a widow living on her own, but not luxurious in its own right. His suite of rooms on the first floor overlooked the driveway and front gardens, with the coach house to the left. His rooms were simply furnished and the bathroom had the benefit of cold running water. Above, he could hear footsteps and assumed that the attic contained the servants' quarters. Feeling clean and refreshed, he made his way downstairs to the room he had been told was the parlour. There, he met Rachel sitting before a table laid out with china cups and a proper English teapot.

'Ah, there you are, Richard. I hope you find your rooms comfortable. Do let me know if there is anything else you need. I can run to a hammock in place of the bed, should you require, but it's in the garden at present.' She smiled cheekily.

'No, everything's most satisfactory, thank you. I'm just sorry to have put you to some inconvenience.'

''Tis no trouble. I shall enjoy the company whilst you're here and the rent comes in right 'andy.'

'Why, of course. How stupid of me. How much do I owe you?'

'Now don't be silly. That's all taken care of. You're a guest of the Russian Navy. They often send me their most favoured guests and what, with the money I get from my English lessons, I do rather nicely outa it. Now how d'you take your tea? I thought you might fancy a change from Russian Caravan, so I've brewed some of my Indian tea.'

'With a little milk and not too strong, please.'

Richard savoured the delicate taste of the tea with pleasure. It made a pleasant change from the thick mixture to which he had become accustomed on the bridge of his submarine.

'Do I detect a blend of Darjeeling and Earl Grey?' he asked.

'Why, how right you are. That's just what it is. My Edmond and I spent the first three years of our married life in Bombay.'

'Edmond was your husband?'

'Aye, that's right. He was a mill manager and went out there to help the Indians set up their own mills. Proved to be the cutting of his throat, mind. When we came back, he struggled to find a job back in the Lancashire mills, so that's how we ended up in Bogorodsk, back in 1904.'

'That's in Russia, I presume?'

'It is. 'Tis near Moscow.'

'May I?' Richard proffered his cup and saucer for a refill. 'So how did you find yourself in Reval, Rachel?'

'I came here about five years back after the Lord was pleased to take my Edmond from me. There were nothing much for me back in Lancashire and I've always hankered to live by t'sea, so... We once spent a lovely summer near here and with our savings I bought this place. Life's much more relaxed here than in the rest of Russia.'

As Rachel chatted freely about her past life, Richard listened attentively. Sipping his tea from English china, sitting in an English-styled parlour, he found it hard to imagine that he was nearly two thousand miles from home. It was now over five months since he had last enjoyed a woman's company and a pang of home sickness overcame him. He wondered what Lizzy would be doing now.

*****

'If you don't mind me saying, dear, you look a little off colour. Are you quite well?'

Elizabeth thought this a little ironic, coming from Emmeline. After all those months in prison and on hunger strike, Emmeline Pankhurst was not exactly bursting with health herself. However, Elizabeth decided to tackle the issue head on.

'I'm with child.'

'Good gracious, Lizzy! That's quite marvellous. And so soon after your wedding, too. You are most fortunate.'

'I suppose I am, Emmeline, but I was not so sure the first few months. I felt sick as a dog. Soon, I will have to buy a new wardrobe. I've already had to have my skirts let out a little.'

'But morning sickness is quite normal, dear. Indeed, it's a good sign, child. I was sick with all three of mine and it all went well. Are you over it yet? And when are you due?'

'Yes, I've been fine since last month, but I'm surprised you couldn't tell. I'm already five months gone. The baby's due in September. I'm afraid he or she will be a honeymoon child.' Elizabeth blushed.

'And is your husband delighted with the news. Richard isn't it?'

Elizabeth looked away and stared blankly through the window into the garden of her home in Crosby. She bit her lower lip before replying softly. 'I'm not sure in all honesty. Of course, I've written to tell him, but he's never referred to it in his letters. I hope it's not yet another burden on him.' A tear slowly streaked down her cheek. She wiped her eyes quickly in embarrassment.

'I shouldn't worry, Lizzy. In my experience, men are obtuse with babies. I swear my husband would have been happier if our girls could have been born at the age of two. Richard's probably too embarrassed to show his feelings.'

There was a minute or two of silence between the women whilst they sipped their tea. Then Emmeline tactfully changed the topic of conversation.

'I so enjoyed my visit to your yard this morning, Lizzy. You're doing wonders for the cause.' Earlier in the day, Emmeline had given a speech to the women of Miller's Yard on the subject of women's rights. 'You're setting a fine example to the world on how women can be absorbed into the workplace.'

'It seems to be working well, but employment doesn't guarantee them a vote when the next election comes around. Even so, Emmeline, I think it was right to offer the government a truce. I know some fellow members of our movement were relieved that our militant activities had been paused.'

'I believe you're right, but don't you worry about the suffrage issue. As more and more women enter the workplace, they're waking up to reality and becoming more independent… certainly more independent than before the war. They're not going to accept being disenfranchised and frankly, my dear, I don't think the majority of men will accept it either. Not now they've seen more of what women are capable. If only I could persuade my daughters of this.'

'But Emmeline, what do you mean? Surely all three of your daughters are still committed to the cause of universal suffrage. Only yesterday, I read a fervent article by Christabel on the issue.'

'It's not Christabel causing me angst, dear,' Emmeline sighed and laid down her cup and saucer. 'It's Sylvia and Adela with their wretched peace protests. Too much blood has already been spilled to persuade the many widows and mothers who have lost their husbands and sons that we should end the war before it is won. And look at how the shortage of labour is improving the working conditions of the women in the East End. Even that rascal Lloyd-George is coming round to our cause.'

'I had noticed that you and he were becoming a bit thick together. Have you really forgiven him?'

'Oh, he's not so bad, really. He's a pragmatist and all he cares about is preventing another Tory government. He's, also, extremely dissatisfied with the all too frequent drunkenness and slackness of the male workers in the munitions factories. I enjoy his company, if I'm honest.'

Elizabeth was not totally convinced by this unholy alliance, so decided to change the subject back to children.

'And how are your orphans?' Emmeline had adopted four three-year-old girls the year before as part of her war baby orphanage project.

'Extremely tiring. I wonder if it was a bit of a mistake at my age in actuality, but Nurse Pine is marvellous with them. She takes most of the strain. And on that subject, how are you going to manage after your confinement? I presume you will hand over the management of the yard to somebody else.'

'Not so, Emmeline. Oh, how clumsy of me.' Elizabeth had replaced her cup on the saucer with such force that she had spilt her tea over her skirt. She mopped herself down with a napkin.

'It would send the wrong message entirely. No, I shall have the baby and be back at work as soon as I can. In any case, we're extremely busy with our war work.'

'But, child, how will you manage?' Elizabeth was surprised by Emmeline's shocked expression. Surely, she saw that if women were to demand equality with men, they couldn't let childbirth interfere with their employment?

'As you saw this morning, unlike most women, I have the privilege of a private and substantial office. I can bring the child with me to work whilst I'm feeding her – or him - but…' Elizabeth hesitated. 'There is something over which I would welcome your guidance.'

'My dear girl. Whatever it is, just say.'

'You mentioned Nurse Pine. Could you advise me how to find a good nurse? As you know, I have no mother… and my mother-in-law and I don't see eye to eye.'

'But surely your mother-in-law is softened by the news she is to become a grandmother?'

'Hardly... Well, actually, I have yet to pass on the news. Richard and I are first cousins and his mother was set against our marriage. I believe she fears we will produce a mongoloid child.'

'Oh dear. How dreadful. But I have just the solution. I shall speak to my friend Isabel. She's the principal of the Norland Institute. I'll ask her to recommend a good nurse. It will necessitate some expense, I fear.'

'Don't worry about that, Emmeline. The yard has never been busier or more prosperous and again, in that I am more fortunate than the women I employ.'

CHAPTER 13
June 1916

The men working on the casing of HMS *E19* came to attention in response to the call of the 'Still' from the boatswain's call. Richard returned the salute of the commanding officer of the departing HMS *E1*, Lieutenant Commander Athelstan Fenner, before the quartermaster piped the 'Carry On'. Despite the exigencies of war, the Baltic flotilla of submarines maintained the age-old traditions of all Royal Navy warships by manning the side and saluting vessels commanded by an officer senior to their own CO. The shrill notes of the boatswain's call were echoed from *E1* before her own ship's company fell out to begin stowing the berthing ropes for sea. In the customary slick and co-ordinated fashion, the ensign on the staff at the stern was lowered precisely as the sea-going and smaller ensign was raised on the bridge staff. Richard raised his hat and waved it to Fenner, who replied with his own cheery wave.

Richard felt a pang of envy for Fenner's freedom to carry out an independent patrol, away from the officialdom of their base port. Goodhart was waiting for him in his cabin on board the *Dvina*, finishing off his hand-over of the responsibilities of administering the flotilla. Worse, Halahan and *E18* were missing. On the twenty-sixth, she had signalled a successful attack on a German destroyer, blowing her bows off, and had been expected to return from patrol on the thirtieth, but she was now two days late and no more wireless transmissions had been heard. Richard looked at the grey and overcast sky before returning to his cabin and office. It was not typical weather for June, but it matched his mood.

'Very well, Francis. Where were we?' he asked on returning to his cabin.

'I was just about to inform you of our new arrivals.'

'Oh, yes. Replacements for the men being drafted back to England. Any issues?'

'None, sir, but we do have a chaplain amongst them!'

'What? A naval chaplain?'

'Yes, sir. The Reverend Anthony Lomax. C of E.'

'I don't believe it, Francis. Of all the officers they might have sent me. Another engineer, a paymaster, a torpedo specialist… It's hard to credit. What's he like?'

'He's all right actually, sir. Pleasant and keen. Moreover, he's not your usual God Squad. He appears to have a relaxed attitude towards religion. The men quite like him already. It turns out he has a soccer blue from Durham. Quite a good left-winger, I'm told.'

'I thought you said he was C of E?'

'I'm sorry, sir?' Goodhart was puzzled.

'I presume, as a left-winger, he favours the left foot? A Catholic like me.'

'Oh, I see what you mean, sir. A left-footer. Very droll, sir.' Goodhart smiled politely at the joke before continuing. 'No, he's definitely Protestant, but the thing is, sir… Whilst we've been out here, several of the men have formed relationships with the local girls. Two of them have now submitted requests to you for the padre to marry them.'

'Really? I suppose I should be pleased they want to make honest women of their liaisons.' Richard stood looking out through the scuttle of his office and former cabin. 'What's the state of stores?'

'It's not so bad on the engineering front, sir. Now the snow's melted, we've received several crates that had been sitting at Archangel since last year. Cash and clothing are our main shortages. You've seen for yourself how some of the men are dressed almost in rags and we're all owed back pay. However, we have had a batch of mail come through, so that's done much for morale.'

'Yes, I could see that from the size of my in-tray. The lack of cash and slops is a worry, though. I'm paying my first call on Admiral Phillimore at Imperial Headquarters on Monday when I go up to Petrograd. I'll raise our issues with him and see if he can put any pressure on the Admiralty to make us an independent command. Now give me an hour to wade through all this *bumf* and then I'll meet you on board *E8*. I'd like to see the progress of your repairs... and you might ask Simpson to be there. He can bring me up to speed on the state of play of the whole flotilla. I want to up the tempo of patrols and try to keep two boats on patrol if possible.'

'Aye aye, sir.' Goodhart made to leave the cabin, but hung back a moment. 'I don't suppose there's any news on *E18*, sir?'

'No, but not to worry. She's still another five days of food and could turn up any day. You know how unreliable the W/T is and she might have been kept down by over-zealous destroyers. I'll call on the Russian Staff this afternoon and ask them to keep an eye out for her... and to report any sightings or W/T transmissions.'

'Very well, sir. As you say, any matter of things might have delayed her.'

After Goodhart had left, Richard crossed himself for the lie he had just uttered. Halahan was a good CO and would have found a way of reporting any delay in his return. Something was awry, but it was just one of several problems on his plate. He added a number of entries to the list of matters he would need to discuss with the Commodore that afternoon. It was already headed by news of *E18*; future operations; ideas and paint for a new camouflage scheme for the submarine hulls; a new gun for his own boat and the protocol and arrangements for his and his officers' investiture on Monday. Now the already long list included clothing and the prospects for a loan of cash.

*****

Richard had briefly met Rear Admiral Phillimore in the Dardanelles the year before when Phillimore had been a captain and the Principal Beach Master at Helles. Now, as the Royal Navy's Liaison Officer at Imperial Headquarters, Petrograd, his surroundings were much grander.

'Sit yourself down, Miller. May I offer you some English tea or have you taken to the Russian form?'

'Either will do nicely, sir.'

'Very well. When in Rome.' He gestured to his steward to pour tea from the samovar sitting on the buffet to the right of his armchair. Once the refreshments were poured, the steward withdrew without instruction.

'You've lost a little weight since I last saw you at Mudros. I seem to have the opposite problem.' The admiral patted his midriff. 'Too many functions to attend. You'll have to watch for that as you grow in rank, my boy.'

Richard remained silent and observed Phillimore as they drank their tea. His direct superior was Commodore Hall in England, the Commodore Submarines, but he hoped the admiral might aid his cause. In his early fifties, Phillimore's slightly pointed beard and hair were greying, but he appeared lean and energetic to Richard, although the admiral was right. He had put on weight since Mudros.

'Your father wrote to me to ask I look out for you. I'm sorry it has taken this long to meet at last.'

'You know my father, sir?' The news did not surprise Richard. He knew Papa was well-connected in Admiralty circles.

'Yes. I was the Commander of *Goliath* on the China Station. Your father had just won his own VC. A family trait it seems.' Phillimore indicated the blue ribbon on Richard's left breast. 'Anyway, I have some news for you. On top of the Tsar's decoration this afternoon, I've just been informed that you're to be awarded a bar to your DSO. It'll be gazetted later this month. Congratulations.' Phillimore rose and shook Richard's hand warmly. 'Let's hope we get this war over before your tailor complains about lack of space for your ribbons.'

Richard was a little distracted by the news. He had only been carrying out his orders, but the thought quickly passed.

'Is there anything for my officers, sir?'

'Absolutely. Both are to be Mentioned-in-Despatches. To have acted so quickly, the Admiralty were clearly impressed by your glowing reference to them in your patrol report.'

'It was no more than they were due, sir.'

'Fine, fine,' Phillimore muttered inattentively as he rummaged through his signal pad. 'I suppose you haven't yet heard about the great battle in the North Sea last week?'

'I've heard rumours that the High Seas Fleet put to sea, but little more, sir. We receive little hard news in Reval.'

'I've only read scant reports myself and the newspapers haven't come through yet. It seems Beatty's squadron met the full might of the High Seas Fleet and was badly mauled, but he managed to draw them onto the Grand Fleet which, conveniently for once, just happened to be at sea. The two fleets came up against each other, but the Germans escaped under darkness. It seems something was wrong with our ships as we suffered badly, losing 6,000 men and fourteen ships, including three battle cruisers, would you believe?'

'But how fared the smaller High Seas Fleet, sir? Surely this was what we wanted? A decisive battle to finish the German Navy, once and for all?'

'Theory and practice differ, Miller, as you well know. The Germans took a pounding, but the battle was far from decisive. Their ships seemed to be better armoured and they lost fewer ships. I fear the knives will be out for scapegoats.' Phillimore paused to drink his tea before continuing.

'However, there's good news on the way. You'll be informed in writing by Commodore Hall in the next mail, but in the meantime, I have a signal here somewhere... Ah, here it is. You're to receive reinforcements in the form of four more submarines.'

'What? That's madness!' Richard checked himself. His mind had been on the news of the awful losses the previous week and he feared for his youngest brother, John. The loss of so many ships and men was the Royal Navy's greatest ever disaster in all its long history.

'I'm sorry, sir, but after what happened to *E13*, I can't see how it could be done. It would be suicide.'

'Miller, I'm aware how young officers believe the intelligence of their superiors is inversely proportional to their seniority, but don't you think our lords and masters have had that same thought. These submarines are being sent overland. That's how I'm involved.'

'Really? But how will that be possible, sir? The boats are surely too big.'

'True, which is why the Admiralty has had a rush of the proverbial to the brain and decided to reinforce you with a smaller class of submarine. I believe they are of the *C*-class, if that makes sense. They're to be towed to Archangel and then packed onto barges for transport by river and canal here. It should make for an interesting sight.'

'Indeed, sir. They're nowhere near as capable as my *E*-boats… they're only propelled by a single petrol engine and fitted with two torpedo tubes… but they'd be ideal in the Gulf of Riga. I applaud the idea.'

'Well, that's something of which you would know more. Thank Heaven for small miracles, but it means a change in organisation, too. Your cries for an independent command have not fallen on deaf ears. From the first of August you are to be known as HMS *E19*. Your suggestion of HMS *Baltic* fell on deaf ears I'm afraid. It means you'll be getting an assistant paymaster, so that should ease the administrative burden.'

'That's something at least, sir. On top of my six *E*-boats, that's going to be another 64 men to victual… well over 200 men in all. I shall write to Commodore Hall and try to persuade him I need more engineering support, but first there is something more immediate you might help me with, sir.'

'Name your price, Miller. If I can help, I certainly will.'

'Our most pressing needs are clothing and cash. Some of my men are in rags and have had to wear thin cotton overalls to hide the nakedness of the land. Despite my entreaties and those of my predecessor, serge and flannel can't be bought at any price. And then I'm short of cash. I can write notes for stores, but I'm very behind in paying the men. I wondered if you could use your influence to negotiate a loan, sir?'

'Mmm. The latter shouldn't present much problem. We can fix a shipment of gold in time, but clothing is more of a problem. The Russian army faces the same issue. I've read of men dressed in rags fighting on the Austrian front. All I can do is reinforce your plea for more supplies.'

'Thank you, sir. I regret the absence of decent uniforms for my officers at the dinner tonight will let down the honour of the Service. We don't have a set of mess dress between us and, other than a fresh collar, we'll be very much dressed in our working uniforms.'

'Actually, Miller, it's a ball tonight. The Russians are rather laying it on for you. But I shouldn't worry about the uniforms. It will give you a sort of *cachet*. Let the dandies of the Imperial Staff show off their frogging and pelisses. You'll be wearing the uniform of battle. I might have to tone down my ball dress to spare me some of my shame for sitting on my backside in this gilded palace. I'd better stick with the lightning conductors, I suppose… Now, let me brief you on the protocol for this afternoon's investiture and the ball this evening. I'm afraid the Tsar won't be attending the latter. He never does on a Monday.'

That news at least came as a relief to Richard.

CHAPTER 14

As agreed with Admiral Phillimore, the officers from HMS *E19* all wore black arm bands to mourn the dreadful naval losses in the great battle the week earlier. Evans watched his captain take to the floor yet again with one of the many ladies keen to court his attention. They seemed attracted to his boyish good looks and the favour in which he was now held by the Tsar. His breast jangled with the VC, DSO and three Russian decorations. At least Menty seemed to be enjoying himself. Earlier, Evans had noted the CO's preoccupation with exactly which ships had been sunk in the recent battle. Now, he suddenly and guiltily remembered that his captain had a younger brother serving somewhere. Actually, he thought, he has two in the Service, but one was an aviator and, therefore, unlikely to have been involved in the battle. That said, he couldn't say for sure. The CO was a closed book when it came to discussing his personal life. Evans, also, had a younger brother at sea, but as an Apprentice in the Merchant Marine, so he assumed he would be relatively safe.

Poor Menty, Evans thought. As if the chap hadn't enough to be worried about with the overdue *E18*. Nonetheless, for now his own attention was more focused on the beauty seated to his right. He wasn't sure he had ever seen a more attractive woman in the world and yet the ballroom seemed full of such beauty. The gilded splendour of the ballroom, its crystal chandeliers, the silk gowns of the ladies and, above all, the glittering jewellery on display, were all a far cry from the Assembly Rooms of Carmarthen. The son of a solicitor with a modest practice, Evans had never seen such a display of wealth. He felt as if he was living in a fairy tale, but he had seen immense poverty on the streets of Petrograd over the past twenty-four hours, too. He knew the war was going badly for Russia and yet the aristocracy seemed untouched by it.

'You seem sad, Lieutenant. Is my company so dull?' The lady spoke French as she knew little English and Evans had yet to learn more than a few basic polite words of Russian.

'I'm sorry, Countess. I was worrying for my captain. He may have had some bad news.'

'Ah, yes. The Battle of the Skagerrak. So sad. So many young lives lost, but we Russians are used to that.'

'I believe we are referring to it as the Battle of... oh, I can't think of the French for it... Jutland.'

'Who can say? At sea there are no landmarks. Your captain is handsome, yes? So tall and dark, but so few medals.'

'I couldn't say, Countess, but as for medals, he is one of the most highly decorated officers in the Empire. Our king doesn't give away medals lightly. Look at me. I have just this one from the Tsar.'

'Our beloved Tsar is, perhaps, better at showing his appreciation to his brave officers. And do stop calling me, "Countess". My name is Sonia... as I have told you. Forget your precious captain for now. Do I not enchant you?'

*****

Gilbert was beginning to think that life in submarines suddenly had its merits. He had rarely had the opportunity to drink champagne, but in Russia his glass was never empty. Come to that, he'd better slow down. He felt confident he would score with the Baroness later and he would need the little man's full attention his works to perform. It was odd how these aristocratic Russians were almost throwing themselves at him whilst their husbands discussed the war amongst themselves or gambled at cards in a side room. From his perspective as the son of a Merchant Marine purser, he had perceived upper class women as unreachable and his many dalliances with the fair sex had been with women of his own class.

He felt the Baroness's hand on his knee and gradually move upwards to stroke his inner thigh. Speaking no Russian and unable to recall much of his schoolboy French, he was finding conversation difficult with the Baroness, but with her broken English and the international language of love, or lust in this case, Gilbert thought he was faring quite well in promoting Anglo-Russian relationships. On another table to his left, he could make out Evans in the company of an equally glamourous lady, his eyes almost on stalks as he fixed on the emerald necklace resting lightly in the 'V' of her gorgeous cleavage. I bet he's a virgin, he thought. The skipper seemed to be making out quite well, too, he noticed. That was his third dance with a different partner, but now he was talking to the admiral and some flunky dressed in the uniform of a diplomat.

'I think you'd better stop there, Baroness,' he whispered. Her stroking of his thigh beneath the table was becoming too sensual. 'Let's not spoil things for later, shall we?' He gripped her right hand and placed it on her lap before gently stroking her gown. He knew too little to say whether it was silk or taffeta. It was smooth and silky to touch, but the crinoline beneath prevented him exploring further.

*****

'Ah, Lockhart. May I introduce you to Commander Miller, commanding officer of our submarine flotilla?' Admiral Phillimore shook the diplomat's hand vigorously. 'Miller, this is Bruce Lockhart, our Consul-General in Moscow.'

'*Acting* Consul-General, Admiral. Delighted to meet you, Commander. Your fame has extended to Moscow, such that my wife was keen to meet you. Regrettably, she is detained in Moscow.'

'I will leave you two gentlemen to make your acquaintances. I see Prince Naryskin is trying to catch my eye. I really must be introduced to his beautiful wife.' Phillimore bustled away into the throng the other side of the dance floor, the gold stripes or 'lighting conductors' of his trousers flashing brilliantly in the bright light of the chandeliers.

'So, Commander, does the war progress more successfully in the Baltic than in the south? I gather your new friend, the Tsar, is having second thoughts about the Western Army's offensive towards Vilna.'

'I'm sorry, Lockhart, I don't know what you mean.'

'You confine yourself to maritime matters then? General Evert was due to launch the army of the Western Front in an offensive last week, but that scoundrel Rasputin apparently had a vision that persuaded the Tsar to focus instead on the south-west. I fear it was a mistake of the Tsar to agree to replace the Grand Duke Nicholas as Commander-in-Chief. He is already attracting the blame for the army's failures.'

'I regret that to date, I have been preoccupied solely with my theatre of operations, Lockhart. But if you don't mind me saying, you seem very well informed on the conduct of the war, considering the distance from Petrograd to Moscow.'

'You meant, of course, for a mere Consul.'

'Not at all. My brother is in the Diplomatic as it happens. I believe he is currently serving at the consulate in Rotterdam.'

'I am sorry should I have appeared over sensitive, Commander. Forgive me. What is your brother's name? I probably know him.'

'Peter Miller. He's a couple of years my junior.'

Lockhart looked bemused for a moment. 'No, I don't think I do know him. Strange, I thought I knew of all the European consular staff.'

'I understand he's a passport control officer.'

Lockhart gasped and then tried hard to disguise his surprise. 'Of course. That would explain it. I don't tend to come across the passport control office types very often. They report to a different head.'

Richard did not miss Lockhart's reaction and after a split second, his spine tingled. A few years earlier, before the war, he had discovered by accident that Peter was working for the Naval Intelligence Directorate. He had then assumed that Peter had resumed his diplomatic duties. Now he wondered if the 'passport control types' might belong to a very different outfit.

'That would explain it,' he replied indifferently. 'But just how is it that you are so well informed on the Imperial General Staff's affairs, Lockhart?'

'Oh, I have my sources. One does well to keep one's ear to the ground. Moreover, I've been trying to persuade the Romanians to enter the war on the side of the Entente. Despite my posting to Moscow, my duties take me far and wide.'

He looked knowingly at Richard. Although, sceptical of the explanation, Richard didn't have time to pursue it further as their conversation was interrupted by two attractive Russian ladies. The brunette addressed Lockhart in Russian and a short interchange of conversation unintelligible to Richard took place between two people who seemed obviously well-acquainted.

'Miller, dear fellow, allow me to introduce a good friend of mine, Baroness Marie Benckendorff.' He gestured to the brunette who bowed gracefully and with a smile. 'This is her friend, Princess Anna Shuvalova.'

Richard had to control himself to avoid gasping. Next to Lizzy, Princess Shuvalova was the most beautiful woman he had ever met. Her long, pale neck could have been that of a swan. Her long tresses of blonde hair were piled up on her head in a pompadour style, topped with a silver chain containing a huge blue sapphire to match the princess's eyes. The way they flashed in excitement reminded him so much of Lizzy. She was utterly enchanting, but breaking eye contact to avoid staring, he took each lady's hand and kissed it as he made a short bow.

'Moura here tells me that the princess was keen to meet you, Commander. Regrettably, Prince Nikolai is with the army of the Western Front where he serves as a major-general. Perhaps, therefore, you might escort the princess to select some dinner whilst Moura and I catch up on old times. Nevertheless, I'd like to meet you again. I believe we might find it fruitful.'

'I'd be honoured,' Richard replied, unsure of himself. However, Lockhart's attention had switched to his lady friend and they seemed to be sharing some private joke as Moura giggled coquettishly.

'*Pardonnez moi, votre… Altesse. Mais je ne parle pas encore la Russe*,' he stuttered.

'Then let us speak in English, *sauf vous préférez continuer en français. Vous le parlez bien.*' Princess Anna spoke English with a heavy accent, but Richard noted that her French accent was faultless.

'As you wish, your highness. But forgive me for saying, you speak French exceptionally well.'

'You think so?' She cocked her head to one side and eyed him confidently. 'My husband was a military attaché in Paris soon after we married. I lived there for three years, but my English is less good. There is so little chance to exercise it in Russia. But you must take the time to learn Russian.'

'I've already taken the first steps, your highness. My landlady in Reval has so far introduced me to the Cyrillic alphabet and taught me a few greetings.'

'That's good, but please call me Anna. The title is my husband's. Let us eat. I am… *affamée*.'

'You mean famished. But of course.'

*****

With alarm, Evans watched the CO go into dinner with the most beautiful woman in the world on his arm. He felt he should warn him, but he was presently locked in the arms of Sonia for his third waltz with her. But he had vital information to pass. He feared for his captain's soul. His attention having wandered, he was quickly brought back to the task in hand by his partner. He had just trodden on her toes. Only minutes before the dance, she had made it plain to him that he was expected to escort her home and spend the small hours in her rooms.

'But what of your husband?' he had asked aghast.

'No problem. He will be with his mistress. A flat-chested strumpet at the *Bolshoi.*'

'But surely? Were he to find out… he would still be annoyed?'

'No. Why? It is the way matters are arranged in Russia. The husbands have their mistresses and we are free to have our little affairs. It is a matter of convenience. Look. Even your beloved captain has caught on. Mark my words. He will be pleasuring the Princess Shuvalova until the dawn.'

Evans's middle-class principles were outraged. 'But he's a happily married man!'

'So is my husband. Let's keep it that way. Now… why don't you take me somewhere quiet? I hope you make love better than you dance.'

CHAPTER 15

Not even the warm sunshine of a beautiful Baltic day could lift Richard's mood as *E19* sliced through the glistening blue sea in the company of her escort. He was becoming sick of this war. There had been no news of the missing *E18* and, reluctantly, he had given the orders for the kit and effects left behind in the depot ship by the ship's company to be packed and stored ready for return to Harwich. Richard himself had cleared Halahan's cabin and the action had a depressing finality about it. Moreover, as he had searched Halahan's effects for any inappropriate items that might have caused embarrassment to his wife, Gwladys, he had discovered Halahan's flying log book. Until then, Richard had had no idea that Halahan had taken a year out of the submarine service prior to the war to qualify as a naval pilot. He felt guilty that he had made so little effort to know the man in life.

Such was the esteem that Halahan and his boat were held in the eyes of the Tsar, he had not only sent a telegram of condolence, but taken the unusual step of awarding the entire ship's company a posthumous decoration. Halahan had been awarded the Order of Saint George, the same decoration the Tsar had personally bestowed on Richard just two weeks earlier. Richard hoped that Gwladys and her two children would appreciate the gesture.

The thought prompted him to reflect on his mother's feelings at present. Richard had received confirmation that his youngest brother's destroyer, HMS *Turbulent*, had been sunk with all hands at Jutland. How could John be gone? Barely twenty years of age and always full of fun, but never again would John accompany him to watch Surrey at the Oval or take delight in taking his wicket with those off breaks. He should be at home to support *Mutti*, but instead he was 1,600 miles away and unable to help. The infrequent mail didn't help either. He had immediately penned a letter to his parents, but he had no idea when they would receive it. Why was it that their Lordships' demands for frivolous reports and returns always seemed to get through, but the flotilla could go without personal mail for months? According to Evans, even Mister Gieve's tailor's bill had failed to make its usual appearance and they always caught up with one. Richard felt cast adrift by the world and longed to hear from Lizzy. Why had she not written? Both Evans and Gilbert had had mail about six weeks earlier, but he had had nothing. Of course, Lizzy would be busy running her shipyard, but surely, she might have had the time to pen him a short note. Was that why he had behaved so badly the previous week, he thought guiltily. Did he secretly blame her?

Evans asked permission to come to the bridge and Richard, having granted it, returned to his guilty memories of the sleigh ride with Anna, the Princess Shuvalova, after the ball in Petrograd. It had seemed like a romantic fairy tale as they had drunk champagne and eaten smoked salmon under the glitter of the chandeliers to the sound of the orchestra. He had found Anna utterly enchanting. She was graceful, lively, intelligent and had an endearing way of teasing him. After the ball, in the early hours of the morning and half-light of the Baltic summer night, he had escorted her home to her mansion in the suburbs of Petrograd. To keep out the morning chill they had shared a fur and she had snuggled close to him for additional warmth. Perhaps it had been because he had been unused to wine, but he had found her beauty, her scent and the warmth of her body irresistible and, without thinking, he had suddenly kissed her passionately. She had responded enthusiastically and it had taken iron will to resist her invitation to accompany her into the house. He had known to what that would have led.

To his surprise, on returning to his lodgings, he had discovered Rachel Henderson up and about at the early hour. Over a strong black coffee, he had learned that she had set up a small section of her home as a chapel and it was her habit to pray there early every morning and last thing at night. Since then, he had tried to join her whenever the preparations for this patrol had allowed. Their shared time together in prayer had offered him comfort, but not been enough to assuage his guilt.

'Good afternoon, sir,' Evans interrupted in a breezy tone. 'And it really is a wonderful day, too, isn't it, sir.'

In his present gloomy mood, Richard found his first lieutenant's newly-acquired constant cheerfulness intensely irritating, but he bit his tongue to prevent emitting the rebuke already formed on his lips.

'Indeed, First Lieutenant.' Richard was reluctant to engage in conversation, but realised this would appear churlish. The piece of paper Evans was carrying gave him an opportunity.

'What's the news on the wireless, then?'

'Good news and bad, I'm afraid, sir.'

'Give me the bad news first then.'

'A signal from the Admiralty about our interception of the *Antarus*, sir. They want a fuller report on our actions. It seems the Germans are claiming we fired upon her in neutral waters and they've raised a diplomatic stink. It's complete balderdash, of course.'

'As if I've nothing better to do with a war on.' Richard searched the horizon for a minute. He could smell the scent of the pine trees being wafted towards them on the gentle breeze. It reminded him of Switzerland and improved his mood. 'Very well, Number One. Ask Pilot to put together all the facts for my report. Full latitude and longitude of when we engaged her, when and where we ceased firing… the full works. I'll submit my report on our return. And what's the good news?'

'A message from Captain (S), sir.' Evans beamed as he referred to it. 'It's in response to your request for the casualty list of *Turbulent*, sir.'

Mention of the name of his brother's ship suddenly absorbed Richard's full attention. Evans had said it was good news. Dare he hope?

'Captain (S)'s staff have clearly worked out your interest, sir, and Captain Waistell has sent a personal message to inform you that your brother was re-appointed to Coastal Forces shortly before the battle at Jutland, sir. He reports him alive and well. Read it for yourself, sir.'

Richard grabbed the proffered signal and read it quickly. It was impossible to believe how so few words could convey so much. He focused on the words, '*alive and well*' and fought to control his emotions. He could feel tears welling up and it would not do to display such weakness in front of his second-in-command, let alone the lookouts. He tucked the signal into the pocket of his reefer jacket without folding it and, hiding his embarrassment, quickly applied his binoculars to his eyes and pretended to take an interest in a feature of the coast. His attention wandered to thoughts of *Mutti*. She would be so relieved, but would she know? Of course, she would, he thought. Papa would have access to the same information and John would have been in touch. No, there was nothing about which to worry about there. His attention was brought back to his present position by Evans's discreet cough.

'There's one other signal worthy of your attention, sir. Ruskie Intelligence reports various changes in the movement of Swedish iron ore. The Germans have given instructions that all masters are to remain in Swedish territorial waters until they meet up with patrols to see them over the open sea to Germany. They're, also, making more use of Swedish registered ships. Accordingly, the Russians will take care of the iron ore traffic themselves from now on and we are ordered to attack only cruisers and larger ships.'

Richard could not help laughing out loud at the news. 'That is good news, Number One. I suddenly feel hungry. Ask the messman to send me up a corned beef sandwich, would you?'

*****

Gilbert raised the periscope again for a routine all-round look. The submarine was operating three feet shallower than the usual periscope depth in order for Gilbert to see above the wave tops. The sea had been whipped up by an earlier storm and the present heavy rain was making watchkeeping difficult.

The weather was not the only tedious element of the patrol in Gilbert's view. For days *E19* had patrolled off the coast of Libau hunting for a target of opportunity, but to date had only come across small vessels. Frustratingly, five enemy cruisers could be seen lying in the safety of Libau harbour. Like a cat at a mouse hole, Menty had ordered that the boat lie in wait for any exit of one of these ships. In the meantime, Gilbert was carrying out a reconnaissance of the approach channels. Yet again, he took a bearing of a prominent landmark and, leaving the periscope raised, checked it against the chart. As well as checking the accuracy of the chart, the boat's officers were plotting the movement of the trawlers and destroyers patrolling off the port in order to draw up a picture of the passages through the mine fields.

As instructed by the CO, Gilbert made a notation to the chart to add a little more description to that printed. When he had done so, he absent-mindedly tickled Terry's ears whilst he reflected on the relative drudge of life on patrol versus that he had enjoyed in Petrograd. It was a sin how the Russian nobility neglected their beautiful wives in favour of their mistresses. The Baroness had been like putty in his hands and eager in her responses to his love making. After two nights, it had been a relief to return to Reval for a rest from her sexual demands, but he looked forward to a return visit. It was obvious to the whole ship's company that the first lieutenant had struck lucky, too. That silly grin had barely left his smug face since the night of the ball.

Life in Reval was looking up, too. Menty had met the British honorary vice-consul at Reval and that seemed to have opened the doors to a wider, expatriate social scene. The submarine officers had been given membership of the British Club in Reval and several of the sailors had been invited into the expatriates' homes. Gilbert hadn't participated in any of the many football matches that had been arranged between the sailors and expatriates - with a few Russian players, too - but he had appreciated the introduction to the wife of a mill factory engineer currently working a long way from home. His campaign to bed her had yet to bear fruit, but the omens were good that he might succeed on his next return to harbour.

'Sorry to interrupt, sir,' one of the control room watch cut in, 'But the periscope's been up at least three minutes now, sir.'

'Damn! You're quite right.' Gilbert rushed back to the periscope and began a much-delayed all-round look. 'Christ!' he exclaimed. 'Down periscope. Wake the Captain.'

*****

Richard didn't need a shake to be roused from his bunk. Some sixth sense that all submariners develop had already woken him and he appeared from behind the wardroom curtain within seconds.

'What's the problem, Navigator?'

'I'm sorry, sir. I must have… I forgot…'

Richard ignored the spluttering Gilbert and called for the periscope to be raised. He spotted the problem immediately, but finished his 360-degree sweep before returning to look at the nearest trawler in high-power.

'Depth of water?' he called out, but nobody answered. Gilbert was frozen and unable to speak. 'What's the depth of water here? Anybody.' He swivelled onto the second trawler to seaward of the submarine. Both trawlers were beginning to pay out a net to block the boat's escape.

'Eight fathoms, sir,' Evans responded from the chart table. He had been asleep, too, but had risen immediately on hearing the commotion in the control room.

'Port fifteen. Group up. Half ahead. Take a look, First Lieutenant. I need to check the chart.'

Evans pushed the petrified Gilbert out of the way roughly as he made his way to the periscope. Richard, meanwhile, surveyed the chart to calculate his available sea room. The trawlers must have had the submarine under observation for some time as they were already positioned to pay out their net across the channel to deeper water. No doubt the net would have explosive charges attached. *E19* was too close inshore and in too shallow water. He started to wonder how Gilbert could have allowed this happen, but cut himself off. There wasn't time now for recriminations. He would have to act quickly if he was to save the submarine and the lives of his men.

Richard took the periscope again and checked the bearings of the two trawlers and then the heading of the swinging submarine. There was just a chance. 'Midships. Steady on two-two-zero. Keep forty feet. Full ahead.'

The motor room staff responded immediately and the submarine quickly built up to her maximum dived speed of ten knots. Full ahead was an emergency order meaning that damage to machinery was acceptable and the motor room staff were giving their CO every amp and revolution they could. Richard checked the chart once again and noted Gilbert's recent fix. There wasn't yet enough water to go deeper and, in any case, they would still run the risk of falling foul of the submerged trawler net. His only hope was to skirt to the south of the left-hand trawler attempting to block his path. The weight of the net would slow it down.

Within the submarine there was a deathly hush. Without any explanation of the circumstances, the ship's company seemed to have sensed that they were in a dangerous situation. Petty Officer Connolly, the Coxswain, had appeared in the control room as if by some telepathic summons and was standing by to take over the helm if necessary. Elsewhere, key personnel were taking over positions as if secretly summonsed to Diving Stations. Outside the hull could be heard the diesel engine noise of the trawler and its steam winch as it manoeuvred itself and its net to trap *E19*. Richard's experienced ear offered him hope. The bearing of the noises seemed to be drawing right. He glanced across to the log and noted that the submarine's speed was ten and a half knots. The motor room crew had exceeded the boat's supposed maximum speed. It would be draining the battery quickly, though.

Evans, the only other person to appreciate the fix the boat was in, broke the silence. 'The bearing's drawing aft, sir. I think we're going to make it.'

Richard spotted the tangible signs of relief from the crew in response to Evans's words. They had not known the nature of the emergency, but had sensed the danger. It was time to ease the tension.

'Half ahead. Revolutions for eight knots. Starboard wheel, steer two-four-zero,' and then muttered aloud to himself. 'We're going to be all right.' It had been a narrow escape and now he wondered what Gilbert had been up to.

CHAPTER 16
July 1916

Not even the impending interview with Gilbert could dampen Richard's mood on *E19*'s return to Reval from patrol. The mood of the ship's company was pretty chipper, too, for awaiting the sailors and officers alike were sacks and sacks of mail. It was going to take some time to sort the mail, but there was no shortage of volunteers for the task and Evans had just handed Richard a huge batch of personal mail, several of which Richard recognised as being from Lizzy.

'You wouldn't believe where this lot has been, sir. You couldn't have made it up.'

Richard was anxious to begin sorting through his mail, but he humoured Evans out of politeness. 'Go on then, Dai. What's the story?'

'It's only been across the Atlantic twice - to Canada and back – and then via Berlin of all places!' Evans stated excitedly. 'It seems that some clever clogs in Blighty had the bright idea to send the mail via Canada. Perhaps they thought it would go overland and across the Barents to get here, but for whatever reason, it was sent back to England. Somebody then had the sense to send it direct to Russia, but the two ships carrying it were boarded by the Germans and the mail confiscated.'

'Berlin you say? It seems a bit rum. So how has it arrived at all, Dai? And how do you know the story?'

'It seems the Hun isn't such a bad chap after all. They've sent a jolly polite note with the mail to apologise for the interference and delay. Their intelligence chaps have opened it, of course, but deemed it harmless and had the grace to send it on.'

It was a strange tale, but Richard began to lose interest in it and started separating out those letters from Lizzy. Evans must have spotted his distraction as he quietly withdrew from Richard's cabin on board the *Dvina*.

'Well, there it is, sir. There's plenty more to come, but I'll leave you to read through that lot.' Richard didn't hear him. He was already taking his letter knife to the first envelope.

*****

One of His Majesty's latest prospective commanding officers alighted from the train at its terminus at Thurso station. Like his fellow officer passengers, he had travelled first-class, but as a lieutenant, he had been the junior officer in his compartment. Only one of his travelling colleagues, a lieutenant commander joining one of the battlecruisers of the Grand Fleet at Scapa Flow, had shared the three-day journey from London. They had met up with the two commanders the previous afternoon at Edinburgh Waverley station. All the naval officers were glad to stretch their legs on the platform, but none more than the fair-haired lieutenant who took time to unbend his six-foot-six-inch willowy frame. His languid air gave no indication that he was a famous cricketer and a good swimmer. However, although now free of the smoky compartment, the Scottish weather was fresher than some had expected. Despite it being early August and the height of summer, Mother Nature was now treating the northern Scottish coast to the might of a full north-westerly Atlantic gale. Only the lieutenant was armed with his greatcoat as he was joining his command for the first time. Moreover, having been brought up on his late grandfather's Scottish estate, he was accustomed to the vagaries of a Scottish summer.

It was not possible to see the sea from the station, but all the train passengers could feel it as the wind blew the rain and spray across the platforms. One of the commanders, also, sported the dark-blue and white ribbon of the Distinguished Service Cross. It was he who suggested they make their way quickly to the shelter of the Railway Hotel and none of his subordinates demurred. As an old hand at making the crossing of the Pentland Firth, the commander further suggested each officer ate a hearty meal before boarding one of the former mail steamers that now acted as troop ships between the mainland and the islands of Orkney. After all, the men were due a 'lumpy' crossing and it was better to have something to bring up should their stomachs fail them.

A few hours later, the lieutenant parted company with his travelling companions in Scrabster Harbour. He was to take the *St Ninian* to the naval base at Longhope, whilst they took another steamer to Stromness. The lieutenant pitied them their longer journey along the west coast of the island of Hoy. As he boarded the bucking steam packet, his new companions were mainly sailors, but with a couple of Wrens and half a dozen soldiers in khaki, too. He recognised a couple of sailors as seasoned hands by the way they adjusted their gait to cope with the roll of the ship. They all immediately headed for the boat davits to sit on the deck, wedged between the posts and rails. Although not knowing the reason why, he decided to join them and stretched his long limbs over the rail. However, as soon as the steamer passed out of the relative lee of Holborn Head, he realised the sagacity of the experienced seamen. The meeting of the North Sea and the swift current from the Atlantic funnelling down the strait had created monstrous green mountains of sea. One minute the lieutenant was gazing at the clouds and the next his feet were almost dipping into the swirling water.

Barely twenty minutes into the three to four-hour voyage, the other passengers, who initially had taken shelter inside the ship, began to emerge and to man the rails, several tars amongst them. One old salt kindly persuaded a soldier to face downwind before voiding his stomach. The lieutenant took no delight in their discomfort. In his early days in submarines, he had frequently 'yodelled the bucket' at periscope depth in the North and Irish Seas. He recalled that on his first storm in a submarine at PD some wag had painted a scale on the inside of the bucket. Each inch of the communal bucket had indicated an increase in the force of the wind. Seeing a half-eaten poached egg in amongst the bucket had been enough to ensure he had heaved with the rest of the unfortunates to need the bucket. Now, he wasn't confident he would be holding down his Railway Hotel kippers for the entire crossing.

A few minutes later, his discomfort was eased a little by a childish giggle at the scene he had just witnessed. One of the Wrens had just vomited and the wind had curled her breakfast or lunch down the rail, past several sailors, before coming back inboard over a green-looking soldier. 'Fuck me,' he had roared. 'I don't mind being sick or someone else being sick on me, but when it's someone four places further down the rail and she missed the three in between, that's what I call bloody bad luck!'

*****

The *St Ninian* eventually discharged its sick and bedraggled passengers at Longhope. The lieutenant was surprised to see a couple of ambulances waiting on the quay. He asked the reason why of the member of the ship's crew helping him carry his baggage down the gangway.

'Och, there's always a few dead ducks on this crossing, especially in rough weather. The authorities ken this is the only way to get some of them back to their barracks,' the seaman replied in his soft Orcadian accent.

Thankful that he had retained his kippers intact during the crossing, the lieutenant asked directions for the way to the wardroom of the naval base. There, he would stay the night before taking command the following morning of HMS *C27.* Although late evening, the sun was still high in the sky in the mountains to the west and there was plenty of light to see the four *C*-class submarines bobbing on the swell alongside the huge tugs that would take them to their new operating base within a few days. With only a single 600-horse-power petrol engine and two bow torpedo tubes, these boats were far less capable than the *E*-boat the lieutenant had just left. Indeed, they were now obsolescent as far as the submarine service was concerned, but they would be ideal for the mission the Admiralty had in mind for them shortly. Moreover, tiny as they might be, the second boat in would be the lieutenant's first command and he felt a huge surge of pride course through him. From tomorrow, he would be responsible for the fifteen men who made up her ship's company.

Checking his pocket watch, he realised he was probably already cutting it fine to change in time for dinner, so he was in no hurry to make his way up to the wardroom. In any case, he thought he needed to give his stomach time to settle down from the violence it had suffered in the crossing of the Pentland Firth. Instead, he left his baggage with one of the storekeepers checking off stores being unloaded from the *St Ninian* and strolled down the jetty towards his new command.

All four submarines were barely recognisable as *C*-boats. The hydroplanes, periscopes and all exterior fittings had been removed to leave only the hulls and fins to suggest the true role of the vessels. The decks of the tugs were piled high with crates of equipment that had been stripped from the boats. To the lieutenant's surprise and anger, the crates were boldly stencilled with the word 'Archangel'. How was it he wondered, when he was under orders not to reveal the nature of his forthcoming mission even to the Vice-Admiral Orkneys and Shetlands, that the destination of the submarines was advertised so plainly to all and sundry? However, there was nothing he could do about it now and he trudged back to collect his baggage. After a bath and early night in a proper bed, he would have an exciting day ahead of him.

CHAPTER 17
August 1916

Despite the August rain, Richard left the Astoria Hotel on Petrograd's Nevskiy Prospekt on foot. Freed of his administrative duties at the submarine base for a few days, he was taking every opportunity to take exercise. Although it was only a mile to the British Embassy on Palace Quay, he figured that if he went via the Warsaw Station, it would offer him a five-mile walk. The Russian summer weather had not improved since his return from patrol the month before. The dampness and grey seemed to match the mood of the Russian people towards the conduct of the war.

He hoped that the walk might clear his head, not just of the cigar smoke of the previous evening, but the facile conversation and, unusually for him, the after effects of the vodka. After dinner the night before, he had fallen in with a mixture of well-dressed army officers and civilians with their ladies. As he was wearing his uniform and Russian decorations, it was, perhaps, natural that he should have attracted their attention. His British decorations now included the bar to his DSO. Whilst drinking champagne and eating caviar, his fellow guests had begun by suggesting that it was the fault of Russia's allies that the war was not going well. They seemed to have little idea of the struggle on the Somme where hundreds of thousands of Tommies and *poilus* were being slaughtered or the horror of Verdun. To the wealthy *bourgeoisie* of Petrograd, war was a romantic game of chess. They shrugged off the slow disintegration of their country's social infrastructure as something that could be put right by a military victory. It was only after they had left for a *soirée* elsewhere that Richard had been approached by a young Cossack colonel missing an eye and hand and dressed in a striking green. He had been listening to the conversations from the bar, but taken no part in them.

'Sir, allow me to introduce myself. I am *Voyskovoy starshina* Konstantin Doroshenko. I come to apologise for the outrageous comments of those people who just left. The officers should have known better.'

‘I’m delighted to meet you, sir. I’m Commander Richard Miller of the Royal Navy. Allow me to say, sir, your English is impeccable. I regret my Russian is still rudimentary.’

‘I was fortunate to have an Indian tutor as a child and, before the war, I served in Persia where English is the er… language of France? I don’t know what that means.’

‘The *lingua franca*, the language of the Franks, but don’t worry about it. And there is no need to apologise. Everyone is entitled to their opinion, Colonel.’

‘But they speak from ignorance. If you want to see how the war go, visit Warsaw Station. See the dirty trains come full of the wounded. Visit the hospitals to see the wards too crowded to take more casualties. See the streets around the stations. There you see the hovels where the starving live. The cripples, the orphans, the widows this war make. The people starve whilst warehouses are full of grain and sugar. I fear thousands will die this winter.’

‘Do you not agree then that it is only a question of time before victory? Somebody was telling me only last month that the latest offensive in the south-west is going well.’

‘Ah, *General roda voysk* Brusilov. Yes, it is going splendid. Brusilov is a clever general, but I fear he will overreach himself. What are we to do with the Austrian prisoners? We can barely feed and clothe our own army. Where are the railways to support him? How do we treat the wounded? Those drugs that are available are too much cost to buy, Commander.’

‘Thank you, Colonel, for your honesty. I’m based in Reval and we hear rumours of the enormous casualties, of course, but the newspapers only print the most optimistic and glorious of stories.’

‘You remind me of something my late father once said. “Never trust what you read in the newspapers, Petrovich. For there are lies, damned lies and newspaper stories.”’ The Russian laughed and raised his good arm to summon a waiter.

'Commander, let me buy you a drink and then I will tell you the truth about our army.' Richard knew enough Russian to understand the Cossack was ordering vodka for them both. He didn't have the heart to tell his companion that he didn't drink. Almost immediately, the waiter returned with a tray of four vodka glasses.

'First we drink a toast to Russia, the mother country.' The colonel raised his glass and swigged his shot in one go. Richard followed suit and almost choked on the fiery liquid. It was worse than the whisky he had drunk before the war. However, he bore it stoically.

'Let me tell you, Commander,' the Russian leant over the table towards Richard conspiratorially. 'The soldiers are starting to talk of peace. Even the officers. Indeed, I can tell you that several officers are overstaying their leave. This war is creating too many widows and orphans. You cannot do that without unrest. The generals know that and so more and more troops are being withdrawn here to protect the Tsar. But you cannot house thousands of men in barracks built for only a few hundred. Soon or later there will be a… boom. An explosion. But now we drink another toast. To our allies.'

Again, Richard gulped down the foul-tasting liquid before pleading an early start and making his farewell to the Cossack colonel. Before retiring, however, he tipped the waiter to ensure the Russian's glass was continually replenished and the costs charged to his room bill.

*****

Richard's visit to Petrograd had taught him much of the conduct of the war and the depth of feelings on the home front. At Warsaw Station he had, indeed, seen testimony of the veracity of the Cossack colonel's claims. Yet he had, also, received good news and, having now had contact from Lizzy, Richard had omitted to inform Princess Shuvalova of his presence in the capital. Admiral Phillimore had informed him of the departure of the four *C*-class submarines from Scapa Flow for Archangel. All being well, they would arrive in

September, and in preparation, his flotilla was to have a full staff, including a medical officer. The new assistant paymaster had already arrived and that would reduce his accounting and payroll headaches. Best of all, he had seen the list of the COs for each of the boats reinforcing his flotilla. In command of *C27* was Lieutenant the Viscount Algernon Steele DSC, his first lieutenant from his former command, HMS *E9*. Richard could not wait to see his old friend and made a mental note to include the news in his next letter to Lizzy.

Now back in Reval, he regarded Lizzy's news that he was to become a father as a mixed blessing. Naturally, he was delighted, but he worried, too. When would he ever see their child and how would Lizzy cope in his absence? He knew she was busy enough running the shipyard without the burden of motherhood. Was Lizzy fit and well enough to bear a child? She had reported herself in good health through her letters, but would she be candid about such a thing? Richard could not help remembering tales of women dying in child birth. And who would care for the child once Lizzy went back to work? He knew his wife and cousin well enough to know that she would return to work at the earliest opportunity. He wondered whether he might have been better off not hearing from Lizzy. Naturally, he had been euphoric initially to have the contact and to know that she was fine and still loved him. But her letters had made him feel awfully homesick and there was nothing he could do about it. What rot, he thought. Of course, he was better off hearing from Lizzy. Had he not been concerned by her lack of contact? It was just that he was unlikely to be granted leave any time soon and so, for now, must prosecute the war as best he could, despite distractions from home. He had enough on his plate already. Even though it was a Sunday, that plate included a pile of official correspondence in need of his attention.

Richard cast aside thoughts of Lizzy and read through the latest letter from Commodore Hall. He reported that Gilbert had arrived safely in England and had been reappointed to a Q-ship. The Admiralty seemed to have been satisfied with his report on the interception of the *Antarus*, but there was now fresh controversy over his capture of the Swedish ship *Caledonia*. The Germans had responded by referring to the stipulation in the 1909 Declaration of London that iron ore was not contraband. Anxious not to upset the only neutral nation in the Baltic with which they could trade, the

Russians had, accordingly, decided to return the *Caledonia* to the Germans. Moreover, after consultation with the Russians, the Foreign Office had agreed that in future his submarines were, henceforth, no longer to board neutral ships. To Richard that was a relief, at least. Hall went on to say that the batteries for the *C*-boats were being shipped separately to the Petrograd Baltic Works at Kronstadt. There, they would be reinstalled into the boats, the boats readied for sea and the submarines would make their own way to reinforce the flotilla at Reval.

Richard laid down the Commodore's letter and made another entry in his notebook. He would need to battle with the Russians to find more accommodation for the crews of the new submarines. They would need new bathrooms as well as mess decks. However, the Russians had been quite amenable ever since the Tsar had invested him with the Order of Saint George. Richard now found it helpful to wear his Russian and British decorations permanently on display. It offered him a certain *cachet* and opened many doors hitherto locked to his flotilla.

Next, he turned his attention to the letter from his prize agent. The Admiralty Prize Court was dragging its feet over his claim for sinking the Turkish troop ship *Gul Djemal* when in command of *E9* the year before. In 1915, the King had re-enacted the old Prize Law of 1708 that offered the Royal Navy £5 for every enemy person on board a ship sunk or captured. Such prize money was normally divided amongst all ships involved in the action or in the vicinity, but in this instance *E9* had operated entirely alone. Richard's agent had submitted that the ship had been carrying 6,000 troops and 200 crew members and, accordingly, lodged a claim for an award of £31,000. Richard's share would be one eighth. Given his father's relative wealth, he was not unduly concerned about the award of such a fortune, but he did care for the men's prospects. If successful, each member of *E9* at the time stood to gain about the equivalent of fifteen years' pay. The agent reported that whilst the claims for the other vessels sunk by *E9* in the Sea of Marmara had been honoured in full, the Admiralty had rejected this claim on the grounds that it could not be proved that the troop ship was an armed vessel. The matter would have to go to court and Richard would be required to appear as a witness in person. Clearly, there was little prospect of that whilst Richard remained in the Baltic.

The news depressed Richard and he wondered how to respond. Perhaps Papa could intervene, not on his behalf, but for the sake of the men who had been under his command. He regarded the whole affair as mean-spirited on behalf of the Admiralty and it left a sour taste in his mouth. He decided to deal with the issue and Commodore Hall's letter when he was in a happier mood, but when might that might be?

The new paymaster, Assistant Paymaster Percy Hayward RNR, had prepared a brief on the 'Requestmen' he was due to see. This formal naval procedure allowed members of a ship's company to request to see their commanding officer in person to state complaints, grievances or, more routinely, to seek formally due advancement or increments in pay following qualification. Now that HMS *E19* was an independent command, he had the authority to hold Requestmen for all members of the flotilla. Two of the 'requests' were from sailors seeking the CO's approval to marry local girls. Moreover, helpfully, Hayward had, also, included in the file a note to inform him of the birth of a baby girl to a leading seaman in *E8*. This news brightened Richard immeasurably. It had always been a matter of pride for him to congratulate the wives of his ship's company on such happy events and it was a habit he was determined to maintain for his flotilla.

He quickly penned a note of felicitation to the new mother, enclosing a Russian mug as a gift to the child. He suggested the girl should be christened with a middle name of Tatiana in memory of her father's service in the Baltic.

Feeling more cheerful at last, he felt ready to begin a letter in response to Hall, but was interrupted by a knock outside his cabin before Dawes thrust his head through the curtain in the doorway.

'Sorry to bother you, sir, but I've just received a message from Lieutenant Commander Fenner, sir. He'd like you to see Seaman Langridge, one of his torpedomen, sir. Young Langridge 'as been in sickbay for a while, sir.'

'Did Lieutenant Commander Fenner stress any urgency in my visit, Dawes?'

'Aye, he did, sir. His first lieutenant's just informed him that the Russian MO wants to admit him to hospital. The Ruskie suspects it's the onset of kidney failure.'

Richard reached for his cap. It was just another facet of life in command of His Majesty's Baltic submarine flotilla and his correspondence would have to wait. 'Very well, Dawes. I'll go and see him now.'

CHAPTER 18

Ten days after leaving the port of Lerwick in the Shetland Isles, Lieutenant Steele, the new CO of HMS *C27*, viewed his command with concern from the after deck of the tug *Hampden*. The passage from Scapa Flow to Lerwick in a north-westerly Atlantic gale had been like crossing a millpond compared with that north of Norway. The strange-looking convoy of four tugs with the *C*-boats in tow astern had the look of toy boats in heavily-disturbed bath water. They had now passed the North Cape to enter the Barents and the weather was unusually atrocious for the time of year. The tugs seemed capable enough of riding the tall, steep waves, but the submarines had a tendency to penetrate the base of the huge waves and disappear from view for agonisingly-long periods. Their batteries had been removed and crated up as a precaution. The holes where the periscopes and forward hydroplanes had been removed had been blanked. Additional ballast had replaced the weight of the batteries and the rudder and after hydroplanes had been locked amidships, but nonetheless, the boats weren't riding the storm well.

Every time his boat disappeared in a plume of white spray and green wash, Steele held his breath, wondering if she would surface again. He had arrived in Scapa too late to join the officers and the majority of the ships' companies. They had sailed ahead to Archangel with an Engineer Commander and naval constructor to supervise the next stage of the journey, but the coxswain and one junior rating from each submarine had been left behind to find passage in each tug. Petty Officer Davis and Able Seaman Stevens were, also, witnessing events from the stern of the tug towing *C27*. Like their new CO and despite it being August, they wore full oilskins to protect them from the heavy rain and spray. The polar wind had backed from the north-east to the north, but the swell still came from the east to cause an awkward and uncomfortable corkscrew motion.

'If she don' sink to the bottom, I reckon she'll slip her tow afore long, sir,' Stevens shouted above the wind.

'Just as well then, lad, you're not still tucked up in your snug fore ends isn't it then?' Davis replied. He turned to his CO. 'Lieutenant Lucy seems to think the storm will blow itself out soon, sir. How do you rate our chances, sir?' Lucy was the RNR master of the tug.

'I fear we'll need to keep our fingers crossed about that. Even if the storm abates, we'll no doubt have a heavy swell for a few days yet.' Steele had yet to meet the rest of his ship's company, but had noted that both Davis and Stevens wore three good conduct badges on their left sleeve, denoting a minimum of twelve years' good conduct, or 'undetected crime' as sailors put it. That made Stevens unusual for a submariner. Whilst Davis had reached the rate of Petty Officer and Coxswain, in a similar period of service, Stevens had remained an able seaman. However, Steele had noted, too, the slightly darker patch of the sleeve above Stevens's good conduct badges. He suspected that once Stevens had sported there the killick-anchor-badge of a leading seaman, but had since been disrated for some serious misdemeanour, albeit long enough ago to have regained the good conduct badges he would have forfeited automatically following his disrating.

He turned away sharply as a burst of spray was carried across the stern and hit him fully in the face. He used his scarf to wipe the salt from his blue eyes, but as he looked back astern, a commotion to port caught his attention. He quickly raised his glasses. Although late in the evening, it was still almost fully light. In these latitudes, the time between sunset and sunrise was barely noticeable. Noting the shift of his gaze, the two ratings looked over to their right, too.

'Your prediction has come to pass, Stevens, but not here fortunately.'

'What is it, sir? I don' see nothin' from this distance.'

'It's *C35*. She's broken adrift. Looks to me as if the towing slip has broken loose. Here. Borrow the glasses.' Instinctively, Steele looked to starboard. The now northerly wind put them on a lee shore, but when the rain squalls permitted some visibility, he couldn't see any sign of land. Even allowing for the drift and leeway caused by the wind, he estimated that the convoy was about twenty miles off the Russian coast to the south. It wouldn't be easy passing a fresh tow in this heavy sea, especially since none of the submarines were manned, he thought.

'I think it's time we turned in with a mug of *kai*. The tug's crew will call us if they need us.'

'Aye aye, sir,' the Coxswain replied. 'All this wind and lumpy stuff is tiring, but it still doesn't seem right to turn in with the sun up. I feel like I'm a child and my ma's putting me to bed early.'

The two sailors headed forward, but Steele remained at the stern looking out over the black shape bobbing in the waves behind and uttered a silent prayer she would survive the journey. Of all the COs on passage to join the Royal Navy's submarine flotilla in the Baltic, he had the most pressing reason to wish to be there.

*****

'Algie, you'd better come on deck… and quickly,' Lucy called to the recumbent CO of *C27*. 'Both *C26* and your boat have slipped their tows.'

Steele quickly rose from his bunk, so much so that he forgot to duck and his head caught the athwartships beam in the deckhead of the tug officers' small sleeping berth. He grabbed an oilskin jacket and followed the tug's master onto the after deck. The wind had dropped, but there was still a nasty swell. The tug was already executing a tight turn back towards the drifting submarine and Steele regretted not having the presence of mind to bring his cap as the wind blew his long blond locks into his eyes. As the tug slowly drifted with the swell back to his submarine, he saw far in the distance, another tug carrying out the same manoeuvre towards her own wayward charge. He was quickly joined by Davis and Stevens.

'Stevens, be a good fellow and collect my cap and binoculars from my cabin, will you?'

'Looks to me as if she's lost a link in the towing pendant, sir,' Davis suggested. 'Can't be sure from here, but if I'm right, it'll be a bastard to recover the tow, sir.'

'I fear you might be right, Coxswain. I just hope Lieutenant Lucy is a good enough seaman to perform some magic.' Steele looked out to port and noted with alarm the desolate coastline only a few miles off. The fin of the helpless submarine was acting like a sail and the wind was quickly blowing the vessel onshore. With the wind and heavy swell 90 degrees apart, it would be a tricky piece of seamanship to manoeuvre the tug close enough to pick up the broken towline.

Seamen from the tug's crew immediately began to rig shock mats at the stern of the tug and then stood by with grappling and boat hooks to fish for the parted tow rope. Lucy deftly manoeuvred the boat upwind of the drifting submarine and allowed the wind to propel it gently down onto the hull. Steele moved to the shelter of the wheel house to observe the tug's manoeuvres. Normally, a boat would have been lowered by the tug to recover the tow, but that would have been suicide in such weather conditions.

'I hope the chaps pick up that tow before too long, Algie. Your precious boat seems to have a death wish.' Lucy indicated the proximity of the shore. The distance was closing rapidly.

Any further conversation between the two COs was interrupted by a cry from the after deck. The submarine CO was relieved to see that a seaman had managed to retrieve the towing pendant from the water with a grappling hook and other seamen were busy fishing it inboard. However, his relief was short lived when a messenger made his report to Lucy.

'Begging your pardon, sir, but the PO's told me to inform you that the mooring ring has parted.'

'The devil it has!' Lucy exclaimed and peered out of the wheelhouse window at the approaching shore line.

'Is that a problem?' Steele asked.

'You're damned right it is, Algie. We had two steel hawsers running from your casing to that ring and our towing pendant connected to it. It must have been some force to shear it.'

'I know that, Roger,' Steele replied impatiently. 'I was the first lieutenant of my last boat. What I meant was, why not replace the mooring ring with another. No doubt you have a spare?'

'Absolutely, old man. But how are we to shackle the hawsers onto the new ring? Your boat's unmanned and judging by the distance to the shore, she'll be aground before long.'

Steele could see for himself that the tug and his boat now lay barely three miles offshore. He wracked his brains for a solution. He just had to get his command to Archangel. Suddenly an idea occurred to him.

'What if I jumped across? You could float across the pendant with a new ring on a grass line and I could connect the existing hawsers to it.'

'It would be sheer folly in these seas. The deck's rolling like a drunken matelot and it would be committing suicide. Come off it, man. The game's up. Accept it.'

'I can't accept it, Roger. I must deliver that boat to Archangel and beyond. I'm going to give it a go. My mind's made up.' Steele grabbed a life jacket from the wheelhouse rail and began climbing down onto the deck below. As he made his way back down to the working deck at the stern, he heard a cry of, 'Man overboard!'

Rushing to the stern, he saw a man in the water between the bucking tug and the rolling submarine. He was thrashing in the water and trying to paddle towards the lifebelt that had already been thrown in his direction.

'What happened?' he barked at the seamen nearby.

'It's Stevens, sir. He didn't give us the chance to stop him. He just tried to jump onto his submarine, sir,' a shocked seaman replied. Steele didn't wait for any further explanation. He cast aside his lifejacket, oilskin jacket and sea boots and jumped into the water himself.

He immediately sank beneath the waves, but didn't panic. After an apparent age, he rose again to the surface and was able to take a gasp of air. Above him towered the transom of the tug and he immediately kicked away with powerful strokes to avoid the propellers. To his left he could see the hull of the submarine and the jumping ladder over the starboard bow, but no sign of Stevens.

'Where's Stevens?' he shouted to the bunch of seamen on the tug's deck above.

'Over there. About fifty yards away,' somebody shouted back, but the waves were too high for Steele to see anything. Moreover, he was struggling to keep his head out of the water. Briefly, he trod water and removed his white pullover before swimming in the direction indicated by the seamen above. He noted that now he was clear of the tug's propellers, Lucy was altering course to put him in the tug's lee. Although grateful, he hoped Lucy would not let the tug drift onto him. The last thing he needed was to be crushed between the tug and the submarine.

Taking breaths only on his left side, away from the direction of the waves, he continued his practised and powerful strokes. After a couple of minutes, he paused to tread water and look for Stevens.

He thought he saw a shape bob up ahead of him, but couldn't be sure before his eyes were blinded by spindrift and a wave lapped over him.

'Keep going, sir.' Several men were cheering him on. 'Only another twenty yards.'

A few seconds later, he almost swam into the life belt that had been dropped for Stevens. 'Stevens,' he cried. 'Can you hear me?' He thought he heard a cry before he switched to side stroke and began towing the lifebelt.

Thirty or so seconds later, he saw another shape in the water and recognised it as a lifejacket with a mop of hair poking out atop it. 'Hang on, Stevens. I'm coming for you,' he cried and made a last effort to approach the floating sailor.

With relative ease, he managed to approach Stevens and place the life belt over one of his shoulders. Fortunately, the lifebelt was secured to the tug with strong manila cord, but the lieutenant quickly recognised that in these seas it would not bear both their weights if hauled in by the tug's crew. There was nothing for it, but to tow Stevens's semi-inert body back towards the tug as the seamen took up the slack and Lucy manoeuvred his command gently towards them.

'How are you feeling, Stevens?'

'Fine, thank you, sir, but I don' reckon I was never much of swimmer at the best of times. Thank the Lord I wis wearin' my lifejacket or I'd a been a gonner. And for you, thanks, sir.'

'But what happened?'

'I tried to jump onto our boat, sir. I figured we needed somebody on board on account of the friggin' mooring ring breakin', sir.'

Steele was beginning to tire. Although an accomplished swimmer and capable of swimming a mile or more normally, his wet and now heavy clothing, the high waves and the almost dead weight of Stevens were counting against him. Despite all his efforts, he still had another fifty yards to swim to return to the tug. To his right he could see the submarine against the background of the shore, about seventy yards away.

'You're mad, Stevens. As somebody told me a lifetime ago, it would be sheer folly. Suicide even. But I've an idea. If I can get you to the boat, are you still up for boarding her and receiving a new tow?'

'No problem, sir. But ain't she a bit far off yet?'

'Leave that to me. It'll be easier to drift down to her with the wind, but have you the strength to climb the jumping ladder?'

'I'll manage, sir. I might not have the prowess of a duck when it comes to swimmin' sir, but I'm a better friggin' monkey.'

CHAPTER 19

Elizabeth was amused to watch the sailors of *E45* passing crates of beer from one to other. It was a continuous chain of men and crates from the jetty to deep inside the bowels of the submarine. 'It doesn't look as if the crew intend going thirsty in this boat, Tom. I hope her first lieutenant is keeping an eye on the draught marks or there'll be enough beer on the bottom of the Mersey to open a public house.'

'You know very well, ma'am, that these navy boys know their business,' Tom Menzies, the yard's general manager replied. 'I suspect it's a compliment to Cain's brewery. The lads won't be supping that in Harwich.' HMS *E45* had successfully completed her sea trials and was due to be commissioned within a few days before heading for her new base port on the east coast.

'At least the poor sods won't be on the Somme. 160,000 casualties in just four weeks! That's slaughter,' Menzies added conversationally.

'Don't go on, Tom. My brother's in France and I dread to think of it.' Elizabeth winced and held her side.

'Are you all right, ma'am? Should I find you a seat?' Menzies asked solicitously.

'No, I'll be fine.' Elizabeth waved him away. 'I think I'll go back to the office. My legs are tired.' In actual fact, Elizabeth felt anything but fine. Now eight-months pregnant, she was finding it hard to make her daily rounds of the yard. She felt like one of those hippopotami she had once seen in Regent's Park Zoological Gardens and could not wait for the baby to be born.

'Mind yourself, ma'am. They're just about to test the new crane.'

Elizabeth moved aside and looked up at the yard's new electric crane. In order to modernise the yard and improve productivity, she was replacing all the old steam cranes with electric versions. Without the need for boilers, the electric cranes were not only lighter, but immediately available as there was no delay whilst steam was raised. To her surprise, of the two slingers preparing the test weight of just over eleven tons, one was a woman. Elizabeth thought she recognised the female slinger as having been working in the print shop. It gave her a sense of satisfaction to see her women work their way up the ladder of skilled trades and she paused to observe them whilst she caught her breath.

The test weight actually comprised four huge, separate square weights arranged in the form of a pyramid with a six-ton weight on the bottom and a quarter-ton weight on the top. The two slingers worked on either side of the stack and started to attach the large straps to it. Elizabeth heard a male slinger shout to the woman, 'Top two', as he secured the straps to the top two weights for the first part of the test. Suddenly, Elizabeth saw something was wrong.

To Elizabeth's horror, the woman had obviously forgotten about the top weight or, being shorter than her partner, failed to see it, because she fastened her straps to the second and third weights. The male slinger signalled to his colleague in the crane to take up the slack and Elizabeth saw what was going to happen. She shouted a warning, but there was too much noise in the yard for it to be heard.

Instinctively, despite her condition and weariness, she ran at the male slinger, gesticulating wildly to warn of the impending accident, but his back was to her. Everything seemed to go into slow motion for her. In the corner of her eye she could see the weights begin to topple as the crane lifted them and still the slinger was blissfully unaware of the danger. Without thinking, she launched herself into the air and slammed hard into the man's back, pushing him a few feet forward just as the test weights collapsed and the two-ton and quarter-ton slabs of metal landed with a grating crash just a foot from where he had been standing seconds before. The effort winded the slinger on whom Elizabeth had landed, but she screamed in pain. She had landed badly and the pain in her abdomen was excruciating, to the extent she was losing consciousness.

As her vision failed, she could still hear a crowd collect around her and a babble of different voices.

'Are you all right, ma'am?'

'Bugger me, Tam. The mistress's just saved your life!'

'For fuck's sake, what happened there?'

'Mind your language, you lot. That's the mistress there.'

'Are you all right, Tam? What about you, love?'

'Christ, her water's have broken! The baby. What's happened to the baby?'

'She's bleeding! Send for an ambulance, for God's sake!'

The baby, Elizabeth thought. Oh my God, what have I done? She tried to sit up, but then everything went black.

*****

'Captain Roschakoffsky is like no Russian I've met in this God-forsaken land,' Engineer Commander Percy Stocker observed to Lieutenant Lucy as the *Hampden*'s master prepared to make his farewell. Thirty-six hours earlier and almost three weeks from leaving Lerwick, Lucy had delivered *C27* safely to the port of Archangel.

'It's my first time in Russia, sir, so I couldn't rightly say. But he resembles a bear to me.'

Roschakoffsky was, indeed, a tall hulk of a figure with a bushy beard and a booming voice he used to great effect to cow those he deemed to be working too slowly. He had a sharp tongue and a colourful choice of language for petty officials he judged to be obstructing him in his task - language he was not afraid to use on higher officials either. That task was to load the four *C*-boats onto barges ready to be towed to Petrograd.

'Take it from me, Lucy, he's extraordinary. Unlike many of his compatriots, he's remarkably efficient and energetic. He's a master of logistical planning, too. The first barge was lashed down in the floating dock and flooded a day before you hove over the horizon. Believe me, that's most certainly not typical over here.'

'I'll have to take your word for it, sir. I'm just grateful we didn't lose our charge in that storm.' Lucy gestured to *C27* sitting on a barge and ready to be towed away by the paddle steamer *Sealnia*. It was a strange sight to see the submarine out of the water.

'I'm no seaman, Lucy, but I'm told that was a remarkable piece of seamanship of yours to recover the tow when the boat was cast adrift. Without it, the boat would undoubtedly have been wrecked ashore.'

'No doubt her CO could have bought the navy a new one, but I can't take the credit.'

'I don't follow, Lucy.'

'His father owns half of Scotland and a fair chunk of Marylebone. Daddy's an earl and Algie's a viscount. Not that he'd thank me for telling you, sir.'

'Really? Why the deuced is he an unwashed chauffeur in submarines then and not a flag lieutenant in a battle cruiser?'

'I couldn't say, sir, but he's no fop. It's thanks to him we saved the submarine. And that reminds me. I wonder if you would be so good as to deliver this report to Commander Miller when you meet up with him, please, sir?'

'You'll have to enlighten me. Just how did he save his submarine?'

'When the towing pendant broke, we had no way of securing it to the boat. One of the submariners tried to jump onto the casing, but ended up in the water. Without hesitation, young Algie jumped in after him. He saved the sailor's life and together they managed to get on board the submarine. Eventually, they made fast the tow, but we couldn't recover them onto the tug until we reached the anchorage at Yukanski. It must have been an uncomfortable twenty-four hours in that floating can. She rolls like a matelot after a run ashore in Guz's Union Street. We had to float them across some dry clothing, along with food and water, or else the poor sods would have perished from the cold. It's all in my report to Commander Miller here, sir. I've suggested they both deserve a medal.'

'Hell's teeth! He's a cool one. I shall look forward to knowing him better when we're both in Reval.'

'He clearly has heart as well as stamina, too. The seaman he fished out of the water… a bit of a rogue, I understand. Lost his hook for insubordination. I'm told he was carrying his life savings - twenty pounds in banknotes - in his pockets when he jumped into the water. Completely ruined by the salt water immersion, of course. The word amongst the ship's company is that Algie's offered to stump up the cash himself to replace it.'

'What it is to be rich, hey? Still, he didn't have to make the gesture, but I'd better not detain you further. Give my love to Blighty when you see her again.'

'I will do, sir. And when do you travel to Reval, sir?'

'22.00. I'll be accommodated with most of the submarine crews on the paddle steamer towing *C26* and *C27*. Roschakoffsky will follow with the other two boats. I'm looking forward to it. Travelling nearly 1,400 miles of Russian inland waterways is likely to be a great adventure. It'll be one for the history books if we make it intact.'

*****

'Zooks, Cox'n! If it gets any warmer, we may have to break out tropical kit.' Steele mopped his brow as he and Davis surveyed the flat, sandy banks of the broad Dvina river between Archangel and Kotlas.

'Aye, sir. It's fair hot after the White Sea. Must be all of 80 degrees by my reckoning, sir. And there we were embarking extra cold-weather gear for this trip.'

'Indeed. I say, Cox'n. Best warn the men not to stay too long uncovered in the sun.' Steele had met up with his ship's company at Archangel, but several of the pasty-looking submariners were taking advantage of the weather and enforced idleness to sunbathe on the deck of the Russian tug.

'Aye aye, sir. Might be advice too late in the case of Stevens, sir. Look at him yonder. He's already looking like a lobster. Don't they have sunshine in his native Suffolk?' Davis chuckled.

'It's no laughing matter, Cox'n. Sunburn is a self-inflicted injury. You'd better dish out some of the zinc-oxide paste.' In the absence of trained medical orderlies in submarines, medical matters fell to the boat's coxswain.

'Yes, sir,' Davis responded, quickly wiping the smile from his face. 'How much longer do you think it'll take to reach Saint Petersburg, sir?'

'The Russians have renamed it to Petrograd now, Cox'n. It sounds less German. There are some saying our royal house of Saxe-Coburg should do the same. But in answer to your question, oh, I'd say at least a fortnight… or so I'm told.'

'Three bleedin' weeks in all? I'd no idea Russia was such a big bloody country, sir. We haven't seen a town in ages.'

'One is never too old to learn, Cox'n. I wonder what the locals think of the sight of four barges passing by, each loaded with 300 tons of submarine under the White Ensign. Now you'd better break out your first-aid supplies. And give the first lieutenant my compliments and ask him to join me.'

CHAPTER 20

Elizabeth could hear voices, but couldn't focus on the people speaking. She felt tired and it was too much effort to concentrate, so she let herself drift back off to sleep. It was later she discovered she was in a private ward of the Birkenhead Borough Hospital.

The next time she woke, she recognised the sounds of Latin. '*Per istam sanctam unctionem et suam piissimam misericordiam adiuvet te dominus gratia spiritus sancti, ut a peccatis liberatum te salvet atque propitius alleviet.*'

The words frightened her. Was she dying? A Catholic by upbringing, she recognised these as the words of the final sacrament for the sick. She felt for the oil on her forehead, but her head was not anointed. The effort tired her once more, but she forced herself to stay conscious.

'She's coming round doctor,' a female voice said. The Latin prayers continued.

'Mrs Miller, can you hear me?' a male voice asked. Elizabeth tried harder to focus and saw that the man leaning over her wore a white coat. All the time, the Latin sentences continued and they started to annoy her. She was not dying. She wanted the priest to go away. She tried to sit up, but hadn't the strength. A gentle hand restrained her.

'Relax, Mrs Miller. Stay where you are. Nurse, bring over the little girl.'

Little girl? Elizabeth suddenly remembered her unborn child and the accident in the yard.

'There you are, Elizabeth,' the female said as she pressed a tiny bundle of flesh to her bosom. 'You've a lovely little daughter. If I draw the screen, would you like to feed her?'

Elizabeth could feel the baby snuggle into her breasts and a wave of tenderness overwhelmed her, but she still felt unable to do anything but nod. After pulling the screen to afford her privacy, the nurse put the baby to one of her breasts. The Latin incantations had finished and she let herself drift off to sleep again. It was a huge relief to her to know she wasn't going to die. That tiny bundle of flesh suckling at her breast needed her too much.

*****

After nearly two weeks travelling through the interior of Russia's vast interior, boredom had set in amongst the ships' companies of the four submarines piggy-backing the Russian barges. Together, the four submarine COs managed to persuade Roschakoffsky to halt the convoy for a few hours in Lake Bieloe, one of the many beautiful lakes they were passing through, so that the men could engage in swimming. Needless to say, it was not long before various competitions had been organised between each submarine, led by the CO of *C27*. The ten Russian soldiers standing guard on each of the barges watched the skylarking impassively. Stocker shared a cigarette with Roschakoffsky on the bridge roof of the tug, their third tug since leaving Archangel as the depth of water in the canals and rivers was becoming ever shallower.

'We have made good progress, no?' Roschakoffsky bellowed, but good-naturedly. 'In a few days, we will enter Lake Onega and into the River Neva. The Neva will take us all the way to Saint Petersburg.'

'You still refer to your capital by its pre-war name then, Captain?'

'Why not? Before the war, I came to like the Germans, despite their arrogant ways. Did you know that after leaving the Imperial Navy I was a diplomatic representative in Germany? I speak the language.'

'No, I didn't know that.' Stocker drew deeply on his cigarette before exhaling noisily. Something caught his eye on the shore. He saw movement and a cloud of dust approaching. After reaching for his glasses, he was astonished by the sight.

'My God, Captain, what is that?' He passed the binoculars to the Russian.

Roschakoffsky grunted as he observed the scene unfolding before them. A huge column of men was on the march, much like the armies of the Napoleonic wars.

'Austrians. At last. The idle bastards have taken their time. I'll soon ginger them up.'

'You'll have to explain, Captain. How have the Austrians made it here?' Stocker took back the binoculars and looked at the massed columns of men with a mixture of apprehension and wonder.

'They're prisoners. 3,000 of them. They've been digging new locks nearby, but I have called them up for a new task. You recall the barge carrying *C35* rammed the last lock gate, yes? She's now leaking and needs repairs. I've ordered that a new lock is dug at the end of the lake so that we can drain it to form a dry dock.'

'Good Lord! But do you not have steam excavators for such tasks? Surely it would be quicker and more efficient?'

'Possibly in your country, Commander. But it would take too long to summon one from Saint Petersburg. But one thing we are not short of in Russia is labour. We make the best use of what we have to hand. Come with me. You can help me explain to those ignorant bastards in charge just what I want done.'

*****

Nearly three weeks after the accident in the yard, Elizabeth was finally allowed to return home with her daughter. She had decided to call her child, Margaret. Only a week before had she learned that Margaret's twin sibling, a boy, had been stillborn and that both children had been delivered by Caesarean section. She had lost much blood initially, but apart from the soreness of her scar, she felt quite well again. As she looked around the ward prior to her discharge, she felt overcome once again by the kindness of the many workers she employed in the yard. The ward was such a veritable hothouse of cut flowers that she had begged the nurses to take many to the other wards of the hospital. The slingers had even constructed a magnificent crib resembling Noah's Ark in thanks for saving the life of Tam Hardy. She had not had the heart to tell them that she had already purchased one for the nursery.

To her great surprise, one of her more regular visitors had been Johanna. Uncle William had been too busy to do more than write, but Johanna had visited at least once a day over the past fortnight. She stood now holding Margaret and smiling broadly.

'Have you told Richard yet, my dear?' Johanna asked.

'Not yet, Aunt Johanna, but I intend to do so just as soon as I am home. Neither you nor Uncle William have mentioned it have you?' Elizabeth asked in alarm.

'No, Elizabeth. We have waited for you to break the news.'

'Good,' replied Elizabeth relieved. 'I don't want him to know about the accident, nor of the death of poor little William. He has enough to worry about. Let him take joy in knowing that he has a healthy daughter. And she is healthy, is she not, Aunt?'

'Oh yes. Quite healthy. She's a lovely, sweet thing. It has worked out far better than I had imagined.'

Elizabeth scowled at the last remark. Clearly, Aunt Johanna meant that she had expected her to have given birth to a cretin. Aunt Johanna must have caught the look as she continued in a worried fashion.

'I'm sorry, my dear. That was insensitive of me. It was just… We all thought we were going to lose you as well as the little boy. Oh, my dear.' She reached out to take one of Elizabeth's hands. 'I know what you are thinking. I have not been a good mother-in-law to you.'

The remark surprised Elizabeth and she spotted the beginnings of tears in Johanna's eyes. 'Nonsense, Aunt. I'm happy enough.'

'You're a good child, Elizabeth.' Johanna dabbed her eyes with a lace handkerchief. 'You have been in my prayers every day since I heard the news.' Tears began to well in Johanna's eyes again. 'Oh, how shabbily I have treated you.' Tears began to roll down Johanna's face. 'God would never have forgiven my actions had you died in childbirth. And now you have…' She began to sob such that her words came out in a staccato fashion. '… a fine and… beautiful baby… girl. Dearest… dear Margaret. Oh, I beg you, Elizabeth…'

Elizabeth crumpled. 'Oh, Aunt Johanna, don't go on.' Her voice quivered. 'Just give me a hug.'

Like Penelope with the disguised Odysseus, their hearts were melted and the tears flowed as the snow wastes upon the mountain tops when the winds have breathed upon it and thawed it till the rivers run bank full with water.

*****

As September marked the end of the Russian summer, Richard had thought life was looking up. Pending the arrival of the four *C*-class boats from their odyssey through the inland waterways of Russia, he had borrowed the navigator from *E1* and taken *E19* to sea for a short, uneventful patrol off Riga. Uneventful apart from being showered by thirty-four bombs from a German aeroplane. Aircraft were becoming an increasing menace to his flotilla as well as the Russians. In the spring, one of their battleships had been bombed from the air. Richard wondered how his brother, Paul, was engaged in this new form of warfare. However, notwithstanding the lack of success by *E19* in engaging any target, the Russians had achieved some successes. One of their submarines, the *Volk*, had sunk three cargo ships and gone on to capture two destroyers. For Richard, the real benefit of the patrol had been the opportunity to escape the accounts and administration of the flotilla command.

He had welcomed with glee the newly-arrived Engineer Commander Percy Stocker and his news of the safe arrival of the new submarines in Petrograd. However, Stocker had other news to dampen his unusually cheerful mood.

'Your request for a torpedo maintenance crew has been granted, sir. They include five torpedo fitters and a Torpedo Gunner's Mate, and should arrive in the next few weeks, sir. My maintenance team is to be supplemented, too, sir, by some technicians from Chloride to care for the batteries.'

'Not before time, Stocker. The boats are beginning to show their age and as it is, *E8*'s battery is playing up again. I'm barely able to keep one *E*-boat at sea at a time, but that should change with you and your team… I confess, Stocker, I have great plans for the *C*-boats. I'm keen to show their mettle to our Russian hosts. I just hope the new accommodation will be ready in time.'

Richard picked up his notebook to check his notes of the last meeting he had had with the Russians on the subject. 'Ah, yes. The officers' cabins are ready, but the new bathrooms won't be ready for a couple of weeks yet. I'm afraid all the work has impinged on your workshop space. Still, it can't be helped.'

'I'm sorry, sir…' Stocker began to fiddle with his cap nervously. 'There's some unfortunate news on the boats' arrival date.'

'Really? And what could that be? If the Russians are not co-operating, I'll have a word with their C-in-C.'

'No, sir. It's not that. The shipyard is putting the boats back together nicely. My assistant constructor is seeing to that. It's a matter of logistics.' Stocker paused, apparently unwilling to speak further.

'Go on. Come out with it, man.'

'Very well, sir. Firstly, the torpedoes have gone adrift.'

'Adrift? But where?'

'I can't say, sir. That's the problem. It seems they were wrongly addressed and could be anywhere in Russia.'

Richard let out a sigh of dejection. 'That is most unfortunate. We're low on mouldies. I've been begging and stealing them from the Russians lately. With a little modification they work, though. I dare say we'll manage.'

Stocker still seemed discomforted, however. 'Sir, I'm sorry to say, but that is only part of it.'

'From the look on your face, Stocker, I can tell I'm not going to like the rest of it. Don't worry, I'm already seated and if it's as bad as your expression suggest, we have a new fleet surgeon on hand to revive me.'

'It's the batteries, sir - for the *C*-boats. They were badly packed in the first place and then somebody stowed them loose on top of the coal in the transporting ship. The plates are damaged.'

'Oh, my Lord! Surely not. How could anyone have been so negligent? Forget I said that, Stocker. How many can be salvaged? We could at least get a couple of boats operational.'

Stocker looked wretched at Richard's words.

'Come on, let's be positive and no pun was intended, man. Could we make up two batteries?' Stocker shook his head. 'No? Just one then? Not even one!' Richard spoke quietly in disbelief. 'You're telling me that not a single submarine can put to sea for the sake of some no doubt idle and irresponsible persons at Chloride failing to pack those plates properly. Words fail me.'

Stocker said nothing, but continued to fidget with his cap. Richard shut his eyes and let his chin rest on his chest. Eventually he broke the silence.

'I have to have those boats by the end of November or else they'll be frozen in. So, I want you to round up all the spare plates here and send them up to Petrograd with the aim of getting at least one boat operational. I'll signal Commodore Hall instantly and demand replacements within the month. If that fails, we'll have to lay up *E8* and rob what plates we can. I need those boats on patrol before the ice comes. You hear me?'

'Aye aye, sir. I'll do the best I can.' Stocker stood and made to leave. Richard halted him.

'I'm sorry, Stocker. It's not your fault. It's the way things seem to be out here. I've not made you very welcome, have I? Let me buy you a gin. That is something we do seem to have in again at last.'

CHAPTER 21
October 1916

Together, Richard and Rachel Henderson kneeled before the make-shift altar in her home and prayed aloud. Then Rachel read out loud her chosen psalm for the day, number 142. As she read it in her soft northern accent, Richard felt the words deeply.

'*... I pour out my complaint before him; before him I tell my trouble. ... In the path where I walk, men have hidden a snare for me. ... No-one is concerned for me. I have no refuge; no-one cares for my life...*'

He barely heard the next line as he reflected on the misery of his current existence, but made an effort to focus on the reading. *'Listen to my cry, for I am in desperate need...'* Tears began to well in his eyes. *'... rescue me from those who pursue me, for they are too strong for me. Set me free from...'*

'Whatever t'is the matter, Richard?' Rachel didn't finish her reading, but rested a hand on his shoulder. He failed to stifle a sob before burying his head in his hands. Rachel laid her arm gently round his shoulders.

'Come now, Richard, lad. 'Tis not like you. Tell me what's up.'

Richard gathered his emotions in check and took a handkerchief to his eyes. 'I'm sorry, Rachel. That was most unmanly of me. Forgive me for embarrassing you.' He turned towards her and managed a faint smile.

Rachel removed her arm. ''Tain't nothin' to be embarrassed about, chuck. Mebbe's yer feelin' 'omesick, like. Nowt wrong wi' that.'

'Quite possibly, but it's more than that. I was imagining David in his cave as he made that prayer and suddenly, I felt as if I was there. I heard recently that my child has been born… a fine, healthy daughter. Naturally, I'm very happy at the news, but it has brought it home to me that I'm nearly two thousand miles from my wife, child and family. For a moment, I felt I had been forsaken by God and would never meet my child.'

Now it was Rachel's turn to become emotional. Her face melted and tears appeared in her eyes. 'Oh, love, don't talk that way. God would never forsake you. 'e loves you just as so many do

’ere. Don’t take on so. Come here.’ She reached out both arms and grasped Richard’s head to her bosom. ‘You’re strong. I know that. So, stop frettin’.’

Richard was astonished by Rachel’s actions, but whether through shock or politeness, he let his head rest on Rachel’s chest. For some reason it struck him how flat was her bosom compared with that of Lizzy and that she wore a beautiful perfume he couldn’t place. It reminded him of the forests. Perhaps it was sandalwood or cedar wood. And there was a hint of spice. Could it be cinnamon and nutmeg? The scent seemed familiar and reassuring. He let Rachel hold him a moment longer before disentangling himself. Somehow, he felt strong again.

‘Thank you, Rachel. I feel better now. Let’s sing a hymn. Singing always improves my mood.’

*****

At last, the first of the *C*-boats arrived in Reval. First, *C32*, under the command of Lieutenant Christopher Satow, and then *C35*, under the command of Lieutenant Edward Stanley DSC. Their arrival coincided with that of the medical officer, Staff Surgeon Kenneth Hole, sadly too late to prevent the death of the sailor from *E1* of kidney failure. Pleased as Richard was to see the two new reinforcements, he quickly despatched them to a new base at Rogekul, in the Moon Sound, closer to the Gulf of Riga to support the Russian forces defending Riga and the Gulf. The small submarines had a limited endurance, but would be ideal for coastal work whilst the *E*-boats worked further offshore. However, with the approach of the winter, there would only be time for the boats to complete one patrol. Richard didn’t envy the crew their new base port. With no sports grounds or canteen, it was a bleak and unlovely place to spend a winter. Meanwhile, Richard still had no batteries for *C27* nor *C26*.

As December approached, he arranged for both boats to be towed down the Gulf of Finland, just as the ice set in and in time for Christmas. Meeting his old first lieutenant was the bright spot in what was turning into a bitter and bleak winter. Steele now wore the blue and white striped ribbon of the Albert Medal, awarded on

Lucy's and Richard's recommendation for the saving of Able Seaman Stevens's life in the summer.

'Algie, my good fellow. Ever since I read your name as being in command of *C27*, I have longed for this moment. Are you well?' The two former comrades-in-arms chatted happily for an hour or more, catching up on events of the previous year. During the conversation, Richard asked after the health of Steele's father.

'Not well at all, I'm afraid, sir. He and my grandfather were very close and Pater seems to have taken his death badly. I took some leave after leaving *E9* and he seems to be letting the estate go. Thankfully, he still has the income from the London properties.'

'I'm sorry to hear that, Algie. It must be a worry for you.'

'Not really, sir. I'm fatalistic about such things and there's nothing I can do it about it out here. I'm just glad to be out of Petrograd… as I believe it's now called.'

'I'm afraid it may be a while before you see action. There's nothing we can do before the spring thaw, so you might have preferred Christmas in Petrograd.'

'Lud, I can't think of a more depressing place right now. Every day sees demonstrations and strikes. I gather there are severe food shortages. Mind you, there seemed to be some joy at the news of the murder of some rascal called Rasputin.'

'I had heard. He was a mendicant who seemed to have a hold over the Tsarina. As for food shortages, take care, Algie. Compared with the Russians, our lads fare quite well for rations, but I fear it's going to cause jealousy and strife afore long. In general, the Russians don't treat their men well.'

''Pon rep', sir, I saw that for meself. All this bowing and scraping the officers demand. Insisting upon being addressed as "High-born excellency". You know, I once saw a young army officer seek out a soldier promenading with his lady… just to accept his salute. Then this officer spat in his face and ordered him to turn round and bend over, whereupon he kicked him in the backside so hard the poor wretch fell over in the filth of the street. It's diabolical. No wonder the chaps are deserting in their thousands and mutinying.'

'Mutiny, you say? I hadn't heard of such things yet.'

'It was about a month after we arrived at the dockyard, sir. Apparently, some strikers began rioting and a couple of regiments were ordered to fire on them. Instead, they turned their rifles on the police.'

'It's come to that has it? My word, Algie, I don't want this shared, but I fear matters may become desperate soon. The country's falling apart and I don't think the Tsar has a handle on it. Now Romania has fallen, I expect further stretch on Russia's southern front. We have to keep Russia in this war or else imagine how that would affect our boys on the Western Front. I presume you've heard about the change in government at home?'

'You mean the Welsh windbag, sir?'

'Don't let my first lieutenant, Evans, hear you say that, Algie. But yes. I suppose the new coalition government might help with the prosecution of the war. It probably can't do worse than the last lot, although I quite liked Asquith. I fear it was the Somme that did for him.'

'I once met his son, Arthur, sir. He joined the Naval Division at the outset and seems to have done well for himself.'

'I didn't know that. My cousin, Charles, must have served with him.' Suddenly, Richard chuckled. 'I've just had a most amusing thought. My wife won't be happy with the new PM. She once set fire to his house on the golf links!'

*****

Elizabeth noted that Christabel had put on weight during her self-imposed exile in France. Whilst soon after the outbreak of war the government had remitted the sentences of those suffragettes in prison and at large under the 'Cat and Mouse' Act, Christabel had feared she might still be subject to arrest since she had not commenced serving her sentence. As a result, she had spent most of the war to date campaigning on a variety of issues from France and New York. This meeting in London was the first time Lizzy had seen her since before the war.

'I am so pleased to see that little has changed at the Ritz despite this dreadful war, Lizzy. It's sort of reassuring, isn't it?'

'There's a strange irony there, Christabel. Here we are, both campaigning for change and you hark on about stasis.'

'You know what I mean, Lizzy. Anyway, you've certainly changed. Mother tells me you have a daughter now.

Congratulations. I'm sure I could never go through the child birth thing.'

Elizabeth hid her distraction by sipping her tea as she reflected on the awkward circumstances leading to the birth of Margaret and the loss of little William. That loss and her considerable discomfort following the birthing operation had been difficult to bear over the past four months, but she had found joy in Margaret.

'Where is the dear thing anyway, Lizzy? You've not left her in a railway station, have you?'

'No, Christabel,' Elizabeth replied, coming out of her reverie. 'It's only boys that get left in handbags at stations. She's at my Aunt Johanna's home with her nurse. I'm spending Christmas with my parents-in-law.'

'How lovely for them. And the baby, of course. I'm sure she'll be spoilt rotten. I'm pleased to hear you have managed to spare time away from your precious shipyard.'

'It is precious, Christabel. And you of all people should recognise that. It's not just the contribution to the war effort, but look at how it's empowering women. It's all very well to write letters and leaflets, or give fine speeches, but I'm offering practical help to women.'

'*Touché*, Lizzy. I'm sorry. I didn't mean it to come out that way. Mother tells me you're being a marvel, although I gather you've been upsetting the engineering unions.'

'I'm sorry, Christabel. I over-reacted. I'm feeling a bit tired, that's all.' Elizabeth reached across to squeeze Christabel's hand affectionately. 'I seem to have the local unions tamed, but I'm struggling with the unions nationally. It's the old problem. Men have to come first. They're worried about competing with women for jobs if employers allow women to take on skilled work. There's to be a big *brouhaha* on the subject in Glasgow next month.'

'Perhaps we should send along a few women to the meeting, Lizzy. I can speak to the local membership.'

'It might be worthwhile, I suppose. I presume you and your mother are pleased that Asquith's resigned? Do you think it will help with the Speaker's conference?'

'Naturally, it's good news. I think L-G will have no truck with the Foreign Office's schemes to negotiate a compromise peace agreement. I have to say that he's very open to suggestions on a whole raft of issues. He's already met with mother.'

'But it was Asquith who set up the Speaker's conference to examine the issue of broadening the franchise to vote, Christabel.'

'Of course, I know that, but I doubt he would have paid it anything but lip service... I say! Look at those marvellous cakes. Should we order a plate?'

'Not for me, thanks, Christabel. I'm still not back to my weight before Margaret came along.'

'Well, it's not as if Richard's going to be home soon, is it?' Christabel covered her mouth in horror. 'Sorry, Lizzy. That was tactless of me.'

'Don't worry. I'm a big girl now.'

'Yes, I suppose you are.' Christabel seemed about to say something, but thought better of it and moved on. 'Anyway, as I was saying, according to mother, the Speaker may recommend extending the vote to more than the six million women we thought. If that's the case, we'll not argue. It will just be a case of debating the terms under which the legislation is enacted.'

'Really? Is that what your mother thinks? I've heard that the Speaker isn't proposing equal rights to vote for men and women. Is there not talk of an age and property restriction for women? I hear tell it might be thirty-five for women of property and twenty-one without any restrictions on men.'

'I can't say, Lizzy, as L-G hasn't seen the proposals himself, but better to have an imperfect scheme that can pass through Parliament. Mother's view is that we should accept whatever he thinks he can get past Parliament with the least discussion.'

'Gosh, Christabel. She has changed her tune. Willing to accept whatever Lloyd George is prepared to allow! I'm not at all sure my women workers would agree with you. They would see it as the WSPU looking after the interests of the middle class and not the majority. But I'll not debate the point with you, Christabel. I've too much else on my plate. And talking of plates… You know, I've changed my mind. Let's order some of those delicious-looking cakes.'

CHAPTER 22
February 1917

Despite regular cheerful letters from Lizzy describing the daily changes in and progress of Margaret, the winter of early 1917 suddenly became ever bitter as Richard read the latest communiqué from Commodore Hall. It contained the news of the deaths of both Goodhart and Gilbert. Gilbert's Q-ship had been sunk with all hands in the North Sea. Richard felt a flash of guilt that had he not been sent home, Gilbert might still be alive. Then he remembered the instances of Gilbert's inattention or laziness to involve himself in detail. Such a lack of efficiency in a submarine officer could cause the death of an entire ship's company and Richard consoled himself that he had made the right decision, even if he regretted its consequences, nonetheless. Sadly, Gilbert was just another casualty of this never-ending war.

Goodhart's death, however, touched him more deeply. He recalled with fondness and gratitude the many ways in which Goodhart, as his second-in-command, had eased his administrative burden over the previous year. As his just reward, Goodhart had then been promoted to commander on New Year's Eve and, in early January, had returned to the UK to take up command of HMS *K14*, a new class of submarines propelled by steam to enable them to keep up with the Fleet on manoeuvres. According to the facts Hall had been able to ascertain, Goodhart had joined his friend Commander Godfrey Herbert on board his boat *K13* for some sea experience. During the trials and on her final dive, the boiler room had flooded and the submarine had sunk. Typical of the man, Goodhart had volunteered to escape to seek help, but as he had passed through the conning tower, he had hit his head and drowned. He had been recommended for the posthumous award of the Albert Medal. It seemed such a waste, Richard thought.

Reading the letter again, he felt a surge of tiredness. He knew he was feeling the strain of command and wondered if their Lordships had been right to give him such a heavy responsibility. After all, whilst Goodhart had earned his promotion by dint of a lengthy period of hard work and efficiency, his own promotion had come with a VC for a foolhardy entry into the harbour of Constantinople and an attack on the ships within it. At the time, he had seen it as an act of great strategy to knock the Turks out of the war, but despite his and the other submarine CO's success in bringing the Turks to within one week of running out of ammunition, the Allies had, nonetheless, withdrawn from the beaches of Gallipoli and so had ended their best hope of opening a southern front. Had the effort and risks been worth it, he wondered.

For some time now, Richard had been having problems with sleeping. It had come to the point where he dreaded going to bed. When in bed, he would lie awake thinking of all the tasks he had left undone. Gradually, he would feel his heart rate increase and his body temperature rise. Then and worst of all, would come the tightening of his stomach as the gnawing pains began. It was as if he had swallowed a rat alive and it was trying to eat its way out of his body.

'I think if it hadn't been for Rachel, I would have gone mad.' He realised he had spoken aloud, but in the privacy of his cabin on board the *Dvina*.

Richard reflected on the present situation. The winter was proving particularly frustrating for him and his men. As sailors, their place was at sea, but the ice had them trapped. To prevent boredom amongst the ships' companies he had organised a series of concert parties and time and time again, he had been amazed at the ingenuity and latent talents of his men on the stage, despite the frequent bad and blasphemous language. During the day, the men were continuously employed trying to keep the boats free from the ice in the harbour and on the casings. The engineering departments under the effective leadership of Stocker were valiantly engaged in maintaining the flotilla of nine submarines, each now gaily painted in the new dappled paint scheme, and preparing the boats for the coming spring campaign.

He and his officers had tried hard to repay the generous hospitality of the expatriate community in Reval, but it was proving an expensive task. For Richard, this had not presented a problem, but he had seen the pecuniary embarrassment of his COs and, accordingly, written to Commodore Hall to request some form of table money for his officers. Many had followed Richard's example in attempts to learn the Russian language and he had engaged the services of a Mrs Kinna for the purpose. She was a Russian widow who had been married to a Scotsman. Thanks to Rachel's efforts and his flair for languages, Richard now considered himself fairly fluent in the Russian language. No longer did he need an interpreter for routine meetings, which was as well since Pavlyuchenko had been appointed as first lieutenant of a Russian submarine and would not be replaced until the spring.

It wasn't just for her Russian lessons that Richard felt grateful to Rachel. Increasingly over the past few months he had drawn strength and comfort from her faith, even though they both took a different approach to attendance at a church service. As a Catholic, he loved the ceremony and rituals of the church, many of which were replicated by the flotilla's Anglican padre in his weekly non-ecumenical Divine Services, but without the 'bells and smells'. Although he had invited Rachel to attend these services, as a Methodist she had declined on the basis that she was content to pray at home and it was better to concentrate on good deeds and virtuous acts to please God. However, Richard's faith, also, required him to attend the confessional to repent of his past sins. This was not something the Anglican padre could offer and so Rachel had introduced him to the local Lutheran community.

As was his daily habit, Richard reached for his Bible and opened it at random to read a few verses. He noted that the page he had chosen was from the Second Book of Samuel. The first line of the sixth chapter caught his eye, '*Again, David gathered together all the chosen men of Israel, thirty thousand.*' It gave him an idea. With the ships' companies of the seven submarines currently ice-bound in Reval together with the support staff, he had over two hundred men under his command. It might set a good impression to the Russians if they were to see his men assembled as a body, on parade for Divisions. Discipline and morale in the Tsar's navy was deteriorating quickly. Only recently had he agreed to have his medical officer take over the running of the *Dvina*'s sickbay because the Russian sailors had refused to be tended by their own staunchly imperialist, though competent, doctor. Anything that might stiffen the resolve of the Russians to persevere with the war effort was worth an attempt.

He was interrupted by a knock at the door. It was Steele.

'Awfully sorry to disturb you, sir, but there's an urgent matter demanding your attention.'

'Think nothing of it, Algie. What's the problem?'

'If you don't mind, sir, I'd like Leading Seaman Stevens to see you and explain in person. He's just outside.'

Richard shot Steele a questioning look to which Steele said nothing before summoning Stevens.

'This is Stevens, sir. He's one of my torpedomen.' Stevens marched in smartly and saluted.

'Stand easy, Stevens. No need to salute. I'm not wearing my cap and can't return it. What's up?'

'I'm sorry, sir. It's a bit delicate. Not sure 'ow to put it.'

'Relax, Stevens. Just tell the CO what you told me. You were sent on an errand by the paymaster,' Steele interrupted.

'Aye, that's right enuff, sir. I wis workin' in the ship's office an' Assistant Paymaster Hayward sent me with the weekly noos clippin's to the admiral's yacht. That's Admiral Canine's yacht I mean, sir.'

'Kanin, Stevens. Kanin,' Steele interrupted. Richard waved his hand to ignore the seaman's malapropism.

'That's what I said i'n'it? Admiral Canine. Anyway, just as I was trottin' up the brow, the admiral hisself starts comin' down, so I waited on the platform 'alf way up, stood smartly to attention and saluted 'im properly, like. You know, showed proper respect, sir. I did, sir. Honest.'

'I'm sure you did, Stevens,' Richard added reassuringly. 'Carry on.'

'Well, the admiral came down the steps an' as 'e passed, he stopped. I thought p'raps 'e wis gona say summat or return me salute, but then 'e gone 'n' spat full in me face. It wis…'

'The admiral spat at you? In the face?' Richard jumped to his feet in indignation.

''e did, sir. Right in me oye.'

'And did anybody witness this act, Stevens?'

'Only 'alf the bloody Russian Navy, sir… and Shiner Wright, sir.'

'Leading Seaman Wright, sir,' Steele added helpfully. 'He's outside, sir. I thought you might like to hear his account in corroboration.'

'Have you spoken to him, Lieutenant Steele?'

'I have, sir, and he verifies Stevens's story, sir.'

'Then I have no need to speak to him, too. Now tell me truthfully, Stevens. Did you offer any form of provocation or insolence towards the admiral? It's a serious accusation you are bringing.'

'You mean jest coz I lost me 'ook for insubordination last time, sir, I might 'a' done the same to the admiral?' Stevens pointed to the recently sewn-on anchor badge showing his rate to be that of a Leading Hand.

'Stevens,' Steele said curtly. 'Don't be impertinent now. The CO doesn't happen to know of your wicked past. Answer the question.'

'No, sir. Sorry, sir. I swear I wiz polite and offered no offence.'

Richard paused to absorb the information and returned to his seat. 'Very well, Stevens. I believe you. Leave the matter with me. I'm sorry. Thank you for bringing it to your CO's attention and now to mine. Carry on.'

Stevens came smartly to attention, checked himself from saluting and swivelled about before leaving the cabin. Richard let out a deep sigh and slumped in his chair.

'I'm sorry, sir, but I thought you should know. Don't worry about Stevens, though. He'll become a minor celebrity over the incident.'

'Thank you, Algie. You're quite right in bringing the matter before me. It's…' Richard delayed finishing his sentence, but came to a resolution and flushed red in the face. 'No. I will not have it. This is unsupportable.' He reached for his greatcoat and cap.

'Where are you going, sir?' Steele asked fearfully.

'I'm going to see Admiral Kanin, of course. I will not have my men treated this way.'

'Would you like me to come with you, sir?'

'No thank you, Algie. What I have to say to the admiral will be for his ears only.' Richard brushed past Steele and headed for the upper deck of the *Dvina*.

*****

Richard stormed up the gangway of the Russian C-in-C's yacht, leaving the sentries little time to prepare the customary ceremonial honours to foreign naval officers. He headed straight for the admiral's outer office, bursting in to the astonishment of the lieutenant and clerks sitting there.

'I wish to see the admiral,' he demanded in his best Russian.

'I'm sorry, sir. His excellency is in a meeting.' The staff officer rose to his feet flustered and started flicking through the pages of the admiral's diary. 'You are not due to meet with him for two days yet, sir.'

'I wish to see him now,' Richard said angrily. 'Tell him to cancel his meeting.'

'But, sir! I can't do that. If you would wait but a minute and I will see if I can bring forward…'

'Cancel it now or I walk through those doors myself to do it,' Richard cut him off in his iciest manner.

The lieutenant appeared to panic and then, still standing, picked up the telephone. Richard could only hear one side of the conversation, but it was clear that the admiral was not happy to be interrupted. The Russian almost pleaded with his superior that the matter was extremely urgent. Sweat trickled from his brow and chin. After several exchanges, he sat down dejected, still holding the two parts of the telephone in his hands.

'The Commander-in-Chief is finishing his meeting, sir, and will see you in two minutes.' Almost as an apology he added, 'I did my best, sir.'

Three minutes later, a pink-faced captain walked from the admiral's office into the outer office. He stared stonily at Richard, but said not a word before collecting his *ushanka* fur hat and departing. The staff officer rose again from his desk, straightened his jacket and walked over to the double doors leading to his principal's sanctum, paused, knocked and without waiting, opened the right-hand door for Richard.

'His high-born excellency will see you now, sir.'

Richard passed through the door in two strides, leaving the Russian to shut it behind him. Kanin remained seated behind his large desk. His normally pale face was oddly flushed and his eyes flashed at Richard in anger. Without rising he addressed Richard.

'So, what is this extremely urgent matter that comes even before my discussions of the next season's mine laying operations?'

Richard noted without surprise that he was not invited to sit, but that suited him fine. It would be easier for him to say what he had to whilst standing.

'Sir, I come to complain about your treatment of one of my men, Leading Seaman Stevens of His Majesty's Submarine *C27.* I understand you spat in his face earlier today.'

Richard noted Kanin wince at the words and his mouth tighten almost ready to snarl. He hurried on to his next sentence.

'Sir, no Royal Navy officer would ever treat one of his men in such an ugly manner and I have come to demand an apology.'

Richard watched Kanin's face turn puce and the veins in his temples throb. When Kanin spoke, his eyes flashed evil thoughts.

'You, a mere commander, have the gall to burst into my office, to interrupt an important meeting and to demand an apology from me over a trivial incident. May I remind you I am the Tsar's Commander-in-Chief of the Baltic, Commander.'

'I know who you are, sir, and your high office demands higher standards of you. That includes respect for my men.'

'Fuck you, Miller. I will do no such thing.'

'You disappoint me, sir. Then I have no choice, but to take this matter to a higher authority.'

'Hah! I doubt Admiral Grigorovich would give you the time of day. You're wasting your time.'

'I didn't have the Minister in mind, sir.' Richard gently touched his three Russian orders almost absentmindedly.

Some of the puce colour drained from Kanin's face and he spluttered before replying. 'You're not serious. The Tsar? Over such a trifling matter?'

'It is not trifling to me, sir. It is a matter of honour and discipline.'

The two men stared at each other before Kanin relaxed his posture and responded. 'Come now, Commander. Let us not fall out over such a… shall we say, cultural misunderstanding? We are allies, after all. Very well, I apologise. Now let us move on.'

'No, sir. It is not to me that the apology is owed.' Richard stared hard at Kanin.

'Shit!' Kanin's puce colour rose again. 'You surely don't expect me to apologise to one of your serfs?' Richard said nothing, but gestured the affirmative with his eyes.

'Miller, I'll rip your arse and poke out your eyes, you shithead.' Kanin jumped up from his seat and approached Richard menacingly.

'Very well, sir. I will take my leave. Please be informed that I will be in Petrograd for the next few days.'

Kanin made to grab Richard, but thought better of it. 'No, mother fucker. I shall have you placed under close arrest and tried Russian style for your insolence. Then you will be shot.' He turned his back and picked up the telephone.

'I was worried you might say that, sir, so I have taken certain precautions.'

Kanin replaced the ear piece of the telephone. 'What precautions?'

'In the event of my arrest, all my commanding officers are under orders to refuse to sail on operations again. I have explained my orders in a sealed envelope to Admiral Phillimore that will then be delivered to him. I am sure the Tsar, as Commander-in-Chief of all Russian forces will want to know why the Royal Navy submarines will not leave harbour.'

Please God, forgive the lie, Richard prayed silently.

'You wouldn't dare. Phillimore and your government wouldn't countenance such an action.'

'Try me, sir.'

Kanin resumed his seat at his desk and examined his options silently. At length he stood resignedly. 'Miller, you walrus penis. One day I'm going to crap in your mouth, but for now you win.'

Richard came to attention. 'Thank you, sir. I will arrange an appointment with your staff officer for you to see Stevens this afternoon.' Without awaiting a response, Richard retired from Kanin's office.

CHAPTER 23
March 1917

Richard found the city of Petrograd dirtier and gloomier than on his last visit, and not because of the snow on the streets. He had granted himself a week's leave, his first since his honeymoon in December 1915. As usual, he was staying in the Astoria. It was a military hotel that catered for foreign officers as well as Russians and just a short walk from both the embassy and Imperial Headquarters.

There was a tension in the air and the people seemed in a hurry to get about their business. On every street there were beggars and long queues for food. He was met at the station by the military attaché, Colonel Knox. Knox warned him that only a few days before there had been a major disturbance at the Renault works. The workers had murdered four of the foremen before taking to the streets singing the *Marseillaise* and breaking windows.

Nonetheless, for the first two days of his leave, Richard witnessed no wholesale disturbances. Occasionally, he had observed small demonstrations by workers carrying placards calling for '*No More War!*'. Usually, the crowds had been broken up quite quickly by the local police or troops from the garrisons. Sometimes, the demonstrators were led away by policemen in civilian clothes, clearly the *Okhrana*, the Tsar's secret police. However, all seemed to change very quickly.

On March the eighth, the third day of his leave, the trams stopped running and initially, the streets appeared quite deserted. The following day, however, crowds of women began to congregate at major junctions. Richard saw them being charged by mounted police using the flat of their swords to disperse the women, but the crowds only seemed to part and reform afterwards. At the embassy he heard reports that riots had broken out in response to the serious food shortages, with bakeries and food stores looted. Only the Cossacks seemed willing to maintain order. Regiment after regiment of the garrison troops were mutinying and joining the mobs on the streets. Richard feared the Russian Navy could be next and considered breaking his leave, but a call to Stocker had informed him that all was quiet in Reval. Knowing he was exhausted, Richard opted to remain in Petrograd.

By chance, staying at the same hotel was Commander Oliver Locker-Lampson RNVR. Locker-Lampson was the MP for North Huntingdonshire and now commanded a squadron of the Royal Naval Armoured Car Division operating with the Russian Army in the south. Richard's younger brother, Paul, had served with the division in Belgium under the command of Charles Samson in Belgium and France, but had returned to England before Locker-Lampson had arrived in theatre. Richard recalled from one of Paul's letters that Churchill's price for allowing Locker-Lampson to join the outfit, disparagingly named by the army as 'Samson's Flying Circus', had been that he was to supply all the cars of his squadron at his own expense. Locker-Lampson had suggested they attend the opera and Richard invite a guest to make up a foursome. Locker-Lampson, a bachelor, seemed to have fallen under the spell of a Russian baroness.

Richard had telephoned Princess Shuvalova. Anna had immediately agreed and, on their meeting, had looked as lovely as ever. It was their first meeting since the ball and he was thankful that the distance of time had cooled her ardour for him. He was, after all, he thought, the father of a toddler now. Otherwise, he might have allowed his feelings for her to have run away with him. The two couples took a pair of cabs for the short journey from the Astoria to the Opera House. Anna was wearing a white fur cape, a diamond tiara and a stunning pendant of diamonds with an icy-blue topaz or similar precious stone atop her deep cleavage. The fabulous display of wealth made Richard feel awkward and not because his mess kit seemed drab by comparison.

'Anna, my darling. Do you think it wise to wear that pendant in times such as this?'

Anna took hold of the pendant with her gloved hand and looked at it admiringly. 'What a strange question? Are you concerned somebody might attempt to steal it?'

'There is that, I suppose. This afternoon I witnessed quite serious unrest. A mob burned down the *Palais de Justice* and most of the prisons after freeing the prisoners. Some of the regiments sent to break up the disturbances sided with the people, disarming their officers or worse, murdering them before mutinying. But that's not my main concern. Just look at the people.'

Anna did as she was bid and looked out at the busy crowds on the Nevskiy Prospekt. The people were poorly-clothed and pinch-faced. Some looked sullen and many just frightened. Others were completely blank and listless.

'Oh, Richard. How dreadful! I never thought. They're starving and here we are going to the opera. Have you any change you could give them?'

'I don't think that would be a good idea, Anna. It might start a disturbance.' The disparity between the poverty of the ordinary Russians and the privilege of his class shamed him. Anna clearly shared his thoughts as she quietly removed her tiara and turned her back to him.

'Richard, darling. Please unclasp my necklace. I'm ashamed to wear it in front of these wretches.'

He unfastened the necklace and felt a tingle throughout his body as he touched the back of her slim neck. He placed it in his inside pocket for safe keeping whilst Anna stored the tiara in her handbag.

'My God, Richard. The Tsar must do something for his subjects.' She covered her mouth with her long-gloved hand before suddenly turning to him. 'Do you think there will be serious trouble? There is talk of rioting and you mentioned mutinies in the streets.' Richard noted a tear in the corner of one of her beautiful round eyes.

'Don't worry, my dear,' he patted her on the arm reassuringly. 'The troops seem to be keeping good order here.'

He glanced down the street and it was true that it was a peaceful scene. The crowds seemed aimless and no threat. A troop of Cossacks watched impassively from the bridge ahead. Even so, the atmosphere was charged, as if everyone was awaiting a thunderstorm. Richard felt the city might be a powder keg about to go off and again he questioned the wisdom of attending the opera.

Taking his seat in a box at the opera house, he gazed at his gilded surroundings admiringly. The contrast of the splendour of the theatre with the plight of the people in the streets was not lost on him. Looking down at the audience in the stalls, he spied the blue collars of a group of four sailors. From a distance, they looked to be of the Royal Navy. Through his glasses, he observed them more closely and recognised a torpedoman from *E8*. Somehow the sight of his men also on leave and attending the opera made him feel more at home. He longed to call to them to let them know his presence, but it would not have been seemly. Instead, he resolved to buy them a drink during the interval.

Soon he was lost in the performance of Puccini's *La Bohème*. It was one of his favourites. The staged squalor of the bohemian garret again reminded him of the world outside, but soon he was lost in the music. As Rodolfo took Mimi's cold hand and sang the aria *Che gelida manina*, he felt Anna take his hand in hers. He didn't resist. It seemed appropriate for the moment. The music absorbed him and he quite forgot his resolution to buy his men a drink at the interval, his responsibilities at Reval, the chaos in the streets and even Lizzy. Tears streamed down his face as the tragedy of the final act unfolded. Despite the sadness of the plot, he felt happy for the first time in months. He was in another world and in the company of a very beautiful woman who clearly admired him. Although he had no plans to be unfaithful, he desperately wanted to lie in her arms and to feel affection once more. When the curtain finally fell on the opera, he felt disappointed. It was as if the gate to a pathway to the Elysian fields had been shut to him. With the rising of the lights, Richard returned to modern-day Petrograd.

He tried to catch the attention of the sailors before they left the theatre, but they were on different levels and were nowhere to be seen as he joined the throng in the foyer. There seemed to be an agitation amongst the other opera goers and many were hanging back from exiting the theatre. Richard and Locker-Lampson managed to carve a path to the exit and were relieved to be in the fresh air. It was cold, but welcome after the enervating air of the theatre.

'I say, Miller. What do you make of that?' Locker-Lampson asked. Outside the theatre there were thousands of people on the march. 'We'll never find a cab in this lot.'

'Quite.' Richard responded. 'Look, it's only a mile to the hotel. Let's walk. I could do with the air anyway. Are you all right with that, ladies?'

Neither lady seemed content with the plan and it was Anna who responded. 'No, Richard. Can you not understand what they are chanting? It's "*Down with the Tsar!*" I think they're heading for the Palace and I fear there will be trouble.'

Richard saw the sense in her argument and pondered their situation. 'All right then. Supposing we head past the park to the Saviour on the Blood. We might pick up a cab there or we could take shelter in the church until matters die down.'

The rest of the party agreed and they headed north on foot, along the embankment of the Catherine's Canal. As they passed the Mikhailovsky Palace Museum, they had to make their way against the flow of several groups of workers, but the mood seemed peaceful enough. Ahead of them was situated the Church of Our Saviour of the Spilled Blood, built to commemorate the death of the Emperor Alexander the Second. Locker-Lampson was captivated by the beauty of its bright-coloured facade and onion-shaped domes. They had paused to allow him to admire its architecture when Richard heard a shout of, 'Sir, please, sir.'

Out of the shadows stepped first one and then the remaining three sailors Richard had spotted in the opera house. 'Thank God, sir. We're in a bit of jam, make no mistake.'

Richard noted that he was being addressed by the torpedoman from *E8*. He now recalled his name was Eastman. The other three sailors comprised another torpedoman, a stoker and a telegraphist. As was customary, none wore a cap tally identifying the name of their submarine, but Richard assumed they were all from *E8*. The side of the face of one of them was splattered with blood. As an afterthought, all four of the sailors wished the ladies and Locker-Lampson a good evening.

'What sort of a jam? It's Eastman isn't it?'

'Aye, sir. We're wondering what to do, sir. We were watching an opera. When we went in, the streets were a bit busy, like, but peaceful enough. By the time we came out, all hell had broken loose. There's been a revolution, sir!' Eastman announced excitedly. 'There's…'

'Hold your horses, Eastman. Who says there's been a revolution?' Locker-Lampson asked.

'A Ruskie policeman, sirs. We were trying to make our way back to the hotel via the Nevskiy Prospekt, but there were hundreds of thousands of people, sir, all screaming blue murder and waving placards. Then the Cossacks started charging on their horses, using whips. But the horses couldn't get through and started trampling the people. Some of them started grabbing at the Cossacks, pulling them off their horses and beating them up. That just riled the next lot of Cossacks and they charged again, but this time hacking away with their sabres. We nearly copped it, too, so we headed back this way for safety.'

'You wouldna'a believed it, sir,' the stoker with the blood speckled face cut in. 'There were bodies ev'rywhere. Whether they wur arl deed or no' is hard to say, but it was offul, sir.'

'That's right, Dinger. Then we met a policeman on the way, sir, and he was the one who said the people were revolting,' Eastman continued. 'We're right glad we saw you, sir.' The other sailors voiced their agreement with the last sentiment.

Richard sat on a step to the entrance to the church and removed his cap whilst he considered the situation. The other members of his party, also, sat on the steps, two of the sailors removing their greatcoats and laying them down for the ladies to sit on. Eventually, Richard made a decision.

'Anna, Baroness, you say the people are chanting, "*Down with the Tsar*"?' Both nodded. 'That would fit with the policeman saying there has been some sort of revolution. I can't say I'm surprised as I've felt it building up for some time.'

'Too true, Miller,' Locker-Lampson interjected. 'I've seen for myself on the Front the deterioration of morale and the mass desertions. I wouldn't treat my dogs the way the soldiers have been treated.'

'True. But the question is what to do tonight. I'm not sure it's safe to allow the ladies home… and in any case there's no transport.'

'You sum up our situation well, Miller. So, what do you propose we do?'

'I'm not sure, but for now, I suggest we rest up here a while to allow the crowds to pass through. The main trouble's likely to be round the Palace, but the Admiralty might attract trouble, too, so I think it would be best to avoid the embassy for now. I say we all head back to the hotel. There are plenty of officers staying there and there's safety in numbers. What do you think, Lampson?'

'Seems a sensible plan to me, but what about your chaps? They might be useful.'

'Agreed. I think they should come with us. It'll be safer for them and we might need the protection. Eastman, do any of you have your seaman's knives on you?' Both torpedomen rummaged in their pockets before holding aloft their knives. 'Are the blades keen?'

For the last question, Richard received a look of reproach from both torpedomen and a response in unison of, 'We be seamen, sir.'

'Sorry, chaps. Nip over to the fence of the park yonder and remove four staves. You can act as an escort for the ladies and stay at our hotel tonight. I have a feeling it could be a lively night. However, slope arms with the staves. I don't want any signs of aggression and you don't use them unless I give the order. Is that clear? You two go and help them.'

The sailors acknowledged Richard's orders and moved over to the shadows of the Mikhailovsky Gardens.

CHAPTER 24

The walk from the Church of Our Saviour of the Spilled Blood was only a mile and a half, even with the detours through side streets to avoid the mob, but it was not without interest. Shortly before midnight, the gas lights went out, an event that ordinarily would have left the streets of Petrograd in darkness, but it was a clear night with a part moon and the light of several burning buildings, especially to the west along the Neva river. The noise across the city was intense; a combination of chanting, screams and rifle shots. The worst scene the naval party and their two Russian ladies encountered was near the Stroganov Palace where they witnessed a pitched battle between a regiment loyal to the Tsar and another that had joined the revolution. However, without exception, the mobs were extremely civil towards the foreign sailors and the Russian noble women. Richard had taken the precaution of transferring his medals to the outside of his great coat and found, not for the first time, that the Tsar's decorations acted as a passport.

It was after midnight when they finally arrived at the main entrance of the Astoria. Outside the hotel a mob had gathered, but they seemed peaceful and allowed the navy men and their guests to pass through without interference. In the foyer, Richard and Locker-Lampson met a very flustered Assistant Naval Attaché, Commander Eady RNVR.

'Thank God you're both safe.' Eady almost wept with emotion. 'I was convinced you'd be murdered on the streets.' Eying the ladies he added quietly, 'And your ladies might have encountered worse.'

'Not at all, old chap,' Locker-Lampson replied. 'We had a splendid escort from our bluejackets here and we have met with no maltreatment whatsoever. Surprising really when one considers the deal the poor blighters have had.'

'Even so,' Richard cut in, 'I think it best the ladies stay here for the night. Do you know if there are any spare rooms available?'

'Yes, I mean no. Every last room's been taken. We've had hordes of Russian officers pour in over the evening to seek protection. General Poole's worried that lot out there might come in after them.'

'Are the Russians officers armed?' Richard asked.

'Only with their side arms.'

'Even that's a pity. It only needs some hothead amongst them to start shooting and we really will have the mob inside. Anna, Baroness, I think it best you sleep in my room tonight.' Locker-Lampson raised his eyebrows at the suggestion, but Richard ignored the gesture. 'Eastman, two of you can doss down in Commander Lampson's room. I want the other two to stand guard outside my room and to protect the ladies, if necessary. Lampson, I think you and I might kip down here – if that's all right with you?'

'Why certainly, but first I'll fetch my revolver. I hope I shan't be needing it.'

As Locker-Lampson left to retrieve his revolver, a Russian officer burst through the doors. He seemed to recognise Eady as he rushed over to him and threw himself on his knees, gripping Eady's thighs.

'Save me, oh save me,' he begged. Richard could not hear the conversation as Eady spoke too quietly, but the Russian calmed down and surrendered his side arm on request. Richard observed the little scene in puzzlement. It seemed odd for a Russian army officer to be on familiar terms with an assistant naval attaché.

About thirty minutes later, with the Russian ladies upstairs out of harm's way under the protection of Eastman and his fellows, a furious mob burst into the hotel foyer demanding to search the hotel. Richard noted that several Russian sailors were amongst the crowd. They were met by General Poole, head of the Military Supply Mission. Poole had twice been mentioned in despatches and held the Distinguished Service Order for his service in several colonial wars. He didn't flinch at the intrusion, but merely stroked his moustache as he quietly observed the proceedings. Only minutes before, he had sent all the Russian officers upstairs out of sight and ordered that none of the foreign officers should appear armed.

Despite the brandishing of a variety of weapons amongst the angry crowd, Poole, a fluent speaker of Russian, listened to the ringleaders calmly. Politely, he agreed that they should be able to search a few rooms of the hotel, but quietly and quickly as there were women with children asleep in the hotel. The mob seemed a little unnerved at such calmness and twenty minutes later began to leave the hotel. Unfortunately, their orderly exit was interrupted by the sounds of shots from the roof of the hotel.

'Some blithering idiot's started taking pot shots at the crowd,' an army officer shouted.

Within seconds, the mood of the crowd changed. The rebels swarmed back into the hotel and began screaming and smashing the furniture. The situation was inflamed when an elderly general and a few other Russian officers began firing on the mob from the top of the staircase. The rebels returned fire, killing the general and an innocent woman was caught in the crossfire. A British officer was savagely beaten when he jerked aside the rifle of a rebel taking aim at civilians on the staircase. The situation was rapidly becoming out of hand.

Richard dived into the crowd and caught the attention of a Russian boatswain. 'For the love of God, you must stop this before it becomes carnage,' he entreated passionately.

The boatswain seemed surprised to have been addressed by a foreign officer in good Russian. His gaze moved from Richard's face, to his medals and a look of understanding passed over his visage. He said nothing in return, but nodded before bellowing for the mob to cease firing. With a voice accustomed to giving commands in the teeth of a noisy Baltic gale, his voice carried across the noisy clamour and sporadic shooting with effect. The mob quietened.

Richard went over to Poole. 'Forgive me, sir, but I've an idea.' Without waiting for Poole's assent, he addressed the angry rebels.

'Gentlemen, we have no quarrel with you. If the sailors among you will offer me your assistance, we will disarm the Russian officers and I will guarantee there will be no more shooting. The sailors may then remain here to ensure that my guarantee is upheld. In return, I ask that the rest of you leave the hotel. There are women and children here with whom you can have no quarrel… and I think we could all do with some sleep.'

Poole understood Richard's words and added his agreement to the proposal. The leaders of the mob talked amongst themselves and with the boatswain. After a few minutes, they seemed to agree and the boatswain called for the sailors amongst them to come forward. Quickly, the rest of the mob dissipated. Immediately, Richard set about organising the Russian sailors with the help of the boatswain.

'Boatswain, if it's all right with you, I would like you to split your men into three sections. The first is to mount a guard on every floor. Nobody is to enter the floors without a room key. I will ask General Poole to issue orders to the Russian officers that none may leave their rooms before the morning. Your men will be on their honour to the Russian Navy to maintain order.'

'Of course, Commander. We are not a rabble.'

'That is abundantly clear and why your help is so necessary. Another section is to maintain a guard on the entrances to the hotel.'

'That is sensible, Commander. And what about the rest of the men?'

'They have a very delicate task and should be selected carefully.' Richard called to the hotel manager, taking shelter behind the main reception counter. 'Take us to the cellar and bring the keys with you.' Puzzled, the hotel manager did as he was bid and joined Richard and the Russian boatswain.

Obligingly, the hotel manager led them down to the vast cellars of the hotel and opened the doors and grates to them. Richard, as a teetotaller, was surprised at the vast space given over to the hotel's wines.

'Boatswain, I think feelings are running high enough without pouring fuel on the fire. I want your men to destroy all this wine.'

The hotel manager shrieked in outrage. 'You cannot do that. There are over 3,000 bottles here, many of fine vintages. It would be sacrilege.'

Richard ignored him and addressed the boatswain. 'I don't care what happens to the vodka, but it is not to be consumed on the premises. Does that make sense, Bos'n?'

The boatswain studied Richard's face intently for a moment before replying. 'You are a wise man, Commander, and I will try to select reliable men for the task. But I do not know all the men personally and this might be like letting kiddies loose in a sweet shop. I offer no guarantees. My authority may not prove much better than that of the bastards we call officers in our navy.'

'Bos'n, I respect your position and I rely on you to do your best.' Richard shook the hand of the Russian warrant officer warmly and gave the whinging hotel manager a look of withering contempt.

*****

Richard barely slept an hour for the rest of the night. However, his night on a couch in the foyer was, perhaps, no less comfortable than that of the attachés in their rooms. Some of them were sharing their rooms with up to fifteen refugees. In the main, he was pleased with the conduct of the rebel sailors. However, some elements had fallen into drunkenness and a few of the officers' rooms had been ransacked in their absence, including Eady's. Eady was unhappy to discover that not just his sword had been stolen, but a precious case of malt whisky.

It was clear to Richard that he could not stay on leave in Petrograd. If revolution was in the air, then it would soon reach Reval, if it had not already done so. He tried to ring through to the naval base, but either the lines were down or nobody was bothering to man the telephone exchanges today. He decided his best course was to head for the embassy for an update on the situation and to find transport back to Reval for him and his four sailors, and out of the city for Anna and the baroness. Commodore Kemp, the naval attaché, agreed to accompany him.

First, he returned to his room to wash, shave and check on the welfare of Anna and her friend. Both were up and dressed when he knocked on their door. Anna immediately rushed up to him, flung her arms round him and kissed him several times. 'Oh, my darling, you're safe.' She kissed him again and clung to him tightly, her head on his chest. 'Moura and I were so worried about you.'

Embarrassed at such a public display of affection, Richard disentangled himself. 'Did you sleep well, ladies?'

The baroness snorted. 'Hardly, with the racket of that rabble outside, baying like dogs… and afraid we might be raped and murdered at any moment. And now we have no fresh gown to wear. One feels so… over-dressed. You must get us away from this awful place at once, Commander.'

'I regret, ma'am, that that may not be possible for a while. Perhaps, in the meantime, some of the other lady guests might spare you fresh clothing and whatever other feminine accoutrements you need. As soon as I've washed and changed, I'll make my way to the embassy and try to procure you some transport home.'

'But, darling Richard. Won't that be awfully dangerous?' Anna looked up into his eyes fearfully.

'It's a case of needs must and I won't be going alone. But for the moment, you must both stay here. I promise you that you'll be quite safe and I hope not to be long.'

Richard ignored the further protests and sought out his day uniform and toilet kit. If he were to meet the ambassador, it would not do to appear unkempt.

*****

When Richard returned to the foyer to meet Kemp, he was met with a sight that angered him. A number of Russian officers, including two elderly generals, were being marched away at gunpoint by rebel soldiers of their regiments to a fate Richard could only imagine. Poole was watching the events with sadness, flanked by the military attachés.

'I know what you're thinking, Miller, and there's no point arguing about it. I find the whole proceedings despicable, too.'

'So why are we standing by to let it happen, sir?'

'Quite simply, Miller, what else would you have me do? Even if I had the men and the arms to hold off the mob outside, it would cause a bloodbath to defend this place and we have women and children to consider. Just let it go, Miller. You did a great job last night, but I'm in command here.' Poole turned away to show that the discussion was over. Richard approached Eady instead.

'What's going on, man?'

'The rebels seem better organised this morning. They sent in a couple of delegates earlier and demanded the hotel register. Before we cottoned on to what they had in mind, that cowardly hotel manager had handed it over. The next thing we knew, the rebels presented a list of about thirty officers they wanted to interview for criminal acts… and before you ask, the general refused initially. Bur he soon recognised that we were in no position to refuse. Either the officers were handed over or the rebels were going to come in and take them. Sadly, a couple of them shot themselves rather than come out. It's a beastly affair, but don't worry, we did save a few.'

'By what means, Alastair?'

'Whilst the general deliberately procrastinated, we tipped off a few to escape over the roof and there's a dozen or so hidden in various parts of the hotel. The rebels insisted on searching their rooms, but found no trace of them. I think they seemed happy enough to take the two generals. Poor blighters.'

Richard recognised Poole's dilemma and accepted that the general had acted for the many and not the few. In any case, he saw Kemp approaching and he had the flotilla to consider.

The two naval officers left the hotel and passed through the assembled crowd slowly and calmly. Both had their greatcoats open to show the absence of weapons concealed underneath. Richard noted that several of the civilians now held rifles or revolvers, too. Kemp cracked a joke and the Russians responded jovially. They seemed good tempered and civil to the two English officers, making way for them to head towards the Admiralty district.

It was only after entering the Voznesensky Prospekt, one of Petrograd's main thoroughfares, that Richard and Kemp found their path impeded. Down the Prospekt's entire length, they encountered opposing armed factions, sniping at each other. It was too dangerous to walk normally down the street and the two officers took to running from doorway to doorway. Nobody seemed to be taking direct aim at them, but it was difficult to tell. Despite the cold winter temperature, both men were perspiring heavily in their greatcoats by the time they reached the Alexander Garden. They took shelter behind one of the posts of a gateway to the park to recover their breath.

'Hot work hey, Miller.' Kemp wiped his face with a red spotted handkerchief.

'Indeed, sir, but I fancy the going should be better for a short distance if we stick to the outside of the park. I fancy I hear machine gun fire ahead, though, sir.'

'I think you're right, Miller. I would judge it's coming from somewhere near the Winter Palace. Come on, let's push on.'

Warily, Richard and Kemp reached the northern end of the park, but as Kemp had feared, at the intersection of the Nevskiy Prospekt the firing became very hot indeed. A number of machine gun nests had been mounted around the Admiralty and the gunners didn't seem to mind who they fired upon. Bodies lay on both sides of the streets ahead.

'What d'you think, sir?' Richard asked of Kemp.

'I think discretion is the better part of valour and I'd like to remain in this doorway for a little, Miller. I've never been so fond of a doorway. Let's see how events pan out.'

Both crouched in their comparative shelter and watched the battle play out before them. Neither could work out which side was which as both contained components of uniformed infantry. After five minutes, the firing became more sporadic and Kemp stood up.

'I've had enough of this, Miller. I'm going to make a dash across the square and take my chances. You up for it?'

'Certainly, sir. You lead and I'll follow.'

'Right. On the count of three.'

With Kemp leading, Richard sprinted across Palace Square towards the Alexander Column. Immediately, bullets spat towards them from two machine guns to their left. Instinctively, Richard ducked and began weaving. He saw the dust fly just yards ahead of Kemp as machine gun bullets raked the square and then, just short of the relative safety of the column, Kemp checked his stride and his cap flew off his head to one side. Richard thought he must have been hit, but quickly realised Kemp was merely changing direction to retrieve his hat. Richard just thundered on and body-charged Kemp, partially flinging himself and the attaché behind the column.

Both men crouched at the base of the column and drew in deep gasps of air. 'Thanks,' said Kemp. 'Can't think what came over me, but…' He was interrupted by chips of stone being flung over his shoulder from the machine gun fire on the Admiralty side of the square.

'I'm not sure this is a good place to hang around either, Miller. Come on. Let's go.' Without awaiting an answer, Kemp sprinted away across the remainder of the square. Richard didn't hesitate to follow. Again, he heard the chattering of a machine gun and the zipping sound of bullets hitting the paving behind him, but he couldn't tell how close. He concentrated instead on running. Mercifully, the machine gun fire either stopped or was redirected elsewhere.

Slowing to a mere trot, they reached the Palace Quay and stumbled past the Royal Marine sentries to reach the plate-glass doors and safety of the British Embassy.

'I hope Sir George will forgive my dishevelment, sir,' Richard gasped.

‘You should worry, Miller. Those buggers shot up my best cap.’

CHAPTER 25

Richard's meeting with the British Ambassador, Sir George Buchanan, was an optimistic one. He informed Richard that the Tsar had matters under control. A provisional committee of the Duma had been formed to take control of the lawless capital and a General Ivanoff was marching on Petrograd with a special force of men from front line units to restore order. Confident these measures would be sufficient, the Tsar had temporarily retired to his palace at Tsarkoe Selo. Sir George seemed confident that the chaos in the streets was a minor event and not a full-blooded revolution. Richard, however, doubted this assessment and determined to return to Reval as quickly as possible. Meanwhile, Kemp sent an embassy car to the Astoria to take Princess Shuvalova and the baroness home to safety. Another would return with Richard's luggage. The fly in the ointment was that no transport was available to take Richard back to Reval and he was advised to take his chances on the trains.

When the car with his baggage returned to the embassy, Richard was shocked to see it contained a blonde-haired passenger.

'Please don't blame me, sir,' the Russian driver protested. 'She insisted.'

'Anna, what on earth are you doing here? I arranged a car to take you home.'

Princess Shuvalova responded to Richard's anxiety by shrugging her shoulders and smiling coyly. 'I couldn't go home. With my husband away at the front, I worried for my safety. In any case, I want to be with you.' She rushed across to Richard and embraced him. The driver tactfully looked away.

'If you are worried about your reputation,' she teased, 'you won't have to keep me as your mistress. I have friends in Reval who will lodge me.'

That at least was reassuring, Richard thought, but he was, nonetheless, concerned for Anna's safety. It was a three-mile journey across a war zone to the Baltic Station and who knew what challenges might lie ahead on the train journey to Reval - should there be any trains, he thought. Then again, if he sent Anna home, even if she were to go, she would be crossing the city alone. He decided it would be easier not to argue and turned to the driver.

'Do you think you could make it to the Baltic Station?'

From the driver's reaction, he was clearly not happy at such a prospect, but he nodded. 'I will try, sir, but it will be very dangerous…' his voice tailed off.

Richard suddenly had an idea. 'What if I could provide you an armed escort?'

The driver's face brightened a little. 'It might help, sir, but the people are erecting barricades.'

'We'll deal with them as and when we face them. First, we need to return to the Astoria to collect our escort.' Richard had in mind the four sailors he had met the night before. Mention of a return trip to the Astoria dampened the driver's new-found enthusiasm, but he started the motor car anyway.

Without instruction, the driver sensibly avoided the area around the Admiralty and Winter Palace and headed instead up the historic Millionaya Street and back towards the Saviour on the Spilled Blood, before cutting south to the Nevskiy Prospekt. There, they encountered their first barricade, festooned with red flags. A rebel army under-officer flagged them down and approached the car.

'State your business, comrade,' the soldier asked brusquely. Behind him a crowd of angry citizens watched suspiciously.

'I am a British officer. I am on my way to the Astoria hotel to collect my men before I rejoin my command at Reval.'

The mention of the word *Britanskaya* changed the mood of the crowd immediately and many pointed at the union flag on the embassy car. Several repeated the word and others cheered. The soldier in charge altered his mood and smiled warmly at Richard and Anna.

'Comrade, you are most welcome, but I cannot let you cross the Moyka this way. There is much fighting on the Nevskiy Prospekt. You will have to go round and try your luck on the Gorokhovaya Street crossing.'

The driver interjected, 'I know it, sir.'

'Comrade,' the soldier addressed the driver sternly. 'We don't use the word "sir" anymore. Since the revolution, we are all comrades. Good luck.'

The driver manoeuvred the car left with some difficulty as so many of the crowd were trying to shake Richard's hand, but eventually amid cheers, he drove the vehicle away to the east. A few minutes later, with only the occasional diversion, they arrived at the hotel. Richard was pleased to note that the hotel was no longer surrounded by the mob. He immediately sought out Eady.

'Thank the lord you're safe, Richard. We've had reports of heavy fighting near the Admiralty.'

'Quite. Commodore Kemp and I can confirm that, but we came back another route. The Nevskiy Prospekt is blocked by the way. I'm here to collect four of my men and find a train back to Reval.'

'Ah,' Eady's face fell. 'Your men left this morning on foot. They had the same idea… to get to the station, but I've heard there are no trains running. However, you see those Russian officers over there? They're keen to get to Reval, too, and have a scheme in mind.'

Hoping Eastman and company were safe and well, Richard approached the officers Eady had indicated. Their plan quickly filled him with misgivings. They planned to seize a locomotive at gun point and take it down to Reval. Richard believed such a plan fraught with danger and decided to try his luck at Baltic Station instead. Eady had disappeared somewhere, so Richard was unable to say farewell, but a Russian naval captain approached him as he made to leave.

'Commander, forgive me, but I could not help overhearing your conversation just now. I am Count Keller. I, too, have need to return to Reval and request your protection to make the journey together.'

'I would be happy to accompany you, Captain, but I fear I can offer little protection. I am not armed and I'm already under the obligation to escort a lady to Reval.'

The Russian winked. 'I understand, Commander, but I believe there is strength in numbers.'

Now a member of a party of four, Richard left the hotel, but, downcast at the lack of an escort, the driver refused to take the party beyond the Mariinskiy Theatre. Richard, Keller and Anna had no choice but to proceed the final two miles on foot. First, Richard removed the union flag from the car and gave it to Anna to wave prominently. He had spotted three Maxim machine guns mounted on the roof of the theatre and had no wish to repeat his experience earlier in Palace Square. Carrying their baggage, they trudged west to the chattering backdrop of machine gun fire and the cracks of rifle shots in response. At the Catholic church of Saint Stanislaus, Richard insisted on stopping to pray briefly and to light a candle for their safety. He noted that the school was shut. The exercise seemed to amuse Keller, but Anna joined Richard in the ritual.

Unfortunately, the prayer seemed not to be answered as shortly after heading towards the bridge over the Catherine Canal, they came under heavy fire. Richard was grateful that Anna had changed into walking shoes as the three of them had to run for their lives as the bullets sprayed the road near them. Grabbing her roughly, Richard dragged and then pushed her into a nearby doorway. Keller took shelter further down the street. Anna waved the tiny Union Flag wildly until Richard restrained her hand.

'I think you'd better put away the jack for now, Anna. I believe the sniper across the road's using it for target practice.' Richard shrank back into the doorway as a chipping from the stonework narrowly missed him. Rifle shots rang out again as Keller ran past them into a nearby alley.

'Can you hear me, Commander,' Keller called out. 'I think there is a route to the canal this way.'

'I'm sorry, Anna, but we're going to have to make a dash for it. Are you ready, my dear?'

'First you must kiss me, darling.' Anna took one of Richard's hands and held it to her breast.

'Steady on, Anna. This is no time for tomfoolery.'

'But it will give me courage… and if we are to die, I want to taste you on my lips as I meet my maker.'

Richard recognised the obstinacy in her face and quickly kissed her on the cheek. 'Right then, can we go now?'

'No, not like that. Kiss me properly.' Without waiting, Anna embraced him and pulled his face to hers. She kissed him passionately on the lips and only when he softened, did she release him. 'There,' she said triumphantly, 'that didn't hurt did it? I'm ready now.'

Within seconds, they grabbed their cases and sprinted the ten-yard distance to the entrance to the alleyway. The move clearly surprised the sniper as the shots after them rang out too late. They followed Keller through the alley between the tall buildings and after a couple of turns, they faced the frozen canal opposite. The bridge lay to their right and devoid of armed rebels, police or troops.

They waited a few minutes, observing the pedestrians crossing the bridge in both directions. 'We must cross that bridge, Anna. After that, it's only another mile and a half to the station.'

'No, Commander. It's not safe,' Keller responded. 'Even if we cross that bridge, we still have to cross the Fontanka.'

'So, what do you suggest, Captain? We can't stay here.'

'I think, perhaps, we should return to the hotel.'

'No!' Anna said emphatically. 'We go on.' She faced them down fiercely.

Keller shrugged his shoulders and raised his eyebrows in acquiescence. 'Very well, then, but I suggest you both go first. I will follow a few yards behind to present less of a target.'

'Agreed. However, Anna, I think we will fare better if you leave one of your cases behind.' To Richard's surprise, Anna didn't argue.

'That's fine. I dare say I'll manage with my reticule and jewellery case.'

'Good girl.' Richard kissed her fondly on the forehead. 'Right, let's go.'

Richard and Anna dashed for the bridge with Keller two paces behind. Just as they started to cross the bridge, shots rang out and they were forced to duck as the bullets hit the stone parapets. Half way across, they heard Keller cry out.

'Keep going,' Richard shouted to Anna and pushed her forward. He turned round to see Keller lying on the road, writhing in pain. Dropping his case, Richard went back to him, crouching to avoid the bullets passing over the side of the bridge. Keller had taken a bullet to the right thigh and shoulder, and blood was seeping onto the paving. Without hesitation, Richard raised Keller to his feet and, with his arm under his good shoulder, forced him to hobble across the bridge. Keller soon seemed unable to offer assistance from his good leg and became a dead weight. Further shots rang out and this time Richard and Keller presented an upright target. Ahead, he could see Anna had crossed the bridge safely and was taking shelter in the doorway of a house on the corner opposite.

Abruptly, he felt a great shock and was thrown forward, losing his grip on Keller. They both hit the ground and Richard saw the gush of blood pouring from Keller's neck. Vainly, he grasped Keller's neck to try to stem the flow of blood, but slowly, Keller's jittering stopped and the light left his eyes. Richard had no doubt Keller was dead and he wasn't going to waste time checking further. He paused briefly to close Keller's eyes and commend his soul to God, before running at a crouch towards Anna.

On reaching Anna's shelter he was met with a gasp. 'Oh my God, Richard. You look as if you've come from a slaughter house.' Anna winced and looked away.

Richard looked down and saw that his hands were covered in blood and that the same blood had spurted over the front of his greatcoat. The best he could do was to take out his handkerchief and attempt to clean his hands. Anna meanwhile, reached into her reticule and pulled out a delicate handkerchief and crystal perfume bottle. She moistened the handkerchief with a liberal amount of perfume and began to clean his face.

Richard protested. 'Anna, you'll have me smelling like a tart's boudoir.'

'Better that than you wander the streets looking like a modern day Saltychikha after murdering her serfs.'

There was little Richard could do so, now unencumbered by a valise, he graciously carried Anna's jewellery case for the remainder of the walk to the station. It was snowing heavily, but they encountered no further trouble until the approaches to the station. There, several gun battles were underway, but Anna's little union flag seemed to keep them safe and yet again, Richard was amazed at the warmth shown by the people towards him as a British officer.

To his further surprise, some of the trains were running. The station seemed to be overflowing with Russian sailors and Richard approached one to ask what was happening.

'We have come from Kronstadt, comrade. We have come to join the glorious revolution.'

'But does that mean the Fleet has mutinied?'

'No, comrade. We have not mutinied. We have merely refused to obey the bastards who have continually shown no care or decency towards us. When we have brought down our oppressors, we will have peace again.'

The last words sent a chill down Richard's spine. Were Russia to sue for peace, it would have a catastrophic effect on the Allies' war effort.

'Tell me, have you seen four British sailors in the station.'

'Four? I've seen several. They came in on the Murmansk train, comrade. I saw them by the booking office. Over there, comrade.'

Richard's heart leapt at the prospect of meeting a fresh draft from England, but he couldn't see any through the swathe of revolutionaries from Kronstadt. Holding Anna tightly against him, he cut his way through the crowds towards the booking office. The sailors seemed good humoured and politely made way for them. Despite the revolution, he could see several hundred soldiers boarding a train in a disciplined fashion. All of a sudden, he heard a burst of machine gun fire at the station entrance. The machine gunner was firing at the roof of a building opposite, but the firing stopped just as suddenly. The babble of excited voices hushed at the noise of the gunfire and to Richard's utter surprise, one voice floated above the thousands of people in the station.

'For fuck's sake, Ivan. Don't they teach you anything in your army? Shove over and let me see the rabbit.'

Richard spotted his quarry. A group of Royal Navy sailors was standing near the machine gunner whilst a petty officer freed the machine gun belt and fed it back into the gun.

'There you are, mate. Ain't nothing to it… when you've been properly trained.' The petty officer slapped the top of the machine gun and took a bow in response to the clapping and cheering from the Russian audience.

Richard was incensed and moved quickly over to the petty officer. 'PO, just what do you think you were doing?'

The petty officer spun round and seeing a senior officer, immediately came to attention, straightened his cap and saluted. 'Begging your pardon, sir, I don't understand your meaning.'

'What were you doing with that machine gun?'

'Oh, that. The belt had jammed and I was just doing the boys a good turn and freeing it. They were having a pop at a police spy the other side of the street. Nobody in their army seemed to know what the matter was with it, sir.'

'But why were you helping them, PO? This isn't your skirmish.'

'Well, mebbe not, sir, but the Ruskies seem a friendly bunch and they've looked after us for the past few hours, so I just thought, one good turn deserved another.'

Richard was confused, but unsure how to respond. He gestured to the British sailors standing by. 'Is this all of you? And where's your kit?'

'No, sir. The rest of the lads are at the platform looking after our kit. And if you don't mind me mentioning it, sir, we'd best get a shift on. The train leaves shortly?'

'You mean there's a train to Reval?'

'Aye, sir, and it's the only one today. Might be the last one, too, judging by the chaos round here. Wouldn't 'a' known about it, but for the help of the Ruskies, sir, not speaking the lingo. Best we hurry along, sir.'

Richard wondered if he was capable of further surprise today and meekly followed the petty officer and the other sailors to the platform. However, there awaited one final surprise for the day as he was reunited with Eastman and his three colleagues.

'Hello, sir. I knew you'd make it. The train's busting, sir, but we've saved you a seat. Didn't expect the lady, though, sir, but we'll sort something out for her. A pleasure to see you again, ma'am.'

Tired, emotionally spent and bloodied, Richard allowed himself and Anna to be led onto the train. Have I gone mad, he thought? Then he remembered a quotation from Lewis Carroll's Alice, '*I'm afraid so. You're entirely bonkers. But I'll tell you a secret. All the best people are.*'

CHAPTER 26

Having parted from Anna at Reval, Richard made his way back to the *Dvina* with utmost despatch. There he was met by Evans in his capacity as the duty officer of the flotilla. Richard was much relieved to hear that life in the harbour was still comparatively normal.

'Actually, sir, I have some other good news.'

'Anything positive would be welcome just now, Dai.'

'It happened before you left on leave, sir. Kanin has been relieved of his command! The word amongst the Russians is that it was down to you.'

'Really? Why would anyone think that?'

'There's a rumour that you and he had a shouting match and you threatened him with the Tsar, sir. Then you went off to Petrograd and people have, naturally, put two and two together.'

'But I last saw Kanin a month ago and you've just said Kanin was relieved before I set off on leave. In any case, I never saw the Tsar. He's had far too much on his mind lately.'

'Well, he must have ordered it, nonetheless, sir, as the admiral has gone and, in any case, why spoil a good story with the truth? The Russians think you a bloody hero.'

'Amazing. So, who's the new C-in-C?'

'An Admiral Nepenin, sir. My sources tell me he's much more dynamic and he's replaced the Commodore Submarines with a Captain Vederevsky. I hear he has the reputation as being quite hot. It bodes well for future operations wouldn't you say, sir?'

'Perhaps, but only if this latest trouble passes over. On that subject, I'd like you to inform all the COs that I want to clear lower deck tomorrow of the whole flotilla. Let's say 11.30, before the hands go to dinner.'

When Evans left, Richard began to prioritise his coming workload. He would need to call on both Nepenin and Vederevsky. With their agreement, he planned to move back on board the *Dvina* until things settled down. He would miss Rachel's company, but the flotilla had to come first. For now, though, his top priority was replacing his lost toilet kit.

*****

The sky was grey above with low, thick clouds and occasional flurries of snow as the men of the Baltic submarine flotilla listened to Richard brief them on the momentous events of the past few days. With the fleet frozen in for the savage winter, there were no movements of ships, but even so, the harbour seemed unnaturally quiet with little work going on anywhere but on the *Dvina*.

'Men, despite these uncertain times, we still have a war to fight. The Germans are knocking on the door of Riga and must be stopped if Russia is to stay in the war. And stay in the war she must. With the stalemate on the Western Front, imagine the difference to the war were Germany suddenly able to withdraw her divisions from the Eastern Front and reinforce those in France.' Richard's last comment drew some murmuring amongst the sailors listening.

'I'm proud to have you all under my command. Sailors and officers of the King's Navy. An efficient and disciplined fighting force. I look to you now more than ever to set an example to the Russians. I accept that some of you may have a modicum of disgust with the treatment of your colleagues in the Russian Navy…' Again, there was a murmuring of accord, but Richard ignored it.

'Whatever your personal feelings, you will take no sides… and I mean that most strongly. Agree to everything and with everybody, but without enthusiasm… and certainly don't offer any criticism. Keep cool heads and calm tempers, no matter the provocation. For some days yet, the situation is likely to be extremely volatile. But remember, the Royal Navy is rightly held in high esteem here and, should you encounter any problems, see or hear anything of significance, then report it immediately to me or any of your officers. God save the King.'

As the cheers subsided, the sounds of the *Marseillaise* drifted across the harbour, almost in response. Sensing trouble, Richard immediately had the men dismissed. He knew the *Marseillaise* was banned and its playing could only mean that the rebellion in Kronstadt had spread to Reval. He and a few idlers who had stayed behind looked across the frozen water to the jetty nearest to the town. A large body of Russian sailors was marching in a demonstration with a brass band at its head. They began chanting slogans and waving red flags, but it all seemed peaceful enough. Even so, the civilian police soon arrived and the officer in charge looked to be trying to persuade the demonstration members to disperse. Richard later heard that this was the deputy chief of police, a popular man in the town. After a stand-off of about fifteen minutes, the mob moved over to the town's prison and an altercation occurred shortly afterwards. Richard had a clear view of the proceedings and was sickened to see the deputy chief of police then beaten to the ground, presumably for refusing to hand over the keys to the prison. Whatever the pretext, a wave of prisoners joined the rebel sailors soon afterwards and they set fire to the building.

An hour later, the procession of rebel sailors, former prisoners and strikers formed up on the jetty alongside the *Dvina*. In anticipation, the CO of the *Dvina,* Captain Nikitin, with some of his officers and more loyal senior rates formed up on the quarterdeck. The crowd on the jetty shouted demands for a republic to be established and for the sailors of the depot ship to join them, but to Richard, it seemed a peaceful demonstration. As the Russian sailors completed their lunch, they appeared on the upper deck and listened to the chanting. Two delegates from the crowd, wearing red armbands, then came up the gangway to address Nikitin and to demand his men join them. Nikitin refused, but even so, some of his ship's company disobeyed and joined the rebels to many cheers from the crowd. By this time, the military governor of the town, Admiral Gerashimoff arrived. Alone, he addressed the unruly crowd and the mob's chanting died down to hear him speak. Again, Richard had no fears the crowd would become unruly.

'My brave, fighting men, I have dramatic news to report,' Gerashimoff called out. 'I have just heard that earlier today, His Imperial Majesty has abdicated.' The news elicited waves of cheering for several minutes. When the hubbub had died down, Gerashimoff continued his address.

'A new government has been formed and I have been instructed by the Duma that the government is keen to restore order. To that end, I insist that you disperse and return to your ships.'

This latest news did not seem to have the same, joyful effect on the rebels and Richard sensed a souring of the mood. One of the delegates called for silence and spoke up. 'Comrade, you are in no position to make demands. The navy is now under the command of the revolutionary council. We will decide what is to be done.'

Gerashimoff flushed angrily at the words. 'Rot! You are sailors and have your duty to fulfil. You will disperse immediately. I have come alone, but if this nonsense is to continued, I will have no choice but to call in the troops to break up and put an end to this madness.'

Richard could see that the crowd was now clearly antagonised and he heard cat calls and shouts of, 'And where will you get your troops from, comrade?' and, 'Who's going to protect you?' It was a disaster for the admiral as very soon the mob set about him and smashed in his face with rifle butts. Having had their fun, the rebels left the injured governor lying on the snow and moved on to begin setting fire to parts of the old Strand port. Staff Surgeon Hole immediately rushed to attend Gerashimoff and have him brought to the *Dvina*'s sick bay. Richard was not alone in being disgusted by the incident.

*****

That evening, Richard again cleared lower deck to assemble his men, but did so in one of the larger mess decks. He had a sentry placed on each of the access points with orders to prevent any Russians entering whilst he held his meeting.

'Some of you witnessed the brutal attack on the military governor this afternoon. No doubt the lower deck scuttlebutt has passed the news on to those who didn't. I'm sorry to say that the deputy chief of police was murdered this afternoon, too, possibly by the same mob. You can see for yourselves the fires in the town and port. Now earlier today, I told you all to keep a low profile. I have to say, therefore, what I am about to ask will be extremely delicate and, possibly, not without danger… I want a hundred volunteers to come with me to the home of the British Consulate.'

Richard noted the nervous glances between some of the men. 'All of you have benefited from the hospitality shown by Mister Gerard and his wife, as well as the wider expatriate community. The fires around the prison are in danger of taking hold of the consulate nearby. I think we could serve the Gerards a good turn by rescuing their furniture and possessions from the fire.'

A sense of relief seemed to sweep through the men that this was all that was being asked of them, but Richard didn't want them volunteering without knowing the risk. 'None of you will be armed and nor will you carry batons. You will only carry fire-fighting equipment and that may expose you to some risk from an angry crowd. Immense tact may be required and it would be better if you avoided contact with any rebels.'

Richard withdrew to allow the men to discuss the matter amongst themselves, but within thirty minutes he had his volunteers.

*****

Tired after an evening of firefighting, Richard's tact and patience was tested to the limit the following day. Soon after breakfast, a deputation of the *Dvina* sailors appeared at the wardroom and insisted on disarming the Russian officers. The leader of the delegation was Richard's Russian former steward, a man called Malenkov. Malenkov decreed that, henceforth, no officer would be permitted to come on board or leave the ship without the permission of the ship's council. In the absence ashore of Captain Nikitin, Richard argued the point.

'Seaman Malenkov, I am not here to take a view on your grievances. Captain Nikitin will, no doubt, make his views known on his return, but I am in command of the British flotilla and I have my duty. Let me make two things clear. One, there is to be no interference with the movement of my Russian liaison officers. Moreover, their safety will be guaranteed. Two, if it is necessary for other Russian officers to come on board the *Dvina* to facilitate my operations, then they must be free to come and go at will. Is that understood?'

Richard could tell that Malenkov was feeling cowed by his strong remonstrations, but felt it necessary to maintain his dignity in front of the men of the deputation. He retired to the passageway for discussions with his fellow sailors before returning and standing stiffly to reply.

'We have nothing but respect for the Royal Navy and you especially, comrade. For now, we are happy to agree to your *request* that your liaison officers have free movement, but with respect to the staff officers, we have a condition.'

'I'm listening.'

'No Russian officer visiting is to have contact with any officer on board this ship whilst on board.'

'Very well, Malenkov. I can live with that.'

*****

Richard was disappointed not to have met Admiral Nepenin. Nikitin brought sad news as the two commanding officers discussed the spreading revolution and mutinies.

'Richard, I and my officers fear for our lives. Everywhere good officers are being murdered or imprisoned. Did you hear about Admiral Nepenin?'

'No, I have had little news beyond that here, Captain.'

'Dead. Shot in the back in Helsingfors after the crews of the two battleships butchered their officers. Mind you, he suffered less than poor Admiral Viren in Kronstadt. All the admirals were murdered, but he fared worst of all. He was tortured and mutilated before his wife and daughter were killed in front of him. The bastards then murdered him, cut his body into small pieces and threw them on the fire.'

'So, is there a new C-in-C?'

'I fear it may be Admiral Maximoff, but I don't know.'

'I've not heard of Maximoff. Is he an ardent officer?'

Nikitin grunted in disgust. 'He is an opportunist. A weak, self-seeking prick. He tried to take over from Nepenin at the outbreak of the revolution, claiming he had been elected C-in-C by the Revolutionary Council. Nepenin threw him out of his office on the grounds that only the new Provisional Government could make such an appointment. Now Nepenin is dead, who knows?'

'I am truly sorry, Captain. But I thought I had persuaded your men that the safety of you and your officers was their responsibility. Why are you still in fear?'

'Oh, Richard. As you know, my crew has long been disaffected and ill-disciplined. If only London had agreed to you and your men taking over the ship last year. It has always been an unhappy ship. You know it was called the *Pamyat Azova* until the Tsar insisted its name change following its part in the 1905 mutinies?'

'I was aware and can see the insult may be felt keenly.'

'But on top of that, the disparity in comfort and freedom the men see in your men has only made matters worse. After all, my men, too, long for freedom. Now it seems the Committee is to court martial my paymaster and there is nothing I can do about it. Mind you, he deserves it. Even by the standards of our paymasters he is overly corrupt, but that is not the point. You should be aware that they intend to try your namesake, too – *Unter Leytenant* Miller.'

'What? When? They cannot. He's effectively under my command.'

Nikitin smiled thinly. 'I thought you would find the news of interest, dear Richard.'

*****

The trials the following day were shambolic, much as Richard and Nikitin had feared. There was no doubt that no verdict other than guilty was expected. Darmaross, the paymaster, faced dozens of prosecution witnesses, all complaining about his acts of impecuniosity and corrupt acts, especially with regard to the catering. There were no witnesses for the defence. Richard watched helplessly as the man was found guilty, stripped to his undergarments and then his beard and hair shaved off. Nikitin watched the proceedings impassively without interference. As Darmaross was marched off to await the deliberation of the court on his sentence, he was jeered resoundingly. Richard chose this moment to stand and address the judges and jury of the Sailors' Committee. Inwardly, he felt nervous as he recognised he was treading a thin tightrope in his dealings with the revolutionaries, but he had decided that firmness was the correct approach.

'Gentlemen. I am not here to speak in Paymaster Darmaross's defence. I accept the court's judgement. But before sentence is passed, I will say one thing. Neither I nor my men will stand by and see murder committed.' Richard stared fiercely into the eyes of each of the five-member committee before resuming his seat.

Much argument then ensued in low voices between the committee members with several glances at Richard. At last, they made their decision and called back the disgraced paymaster before their leader announced sentence.

'Comrade Darmaross, a late plea for clemency has been submitted on your behalf and this court has decided to show you more mercy than you showed your fellow man. For your crimes, you will serve one month's imprisonment. Take him away.'

As the paymaster was led away, there was a hush from the audience. Darmaross seemed puzzled and then suddenly fell to his knees. With tears streaming down his face, he turned to Richard and shouted, 'Thank you, sir. Oh, thank you. May God protect you.' His escort then dragged him away.

Next, Lieutenant Miller, the Russian liaison officer, was brought for trial. This time, before the charges were even read out, Richard again stood to address the court. 'Gentleman, I submit you have no jurisdiction to conduct this trial. This officer has been seconded to the Royal Navy for liaison duties and is under my command. As such, he falls under the Naval Discipline Act of Great Britain and only I may apply for his court martial.'

The members of the Sailors' Committee protested loudly in outrage and again discussed matters amongst themselves. The court president then appealed for silence and responded to Richard's plea. 'Comrade, this man is universally unpopular with your own men as well as ours.'

'Unpopularity alone is not a criminal offence. Indeed, were it so, I cannot think of many in authority who might escape court martial, myself included.' The audience laughed at Richard's reply.

'Very well, comrade. Let us ask your men what they think. You. Stand up.' The president pointed at Leading Telegraphist Dawes. 'What would you and your comrades do with the lieutenant?'

Richard tensed in anticipation of the answer. It was true that Miller was not popular and especially amongst the telegraphists of the flotilla. Dawes looked across to Richard and then to the liaison officer before answering, 'We would obey the orders of our captain.' The Royal Navy sailors cheered until the court president called again for order.

Addressing Richard, he said, 'Very well, comrade. But you must deal with him. This trial is over.'

As everyone made to leave, Lieutenant Miller turned round to Richard and made to thank him. Richard cut him off.

'Don't thank me, Miller. My cabin, now. We need to get you transferred off this ship and very quickly.'

CHAPTER 27
May 1917

The snow was still thick on the jetties and rooftops as *E19* put to sea in company with four Russian submarines, the first vessels of the Baltic Fleet to leave Reval since the winter. Richard looked across to the surface ships, the splashes of colour from the red flags and rebel bunting contrasting gaily against the grey of the sky and the ice-encrusted yardarms. It had been a savage winter and the thaw too long in coming.

'This ice is still pretty thick, sir,' Evans warned him in muffled tones through the scarf covering his face. It was bitterly cold on the open bridge of the submarine.

'I know, Number One, but it'll ease as we head further south.' Richard knew that he was taking a gamble in leaving harbour so early, but there were many factors that had persuaded him the risk was worthwhile.

The Germans were operating in ice-free conditions further south and still putting pressure on Riga. Were Riga to fall, then Richard didn't have much confidence that Reval would not be threatened, too. More importantly, some example had to be set to the Baltic Fleet to keep the war going. Richard had doubts that the battleships of the Russian fleet would ever sail, so riven were they with revolutionary fervour, but Admiral Vederevksy was energetic and popular, too. He had agreed with Richard that the sooner the Russian Navy was back at sea fighting the Germans, the sooner the madness of the rebellion might cease.

'I don't mean to sound impertinent, sir, but might you not have sent one of the other *E*-boats out on this first patrol? You've had, after all, an exhausting couple of months and there is the whole flotilla to consider.'

'I know full well my responsibilities for the flotilla command thank you, First Lieutenant. I don't need you to remind me of them,' Richard snapped.

'Of course, sir. I apologise.'

Richard regretted his sign of temper. Evans was only trying to help, after all, he thought. I'm edgy and he has a point, but I can't share the real reason for choosing *E19*. In his last letter to Commodore Hall, Richard had expressed just those concerns. He had admitted to feeling depressed with the situation in Russia and that he had not been able to turn in before 03.00 since his return to Reval. He had gone on to suggest that he be relieved of his command of the flotilla by a more senior officer. After all, his equivalents in the Russian Navy were all captains or commodores. Failing that, he requested he be relieved of his command of the submarine to concentrate on the increased demands of leadership of the flotilla. He had not mentioned in his letter that he had Evans in mind to command *E19*, but first he wanted to test him more fully.

But was that the real reason, he wondered. He could not help but feel suspicious that, perhaps, going to sea was the easy way out - a respite from the problems of Reval. Guiltily, he reflected how the time on patrol would give him time to catch up on his personal correspondence, too. He suspected that the mail system between Russia and Britain would now be even more erratic.

'Are you aware, sir, that you have acquired a nickname ashore?'

Richard realised that Evans was trying to make amends for his last remark. Poor Evans, he was the most loyal of officers and hadn't deserved his response, Richard chided himself. Throwing off his slough of despondency, he tried to appear cheerful.

'You mean I'm no longer to be known as "Menty" then, Number One?'

Evans flinched. 'Ah, I hadn't realised you were aware of that soubriquet, sir,' he responded sheepishly.

'So, go on, explain, Number One. How am I known ashore?'

'After your efforts over the past two months, sir, the expatriate community and a few Russians besides, have christened you, "The Blue Pimpernel".

'Good gracious. I'm flattered.' Richard did, indeed, feel honoured. Following the fire-fighting exercise to save the Honorary Consul's furniture in March, he and his men had mounted many similar expeditions to save furniture and possessions from looting or fire. They had produced escorts to the railway station for those seeking to flee Reval and even provided safekeeping facilities for money, jewellery and other valuables. At the head of Richard's list to be protected was Rachel and Anna. He had not had the time to see either of them alone recently, but so far, they were being spared the worst effects of the revolution.

'In all honesty, Number One, I feel bad about keeping back the men who had been due to go on draft, but the extra manpower has been useful.'

Evans looked back at the line of submarines following in *E-19*'s wake. It included two of the *C*-boats, both joining their sisters in their base port at Rogekul. 'I forgot to tell you, sir. The *Bars* has a new first lieutenant. It's none other than our very own Sacha.'

'Thank you, Number One. I hadn't heard. I'm sure he has the necessary zeal to do well as a first lieutenant. Let's hope something good comes out of all his annoying questioning last year. How has his successor bedded in?'

'He's a little quiet and studious for my liking, sir, but he seems amiable enough. I suppose it's natural as newcomers, but he and the new pilot seem to have hit it off. They're both avid chess players.'

Lieutenant 'Shuggy' Hughes had joined as the new navigating officer. Unlike his predecessor, he was a career naval officer who had volunteered for submarines after experience at sea as the navigating officer of a torpedo boat.

The *Bars* was one of the Russian submarines in the convoy astern and Richard took his glasses to look over to it for Pavlyuchenko, but could not make him out from the other heavily clad figures on the bridge. He waved cheerfully, nonetheless.

'Right, Number One, she's all yours. You have the submarine. I'm going below to write some letters.'

'Aye aye, sir. I have the submarine,' Evans responded and made way for Richard to pass through the conning tower hatch. 'Control room, bridge. Captain coming below.'

*****

A few days later, having written to Lizzy, Richard turned his attention to his mother's latest correspondence. Hughes had the watch under Evans' supervision and the submarine was lying off Libau, watching for any German movement or build-up of forces.

As the war had progressed, he had noted that it was *Mutti* who now wrote to him. Previously, it had always been Papa. He understood why. Other than his official correspondence, Richard barely had the time even to pen letters to Lizzy. Whilst Papa's letter had always been fairly matter-of-fact and discussed the conduct of the war, *Mutti*'s letters always complained about how little she saw of Papa and her sons, and her disappointment that none of her sons could be bothered to write. Her latest letter carried on in much the same vein, but this time she seemed genuinely concerned about Papa's health. She feared that his duties of Chief of the War Staff were driving him to an early grave. Paul was in France and was likely to receive another decoration for his successes in dog fights over the Western Front, but she'd only heard that from Murray Sueter as Paul never bothered to write. John was still based in Essex and so the only one to visit London on a regular basis. She was despairing of Peter…

Richard laid down the letter as he heard a change of routine in the control room on the other side of the wardroom curtain. In an instant he joined Evans and Hughes. Evans was on the periscope with Hughes by his side.

'Something up, Number One?'

'The pilot claims he can see smoke to the south, but I'm buggered if I can see it. I've altered course to take a closer look anyway, sir. Would you like a look, sir?'

Richard took the periscope and, after conducting an all-round sweep of the horizon, focused on that to the south, but could see nothing. 'Put me on the bearing, Pilot.'

Hughes took the periscope and, after altering its angle, handed it back to the CO. 'That's the bearing, sir. It's definitely there, sir.'

Richard looked again and thought he might have seen a slight distortion on the horizon. He moved the periscope from right to left in high power and then he saw it - a faint line above the horizon. It was smoke. After another all-round look, he ordered the periscope to be lowered.

'Very well, Hughes. I like your eyesight. Number One, close on the target and call me when you've identified her.'

Richard returned to writing to his mother, but couldn't concentrate on the task. In any case, what could he write of his life in Russia without worrying her? He listened to the orders being given by Evans in the control room. The Welshman was hardly raising his voice and the crew were responding efficiently. Richard took pride in the way his submarine operated smoothly like a well-oiled machine. It gave him an idea.

Twenty minutes later Evans called Richard. 'It's a warship, sir. A light cruiser, I would say, with an escort of two torpedo boats. She's chucking out a load of smoke, so I can't be sure, but she's two masts and I think she could be of the *Gazelle* class. She's certainly an elderly beast. I estimate she's at a range of 7,000 yards.'

Richard's peremptory glance through the periscope verified Evans's identification. 'Very good, Number One. I don't think she's making for Libau. Her track's too northerly. However, we'll take her all the same. You can do the business.'

'You mean, you want me to conduct the attack, sir?' Evans asked astonished.

'Quite. It's time we blooded you. Let the Cox'n manage the trim.' Richard was pleased to see the smiles around the control room at the first lieutenant's discomfort. Instantly, Evans seemed to grow two inches.

'Right then. Aye aye, sir. Group up. Half ahead.'

Richard fetched his camp stool and sat over by the navigator's chart table to observe Hughes at work whilst cradling the cat on his lap. Evans manoeuvred the submarine to close the elderly cruiser and Richard noted how the crew appeared to be putting in just a little extra effort in all their actions. They clearly wanted their first lieutenant to succeed and, not for the first time, Richard was envious of Evans's ability to engage with the lower deck. However, it confirmed his judgement that Evans was probably now ready for command.

Once more, Evans called out the bearings of each target to aid the target set up, before lowering the periscope and increasing revolutions for a sprint into his ambush position. He approached the chart table to check Hughes's plot.

'Sir, I'm heading for this position, here.' He pointed at a space on the plot. 'That should allow me to fire from 1,200 yards, but the starboard escort may be on the bearing so I'm going to set the torpedoes to run at twelve feet.'

Richard wasn't sure if Evans was seeking permission for his plan, reassurance or politely informing him of his intentions, but decided to take a reassuring line.

'That all looks sensible, Number One, but you might have the after ends prepare a mouldie to run at the shallower depth. Just in case you have trouble with the escort.'

'Good point, sir. Thank you.' Evans issued the necessary orders.

Meanwhile, Richard continued fussing the cat, trying hard to avoid interfering with the control room routine. If anything went wrong with the attack and the escorts were carrying depth charges, then it would not be Evans who would face court martial, but him as the commanding officer. He longed to have just one look through the periscope to check Evans's calculations, but to do so might damage his second-in-command's confidence or his standing with the control room crew. In any case, the plan looked sound, although he might have been tempted to go in slightly closer and inside the escort to give less warning to the target. Unobtrusively, however, he checked the timing of Evans's final run-in against his own stop watch.

Evans stared at his stop watch and Richard could see a flush in his face. As Evans pushed back his cap, sweat began to trickle down his temples. The whole control room crew was tense and the only voices came from the low murmurs of the hydroplanes' men as they co-operated on the depth keeping and the reports from the torpedomen concerning the preparations of the torpedoes and tubes. Finally, Evans broke the tension.

'Slow ahead. Revolutions three-zero. Starboard fifteen. Steer two-three-zero. Periscope Depth. Put me on the bearing. Raise periscope.'

Evans crouched on his haunches, the way the Cossacks danced, as the periscope came up. Richard could see the disc of light reflected on his face as the periscope broke surface. He imagined the view through the periscope. The cruiser and escorts should be to port and crossing from left to right, but the target might have zigged and be way to port instead.

'Port five. Steer two-zero-zero. The target's a bit slower than twelve knots, sir. Probably covered in barnacles. Stand by to fire.'

Richard was pleased to see that Evans didn't forget to conduct an all-round look. In the excitement it would be easy to focus on the target and forget to look out for an approaching aircraft overhead.

'The Gods are with me, sir,' Evans called. 'The destroyer's fallen astern to give me a clear shot. Fire One! Fire Two!'

The submarine rocked as both torpedoes left their tubes. The trim board operator quickly compensated by flooding water whilst the 'planes operators reacted by putting dive on the 'planes to maintain depth. Everyone could feel the pressure on their ear drums as the high-pressure air used to launch the torpedoes was vented into the boat.

'Both torpedoes running true. Shut bow shutters and bow caps. Group up. Half ahead. Time to run… 70 seconds. Down. Starboard fifteen. Steer three-five zero. Revolutions six-zero.'

Richard approved of the plan to make the starboard turn. Were the escort to see the torpedo tracks, the captain would automatically look for the submarine down the bearing of the tracks. Openly this time, he checked his stop watch. The clock ran down… thirty seconds… twenty seconds… ten seconds… nothing! Had Evans missed? Had the mouldies failed? Ten seconds later though, everyone heard an explosion that was quickly followed by another. Richard could contain himself no longer. He gave the orders to slow down and raised the periscope.

The cruiser was on fire and her stern had been blown off. Men were jumping into the water, but the destroyer nearest her was bravely manoeuvring alongside the burning hull and taking off men. The action relieved Richard's conscience and he passed the periscope back to Evans.

'Well done, Number One. Take a look at your handiwork. Your first kill.' The men cheered and congratulated Evans pleasantly, but the voices were cut off suddenly by the noise of a tremendous explosion that rocked the boat. Evans confirmed their suspicions.

'The after magazine's gone. She's going down fast. The destroyer's copped it, too, but she's still afloat and…' Evans voice broke and he finished speaking mid-sentence. Richard put a hand on his shoulder.

'I know how you feel, Dai,' he said softly. 'War's not all glory is it? Go and get a cup of tea. I'll take her back to our patrol line.'

CHAPTER 28

On *E19*'s return to Reval, Richard found several surprises in store for him and most of them not pleasant. There was some positive news, however. The United States had declared war on Germany in response to the publication of a telegram from Germany's Foreign Minister outlining a plan to encourage Mexico to invade the southern states of America. Richard wasn't sure what difference the United States entry into the war would make, but it was positive news, particularly in light of the deteriorating military situation in Russia.

Then he had discovered that a fresh batch of sailors had joined the flotilla, having sailed from Liverpool via Belfast to Murmansk, before taking the train to Petrograd. With them came mail. These days, Richard dreaded the mail as it always contained a plethora of demands for more accounts and reports. However, he was pleased to note a letter from Commodore Hall praising his efforts, but rejecting his suggestion that a senior officer take command of the flotilla. Hall had made it clear that he wanted nobody else in command of the flotilla at present, but he would sound out the prospects of offering Richard an acting promotion. However, he had offered some good news and Richard immediately instructed Evans to clear lower deck of his submarine's ship's company.

'Men, amongst the latest mail, I've received some cheery news at last.' Richard knew his ship's company was already upbeat following a fresh delivery of mail and their sinking of the light cruiser.

'I've received notice that I am to be relieved of the command of our submarine with immediate effect.' A groan resounded around the workshop where the men were assembled and Richard could see a look of panic on Evans's face.

'However, here is the bad news. Yes, TI, I can see your look of glee.' Petty Officer Stockman had in fact appeared crestfallen at the news. 'The bad news is that I shall be staying on in command of the flotilla.' The news brought a cheer and Richard couldn't help feeling a glow of pride within him, or was it conceit, he wondered.

'As for the new commanding officer, I have been delegated the authority to appoint somebody of my own choice.' Some of the men began to exchange glances, wondering who would be their new CO. Hughes nudged Evans encouragingly.

'Naturally, command of such a rabble as I have had the misfortune to serve alongside in this submarine, is not a job for a mere lieutenant.' Richard smiled as he saw Hughes's face fall, but there was no reaction from Evans.

'Accordingly, before I announce the name of my successor as commanding officer of *E19*, I have one other announcement to make first. Acting Lieutenant Commander Dai Evans, you are improperly dressed.' For a moment there was silence and confusion on Evans's face and then the penny dropped almost simultaneously with the whole ship's company. Cheers erupted with cries of, 'Three cheers for the Jimmy'.

Richard let the tumult continue for a minute before holding up a hand to calm the assembly. 'I think your new commanding officer needs no introduction.' Richard stepped forward to shake the hand of and congratulate the stupefied Evans. The cheering recommenced.

'Well done, Dai. I couldn't have chosen a finer successor. Just make sure you look after her.'

*****

After handing over command of *E19* and removing his kit from on board, Richard turned to the latest developments in Russia during his absence on his final patrol. At Easter, the *Dvina* had been renamed the *Pamyat Azova* and now flew the imperial ensign. It struck Richard as odd that one of the most revolutionary ships in the Russian Navy no longer flew the red flag. However, pride in the resumption of the ship's old identity had at least persuaded the sailors on board to smarten her up with some paintwork and cleaning. Richard had high hopes that she might be fit for sea.

Concerned about the possible threat to Reval, he requisitioned a lighter and gave orders that all the stores and torpedoes be moved on board. He then booked a call on the C-in-C, Admiral Maximoff, and learned with mixed feelings that Admiral Vederevsky had been relieved as Commodore Submarines and promoted to become Chief of Staff to the C-in-C. Knowing

Maximoff's reputation, Richard arranged instead to call on Vederevsky.

'Sir, I request your permission to take the *Pamyat Azova* to sea.'

'Really, Commander. How very optimistic of you. And just where do you propose taking her?'

'Hango, sir.'

'An odd choice, if I may say. But first tell me why?' The admiral leaned forward with interest and Richard noted how the weak May sunshine reflected off Vederevsky's bald pate.

'As you already know, sir, there are signs that the Germans are intensifying their attacks on Riga…'

'Indeed, Commander. I congratulate you on your success in sinking the *Undine*. Alas, our submarines have not been as successful, although, thanks to your example, they are at sea, at least. But I digress. Pray continue.'

'I worry about the possibility of the base at Reval being overrun, sir. I want to take the depot ship and my flotilla where I can be sure I will have freedom of action.'

'I share your fears, Commander, but why Hango and not Helsingfors where we have better facilities?'

'It's too much a hotbed of revolutionary fervour, sir. I want to keep my men free of it all.'

'I see.' Vederevsky stood to survey the chart of the Grand Duchy of Finland and the Gulf of Finland.

'It makes sense and ordinarily, I would approve your request, but there is a fly in the ointment. Such a move would require the consent of the Centrobalt.'

'I'm sorry, sir. The Centrobalt?'

'Ah, you have been fortunate to be at sea these past two weeks. There is no end to the mischief of our rebellious sailors. We are now all at the mercy of the Central Baltic Sailors' Committee. Amongst other things, they have now decreed that officers will be elected and promoted by the crew, work will only take place between 09.00 and 15.00 and that all matters of routine will be decided by the ship's committee. I am, at least, permitted to continue to be called "Admiral" in place of the undignified "Comrade". I regret that it will be necessary for you to plead your case to the Centrobalt. It is no way to run a navy and especially one at war.'

Richard was alarmed at the latest development. 'Do you think Russia will still fight, sir?'

'Who knows? For now, yes. Kerensky and his Provisional Government have declared it its aim and, for the moment, the Bolsheviks, Mensheviks and whatever other viks are of the view that to protect their revolution, they need to prevent a German defeat. But I fear sinister moves are afoot.'

'I would welcome you sharing your thoughts, sir. It is a while since I was last in Petrograd and so I have not been keeping abreast of the latest political developments.'

'You would not have heard of a Vladimir Iylich Lenin. He is a revolutionary who, until recently, lived in exile in Switzerland. He and about thirty other revolutionaries struck a deal with the Germans to allow them to travel in a sealed train across Germany to Sweden. I can only imagine the price the Germans exacted was a promise to campaign to stop the war. This Lenin and another of his acolytes, Leon Trotsky, are now in Petrograd. However, we must cross bridges as we come to them. Together, we will approach the Centrobalt on bended knee.'

*****

A month later, Richard bade farewell to another submarine setting off on patrol. Since taking command of the Baltic flotilla, it was not an unusual occurrence, but this time it was different. He was waving farewell to Evans, taking *E19* out on patrol for the first time in command. The thin intertwined gold rings in between the thicker rings of his sleeve shone brightly against their green-tarnished neighbours. It would have been normal to have all the gold lace replaced, but the nearest naval tailors were nearly two thousand miles away. Richard felt both proud to see his *protégé* achieving his own command and, also, fearful. The failure of the *Bars* to return from patrol the previous week was a stark reminder of the hazards his boats faced. Richard was sad that Pavlyuchenko had had his promising submarine career cut short so early. He had heard that Sacha's father had shot himself on hearing the tragic news.

Despite many meetings, he had yet to persuade the Centrobalt to allow him to take the flotilla and depot ship to Hango. Moreover, life in Reval was becoming no easier, despite the port now being completely free of ice. The news was becoming worse day by day, he reflected. Across the country there were reports of murders, arson and robberies as the peasants rose up against the landed gentry. In the light of such reports, he had tried to persuade Anna and Rachel to move into the town, but both thought themselves safer where they were.

However, he had more immediate problems to address, he thought grimly as he made his way back to his cabin. He had been able to lend *E1*'s first lieutenant to *E19* for the time being as *E1* was proving mechanically troublesome after two years absence from Britain. Despite the engineers' best endeavours, the boat was proving to be a sick lady and the sailors were already calling her 'The Wallflower'. On returning to his cabin, Richard was on the point of summoning Commander Stocker for an update when he thought better of it. Better to see for himself, he thought, and he clambered down to the submarine.

He found her CO, Athelstan Fenner, in the control room with Stocker. Like the engineers, he was wearing overalls and lending a hand. A man after my own heart, Richard thought. The willingness of submarine officers literally to get their hands dirty and involve themselves in technical issues was one of the reasons why they were regarded with disdain by their fellow officers in the Royal Navy's capital ships.

'Morning, Percy, Stan. Have you found the problem yet?' Pieces of the submarine's hydroplane controls were littered around the deck of the control room in a pool inches deep of red hydraulic oil.

'We think we've found the problem,' Stocker replied, 'But until we've stripped the whole hydraulic system down, we can't be sure.'

The submarine had been having problems with its hydroplanes, but they only occurred below periscope depth.

'So, what do you think it is then, Percy?' Richard asked as he tiptoed around the control room to avoid the oil overlapping his shoes.

'It was Stan's Chief ERA that put us on the right track. He took a magnet and a microscope to a sample of the hydraulic oil. Clever chap that. We're getting sea water contamination, probably due to the return line pressure under the casing. It seems low and at any sort of depth, the external seawater pressure is higher, so it seeps into the holding tank. As you can imagine, sir, once water's in the system it's a devil. It doesn't just corrode the pipework, but the seals and control valves, and that's where we're seeing the drop in pressure.'

'If you're right, Percy, how easy is it to fix?' Richard asked.

'Difficult to say, sir. To be honest, it's a bugger. We can sort out the return line pressure, drain and flush through the system, but it'll be tricky to remove the water and the debris it's caused from the dead legs of the system. You can see what it does to the oil for yourself, sir.' Stocker pointed to the foaming of the oil swilling on the deck.

'Quite,' Richard replied. 'Well, do your best. I still intend taking the flotilla to Hango and I'd hate to leave this boat behind. Not after all she's been through hey, Stan?'

'Absolutely, sir. But I'm afraid the hydraulics are not the only problem I need to report, sir,' Fenner added quietly. 'I'm sorry to burden you with further problems, but might we have a private word?' Fenner gestured upwards with his eyes.

'Certainly, Stan. Why don't we take a breath of fresh air?'

Fenner, still clad in his overalls, and Richard perambulated the upper deck of the depot ship. Fenner seemed reluctant to raise the issue, so Richard opened the conversation.

'A good man your Chief. A problem identified soon becomes a problem solved.'

'Goodman's indeed a good man, sir.' Fenner smiled at the weak joke, but it was enough to make him open up.

'It's a pity I can't say the same about my Russian telegraphist, sir, Chernyshevsky. He's stirring up things. I've tried to sort him out myself, but he refuses to accept my discipline anymore.'

Richard was both angered and dismayed to hear Fenner's report. Discipline was the keystone to a successful submarine and he was surprised Fenner was not able to sort out the trouble. Fenner was a good CO and he was right, Richard thought. As the commander of the flotilla, he could do without having to deal with disciplinary issues.

'In what way is he stirring up things, Stan?' he asked patiently.

'It started off that he was saying Jack shouldn't obey his officers. The ship's company soon gave him short shrift over that, but his latest antics include trying to persuade the other telegraphists from going on board their own boats. Frankly, sir, I'd like to be rid of him, but that's your prerogative, sir, and I'm sensitive that these are awkward times.'

Richard thought that an understatement, but appreciated Fenner's concern. Any trouble in Anglo-Russian relations needed to be nipped in the bud quickly. He continued his circuit of the *Pamyat Azova* in silence before coming to a decision.

'Very well. I'll deal with it this afternoon, but first I need to pay another visit to the Centrobalt.'

*****

'Leading Telegraphist Chernyshevsky, to see the Commanding Officer, sir,' *E1*'s coxswain bawled. 'Off cap.'

The proceedings were unusual. Normally a commanding officer would investigate misdemeanours committed by 'defaulters' in private and a formal charge would be read to the accused. However, Richard had decided to see the Russian in front of an assembly comprising the ship's company of HMS *E1* and all the Russian officers and sailors under his command. Moreover, as no charge was to be read, Chernyshevsky should have been allowed to continue to wear his cap, but Richard was determined that this meeting would be treated as a disciplinary event, notwithstanding the absence of a formal charge.

'Chernyshevsky, I understand you are not prepared to accept the discipline of your commanding officer. Is that true?'

'He is not my commanding officer, comrade. He has not been elected...'

'Silence,' Richard cut in. 'You will address me as "Commander" in line with the proclamation of the Central Committee. In accordance with the proclamation, officers no need to be addressed as "High-born excellency", but are to be addressed by their rank. Proceed.'

Chernyshevsky shrank before Richard's rebuke, but remained defiant. 'Very well, *Commander,*' he sneered. 'It was, also, announced by the Central Committee that all officers were to be elected and promoted by the crew. Comrade… *Commander* Fenner has not been elected and, indeed, no ship's committee has been appointed to do so.'

'Thank you, Chernyshevsky, for making that so clear. However, let me make something else clear. Whilst under my command, you enjoy certain privileges denied to your colleagues or comrades serving in Russian ships. These include better rations, a daily allowance of vodka and a share in any prize money. Is that so?'

'Yes, Commander.'

Richard was pleased to see that the Russian looked less cocky. 'However, with those privileges come responsibilities and submission to our Naval Discipline Act. Were you a Royal Navy sailor you would now be facing a charge of wilful disobedience, the punishment for which is a minimum of twenty-eight days of detention.'

Richard paused to allow the import of his words to sink in, but the Russian was again defiant. 'But that is not right. I am not subject to your discipline. All punishments can only be awarded by a committee of three men and one officer.' He glared at Richard defiantly.

'Not under my command!' Richard barked. 'And I have raised the issue with the Centrobalt. You will no doubt be pleased to know, however, that with immediate effect, you are no longer under my command.'

Chernyshevsky smirked and looked round to his fellow Russians for approval. 'Eyes front,' the coxswain shouted.

'But before you are dismissed, Chernyshevsky, let me advise you of two small matters. Firstly, you are no longer entitled to wear the Distinguished Service Medal awarded to the whole ship's company of *E1*…' In a flash, the coxswain deftly removed the highly-prized medal proudly worn on the Russian's chest. 'And secondly, you now forfeit your share of any prize money accrued by your former shipmates.'

The Russians in the assembly gasped at the news. British prize money was a small fortune to them.

'But, *comrade,*' the telegraphist replied insolently, 'You have no right to remove me. No man is to be removed from a ship without the approval of the ship's committee.'

'Really, Chernyshevsky? You might be correct in a Russian ship, but I've already met with the Central Committee. I have given the Centrobalt forty-eight hours to remove you from this ship. Alternatively, I will report the incident to my ambassador in Petrograd and he will inform the British Admiralty. In which case no doubt, there will be severe repercussions for my men's continued involvement in the campaign to save your motherland from the Germans. The committee seemed inclined to comply with my request. Carry on, Cox'n.'

'On cap. About turn. Quick march,' the coxswain responded. Chernyshevsky didn't appear quite so cocksure now.

CHAPTER 29
June 1917

The last time Elizabeth had taken a sea crossing with Emmeline Pankhurst had been in October 1912. Even on the relatively short crossing of the Channel, Elizabeth had noted that Emmeline was prone to the *mal de mer*. Elizabeth was more fortunate. She had often accompanied her father on sea trials and had developed a cast iron stomach, even in the roughest of weathers. On the second day of their voyage from Aberdeen to Norway, Emmeline was still resting in her cabin, leaving Elizabeth to promenade the ship's decks alone.

Emmeline had told Elizabeth that she had been sent as Lloyd-George's unofficial special envoy to the Kerensky government. Apparently, the government was concerned that the steady collapse of the social and political system in Russia might lead to another revolution. Were the Bolsheviks to gain power and capitalise on the war weariness of the Russian people, the government feared Russia might withdraw from the war. Elizabeth's involvement had been last minute when Jessie Kenney had succumbed to another bout of her recurrent lung disease. Needing a French speaker to assist her with the meetings, Emmeline had quickly persuaded Elizabeth to accompany her.

As she stared at the grey sea beneath the overcast sky, Elizabeth couldn't believe her luck. Finally, after a separation of eighteen months, she would soon see her beloved Richard again. Would he see her changed, she wondered? She had managed to lose the weight she had gained during her pregnancy, but she had detected the beginnings of lines in her face. Well, there's nothing I can do about it now, she thought. She just hoped Uncle William had been able to warn Richard of her fleeting visit to Petrograd.

*****

Richard didn't trust his eyes. He read the signal again. Lizzy was on her way to Moscow and would be arriving in Petrograd that evening. How could this be so, he wondered, but the signal only gave him the bald facts. There was no time to lose and he began to pack his bag for the train journey to Petrograd. His official correspondence would have to wait a few days.

He heard a knock at the door of his cabin and saw Fenner's head poke through the curtain.

'Excuse me, sir, but sorry to bother you. There's something you should know.'

'Good morning, Stan. Could it wait? I'm a bit pressed for time.'

''Fraid not, sir.'

Bother, Richard thought, but he had no choice. 'Come in then, Stan, and take a pew. What's up?'

'It's the old bo's'n of the *Pamyat Asova*, sir.'

'I thought that matter was settled. The last I heard, he'd been acquitted by the Centrobalt and sent to another ship.' The elderly warrant officer had been a popular figure with the Royal Navy sailors and they had expressed concern when the man had been charged with not taking any part in the mutiny on board in 1905.

'True, sir, but it hasn't been settled. The ship's committee are defying the Centrobalt and have dragged him back on board to face a fresh trial. Jack, as you would imagine, is not very happy and I fear some trouble may lie ahead.'

Richard understood Fenner's point. Jack was spoiling for a fight and this might be the ignition point. It was a matter that needed intervention, but even so, it would have to wait until he returned from Petrograd.

'Quite. You're right to bring it to my attention, Stan. I have to shoot up to Petrograd for a few days, but I'll speak to the Ship's Committee immediately on my return.' Richard removed some clean shirts from his sea chest, but Fenner made no moves to leave the cabin.

'Is there something else on your mind, Stan?'

'Sir, it's just the new trial is set for this afternoon. I don't think the matter can wait.' Fenner seemed embarrassed to impart the news.

At first, Richard was inclined to let matters lie. It was a matter for the Russians, after all, and he had already gained a reputation for interference. He paused his packing for a moment and thought about the matter more deeply. Dick, you know you can't walk away, he thought. The members of Ship's Committee of the

Pamyat Asova are some of the most extreme revolutionaries and they'll stop at nothing short of a lynching this time. Stan's right. Were that to happen, Jack would more than likely intervene with dire consequences. He checked his watch. If he took the next train, he could meet Lizzy at the Astoria this evening and spend a blissful night in her company. Were he to attend the trial, he could catch the evening train and still be in Petrograd in time to see Lizzy before she caught her train to Moscow in the morning. It wouldn't be the same, of course, but barely fifteen minutes earlier, he had had no idea when he might see Lizzy again. He made up his mind. His duty must come first.

'Very well, Stan, I'll attend the trial and go on to Petrograd a little later than I had planned.'

'Thank you, sir. I hope the delay won't inconvenience you,' Fenner replied in a relieved tone.

'No, Stan. It was just some private business.'

*****

It seemed a matter of *déjà vu* as Richard attended the trial of the former boatswain of the *Pamyat Asova*. It had been only three months earlier that he had intervened in the trials of the depot ship's paymaster and Lieutenant Miller. However, this time, although permitted to attend the trial with members of his flotilla, Richard had not been allowed to speak on the warrant officer's behalf before the verdict. Despite some obvious bruising to his face, the old man stood proudly erect as the verdict was announced. It came as no surprise that it was one of guilty. The boatswain was then sentenced to be disrated and imprisoned in Kronstadt. However, it was when his shoulder boards were ripped off and the man forced to strip and don a pair of canvas overalls that the trouble started.

Several of the Russian ship's company of the depot ship began to call abuse and some spat on him. Then an angry crowd began to mob him and assault him with punches and kicks. Richard felt sure that at any minute the mob intended a lynching, but as suddenly, some of his own sailors began to weigh in to protect the prisoner. Richard knew he had to act quickly if he was to prevent a riot.

‘Ship’s company, Ho!’ he called loudly. Immediately, the Royal Navy sailors sprang to attention and the Russian sailors looked back at Richard in puzzlement.

‘Mister President,’ Richard addressed the court. ‘I put it to you that under your own regulations, this court has only the power to award summary punishments. The punishment of imprisonment can only be awarded by court martial… and only the Centrobalt has the right to convene a court martial.’ Richard’s words caused much muttering and dissension amongst both the court members and the lynch mob.

‘Mister President, I make no judgement on the rights or otherwise of this court to judge this case and come to the verdict it has, but if the new Soviet Republic is to herald a new era of equality and justice for all, then its laws must be *seen* to be applied scrupulously. I submit that the sentence of this court should be suspended and the matter placed before the Centrobalt for a decision. That would be the way of the Royal Navy.’

Richard gambled that the last remark might hold some sway as he knew the sailors of the depot ship still held his men in some regard. The ploy worked. After some noisy and heated exchanges, the president of the court responded.

‘The court has heard the intervention of Commander Miller. In the interests of demonstrating to our friends and allies of the Royal Navy that justice is applied mercifully and fairly in the new Soviet Navy, the sentence of imprisonment will be referred to the Centrobalt for confirmation, but the sentence of disrating imposed by this court will still apply.’

Richard heaved a sigh of relief. He knew that the Centrobalt had already acquitted the old boatswain, so he doubted the sentence of imprisonment would stand. For now, he had a more pressing problem. He had a train to catch.

*****

By comparison with the Finland station, at which she and Emmeline had arrived the day before, Elizabeth was impressed with the architecture of Nicholaevsky Station, but there the favourable comparison ended. Both women had been shocked by the squalor of the people milling about the Finland Station on their arrival in

Petrograd. The people of the East End of London seemed well-off by comparison. If anything, the Nicholaevsky Station was an even sadder place, though. It, too, was thronged with miserable-looking Russians, many dressed in little more than rags. Moreover, several women bore placards seeking news of their loved ones. Worse was the misery of the lengthy lines of the wounded arriving in Petrograd from the front at Riga. However, at least the station building itself offered a grandeur that the Finland Station lacked. Its large windows, Corinthian columns and huge clock tower reminded her of the great Italian renaissance buildings she had seen on her Grand Tour many years earlier. Even so, the relative grandeur of the station did nothing to brighten her mood. Elizabeth's first impressions of Russia were depressing and she had been hugely disappointed not to have met up with Richard the night before. Perhaps he's at sea, she thought, or perhaps Uncle William had not been able to send news of her short-notice arrival. Whatever the case, there might be another opportunity to meet on her return home through Petrograd… whenever that might be.

*****

Richard was becoming increasingly frustrated by the rail journey from Reval to Petrograd. It was already after 09.00, he was hungry and the journey still had at least another hour to run. If Lizzy was to take the morning train to Moscow, she would be gone by the time he arrived in Petrograd. He had hoped to arrive in the early hours of the morning, but the train had been terminated at Narva to allow a hospital train to pass through. It had taken a good few of Richard's diplomatic skills and the sight of his medals to persuade the Russian transport officer to allow him to board the hospital train as a supernumerary. If only he had not had to attend that trial, he thought. Then again, had he not, the consequences might have been unimaginable.

An hour and a half later, the hospital train rumbled into Nicholaevsky Station. Richard knew he was already too late to catch Lizzy, so he gave a hand with unloading some of the walking wounded. Some of the men were in a pitiable state with dirty scraps of clothing for make-shift bandages and rags for uniforms. It reminded him of a painting of Napoleon's retreat from Moscow. It caused him to wonder once more how the Russians would be able to continue to fight the Germans. He had decided to make his way to the British Embassy to make his journey worthwhile, but the rumbling in his stomach reminded him that he had not had breakfast, so he first made his way to the former first-class restaurant. There, he bought himself some thick tea and black bread as eggs were not available.

Outside the window of the restaurant, he noticed the station master parading about and looking important. Richard thought it worth checking that Lizzy and Emmeline had arrived safely the night before and were now safely on their way to Moscow. He felt sure they would have stood out amongst the local populace, so he opened the window and called to the station master.

'Comrade, did two English ladies catch the train to Moscow earlier this morning?'

'The train to Moscow?' The station master checked his watch. 'No, the train to Moscow has not yet left. Everything is in a muddle today… but then that's normal. I think it might leave in twenty minutes or so… from platform Five.'

Richard dropped his cup at the news, spilling his tea. 'It hasn't left yet?'

'I'm sorry, comrade.' The station master pulled himself up to his full height defensively. 'We have been extremely busy with the hospital train. There is a war on.'

'But have you seen two English ladies?' Richard asked hopefully.

'You mean the guests of Prime Minister Kerensky? But of course. I could not allow such honoured guests to mix with the er…' The station master looked at the crowds disapprovingly and sought the right words, but Richard interrupted him.

'So where are they, comrade?'

'They are in my office, taking some refreshment whilst they wait for me to call them for the train.'

Richard's heart leapt. 'Don't move. Wait there,' he shouted before rushing to the restaurant exit.

Five minutes later, he set eyes on Elizabeth for the first time in over eighteen months. He wanted to rush over and embrace her, but suddenly, he felt shy and unsure what to do.

‘Hello, Lizzy. I’m sorry I’m late, but…’ He never finished his sentence as Elizabeth rushed to him and began showering him with kisses, tears welling in her eyes.

‘Oh, Dick, I thought I wouldn’t see you again.’ She squeezed him hard.

Richard felt awkward at this public display of affection and merely patted Elizabeth’s back fondly, but Emmeline was quick to catch on. It was only as she spoke that Richard really noticed her.

‘I think I’ll just powder my nose before we board the train, Elizabeth. Station Master, could you show me the way?’ She addressed the station master in French, but Richard could see he didn’t understand.

‘Comrade, would you show the lady to the bathroom, please?’ he asked in Russian.

As Emmeline shut the door to the station master’s office behind her, Richard felt no inhibitions and kissed Elizabeth passionately, squeezing her tightly.

CHAPTER 30
September 1917

Steele wondered if he would ever have a shot at the enemy. All summer his and the other three *C*-boats had mounted endless patrols in the Gulf of Riga and Irben Straits, without a sniff of any enemy vessel. Then the long anticipated German assault on Riga had materialised and despite stiff resistance for the first twenty-four hours, it had quickly fallen. Since then, both *C26* and C27 had been conducting the extremely hazardous tasks of mine reconnaissance. Now *C27* had broken down and unable to withdraw to Reval under her diesel power, was under tow.

Nobody had been sorry to leave Rogekul. It had been a dull base port and the only breaks in the ship's companies' tedium was the occasional visit to Reval or, latterly, Hango. The flotilla had finally moved there in August.

'I say, sir,' Lieutenant Morse piped up. He was Steele's first lieutenant and even less experienced than Steele recalled he must have been when appointed to *E9*. 'The Russians are laying it on a bit thick, what? Not just an ice breaker in the height of the bally summer, but an escort of twelve trawlers.'

Steele, too, had been surprised to be allocated an ice breaker in place of the usual tug.

'I can only surmise that the Russians hold us in great esteem.'

'Rather. I can see the breakwater now, sir. We'll soon be alongside. I must say, sir, the chaps are looking forward to the flesh pots of Reval after a winter in dear old Rogekul.'

'Just see to it, Morse, that the men are kept busy. Relations ashore are more than a little volatile at present. A bit of sport... What the deuced? Take cover.'

To everyone's astonishment, the ice breaker towing the submarine had just blown up and debris from the ship was raining down on the submarine astern. Seconds later, one of the escorting trawlers blew up, too.

''Pon rep', the Russians have only gone and led us through one of their own minefields, first lieutenant. That is most unfortunate.'

'What on earth are we to do, sir?' Steele could see that Morse had lost the colour from his face.

'Let me think upon it a little.' It suddenly dawned on Steele that for the first time in his command, he was in a life-or-death situation and the responsibility for action in the next few minutes was his alone.

*****

As *E19* returned to periscope depth after a night on the seabed, it was obvious to all that the rough weather they had been experiencing all September had not departed. The boat was rocked by the waves and the men knew they were in for several more uncomfortable hours of watchkeeping. Designed to sink, submarines are unstable at periscope depth and soon the control room buckets would be back in use for those unfortunate enough to suffer the worst effects of *mal de mer*. Evans noted that in one bucket some wag had placed part of a 'baby's head', the navy's tinned steak and kidney pudding, to discomfort his shipmates.

Evans had a good stomach, so his irritation with the weather was that it made accurate depth keeping difficult, with the constant risk of broaching in front of the enemy. Moreover, the agitated sea and the continuous rain were preventing him approaching the port of Libau close enough to observe any build-up of German naval forces. A sweep of the horizon showed no evidence of shipping and he came to a decision.

'First Lieutenant, maintain this course and speed. I plan to surface in ten minutes. Warn the lookouts it's cold and wet up top. I'm going to change.'

Evans knew that he was at greater risk of detection on the surface, but the increased height of eye from the bridge would offer him better visibility. Moreover, with the low cloud cover, there would be no risk of the Germans putting up any reconnaissance aircraft.

*****

'Yes, I have it. We've a full battery charge, have we not?' Steele asked Morse.

'Yes, sir. 90 percent.'

'That'll do nicely. Go below and rouse the men. I want everyone on the casing, just in case we're the next unfortunate blighters to run into a mine. They might as well slip what's left of the tow. I shall need a volunteer to stay below in the motor room. I'm going to get us out of this mess on the electric motors and I'll need somebody on the switchboard.'

'I'll do that myself, sir,' Morse replied and a little colour returned to his face.

*****

E19 was rolling like a pig and her new and temporary first lieutenant had wisely put the stove out of action to prevent scalding water being thrown about. Evans didn't mind his cold lunch of corned beef sandwiches, but he was desperate for a warming mug of tea. It had been bloody cold on the bridge, but the Third Hand had the watch now. Mind you, it wasn't much warmer in the control room either. With the diesels running, the engines were sucking in a huge, cold draught of air through the conning tower hatch. Whilst he had removed his oilskins, he retained his duffel coat. Although in his opinion the Belgian fabric was no warmer than that of his former submarine blazer, he liked the convenience of the duffel coat's hood and large pockets.

Evans had just started on the second of his thick wedges of a sandwich when the klaxon sounded and within seconds the deck dropped beneath him as the boat dived in emergency. By the time he was in the control room to man the periscope, the first two lookouts were at the bottom of the conning tower hatch. The second, impeded by his colleague was too slow in moving away and found himself flattened by the third and fourth lookouts as they dropped rapidly down the ladder. Automatically, Evans began to sweep the horizon in low power as he heard the Officer of the Watch and navigator, Sub Lieutenant Parkes call out, 'Upper lid one clip… second clip on.' Thirty seconds later, Parkes joined Evans at the periscope.

'Red seven-zero, sir, range six thousand yards. A battleship, light cruiser and some transports, sir.' Evans already had them in sight through the periscope.

'I'm sorry, sir,' Parkes added. 'I saw them late. The visibility suddenly improved and there they were.'

'Port thirty, steer one-seven-zero. Group up, half ahead.' Evans was not ignoring Parkes, but had to act quickly to get into a firing position. Parkes was right. The visibility was markedly better and he hoped the enemy force had not spotted the submarine, too.

'There's one other thing, too, sir. Just before we eyed the ships, I spotted several ships in Libau, sir, including a battleship. I think it was one of the *Deutchland*-class, sir.'

*****

Evans closed the range of the enemy force and ordered the torpedo tubes ready before bringing *E19* back to periscope depth. As soon as the submarine slowed down, it became obvious from the noise levels that the number of vessels above was significant.

'Bloody hell, boys,' Evans chirped. 'It sounds like the whole bloomin' IGN's up there from that racket. Standby target set up. Up. Bloody hell! It's like Carmarthen Park on a Saturday afternoon!' He began reeling off the ranges and bearings of four battleships, five transports, a quartet of destroyers and so many trawlers he couldn't count them.

'Standby to fire one and two bow tubes. I'm going for a nice, juicy *König*-class battleship, but we'll have to be quick.'

As soon as the fore-ends crew made their reports of ready, Evans ordered both torpedoes to be fired. He, like the rest of his ship's company, waited anxiously for the noise of an explosion, but in vain. The torpedoes had clearly missed the target. In response, Evans ordered the submarine deep and the tubes to be reloaded. Above, the whining of destroyer turbines could be heard nearby and then the crash of two depth charge explosions reverberated through the boat.

'Sounds like the Huns have those new-fangled depth charges, sir,' Petty Officer Stockman opined unnecessarily.

'Maybe you're right there, Cox'n, but they couldn't knock the skin off a rice pudding,' Evans replied unconcerned. Patiently, he bided his time as the torpedomen prepared and heaved two fresh torpedoes into the bow tubes. As soon as they were ready, he returned the boat to periscope depth and swept the horizon with the periscope.

'Bad news, boys. We seem to have chased away the battleships. They're too far east for us now, but we've still a chance at the transports. Port ten. Steer one-zero-zero. Range that.'

Again, Evans called out the ranges and bearings of the vessels. The submarine was surrounded by ships and he was intrigued to note the trawlers were heaving out some form of heavy equipment into the sea. However, his immediate concern was the destroyers, one of which had just opened fire on him.

'Bearing that. Range six hundred yards. Down. Keep sixty feet,' he ordered. 'Destroyer coming straight towards us. We'll let him pass over us and come back to PD for our shot at the transport.' Evans removed his cap and wiped the sweat from his head. He was trying to emulate his mentor and previous captain's cool demeanour, but he could feel his heart racing and his stomach knotting. The sight of the destroyer screaming down his throat had unnerved him more than a little.

'I suspect the after-ends crew are about to have their sleep disturbed, boys,' he joked. Sure enough, shortly after the destroyer had passed overhead, the control room crew heard two clicks in the water to starboard.

'What was that noise?' Stoker Burridge asked, but before anybody could answer, the boat was rocked by two massive explosions. The lights dimmed, gauges shattered and small jets of water sprung from water pipes. The whole control room crew were covered in shards of cork from the deckhead. Evans, wedged between the bulkhead and the periscope called out,

'First Lieutenant, pass through the boat and report any major damage or casualties. Anybody hurt in the control room?'

Only Burridge had suffered in the explosion. The side of his face was bleeding from a few splinters of glass. The ERA carefully removed the glass and wiped away the blood as Evans examined him.

'You'll live, Burridge. And for your information, those clicks were the hydrostatic firing mechanism of the depth charges operating. It's not a sound I fancy hearing that often.'

'Captain, sir,' the First Lieutenant, Lieutenant Ainscough interrupted. 'No significant damage or injuries, sir. A few leaks, but under control and a few bruises. Otherwise, we're fully shipshape, sir.'

'Thank you, Number One. Let's get on with the war then. Periscope Depth, please.'

Evans had a feeling of dread as he conducted his extremely rapid all-round look. He identified the target not as a transport, but a cruiser converted to some form of depot ship. It was in the perfect position for him to sink her, on the starboard bow at a range of only 800 yards. His mouth dried such that he could barely swallow at the sight of two destroyers lining up to attack at right angles. With horror, it dawned on him that the Germans had known exactly where to expect *E19* to be, but he had no time to consider that now.

'Fire One.' As soon as the first torpedo was away, he didn't wait to fire the second. The huge bow wave of the destroyer to port was barely two hundred yards away.

'Down. Ten down. Full ahead. Keep 120 feet.'

As the angle came on the boat and it descended into the depths, Evans ordered a forty-degree course change in an attempt to throw his attackers. It was now clear to him that the heavy equipment he had seen being lowered into the water by the trawlers was the new hydrophone. He decided it was not the time to share the news with his ship's company.

Seconds after the destroyer rushed overhead, he and the men heard the splash of depth charges entering the water above. 'Brace yourselves, boys,' Evans shouted. 'Standby for depth charge attack.'

Stockman intoned in mock prayer, 'For what we are about to receive, may the Lord make us truly thankful,' but nobody laughed. Indeed, nobody even cheered as an explosion could be heard in the distance. Their torpedo had struck home.

Again, the unnerving clicks from the arming mechanism could be heard before the boat was lifted violently by the shocks of the double explosions. Down aft could be heard the shouted warning of a fire breaking out, but almost as quickly a report came forward that the fire was out. Evans ordered another distinct alteration in course and tried to figure out his options before the next attack.

He had not experienced the use of hydrophones before, but he knew the Germans must be tracking the submarine's noise. That would have to be cut, but he needed the motors to evade. What would old Menty have done, he wondered. Then he recalled a conversation they had shared a few months earlier after they had sunk the *Prinz Adalbert.* It would be dangerous, but they couldn't leave the initiative with the Germans. When the next attack came, he knew just what he had to do.

CHAPTER 31

Carefully, with steering controlled from the bridge, Steele manoeuvred *C27* on the electric motors a mile astern, along the track the submarine had just followed. He had no idea of the extent of the Russian minefield, but the icebreaker had not triggered any mines on that path so he reckoned it would be safe. To port he could see one of the trawler escorts inching its way across to join him at very slow speed. When in hailing distance, the Russian skipper called for him to stop. Steele called for an interpreter to come to the bridge.

'Stay where you are, Captain. I will fetch help,' the Russian skipper called and Steele noted that a small boat was being lowered. The Russian telegraphist continued to translate the trawler skipper's words.

'Lend me two of your men. I am short-handed and can only spare two men. Together they can row into the harbour and summon a guide.'

In the absence of any better ideas, Steele readily agreed.

*****

Evans waited with bated breath as the next destroyer charged in towards them. He was pleased to note that the men seemed less anxious this time, but it amused him that they all looked upwards as if expecting to see the ship cross overhead. The destroyer went through the same procedure for its attack. Again, the boat was rocked by the explosions, but no worse than before. However, this time Evans responded differently.

'Full ahead. Port thirty. Silence through the boat. Switch off the fans,' he ordered.

'But, sir? What about the batteries?' the ERA asked. The fans ventilated the batteries to remove the deadly hydrogen gas from beneath the deck plates. The gas was extremely explosive.

'It's a risk we'll have to take,' Evans replied. 'I don't suppose the smell will be worse than the farts in the senior rates' mess. Stop engines. First Lieutenant, take her down to 180 feet, but I don't want you using the trim pump. You'll have to do it on the 'planes.'

Ainscough gave his CO a quizzical look, but made no argument. Evans knew that the ship's company would worry about going deeper than the boat's designed depth and decided to offer reassurance.

'Don't you go frettin', boys. Commander Miller once told me he once took his boat down to 200 feet to avoid the Turks and he came back all right. Remember this boat was built by Vickers, too.'

In the absence of the ventilation fans the boat was deathly quiet as she hovered at 180 feet. The only sounds were those of the telemotors operating the hydroplanes as the operators ensured the boat went no deeper. This time, as the next destroyer lined up for its attack, the engine noises were quieter. Evans hoped that he might have confounded the hydrophones operators by his sprint and alteration of course whilst the water was disturbed by the depth charge explosions. Sure enough, this time the metallic clicks of the hydrostatic firing mechanisms were not heard before the depth charges exploded further away. The noise still reverberated around the boat and the shock waves rolled her, but it was not enough to draw sweat.

'Full ahead. Switch on the fans.' Evans took further advantage of the disturbance the depth charges had caused to the water. Twenty seconds later, he changed the order to slow ahead.

'We'll stay on this course and speed, First Lieutenant, until we've evaded the enemy, but I still want silence in the boat until further notice. You can leave the fans on, PO. I dread to think how foul the air would be in the senior rates' mess otherwise.'

*****

'Welcome to Hango, Algie.' Richard returned Steele's salute as he stepped ashore after the short crossing from Reval. 'I'm hoping you'll find life a little quieter here.'

'Good afternoon, sir. I'm mighty relieved to be here. I was beginning to fear we'd be iced in before my bally engines were fixed.'

'It's good to see you safe and sound, Algie. Fancy stretching those long legs of yours? I can show you the town. I could do with a break from my desk for a short while.'

'Absolutely, sir. Lead me on, but I'll just let my Jimmy know where I'm off first.'

A few minutes later, the two tall submariners headed into the Russian town.

'How is life here, sir? Less fraught than in Reval, I trust?'

'Quite. But it has its minuses as well as its pluses. The political temperature is less heated here, but money and food's a problem. I'm sorry, Algie. I know you had a hot time of it down at Riga, but I'm going to send you out again soon… and with emergency rations, too!'

'Things are that bad are they, sir?'

'Do you mean the food or the operational situation?'

'Both, I suppose, but I've seen for myself the problems at sea. The Germans are showing complete contempt for the Russians. I swear I saw 200 bombs dropped on the forts at Dago and Osel. Their seaplanes just taxied in on the surface and only took off at the last minute to drop their infernal bombs, almost without so much as a by your leave from the Ruskies. And don't speak to me about mines.'

'Yes, I had heard about the mines from Satow in *C32*. I gather it's pot luck now as to whether you hit a Hun mine or a Russian one in the Irben Straits. Is it true the Huns are dropping mines with aircraft now?'

'I couldn't rightly say, sir. I had my own skirmishes with aircraft and didn't stay on the surface long enough to ask if they were dropping bombs or mines on me. I say! Are those tennis courts, perchance?'

'They are, but it'll be a while before it's warm enough to play tennis again, I fear, Algie. But you'll like Hango. Compared with Reval, it's extremely clean with a lovely coastline full of small bays and inlets. It has some beautiful walks and beaches and serves as a spa town for the Russian nobility. The trouble is that only one of the hotels is still open and Russian's of little use here. All the locals speak Swedish. Let's cut left here and I'll take you to a good view point of the Gulf whilst I update you on the situation here.'

'I'm fair agog, sir,' replied Steele with a huge grin.

'Don't confuse liberty with licence, Algie.' Richard swiped Steele on the arm playfully. 'However, I'll not hide it from you, old friend. Things are getting desperate. The Hun more or less has command of the sea and judging from Evans's last report, they could well launch an amphibious assault on the islands off Riga. After Riga, Reval's likely to fall next and then the Huns will be on the flank of Petrograd. None of this should have come as a surprise to the Russian staff. We've been warning them for months, but they're paralysed by this blasted revolution. Quite frankly, I'm worried Jack's boiling up for a fight, not with the Hun, but with the Ruskies.'

'Really? How so, sir?'

'You know Jack. Give him something to beef about and a good fight and he's a happy lad. Now he's got plenty to beef about. We're short of food to the point I've given the Russian Staff a week's notice that I plan on standing down the flotilla unless they do something about it. Then there's the contempt our boys have for their allies' lack of fighting spirit. The Russian Army's not putting up much of a show around Riga and there are no Russian boats in the Gulf of Riga.'

'I suppose at least that saves the fight for us then, sir. That should keep the men happy, sir.'

'You would think so, wouldn't you, but sadly discipline has already started to break down. I'm having to send Tod home. Downie has taken over command of *C26*.'

'Good gracious, sir! Surely Eric's not been giving you trouble, sir?'

'No. No, not at all. He's escorting one of his men home to DQs. I had to give the stoker 90 days for punching a Russian quartermaster.'

'But why, sir? Our lads have always been extremely tolerant of the Russians.'

'Less so now, Algie. It was the fifth disciplinary case I've had to deal with in a month. I gather it started with an incident concerning Lieutenant Commander Vaughan-Jones. He was out with his Estonian girlfriend a few weeks back when they were both insulted by a passing Russian sailor. Jones managed to persuade two of the Russian's shipmates to take him away, but two minutes later he returned and slapped both Jones and his girlfriend.'

''Pon rep', sir. Did our boys lynch the miscreant?'

'No. Fortunately, there was no need. The crowd intervened and the following day, the man was brought before me and Jones on his knees to apologise. His ship's committee then sentenced him to twelve years in Siberia.'

'Dash me wig! Twelve years! It seems a little extreme even for so rude a fellow.'

'Quite. I thought so, too, and pleaded the man's case for clemency. He still ended up with four years in Siberia, though. However, I don't think it was enough for Jack. Anyway, what do you think of the view?'

'Good gracious. It's magnificent. I rather fancy I might enjoy a swim here.'

'Algie, you're mad. Have you any idea of the temperature of the water? And it's not even winter here. Just the thought sends shivers down my spine. I'll stand you a hot chocolate at the hotel if you like and then I need to head back.'

'Better not, sir. I'm bound to be a bit niffy after my patrol and I ought to take a hot bath and change before I do much else. I presume the Russians can still lay on hot water for a chap off patrol?' Steele sniffed his armpits.

'Er, barely. I've had your kit moved to lodgings ashore, along with all the other officers. Apart from the difficult atmosphere with our Russian friends, both depot ships are filthy and riddled with bugs. So much so that some of the men prefer to sleep on board their boats.'

'By Jove, what a state we live in today. Are my digs within walking distance?' Richard nodded. 'You'd better lead the way then, sir. But you were saying that there are no Russian boats on operations at present, sir. How so? Before I went away, the Russian submarines were about the only part of the navy still working.'

'True… and it remains the case. The trouble is that the Russians are finding excuses to abort their patrols due to mechanical problems. Our men suspect their allies are more concerned with a safe and quick return to harbour than conducting operations against the enemy. It may be true, but it's not helped by the fact some of the boats' *committees* have dismissed their engineers and not been able to replace them with good revolutionary technicians. Do you know, in one boat I heard that the only person with any idea how to start the diesels was the cook?'

'Lord, sir. I had no idea it was that bad. Maybe I'm better off at sea, after all, despite the Hun's bally mines and aircraft. How soon do you want me back on patrol?'

'The end of the week, I'm afraid. I'll send an *E*-boat and *C32* with you, but I have nothing else fit for sea. *E1*'s stuck to the wall again and Helsingfors is too busy with big ship work to take the boats for repair work. It's one of the reasons I'm resisting the suggestion we move our base there. I'm none too keen either at the prospect of our men mixing with 50,000 revolutionary sailors. At least here I have the town with me. In Helsingfors I would carry no weight.'

'I fancy I'm with you there, sir. This looks a jolly decent place to hole up for a while.'

CHAPTER 32

Richard and Lizzy took their breakfast in their room. To Richard, it seemed a real indulgence in such revolutionary times, but after eighteen months apart, Lizzy would not hear of joining the other guests in the Astoria's dining room on their first morning as a couple again. She and Emmeline had returned from Moscow the night before and this time, thanks to Lockhart, she had been able to give Richard ample warning of their visit.

As Richard knotted his tie and adjusted his collar stud before joining her at the table, Elizabeth noted for the first time that his temples were greying. It gave him an air of gravitas, but it seemed premature for a man of his age, nonetheless. He, also, seemed thinner and lines were forming around his eyes.

'I do feel sorry for Mrs Pankhurst, Lizzy. I'm not sure it's right for her to be breakfasting alone in a foreign country.'

'Don't start on that again, Dick. We had dinner together last night and we'll be spending all day with her later. Where was it you said we were going, darling?'

'The Hermitage Museum, as you very well know, since it was you that asked me to fix it. You're just changing the subject.'

'Well, really. I thought you'd be pleased to spend some time alone with me. In any case, I haven't finished showing you the photographs of Margaret. I'll be gone again in two days.'

'Of course, I'm pleased to be alone with you, Lizzy. Although we did spend last night together, I recall.' Richard giggled and took Elizabeth's hand fondly.

'And why not?' Elizabeth retorted, blushing. 'We are married, after all, and you weren't complaining. I'm surprised you were so interested after all your talk to Emmeline last night of the Russian princesses and baronesses with whom you've been socialising. A mere cousin must seem rather dull company by comparison.'

'Don't tease me, Lizzy.' Richard had a fleeting pang of guilt at the memory of the night of the Tsar's ball and Anna's behaviour during their dash across Petrograd. 'You know there's nobody but you in my heart, don't you?'

'Stop fretting and eat your eggs. They'll be cold by now.' She kissed him tenderly on the cheek.

Richard sliced off the top of one of his boiled eggs. 'I forgot to tell you last night. Mrs Pankhurst won't be joining us for dinner tonight, after all. Sir George and Lady Georgiana have invited her to the embassy for dinner. We were invited, too, but I declined and Lady Georgiana was most understanding about it.'

'Why, Dick, that's marvellous. Why ever didn't you tell me?'

'I seem to recall, I had other business in hand.' He laughed salaciously. 'Now tell me something of your visit to Moscow. Mrs Pankhurst seemed to express some disappointment with it.

'Darling, I wish you would call her Emmeline and not Mrs Pankhurst. She is one of my dearest friends.'

'Very well, *Emmeline* suggested last night that the visit had not been a great success. I gather you ended up being described as "bourgeois women" by anti-government forces and feared for your safety.'

'I don't know. I was merely the interpreter for when Emmeline's French ran out. She certainly addressed several meetings and we were made most welcome by Kerensky. I found him quite charming on the surface, but Emmeline didn't take a liking to him. She didn't find him inspiring. I fear she regarded the poor fellow as not being sufficiently revolutionary. Certainly, he's completely obsessed with the *counter* revolution. Moreover, he seems more interested in killing fellow Russians than Germans... And he forbade us from accepting the Tsar's invitation to call on him. A pity as I had rather hoped to meet the Tsar.'

'I fear your Emmeline's opinion of Kerensky may not be far off the mark, dear, but heaven forfend! To have refused you permission to visit the Tsar. How could he be forgiven, darling?'

'Don't mock me, Dick. However, as it happens, we did mix with Russian royalty. Were I to stay longer in Russia, Dick, I might be swept off my feet by a handsome Russian count or prince. After all, dear, what's good for the gander's good for the goose. We met a charming man called Prince Youssoupoff. He claimed that it was he who killed that scoundrel Rasputin.'

'Un-Christian as it might sound, Lizzy, I think he did the Russian people a favour. His influence over the Tsarina was an unhealthy blight on the Tsar's reign.'

'I had read such reports in the newspapers, but I fear for her and the rest of the Tsar's family now, Dick.'

'How so, Lizzy? My understanding is that he is only under house arrest until his children recover from measles and then he'll be shipped off to England. I'd say he and his family seem to have come out of this revolution rather well.'

'But you haven't heard, dear? That's all changed.'

'Not according to Sir George Buchanan, it hasn't, Lizzy. He told me himself not too long ago that we will likely send a cruiser to collect him and his family. Thereafter, the King will offer him safe lodgings.'

'How strange. When we met Kerensky, he said that the King had withdrawn the offer of asylum whilst the war progresses. He thinks it an excuse.'

'An excuse? But why on earth would the King or the government give back word?'

'I don't know Dick. Emmeline thinks that it could be a response to the rise of socialism in Britain… or the increasing labour unrest.'

'They can't lay that at the feet of the Tsar, though. Surely?'

'I'm just telling you what Emmeline thinks, that's all, Dick. Already the Press are dubbing the Emperor as "Bloody Nick" after his handling of the demonstrations of 1905. Perhaps, the government thinks the Tsar's presence on British soil might damage the reputation of our own monarchy. You know that since I came out here, the King has changed the name of the family to Windsor on account of the anti-German feeling?'

'I had heard, but I don't know about the rest, Lizzy. I never concern myself in politics – that's always been your line. But even if I could believe it of the government, I would find it hard to credit that our King would renege on an invitation. Anyway, let's change the subject. Tell me more of your visit to Moscow.'

'As Emmeline said last night, it was a bit of a disappointment really and quite dreary at times. It started off all right. Emmeline met several journalists and addressed a multitude of gatherings - mainly women's societies. She rightly represented herself as a fellow revolutionary, but how she still backed the war effort, nonetheless. She seemed to be quite well received, but the common question was what more patriotic women could do for their country.

That led to a meeting with a quite frightful woman.' Elizabeth shuddered at the memory.

'And who was that?'

'They called her Yashka, but I think her real name was Maria. She scared the life out of me, I don't mind admitting, Dick.'

'That doesn't sound like you, Lizzy? What did she do to scare my normally courageous heroine?' Richard tickled the underside of Elizabeth's chin affectionately.

'If you must know, Dick,' Elizabeth blushed and laid down her cutlery carefully, 'I think she had designs on me.'

Richard burst out laughing. 'One could hardly blame her, Lizzy. I find you irresistible.' He reached out to take her hand, but she withdrew it quickly.

'Don't joke about it, Dick. She was a brute of a woman. She founded and commanded a group of women volunteers to fight on the front.'

'Women fighting on the front! My word, Lizzy!'

'Indeed, Dick. They called themselves the Women's Battalion of Death. The idea was that the presence of women on the front would shame the men into fighting more bravely. She's a fearsome woman, Dick, and I've since heard she showed great courage on the battlefield.'

'She sounds like just the sort of person to put the wind up the Germans. Perhaps Emmeline could suggest the idea to Lloyd-George. A battalion of harpies, harridans and termagants might cut a swathe through the German lines.' Richard chuckled at the thought and then became more serious again. 'I can't imagine such a battalion being popular with the men, though. The women would probably not give up ground so easily and the average Russian soldier would resent that.'

Richard rose from the breakfast table. 'The thought of your Yashka has quite stifled my appetite, Lizzy, and in any case… we need to be making a move if we are to see even a quarter of the Hermitage. I'll go call on Mrs… Emmeline. How long before you think you could be ready?'

*****

Three days later, crammed in the corner of a compartment on the train from Petrograd to Reval, Richard was lost in thought as he gazed at the framed photograph of Margaret. In the photograph, her short, straight, shoulder-length hair looked fair, but Richard knew it to be red, a colour inherited from her mother. The photograph was slightly blurred as the Crosby photographer had not been able to persuade the tot to remain still long enough for the exposure of the camera, despite numerous bribes, but it was good enough for Richard. The expression on Margaret's broad face betrayed a feeling of impatience with the sitting, but even so, she looked angelic in her sailor costume.

Saying farewell to Lizzy had been even harder than when he had sailed from Harwich. Her presence in Petrograd had been the only light in his life for over a year and, as that light had departed, the shadows of his troubled command had enveloped him once again. Moreover, as they had made their emotional and passionate farewell, a sinister thought had befallen him. It was almost a premonition that they would never see each other again. He would not settle until he had word that she had returned to London safely. His only comfort was that she was travelling in company with Mrs Pankhurst.

CHAPTER 33
October 1917

With one exception, Richard's meeting with Hayward, his paymaster, had not gone well. Hayward had just informed him that roubles were no longer being accepted in Hango as the local residents eyed with concern the increasingly volatile political situation in Petrograd and the rest of Russia. It was widely assumed that Kerensky's government was doomed and relations between the Finnish Parliament and the Russian Duma were becoming increasingly strained. Members of the British expatriate community had informed Richard that following the occupation of the Finnish Parliament by Russian troops in the summer and the forced elections, many Finns were now talking openly about a declaration of independence from the Russians. Whatever the politics, however, it left the Royal Navy with a cash problem. Not only did Richard see no point in paying his men roubles if they would not be accepted ashore, but his paymaster needed Finnish marks to buy supplies. Reluctantly and very much against his values, he had just authorised Hayward to sell Admiralty stores on the black market to raise local currency. The only bright spot was that after six weeks without pay, the majority of the Russian sailors had returned to Reval.

However, Richard had more serious concerns, including the future of Reval. Outside his cabin waited Lieutenant Christopher Satow, the recent commanding officer of HMS *C32*. Normally, Richard would have given one of his COs precedence over the assistant paymaster, but on this occasion, he had made Satow wait. Satow, two other *C*-class COs and an *E*-boat CO had just returned from an ill-fated patrol trying to prevent the Germans' amphibious assault on the Gulf of Riga and the west of Estonia. Now Satow faced a possible court martial as well as Richard's fury.

'Come in, Satow. Take a seat.'

The ashen-faced Satow sat gingerly on the sofa bunk of Richard's cabin. On his lap he held the log of *C32* and the first draft of his patrol report.

'Very well, Satow. Give me a brief summary of the circumstances leading to the loss of your submarine. I don't want the whole nine yards. I can read the details for myself from your patrol report.' Richard worked hard to control his anger. Thanks to the actions of this inexperienced commanding officer, he had lost twenty-five percent of his inshore submarines. Satow cleared his throat nervously before replying.

'I sailed from Rogekul on the twelfth and entered the Irben Straits as you instructed, sir. That afternoon, I encountered a German U-boat on the surface. She engaged me with her deck gun, but I dived without sustaining any damage. I tried to attack her, sir, but we lost each other.'

'And how did the U-boat steal a march on you?'

Satow winced at the question. 'I'm not sure she did, sir. She just surfaced on my starboard quarter and opened fire. As I didn't have a gun to return fire, I dived in the hope of putting a torpedo into her, sir.'

'I'll be interested to discuss the vigilance of your bridge lookouts at some stage, but we'll leave it for now. Carry on.'

'Thank you, sir.' Satow fidgeted with his log book. 'The following evening, I again came into contact with the enemy, but couldn't attack as the ships were the other side of a minefield. Instead, I presumed them - from their course and formation - to be heading towards Moon Sound. Remaining on the surface, I headed north across the Gulf of Riga in the hope of regaining contact, sir. This I did, on the fifteenth, sir. I spotted a four-funnelled cruiser, probably the *Strassburg*, and made to attack her. Unfortunately, just as I was approaching my firing position, I was attacked by a German seaplane. I was dived, sir, but she still dropped several bombs quite close to me and I was forced to break off the attack and to go deep.'

'The Hun would no doubt had had a good view of your silhouette through the clear water, Satow.'

'Yes, sir. That's what I figured. By the time I was able to return to PD, the cruiser had gone too far into the Sound for me to pursue, sir. I remained on patrol in the Gulf of Riga and tried to attack a transport, but my mouldie either misfunctioned or I missed, sir. It was then quite uneventful for a few days, sir, but my problems started on the twentieth. I came across another large transport with an escort of three trawlers. It was flat calm, sir, so I approached to within 600 yards of the transport to have a better chance of sinking her before my torpedo tracks were spotted. However, that put me extremely close to the trawler escorts. Indeed, sir, I was so close to one, I could see the faces of the crew on deck and my first torpedo passed underneath her. Unfortunately, as I fired my second torpedo, I was spotted by the trawler and had to go to sixty feet to avoid being rammed. Nonetheless, sir, I must have hit the transport as I heard two explosions on the bearing.'

'That's something I suppose. I'll ask the Ruskie intelligence bods to try to provide a damage assessment.' Richard made a note in his journal.

'The Germans then counter-attacked with depth charges, sir, and I don't mind admitting we had a sorry time of it. Apart from the usual lighting failure and leaks, my compass was put completely out of action.'

'Difficult for you.' Richard had not heard that news before and his anger towards Satow began to abate a little.

'I waited deep until darkness fell and surfaced to repair the compass, but we were unsuccessful, sir. I knew I hadn't a hope of navigating through the minefields to exit the Gulf through the Irben Straits without a compass. That only left me the Moon Sound, but I had already seen the size of the German forces there, so I assumed it would be blocked to me. Similarly, I assumed all the ports would by now be in the hands of the Hun… wrongly as it turned out, sir.'

'That's an understatement, Satow. You could quite easily have gone to Pernau,' Richard replied acidly.

Satow bit his lip in anguish. 'Yes, sir. I know that now, but I made the decision to scuttle the boat and save my ship's company from internment. I beached the boat in Vaist Bay and made my way inland with my men, aiming to reach Reval overland. You can imagine my surprise when I came across Algie and *C27* in Pernau, and that the Russians still held the coast. I assure you, sir, I was quite mortified.'

'And so you should have been, Satow. Steele's boat was knocked about far more than I suspect you were, but if you'd waited for him to effect his repairs, he could have led you out of the Gulf.' Richard could feel his anger rising again. From his written report, Steele had in fact been most enterprising and Richard fully intended recommending him for a bar to his DSC. Relentlessly pursuing the enemy in the shallow waters of Moon Sound, he had run aground, been hunted mercilessly for several hours and then, with damaged hydroplanes and propellers, and his boat barely afloat, he had negotiated the minefields to reach Pernau. There he still remained carrying out the repairs necessary to return to Hango.

'I'm sorry, sir. I take full responsibility for my mistake. As soon as I realised my error, I did return to my boat with a tug and attempted to recover her from the shore, but the tug wasn't powerful enough. I then had no choice but to scuttle her with explosive charges.'

'Under the misapprehension that the Germans had already occupied that coastline, you should have scuttled the boat immediately, Satow.'

'Yes, sir. I'm sorry, but it just didn't occur to me at the time. I was too focused on avoiding capture of my ship's company.'

Richard left Satow in the obvious discomfort of silence for several minutes whilst he considered his options. He was still extremely annoyed with Satow. The loss of *C32* would make his task in command of the flotilla more difficult. But he had to accept the COs of the *C*-boats were inexperienced and any fault in them lay at his door for giving insufficient guidance. Moreover, what advantage lay in a court martial for losing his ship. It was obvious that Satow was truly remorseful and the comment about Steele had visibly stung. What would be the point in breaking a man who in time might have the makings of a fine commanding officer.

'Listen, Satow,' Richard's words relieved Satow's clear misery. 'It's plain that you quite unnecessarily destroyed your submarine, an asset I dearly valued in these difficult times. I confess, I'm disappointed in you.'

'I'm really sorry, sir,' Satow mumbled in anguish.

'However, the whole show was a shambles and your poor judgement just a part of it. The two most precious things to a submarine commanding officer are his boat and his men. The only two reasons I'm not going to recommend you be court martialled for losing your ship are that I could do without the distraction and you acted for the best for your men. Someday, I hope you will be given another chance to command. Should that come to pass, reflect on and learn from this experience… And remember one thing.'

Satow had straightened from his hunched position at the news he was not to face disciplinary action. 'Yes, sir, Thank you, sir. What is that, sir?'

'Remember, Satow, that even the best of men will make mistakes, but when they do, exercise tolerance and forgiveness. Now let me treat you to a pink gin. The paymaster just brought me a signal to tell me I've been promoted to acting Captain with immediate effect, so let's celebrate.'

CHAPTER 34
November 1917

The news of the Bolshevik coup in Petrograd and the fall of Kerensky's government had a monumental impact on the future of the Royal Navy's Baltic submarine flotilla and Richard lost no time in travelling to the capital. It was his first visit to Petrograd since the start of the March revolution and he found it even more depressing. What he had once regarded as a beautiful, white city, now looked grey. Even the snow was no longer white, mixed as it was with the brown of horse manure and the filth of uncollected rubbish. Although dark, few lights shone on the streets or the houses. The only clear colours were the red and orange emanating from the vivid red banners and flags flown from several buildings or carried by the grey-clad former soldiers and factory workers standing around small braziers for warmth. Moored by the Nicholaevsky Bridge flanked by a couple of destroyers, lay the cruiser *Aurora*, the ship said to have started the coup by firing a blank round. However, unlike in March, the streets were devoid of violence and shooting. The people seemed to be waiting on a knife edge, wondering if Kerensky would launch his much-vaunted counter-attack on the city.

Another change since his visit in March was that Richard was not staying at the Astoria, but as a guest of the British Ambassador, Sir George Buchanan, and his wife, Lady Georgiana. As Richard sawed at his tough, roasted mutton, he felt some guilt that he was eating better than his men, now based in Helsingfors. He had lost the argument against the move from Hango with Admiral Vederevsky. In the summer, following the suicide of Commodore Vladislaveff, yet another Russian Commodore Submarines, Richard had found himself in command of all Russian submarines as well as his own and the new C-in-C had wanted Richard close by. Seated to his left at the dinner table was Lockhart, the acting Consul General in Moscow and opposite, Admiral Stanley, the new British Naval Liaison Officer, and the Buchanan's daughter, Meriel.

Richard refused the meagre dessert on his customary grounds that he never ate pudding. After a career in submarines, his teeth were in a poor state and sensitive to sweetness. As the plates were cleared for the port, Lady Georgiana seemed compelled to offer some form of explanation for the mutton.

'I'm sorry, Richard, that we cannot offer you our usual standard of fare, but food is increasingly hard to come by in Petrograd these days. It's a shame you don't drink as Sir George still has a fine cellar.'

'Think nothing of it, Lady Georgiana,' Richard replied graciously. 'To a submariner, this is a wonderful feast. I'm just sorry that you've had to postpone your return to England on account of the coup.'

'For a few weeks only, I hope. Sir George needs a rest. You must look after your health, dear,' she added addressing the ambassador. 'Now, Meriel, I think we must look in on our naval cadets and leave the gentlemen to their port and discussion of politics. Come now. Don't drink too much, George. It'll keep you awake again.'

After the ladies had retired and as the port was being passed, Richard opened the conversation.

'Sir, what was the reference of Lady Georgiana to naval cadets?'

'Ah, you mean our house guests. Eating us out of house and home. They were kindly sent to provide us with a guard. We've fixed them up with camp beds and they're living in the basement. Quite a decent lot actually.

'I suppose you've all heard that the Bolsheviks have made Trotsky their Foreign Commissar and he's advocating peace with Germany. Would have been better if the navy had left him in Halifax.' Sir George sipped his port wistfully.

'And what are my orders if peace is to be negotiated, sir?' Richard asked of Admiral Stanley.

'Well, obviously you can't stay here and you'll never get your *C*-boats out back overland. I can't see you've much choice but to scuttle them and take your *E*-boats home through the Kattegat.'

'Hardly a promising prospect, sir. It was hard enough getting in with the element of surprise. The Germans will find it like shooting fish in a barrel if we try to leave the same way.'

'True, Miller. I hadn't thought of that. I suppose you could head for Sweden and accept internment for the rest of the war. At least you and your men would survive. The alternative is to scuttle all your boats. Rest assured I've raised the subject with the Admiralty. By the way, have you heard? Your father's the new

Director of Plans. It'll be for him to suggest a way forward if the worst comes to the worst.'

'It's not over yet, gentlemen,' Lockhart intervened. 'I'm in touch with several Tsarist officers who have no intention of seeing this Lenin character and his Bolsheviks sell out their country to the Germans. I'll discuss it with you in detail later, Sir George, but I think the Foreign Office should make some contact with the leading elements of the anti-Bolshevik forces.'

'Perhaps, Lockhart, but the present policy is to wait and see if Ulyanov and his cronies succeed in holding on to power and, if he does, to encourage Bolshevik Russia to remain in the war.'

'But, Sir George, isn't it obvious that the Bolsheviks have no interest in maintaining the war?' Lockhart protested. 'Why else would the Germans have let Lenin and his comrades pass through Germany to return to Russia? My sources tell me that the Bolsheviks are more interested in putting down internal rebellion and consolidating their grip on power than fighting an external foe. Some form of Allied intervention might be enough to topple these Reds and stop them selling out… At least until the Americans arrive on the Western Front anyway.'

'Really, Lockhart!' Sir George snapped. The dinner table is not the place to debate foreign policy. I've told you before…'

'Do we know how the Tsar and his family are keeping, sir?' Richard interrupted to defuse what had the makings of a tense discussion. 'I understand he and his family are under arrest in Tobolsk. Is that right, sir?'

'You'll have to address that question to Lockhart, Miller. He seems to be the one with the sources,' Sir George said sarcastically. Lockhart ignored the jibe.

'I understand the Romanovs are living a life of considerable comfort in the former governor's mansion, but the Tsar is still anxious to find a safe place of exile,' Sir George added.

'But surely, the King has already offered him refuge in England?' Richard asked innocently.

'Never trust a politician to keep his word, Miller,' Stanley opined. Richard could see Lockhart trying desperately to catch the admiral's eye, but Stanley was staring at the table. 'The King was persuaded to withdraw the offer to his cousin by our so-called *Liberal* government.'

'That will do!' Sir George slammed his port glass onto the table with such force, the contents spilled over to stain the damask table cloth. 'The government acted on *my* advice. The left wouldn't hear of the Tsar's family being offered our protection. There would have been uproar. The last thing the government needed in a time of war was another Easter rising.' The emphatic outburst was met with embarrassed silence.

'And one more thing, gentlemen. You breathe not a word of it. The King is in enough anguish about the decision without it reaching the ears of the news scribblers. Now if you will excuse me, I think I will follow my wife's advice and retire early.' Sir George rose from the table and made his way to the dining room doors. 'I really am feeling most awfully tired after the events of the past few days. May I suggest, you gentlemen, adjourn to the library where Wilkins will see to your needs. I still have a good selection of fine cigars and malt whisky. Forgive me.'

Sir George showed the two naval officers and the consul to the library where a good fire blazed. Richard seated himself on the fender whilst the other guests helped themselves to whisky.

'I'm sorry, Lockhart,' Stanley said. 'I had no idea of the insensitivity of my remark concerning the Tsar's fate.'

'No, sir,' Richard interjected. 'The fault was mine for raising the topic.'

'Calm yourselves, gentlemen,' Lockhart responded. 'I'm afraid Sir George's advice may well have been correct to leave the Kerensky government to seek a neutral country willing to offer refuge to the Tsar and his family. However, I fear it is too late now.'

'How so?' Stanley asked.

'Regrettably, I doubt the Bolsheviks will allow him to go into exile. Indeed, I have heard talk of putting him on trial… and given our own history, we can guess how that might turn out.'

'You mean the Tsar might suffer the fate of Charles the First?' Richard exclaimed. Lockhart nodded. 'But surely his family would be spared?' Richard was appalled at the prospect of the execution of the Romanov family.

'No, I don't think it would come to that, Miller. Even the Bolsheviks have scruples. Their leaders are educated men, after all.'

'I gather you and the ambassador are at variance over Britain's policy towards the Bolsheviks, Lockhart.' Stanley topped up Lockhart's glass before settling on the end of a sofa.

'I regret Sir George and his staff have been too optimistic about the current situation. They have been too close to Kerensky and the former Imperial Court. I knew Kerensky very well, of course, but in the far reaches of Moscow I have tended to mix with what Sir George would deem, the less desirable elements of Russian society. Indeed, unbeknown to Sir George, I have been summoned to London to brief the Prime Minister in person on my thoughts on the Bolshevik government.'

'Do you have much hope of keeping Russia in the war, Lockhart,' Richard asked. 'After all, my experience is that the Russian officers seem more focused on the revolution than the conduct of the war.'

'To be absolutely honest, I cannot say. Lenin has promised elections later this month and I'm not sure he'll win. Even so, I can't see him giving up the levers of power. This latest revolution is too well organised. We'll have to see what Lloyd George and his government decide. But what I can say is that the longer the Royal Navy stays active in the Baltic, the better the chances of the Russians hostile to the Bolsheviks prevailing.'

'There's little hope of that at present, Lockhart. Quite apart from my doubts over the Russians' will to provide me the facilities to repair my flotilla, you forget that the Gulf of Finland is icing up already.'

'A fair point, Miller. But I have it on good authority you are still highly respected by the Russians. Anything you could do to bolster their backbone would only be to the good. Moreover, keep your ear to the ground about the Bolshevik intentions. If my meeting with L-G goes the way I hope, I'll have need of a good pair of ears.'

'You mean… spy on the Russians? Surely not?' Richard protested.

'Steady on, Miller,' Stanley interjected. 'You're our best-placed man to keep up with Russian naval developments. In any case, depending on the fate of your flotilla, you might be the ideal man to take over as our naval attaché here. Information gathering would be part of your duties then.'

'I, the NA? Surely not, sir? I mean I'd rather not, sir. I've not been home for nearly two years and intelligence is hardly my game.'

'I thought it ran in the family, Miller,' Lockhart responded.

'In the family? I don't follow,' Richard remarked in surprise.

'Come now, man. Your father was a very successful head of naval intelligence up to the outbreak of war and your brother's one of Cumming's lot.'

That his father had been the Director of Naval Intelligence didn't surprise Richard. He had had his suspicions since a lapse of security when conducting an intelligence operation before the war, but he didn't understand the latter part of Lockhart's statement.

'I'm sorry, who is Cumming and to which brother do you refer?' As he said it, however, he knew it was something to do with Peter. It had been Peter his submarine had landed on the island of Heligoland several years earlier and now Richard recalled an earlier conversation with Lockhart - a lifetime ago it seemed - about Peter's role in a Dutch consulate.

'Captain Cumming is the head of the Secret Service. After we first met and you said you had a brother in passport control in the Netherlands, I made a few enquiries. All the passport control officers are working for Cumming. Eady, too, as it happens. So, spying, intelligence or just plain information gathering is hardly out of your league, old man.'

CHAPTER 35
December 1917

Outside his cabin on the depot ship, Richard could hear Steele's commands as he led several of the men in Swedish Drill. Richard recalled fondly how Steele had introduced this form of exercise to the men of *E9* during the summer of 1915. Then it had been warm and Steele had usually completed the sessions with Hands to Bathe. Nobody in their right mind would be bathing in the Gulf of Finland today. The air temperature was barely above freezing and it was snowing lightly. It wasn't the weather to be stripping down to a singlet, but what had started as compulsory exercise for the dozen men of *C27*, had now attracted about thirty volunteers from the rest of the flotilla. Although Richard took no more exercise than brisk walks for himself, he approved of the ritual. It always drew a crowd of onlookers from the Russians and demonstrated the difference in discipline between the navies of both nations.

He had been pleased to see Steele bring his boat into Helsingfors a couple of days earlier. Not only was it a relief to have Steele's company, but more importantly, there had been a danger of the boat being destroyed along with *C32* to avoid it falling into the hands of the Germans. Despite Stocker sending a team of engineering ratings down to Pernau to assist with the repairs, it had taken three attempts by Steele to take his boat to sea. On the second, petrol in the engine room had caught fire and the ship's company had been forced to abandon ship just a few miles from the enemy, in bitter weather and standing only in the clothes they had been wearing below deck. Somehow, and with the aid of a hand-made wooden pulley to drive the petrol pump, the leaking *C27* had managed to exit the Gulf of Riga and make her way to Helsingfors. It had been a magnificent display of courage and determination that had even drawn praise from the demoralised Russian fleet members, admittedly only after the Centrobalt committee had finally given its permission for the passage to take place. To his intense annoyance, Richard had met with resistance on the grounds that the transit might upset the peace talks in which the Russians and the Germans were now engaged. Richard had had to issue a guarantee that Steele would take no offensive action during the crossing. It had been as well that Steele hadn't come across the Germans as Richard harboured doubts that young Algie wouldn't have undertaken some form of suicidal action to damage the enemy.

The thought reminded Richard of his impending call on the C-in-C, but he still had time to complete reading his latest correspondence. Despite the disorder throughout the country, a batch of mail had reached the flotilla, including a letter addressed in a hand writing so familiar to Richard. He placed Lizzy's letter in his pocket to read at leisure. His attention for now was on the official letter from his father. Stanley had been right, he thought. Papa was, indeed, the new Director of Plans, heading a new division established not just to plan operations, but to look at the future strategy and shape of the Royal Navy. In his letter, he had responded to Stanley's request for instructions for the flotilla in the event of the Bolshevik government entering peace talks with the Germans. Papa's orders were quite clear. Sink the submarines in deep water and bring the men home.

The baldness of the orders caused a ball to form in Richard's stomach. Almost two years to the day since he had left Lizzy in *E19* for the Baltic, the game could well be up. He thought of all the hardships he and his men had faced. The loss of *E13* and then Halahan and *E18*. Tears welled in his eyes at the thought. Of the youthful and inquisitive Sacha Pavlyuchenko. Had it been worth the sacrifices? Suddenly, he felt tired. To face the humiliation of defeat. A defeat not through the want of courage and fighting determination of his own men, but by a self-inflicted wound of their allies. The tiredness gripped his whole body such that he couldn't move a muscle. Had he been able to move he would have wept, but his brain was numbed and telling him to let go. Let yourself sink into oblivion. Sleep.

His fit of depression was interrupted by a knock at the door and Hayward's face appeared through the curtain.

'Sorry to disturb you, sir, but three delegates from the Centrobalt are here demanding to see you. I've put them in the wardroom.'

Richard heard Hayward, but his brain wouldn't instruct his body to move. It was as if his brain was split into two. Part of it was telling him to shake himself out of it, but the dominant force was saying to let go. To fall into that black void of oblivion seemed so comforting. It was like a drowning man giving up the struggle.

Somehow, after a short delay, his will managed to persuade his brain to instruct his head to move and his speech to return.

'Very good. I'll come right up.' From there it was an easy battle to persuade his brain to press his body into action and he began to rise from his desk.

'I should warn you, sir. The lead delegate is our friend Comrade Malenkov.'

'Oh dear,' Richard replied. Malenkov was not just one of the most hard-line members of the Centrobalt, but seemed to take inordinate pleasure in making life for Richard and his men as difficult as possible.

Malenkov now wore gold-rimmed spectacles on the end of his long nose and was filling out. Clearly, the new equality of socialism was more equal to some than others, Richard reflected. Malenkov didn't rise to greet him, although his two colleagues had started to.

'At last, comrade. I and my men have been waiting fifteen minutes and…'

'That's not true, sir,' Hayward protested, but Richard held up his hand to quieten him. Hayward, also, spoke Russian and that had made him a useful secretary.

'… as members of the Centrobalt Committee we are busy men. It is very disrespectful of you, comrade.'

'We have been through this before, Seaman Malenkov. Your own committee has issued a proclamation that officers are to be addressed by their rank. Kindly address me as "Captain".'

Richard had the satisfaction of seeing Malenkov's discomfort at the rebuke.

'Very well, *Captain*. We have not the time to debate such matters of *bourgeoise* protocol.' Malenkov then produced two documents from an expensive-looking leather briefcase.

'I have two documents here that require your signature. One is a translation of the other into English to avoid any misunderstanding.'

'I am very comfortable with Russian, Malenkov.' Richard passed the English copy to Hayward and read the Russian version. It was a declaration that he would in future accept orders from the Centrobalt above those of the Russian Baltic C-in-C. It was an old chestnut and those Russian officers who had refused to sign it had been marched off their ships and shot in the back as they descended the gangway. Richard returned his version to Malenkov.

'I have discussed this before with the Committee,' Richard responded tiredly. 'I and my men have been placed by my Admiralty under the orders of the Commander-in-Chief. I, my officers and men, including those of your countrymen under my direct command, can be answerable only to the Admiralty.' Richard could see his words had riled Malenkov and he wondered if he had pushed his luck too far.

'Come, comrades,' he adopted a more conciliatory tone. 'Why argue over mere words. The important thing is that I will always be willing to stand alongside you to fight our common enemy.'

Malenkov's two colleagues seemed to accept this, but Malenkov merely glared at Richard menacingly over his spectacles. Richard thought quickly. He knew that Malenkov and a few others would cheerfully put a bullet in his back.

'Hayward, fix us a tray of vodka and some glasses. Gentlemen, let's drink to the spring offensive.'

Richard thought he would choke on his three glasses of the fiery liquid, but it seemed to smooth the mood of the Russian delegates. Taking the partially-drunk bottle of vodka with them, they left the depot ship with their proclamations unsigned.

*****

As Richard walked through the snow to call on the C-in-C, he reflected that life in Helsingfors had not proved as bad as he had previously feared. His flotilla's disciplinary problems were behind him. Their Russian hosts seemed to have respected the Royal Navy for being the only effective offensive force in the Baltic over the previous two months and the British sailors preferred life in Helsingfors to that in Reval or Hango. As the Finnish capital, it still retained a high degree of civic order with clean streets, restaurants, theatres and cinemas.

Richard had lost count of the number of C-in-Cs he had met over the past year. Maximoff had been sacked in the summer and replaced by his Chief of Staff, Vederevsky, who had then been promoted to become the Minister of Marine. The new C-in-C was

Admiral Rasvosoff, an officer Richard had only met twice previously. At this latest meeting, Richard explained the orders he had received from the Admiralty.

'That is a great pity, Captain. In my short time in command, I have greatly admired the valiant war service of your English flotilla. You should be proud of the brilliant accomplishments of your officers and men. Tell me, what are your thoughts on your latest orders? Are they fixed?'

'No, sir. I am directed to use my discretion, but I have the authority to sink my submarines to prevent them falling into the hands of the Germans.'

'Interesting and a wise precaution, my friend. However, I would urge you not to take any precipitate action.'

'Certainly, sir. But can you offer any hope?'

'Perhaps not hope, but the alternative is unthinkable. Were you to follow your orders, it would have a catastrophic effect on the already fragile fighting spirit of the Baltic Fleet. And the word is that the peace talks at Brest Litovsk are not going well. The Germans demand too high a price, even for the Bolsheviks. I wonder whether we might amend your orders a little?'

'Willingly, sir. I'm none too happy about them either. But what can I do?'

'Perhaps we could effect a compromise, although I grant it would be difficult. The Finns have just declared independence from Russia and are demanding the withdrawal of all our forces from their territory. However, no such independence has yet been agreed. Mmm, it is difficult, but I have an idea.'

'You have a willing listener, sir.'

'The Admiralty reasons correctly that for the remainder of the winter you don't have a fighting force. Suppose we were to lay up your submarines for the winter and send most of your men home to England? Some could remain behind for care and maintenance and, should the peace talks fail or the anti-Bolshevik forces prevail, your men could return in the spring and take up the war again. If I was to propose such a plan to Admiral Stanley, do you think your Admiralty would agree it?'

Richard considered the idea for a moment and regarded Admiral Rasvosoff with some respect. It was a shrewd plan that kept his flotilla in the game and yet would meet the Admiralty's objectives, too.

'I think there's every chance, sir. As I have said, I have been given discretion to act as I see fit. I will write to my superiors immediately on my return to the *Dvina*, sorry, I meant the *Pamyat Azova*.'

'Very well, Captain. Let us drink to success.'

Richard was spared the embarrassment of refusing the admiral's drink by the sound of shouting in the outer office, followed by the doors to the inner office bursting open. Four armed sailors wearing the arm bands of the Centrobalt strode in followed by an anguished ADC.

'Comrade admiral,' their leader announced waving a piece of paper. 'I am here to place you under arrest. This piece of paper confirms that you have been dismissed by the Soviet government. With immediate effect, your duties will be conducted by a committee of the Centrobalt. You are to come with us.' The sailor stood to one side to allow the admiral to pass, but Rasvosoff remained at his desk and read the proffered paper. The blood drained from his face.

'Very well, comrade,' he sighed. 'I accept you have the authority of the government and I have always been a servant of my government. However, I trust you will indulge me with just another minute to complete my meeting with our brave English ally. Please wait outside and I will join you in a moment. I can promise that I will not be going anywhere.' Rasvosoff handed over his side arm.

The Centrobalt guard accepted it and withdrew to the outer office. As the doors were shut behind them, the admiral scribbled a note and came round to Richard's side of the desk.

'Captain Miller, I fear I have not much longer to live. Although wary of you, the Centrobalt still trust and respect you. If you can, please try to rescue my wife and daughter and send them to this address with my love.' Richard took the note with anger in his heart. How could the Centrobalt be so stupid as to treat such a brave officer this way.

'Sir, it would be an honour.' Tears welled in Richard's eyes.

'Captain Richard, now it is you who will have to write to Admiral Stanley. Please accept my deepest thanks for the great help you have given to Mother Russia during the present war. God bless you.' The Russian embraced Richard, kissed him on both cheeks and reached for his *ushanka* and sword, but hesitated.

'Captain, I will not have need of this where I am going. Take it in my memory. This winter may be a long one.' Rasvosoff handed Richard his *ushanka* and placed his cap squarely on his head in its place. After then buckling on his sword, he marched out to his outer office and fate.

CHAPTER 36

Two days later, Richard received a note with the good news that Steele and his men had placed Rasvosoff's wife and daughter on a train to Moscow, but his other news was depressing. Mrs Rasvosoff had reported to Steele that her husband had been shot in the back of the head the previous day without trial or even a charge. More disconcerting was the news Richard later received from his source within the Centrobalt.

Is this what Peter has been doing, he wondered. Setting up and running a network of informants? Had Peter gone behind enemy lines to collect his information? It was odd how incredibly homesick he now felt. He supposed it was all part of his general state of depression. Now was not the time to have such thoughts, though. He needed to summon all his COs for a secret meeting.

Thirty minutes later, the six COs mustered in Richard's cabin with an armed sentry outside to keep away snoopers. There was insufficient room for all of them to be seated so Steele, as one of the junior officers present, bent his tall, sinuous frame against the bulkhead.

'Gentlemen, I will not beat about the bush. My relations with the Centrobalt are becoming increasingly fraught and I can't be sure how long their patience with me will prevail. At best, I would say we enjoy a hostile truce. However, I have just heard some extremely disquieting news that I consider must be acted upon forthwith, even to the further detriment of our relations with the Centrobalt.'

Nobody spoke to interrupt Richard's flow. Whilst some appeared anxious to hear his news, Richard noted that Steele appeared completely impassive or even bored, as if the meeting was a minor interruption in the prosecution of his war.

'I understand that the Centrobalt have designs on taking their battleships to sea and heading for Kiel.'

A few of the COs gasped, but Fenner took a different approach. 'Do you think they could find their way, sir?' he asked, causing the other COs to snigger at the suggestion.

'That's hardly the point, Stan. It's their intent that concerns me. Far from taking the offensive against the enemy, their plan is to fraternise with the enemy in the hope of spreading their revolutionary fervour amongst the IGN.'

'Might that be a bad thing, sir,' asked Lieutenant Downie, the new CO of *C26*.

'Completely. It would place those powerful vessels in the hands of the Hun and set a disastrous example to the rest of the Baltic Fleet. No, it will not do and this is my plan. I want you all to prepare a couple of torpedoes for firing. Those of you who need to load torpedoes should take pains to ensure you have an audience for the evolution. When you are ready, I shall board the flagship with an engineer officer and signalman. I will inform the Committee that either I be allowed to put the main engines of the ships out of order permanently or else, at my signal or absence of it by a pre-arranged time, you will all sink each ship, one by one.'

'My God, sir. That's bold, but I wouldn't want to be in your shoes when you tell them,' Vaughan-Jones said. 'Should you not take an armed escort with you, sir?'

'If events were to go as badly as your pessimism suggests, Hubert, I'll be a dead man anyway and there's no point risking further loss of life. Now, return to your commands and report to me when you're ready to move.'

*****

Richard, an engineer lieutenant and a leading signalman were escorted with courtesy to the admiral's cabin of the battleship, *Petropavlovsk*, where they were met by the Flag Captain, Captain Schastny, and several members of the Committee. Richard was relieved to see that Malenkov was not present. Quickly, he requested that the Committee cancel their plan to take the battleships to Kiel, but he held back his ultimatum. As he had expected, his plan was not well received. Schastny said nothing initially, but a former senior boatswain with whom Richard had already had several dealings, responded.

'What is to stop us having you and your men shot immediately for such anti-revolutionary talk?'

'Nothing, of course, but it would hardly be in the spirit of our long history of mutual co-operation.' Richard turned to Schastny.

'Captain, I have to tell you that I have been ordered to send most of my men home for the winter.' Richard regretted the lie. Although he had written to his father, Commodore Hall and Admiral Stanley outlining Rasvosoff's compromise solution, he had still to receive a reply. 'Would it not be an insult to the efforts of my men if the last memory of their Russian friends was of them cavorting with the enemy? Remember, this enemy is still intent on overrunning your country.'

'We don't need an Englishman to remind us of our patriotic duty,' the boatswain interrupted.

'No, comrade. That is true and I have seen for myself the treasure and blood your countrymen have lost in fighting the enemy. But I understand your revolution is about freedom. Indeed, the Russians under my command tell me they aspire to have the same levels of freedom that British sailors enjoy. Don't let my men return home ashamed of their Russian friends.'

Richard waited with bated breath whilst the Committee discussed his words heatedly. It was obvious to Richard that Schastny was at odds with the Committee members. Eventually, Schastny called the meeting to order and addressed Richard.

'Captain, as one captain to another, I have too much respect for you to see us part as anything other than proud comrades in arms. The ships will remain in Helsingfors. You have my word.' Schastny shook Richard's hand before embracing him.

Richard was relieved he had not had to issue his ultimatum, but still had more to achieve from the meeting. 'Captain, I have one more favour to ask of you and the Committee.' Schastny raised his eyebrows at Richard's coming request.

'Soon, 150 or so of my men will be leaving Russia. Will you guarantee them safe passage from Petrograd to Murmansk once the necessary arrangements can be made?'

Schastny didn't even discuss the matter with the Committee members, but answered without hesitation. 'Of course. What else could we do for such gallant men?'

As Richard shook hands with all present, he silently thanked God.

*****

It was ironic that just as Richard received approval for his plan to lay up his submarines and send most of the men home, after months of shortages of food and spares, his stores finally made their way through to the flotilla. Now with no operations planned, ridiculously he had six months' worth of stores. He immediately tasked his Canadian assistant paymaster with the task of selling much of the food and stores on the black market to raise much-needed funds for his ships' companies, but not before taking care of the needs of the many civilians in Helsingfors and Petrograd who had supported the British flotilla. Assistant Paymaster Baker RNR was a great bear of a man from Winnipeg and Richard knew that there would be no serious haggling with him.

Having made these arrangements, he accepted an invitation to dinner in one of the international hotels with a group of local Russian businessmen. Their spokesman was Andrei Kapitsa, from whom Richard had had some support in buying food for his men. He came to the point of the meeting over the main course.

'Captain Richard, we represent a group of White Russians and wish to make you a proposition.'

'Sorry, Andrei, but what do you mean by "White Russians"?'

'We take the name "White" after the French royalists during their revolution and to distinguish ourselves from the Bolshevik Reds.'

'Thank you for the clarification. It is not a term I had previously heard. How may I help you?'

'You will have heard, Richard, that the Finns have declared independence and demanded all Russian forces leave Finland. As yet, we have not heard the Bolshevik response, but my colleagues and I believe we have in any case sufficient forces at our disposal to deal with the Red Guards in the city. Our problem, however, is the 50,000 sailors of the Baltic Fleet who might come to the aid of their comrades.'

'It sounds an audacious plan. What is my involvement?'

'Time after time we have seen the Royal Navy act as the *bogey policeman* of the Fleet. We seek your help in using your men to maintain naval order in the harbour and preventing the rebel sailors from leaving their ships. For this, we are willing to offer you the equivalent of £50,000 sterling. We know you are selling stores to raise funds. What you do with the money is entirely your private affair.'

Richard was not only astounded by the offer, but could see a potential problem with it. 'The offer is certainly tempting, Andrei. You are correct in surmising that we are in sore need of cash, especially now the rouble is no longer accepted.'

'But I have not finished yet, Richard. We know you are planning to send your men home soon. Your submarines will then be of no use to you. We assume you plan to scuttle them to avoid them falling into the hands of the Germans should they reach this far up the coast.'

Richard was impressed with the shrewd reasoning, but said nothing and kept his face neutral.

'Sell us the submarines and we will offer you £5,000,000 sterling. You could report the submarines as scuttled and become a very rich man.'

Richards was completely staggered by the scale of the offer. Even by his family's standards, this sum of money was a fantastic sum, but he made up his mind very quickly. Kapitsa had pushed his negotiation too far and offended Richard's moral values. No longer was he tempted to assist the White Russian cause in this way. His reply was full of indignation.

'I am sorry, Andrei, but I must decline your offer. For now, I still hope to recommence submarine operations in the spring and so my submarines are not for sale. As for the offer to keep the Russian sailors on board their ships, I can see the advantages, but must again decline my co-operation. Without a doubt it would damage my relations with the Centrobalt and I need their guarantee of safe passage for my men to Murmansk. My men, I can assure you, are very eager to go home.'

Richard didn't wait for the dessert course and returned by car to the naval base. He wondered if he would regret turning down the best offer of his life.

CHAPTER 37
January 1918

On the morning of the fourth, Richard passed through the three ranks of his men, packed and ready to set off for the long journey home. At their feet, each had laid his kitbag and an odd variety of parcels and souvenirs of their time in Russia. Several of the men had not neglected to rescue the cages of white mice from their submarines, the rodents that gave warning of carbon monoxide warning when at sea. Another held a young black dog on a lead and Dawes cradled Terry, the cat from *E19*. Richard had to work hard to stifle a tear as he shook each of the 150 men by the hand with pride. The men had organised a special concert party to celebrate the turn of the year and, for once, had been able to take their fill of food and alcohol. Then they had spent three days cleaning, painting and polishing their submarines, possibly for the last time. Spotless deck cloths had been laid out and the brass work gleamed brightly. The contrast between the state of the Royal Navy boats and its sailors' own appearance now on parade with that of the Baltic Fleet could not have been greater. Richard thought his men the very best on Earth.

To one side stood the care and maintenance party of the twenty-five men who had volunteered to remain behind. At their head stood Steele, Engineer Lieutenant Simpson, Assistant Paymaster Baker and *E19*'s coxswain, Petty Officer Connolly.

Finally, his farewells complete, Richard stood on a crate to address his men for the final time.

'Gentlemen, together we have been through a great adventure in an alien land. It has not been without glory, nor danger and disappointment, but you can all be proud of the manner in which you have conducted yourselves. Many of you, I trust, will one day have grandchildren and, when they ask what you did in the war, you will be able to relate your experiences with all manner of pride. Some of you I have known for over a year and others just a few months, but one thing you all have in common is that I feel immensely privileged and proud of you. My only regret is that I cannot return home with you.'

The last sentence was greeted with a murmur of surprise, but Richard quelled the interruption by raising his hand.

'Yesterday, I received a signal appointing me as the naval attaché in Petrograd. Of course, like you, I am anxious to return home, but I am determined to see this thing through. In any case, I hope to see most of you back here in the spring. Who knows, by then the Americans might have arrived in Europe. But before you begin your long journey home, I wish to read you one last prayer.'

Connolly brought the parade to attention and ordered the men to remove their caps before ordering 'Stand Easy'.

'*O God, our heavenly Father, whose glory fills the whole creation, and whose presence we find wherever we go: preserve those who travel; surround them with your loving care; protect them from every danger; and bring them in safety to their journey's end; through Jesus Christ our Lord. Amen.*

'Farewell, gentlemen, and God Speed.'

Once the coxswain had ordered the men to replace their caps, Fenner piped up, 'Three cheers for the captain. Hip hip, Hurrah. Hip hip, Hurrah. Hip hip, Hurrah.'

This time, as the men cheered, Richard could not prevent tears of pride and sadness welling in his eyes. As he watched the men march off the jetty towards the railway station, it suddenly struck him that the feeling he had for his men was more than pride. It was love. He had always felt apart from his men and not just because as their commanding officer he had to maintain his distance. They were of a different class. The men were often coarse; swearing, drinking like fish at times and happy to break wind in public. But they had self-respect, a pride in their work and a willingness to accept discipline. They bore the frequent danger and privations with a quiet dignity and, often as not, with great humour. Above all, they looked out for each other. They weren't just a close-knit team. They were a family and he desperately wanted to be part of that family. Why had it taken him so long to realise it? The tears rolled freely down his cheeks now and he struggled to avoid weeping in front of the maintenance party.

Somebody struck up a tune on a mandolin to accompany the sound of 150 pairs of naval boots marching in step. Instantly, Richard thought himself the loneliest man on Earth. Just then, Terry freed himself from Dawes's clutches and ran back to Richard. Dawes made to retrieve the cat, but Evans restrained him. Richard looked down at the little cat rubbing himself around his ankles and could not resist picking him up. As Richard tickled his ears, Terry responded by licking Richard's hands. Something loves me, after all, he thought and he decided he would be grateful of the little cat's company in the coming months.

*****

With the departure of the majority of the flotilla to Murmansk and Richard to Petrograd, it was Steele's turn to feel lonely. His party now formed only a small percentage of the ship's company of the *Pamyat Azova* and, as a consequence, the Russians now demanded a share of the Royal Navy victuals and stores. Time and again, Steele argued with the Russians that the stores were being held back for when the men from the flotilla returned in the spring, but the situation was becoming menacing. He began to appreciate the tiresome diplomatic load that Richard had quietly borne. Now, faced with a threat of dire consequences were he to fail to hand over the key to the stores immediately, he held a council-of-war with his engineer, paymaster and coxswain.

'Could we not negotiate with the Ruskies, sir?' Connolly asked. 'After all, if and when the rest of the flotilla return, we could always requisition new victuals, sir.'

'I don't agree, sir,' Baker chipped in with his powerful, Canadian drawl. 'I agree, we're well set up at last, but I'm going to put some of the clothing and tobacco to another use.'

'And what might that be then, Kenneth? I suppose we might have to spare a few of the slops to cover your massive frame, but you don't smoke.'

'That's not what I meant and you darned well know it, sir. I've no funds left to pay the ship's company. Now the Finnish Reds have taken control of the city, I can't cash any more Navy Bills. I figure I'll have to go back to the black market with some of the surplus clothing and tobacco.'

'Ye gods, old chap. That would be highly illegal.'

'Mebbe, but I've done it before… with the CO's permission, of course.'

'Zooks, I had no idea our dibs were so out of tune. I suppose if such *skilamalink* activities were fine for the boss, then they'll do for me, but it's not going to help us resist the Russians' threats.

They seem of a mind to slit our gizzards any night soon. What say you, Cecil?'

'I'd be fine with trading the slops and tobacco for cash, but I'd not give them away,' Simpson replied. 'If the Russians had a whiff of what we have, they'd demand the lot. I'd certainly not let them lay their filthy paws on my engineering spares either, but an idea has occurred to me.'

'Let's hear it then,' Steele asked. 'All ideas gratefully received.'

'Are you up for a game of bluff, Algie?' Simpson responded.

'Canasta, whist and cricket are more my line, but I'll give anything a go, old chap.'

'Supposing we wired up the store room handle to a battery? Any attempt at petty larceny might prove extremely… *shocking*.'

'I like that idea, sir. I'd love the bastards to just try, sir… and fry, too,' Connolly said.

'But forgive me, Cecil. That might just antagonise the Ruskies more. I don't know about you chaps, but I have to consider a generations-old duty to provide an heir.'

'Don't worry, Algie. We'll try to ensure the future of the aristocracy. As I said, a little bluff will be required. My idea is to make a big fuss about taking timers, fuses and explosives on board the boats. We pretend to booby trap the torpedoes and let on to our *noble* allies that unless somebody goes on board from time to time to reset the charges, the mouldies will go off and take their damned depot ship with them.'

The idea was met with laughter and a murmur of approval from Connolly and Baker.

'That's jokes!' Baker boomed in his Canadian slang. 'That's bound to cause a real kerfuffle, eh?'

'Very well. Coxswain, I'll leave you to organise a working detail to set the charges. Once it's done, I'll inform the Committee.' Steele closed the meeting.

*****

As January drew to a close, Richard was surprised to discover Lockhart back in Petrograd as Lloyd George's envoy to the Bolsheviks.

'So here we both are, Miller. Our fortunes have changed since our last meeting, although there seems to be no evidence of fortune in your choice of apartment.' Lockhart didn't hide his look of disdain for Richard's accommodation, but smiled at the sight of the cat asleep by the stove.

'The cost of living has risen substantially in your absence, Lockhart. Rent's not the problem, but the cost of heating eats up almost my entire naval salary.'

'That is hard cheese, dear fellow. In the absence of the ambassador, I might be able to arrange - should you wish – perhaps, to put you on a more equal footing with the Diplomatic Service under the circumstances.'

'Thank you, Lockhart, but I'll manage. So, to what do I owe the pleasure of your company?'

'I thought you'd be interested to know that I called on Cumming in London. He's suggested a few ways you might help him.'

'But as you must know already, Lockhart, I don't work for Cumming's outfit. I report to our Director of Naval Intelligence, Admiral Hall, and he's been quite explicit in the work he expects me to do. It largely concerns itself with persuading the Russians to stay in the war in any way possible, at least until the Americans can send troops to Europe to reinforce the Western Front.'

'I think I might be able to persuade you to take on a broader role, Miller… if you'll hear me out.'

'Very well, I've nothing else pressing. I'm listening.'

'My sources tell me the peace negotiations aren't going too well in Brest Litovsk at present. Lenin feels Kűhlmann's demands are too monstrous, but he knows he'll have to give way eventually. He's sent Trotsky to delay things a little.'

Richard wondered who these sources were and how Lockhart came by them.

'The point is, you might find it profitable to engage in a little propaganda for now, but your role in seeking to persuade the Bolsheviks to remain in the war will soon be over. London's increasingly concerned that this revolutionary movement could spread like a cancer and wants it cut out. For that we will need more intelligence of the movement.'

'Given that what you say is likely to be true, Lockhart, I'm hardly equipped to become a secret agent or spy. I'm a submariner, used to working with a tight-knit team, not a loner. I wouldn't know where to start.'

'I understand, dear fellow, and that's just why I've come up with some help, although I'd say you've not made a bad stab at it already. But Cumming's engaged a mining engineer with good contacts in the Black Sea area, Ernest Boyce, to work for him. He's made him a reserve commander. Furthermore, Cumming's sending over two of his top agents to form a network of informants on Bolshevik activity. One of them is Russian-born, so will have no difficulty with the language. The other is a gifted linguist with good German, but no Russian. 'C' wants him to lie low for a while until he's picked up the language and thought you might suggest a good Russian tutor.'

'Why would Cumming ask *me* for a recommendation. Surely, you're far better qualified to do that, Lockhart.'

'Because I've saved the best news for last. I told you Cumming was sending two of his top agents. The first agent's a chap who now calls himself Reilly. Apparently, he's done some good work in Germany and latterly the US. I'll introduce him to you in due course. The second, however, is a result of my recommendation and request. It's none other than your brother, Peter! Now might you help?'

CHAPTER 38
March 1918

Felix Dzerzhinsky had henchmen to interrogate prisoners, but this one was of special interest to him. He looked on the figure before him without pity. That figure was only recognisable as a human being by his outline. His features were barely visible through the blood, bruising and swellings that covered his naked flesh. Different elements of the *All-Russian Extraordinary Commission for the Suppression of the Counter-Revolution and Speculation*, of which Dzerzhinsky had been personally appointed the head by Lenin the year before, were devising their own methods of interrogation, but Dzerzhinsky had learned from his years in Tsarist prisons that simplicity was often the best measure in most cases. A severe beating was usually effective, but what was left of this prisoner certainly had courage.

Dzerzhinsky stroked his beard carefully. In this case one of the more elaborate methods of interrogation was required. The prisoner knew he would die, but it had to be impressed upon him that his death could take many forms. It was minus four degrees outside Number Two Gorokhovaya Street, too warm for the favourite of his more drastic methods. The Russian title of Dzerzhinsky's organisation had been shortened to the simple *Cheka* and he had encouraged his men to be utterly ruthless in their counter-revolutionary methods such that the word '*Cheka*' was spoken in hushed tones and with fear. Had it been colder, he would have ordered his prisoner to be doused with water from a fire hose and left to freeze naked on the street as an example to other counter-revolutionaries. Further east of Petrograd, the Cheka was forming an impressive collection of ice statues. Dzerzhinsky decided to give the sailor, until recently a member of the Centrobalt, one last chance. He motioned to his henchmen to lift the prisoner's head.

'Comrade, be in no doubt you will pay for your treachery with your life. But you have a choice over the manner of your death. Give me the name of your contact and I will have a bullet put through the back of your head. Otherwise, I have something far more painful, messy and slower in mind for you.'

What was left of the man merely moved his eyes from side to side and returned Dzerzhinsky's look with a mixture of malevolence and defiance.

'You're a fool,' Dzerzhinsky replied and turned to one of the guards to his side. 'The Chinese method then.'

It was extremely cold in the basement of the *Cheka* headquarters, but the head of the Russian secret police knew it would warm up very soon. He stood to one side as his men brought in a brazier, lit it and placed it before the sailor, his arms now bound to the meat hook hanging from the ceiling above him. Two of the guards then positioned two lengths of metal pipe over the brazier and kept them in place with blacksmith's tongs whilst another held the prisoner's stomach against one end of each pipe. Dzerzhinsky was pleased to see the look of puzzlement and fear on the prisoner's face. He despised informants.

It took several minutes for the metal tubing to heat up, but then it was time for the guard in charge of the interrogation to introduce his *pièce de résistance*, a cage of rats. The prisoner still looked puzzled, but Dzerzhinsky knew that look would soon change to one of terror. The guard donned a heavy gauntlet and delved into the cage to select a rat from within. Expertly, he then squeezed the rat down one end of a tube and whilst he fetched another, a colleague sealed up the end with wire netting. As the second rat was loaded into the second tube, the prisoner suddenly began to struggle to separate himself from the other end of the metal tubes. The tubes were now becoming too hot for the rats and there was only one exit for them. They would have to chew their way out.

The former sailor screamed in terror and pain as the rats began gnawing at his stomach, but the guards were remorseless in keeping his stomach tight up against the open end of the pipe. Dzerzhinsky knew it would not take long and sure enough, barely three minutes had passed before the prisoner indicated he was willing to talk. However, Dzerzhinsky let the man suffer further until he was sure he had the name correctly. It was not somebody currently known to the *Cheka*, but he didn't doubt the veracity of the information. Satisfied, he drew his own pistol and positioned himself behind the unfortunate sailor, now writhing in agony. Without hesitation, he squeezed the trigger of his pistol and ended the prisoner's suffering. As the corpse flexed and relaxed, it gave the two rats, whose heads were already inside the stomach, the chance to escape. Dzerzhinsky looked at the mess they had created with disgust. The only things he hated more than informants were rats.

*****

Richard knelt in front of a chair of his apartment on which lay his precious Bible. It was a full three months since he had last attended church and he wondered if that was why the Lord appeared to have forsaken him. In that time he had received no mail from home and he missed the fraternity of his flotilla. He had once paid a visit to Reval to try to persuade Rachel and Princess Anna to leave before the city was overrun by the Germans, but both had insisted on staying put. He had enjoyed seeing Rachel again and praying with her, but his visit to Anna had sorely tested his marital vows. Desperate for the tenderness of a woman's company, he had almost succumbed to the temptation of her warm embraces and invitation to comfort her for the loss of her husband after a revolutionary kangaroo court martial. At least he had the pleasure of receiving correspondence from Reval and Rachel had informed him that she now had a new student of the Russian language. Richard alone knew this to be his brother, Peter, and would dearly have loved to pay another visit to Reval to see him for some contact from home, but recent events demanded his attention in Helsingfors.

Although the ice in the Baltic was beginning to thaw, there was no prospect of the submariners returning to Russia. Earlier in the month, the Germans and Russians had concluded their peace treaty and with it came disquieting news. As a term of the agreement, the Germans had demanded the Royal Navy's six submarines be handed over to the advancing German forces and a division of those forces was rapidly approaching Hango. Richard was determined his precious boats would never fall into German hands.

He selected Psalm 143 as his choice for the day as it seemed to suit his mood. He read it aloud.

'Hear my prayer, O Lord, give ear to my supplications: in thy faithfulness answer me, and in thy righteousness... For the enemy hath persecuted my soul; he hath smitten my life down to the

ground; he hath made me to dwell in darkness, as those that have been long dead. Therefore, is my spirit overwhelmed within me; my heart within me is desolate. I remember the days of old...

'Deliver me, O Lord, from mine enemies: I flee unto thee to hide me... And of thy mercy cut off mine enemies, and destroy all them that afflict my soul: for I am thy servant.'

Finally, he offered a prayer to his God.

'Everlasting and Eternal Father, I need You every day, every hour, every minute. Pour out Your unconditional love upon my life. I ask that You bless and protect me today as I go out into this harsh and cruel world.'

Back on his feet, he cast a final look about his apartment and wondered if he would live to see Petrograd again. With no regrets over his latest decision, he picked up his valise, tucked the cat into his greatcoat and went down below to meet the driver taking him to the railway station to catch the train for Helsingfors.

CHAPTER 39
April 1918

'Is everything ready, Algie?'

'Just as you ordered, sir. We couldn't load all the stores onto the torpedo barge - you know the bigger stuff, such as the spare armatures and propellers - so I've arranged a detail with sledgehammers and explosives to deal with them.'

'What about the boats?' Richard felt more cheerful than he had in weeks to be back in Helsingfors amongst men he could trust. He had quickly learned that in the intelligence world, men willing to betray their country or principles for money could not be trusted.

'We'll use charges comprising two Mark Eight warheads with a twenty-pound gun cotton charge as a primer. I've instructed the men to place three in each boat; one forward, another aft and one amidships. They'll be fired electrically, sir, using a timing device.'

'A timing device? What sort of timing device, Algie?'

'You'll like it, sir. Leading Seaman Stevens came up with the idea. We'll use good, old-fashioned alarm clocks. When the alarm strikes the bell, the firing circuit will be completed and boom! It'll be a bally show Guy Fawkes might have envied.'

'Ingenious, Algie. Well done.' Richard found it refreshing to return to a world of such efficiency. 'And where do you plan on sinking the boats?'

'Here, sir.' Steele pointed to a spot on the chart one and half miles south of Grohara Light. 'It's fifteen fathoms deep there, sir. And one other thing, sir. I forgot to mention the spare mouldies in the Russian submarine salvage ship. There are forty stowed there. We'll remove the swirlers and sinking gear of each torpedo, blow them through with acid and let the stokers smash them up with sledge hammers. Does everything meet with your approval, sir?'

'You seem to have thought of everything, but I might amend the plan just slightly.'

'Certainly, sir. What have I missed?'

'Nothing of the sort, Algie. I'd like you to spare your boat from destruction for now, just in case we have any problems with the Russians.'

'It would be a pleasure, sir.' Steele brightened visibly.

'I thought it might, but she'll have to follow the way of the rest eventually, dear friend. Right, let's go and see the dockyard captain to organise an icebreaker and tug.'

*****

'I am sorry, comrade, but I cannot spare you either an icebreaker nor a tug.' Richard thought the Russian harbour master a weasel of a fellow with his shifty eyes and officious manner. Such obduracy had been commonplace for the past year, but Richard knew better than to argue.

'Very well, Captain. I understand fully your difficulties.' Richard deliberately looked over at the two tugs lying idle alongside the equally unemployed icebreaker. 'However, I have my own difficulties and will not let my submarines fall into the hands of the Germans. It's a pity your house will have to be sacrificed in my cause.'

'My house? What has that to do with it?' the harbour master enquired nervously and excitedly.

'Surely, that's obvious. Now I'll have to blow up the submarines where they lie. Naturally, when the torpedoes on the barge explode, there'll be some unfortunate damage to your dockyard and the ships nearby. I fear your house will be mere collateral damage. Thank you for your time… and personal sacrifice for the Motherland.' Richard replaced the *ushanka* on his head and stepped through the door Steele had opened for him.

'Wait,' the Russian called after him with alarm. 'Perhaps, tomorrow, I can arrange an icebreaking tug.'

Richard held back and turned around to the harbour master. 'I fear that will be too late. Already, the Germans are a bare hundred kilometres from here. I cannot afford so long a delay. I'm sorry.'

'No wait! I have an idea, comrade. Give me half an hour. Please!'

'That will do nicely, Captain.'

*****

That afternoon, Richard and Steele proceeded to sea with a convoy of the three *E*-boats towed astern of an icebreaking tug. Richard took command again of *E19* for the last time with Steele in *E1*. Two Russian officers took command of the other boat.

With great sadness, from the safety of the icebreaker, both the British officers watched the destruction of the first two submarines. Richard regretted that his force had not inflicted as much material damage on the Germans as he had hoped, but they had at least been a thorn in the side of the enemy. He thought it ironic that he had turned down an offer of five million pounds for these submarines and yet the parsimonious government paid him little enough from his naval salary to cover his living costs in Petrograd. Fortunately, he had his private income.

'Did you know, Algie, that the Germans referred to us as "the English pests" and were forced to keep a special force at sea to counter us?'

'No, sir, but I imagine we were somewhat execrated by the High Command.'

'Indeed, Admiral Altfata, one of the Russians negotiating the Brest Litovsk peace accord, reported the Germans as saying they considered the sinking of a single British submarine as worthy of that of a Russian armoured cruiser.'

'It's a deuced shame to see the boats go this way, sir. I wonder how the chaps are getting on back home. Hang on, why's *E8*'s charge not detonated?'

'You did set it to Russian time and not London time, I presume?'

'Tchah. I'd better go and investigate.'

'No, Algie. You already have a bar to your DSC. Send one of the torpedomen.'

Whilst the torpedoman was rowed across to *E8*, Richard broke some sad news to Steele.

'I'm afraid Fenner's dead, Algie. I had a telegram at the embassy. Went a similar way to Goodhart.'

'What? Not in one of those bally steam kettles?'

'I regret it was so, but again not in his own submarine. I gather it's being called the Battle of May Island. Fenner sailed with an oppo in *K4* as part of two flotillas of *K*-boats departing Rosyth in company with the Grand Fleet. I gather it was bad weather and one of the boats had a steering failure. The result was poor *K4* was rammed and sunk with all hands. Another *K*-boat was sunk, too, and two severely damaged. Not the submarine service's finest hour.'

'They're a bally menace. Steam boats will never catch on and I just hope I'm not sent to one after this show.'

'It seems such a waste, Algie. I only lost one CO in action, Robert Halahan in *E18*, but both Francis Goodhart and Stan Fenner were lost at home in accidents.'

The torpedoman returned to the icebreaker and reported a defective alarm clock was responsible for the failure to detonate the charges. Richard noted it was Leading Seaman Stevens from Steele's submarine. It had been a brave act to step inside a potential time bomb and Richard made a mental note to mention it to Commodore Hall.

'That's Russian engineering for you, sir,' Steele remarked as they counted down the time to the next attempt at detonation, but yet again, there was no explosion.

'At this rate, you'll have to come out and put a mouldie into her, Algie. She doesn't want to die. Can't blame her after all she's been through, though, can we?'

Steele was on the point of sending Stevens across once more with a new alarm clock when the master of the icebreaker approached Richard.

'It's going to be dark soon, comrade. I cannot risk remaining out here. We must return to harbour.'

'But, skipper, I only need another half an hour and the job will be done,' Richard remonstrated, but the skipper would not be moved. Richard turned to Steele.

'Very well, Algie. We'll spare her another night. Leave her here and we'll try again in the morning, but early mind. We don't have much time.'

'Leave it to me, sir,' Steele replied.

*****

Soon after first light, the icebreaker towed *C26, C35* and the torpedo barge out to the stubborn *E8*. *C26* was secured alongside *E8* and the two boats blown up together. *C35* was tied alongside the barge, but again the charges failed to detonate and the master of the icebreaker insisted on returning to harbour. Richard received the news gravely as the Germans were now only thirty miles distant.

'Algie, we can't afford another clock failure tomorrow. The ice will be less thick now so you'll have to take a risk that the icebreaker can evade the area without difficulty. Take *C27* out with you tomorrow and use Bickford charges on the fifteen-minute fuse to sink the barge and *C35*. If that fails, sink her with a torpedo and scuttle your boat. I'll come with you in *C27* to lend a hand where necessary.'

Fortunately, since the Germans were now only twenty miles outside Helsingfors, the last two submarines and the barge were sunk without mishap this time. By the time the care and maintenance party boarded the train to Petrograd that evening to begin their long journey home, the Germans were only five miles away. As in January, Richard had been there to say farewell to his men. This time Leading Seaman Stevens had firm hold of *E19*'s former mascot.

'I thought you were coming with us as far as Petrograd, sir.' Steele was puzzled by the change of plan. 'There's nothing else for us left to do here now, sir.'

'I've changed my mind, Algie. You recall there are three British-registered merchantmen in the harbour and I would be grieved for them to fall to the Hun.' The fact was true and nor was he in a rush to return to Petrograd. He had had word that he was coming under suspicion from the *Cheka* for his anti-revolutionary activities and it would be dangerous for him to return to Petrograd.

'Then you'll need us to help, sir.'

'No, Algie. As you said. You're all skilled men and England needs you to carry on the fight back home.'

'Well, at the very least, sir, let me stay. I can help you with the job and follow on later.'

For a moment, Richard was tempted to agree to Steele's offer. He could see that he might have need of the former MCC cricketer's swimming prowess, but he resisted the temptation.

'No, Algie, you need to take command of your men. It won't be an easy journey to Murmansk and the men will look to you for firm leadership. Besides, I've had a telegram to say that you are urgently required for another command. I have no other information, so farewell and good luck, dear friend.' Richard shook

Steele's hand and was reluctant to let it go. Parting from Steele would be like losing a part of him and again he was tempted to take up his offer to stay and help sink the merchant ships, but then he recalled the telegram he had lately received. The Admiralty wanted Steele back in Britain with utmost despatch. At least Steele had the chance to progress the fight against the Germans. Steele in turn had tears in his eyes as he stood to attention and saluted smartly.

'Good bye, sir, and good luck.'

As the crowded train pulled out of the station, Richard shuddered. Something told him he would never see his friend again, but then, he had had the same feeling when saying farewell to Lizzy and yet she had returned to England safely.

CHAPTER 40

Captain Pettifer, the master of the SS *Cameron*, one of the three British-registered ships stranded in Helsingfors, had no objection to the destruction of his ship. Richard had discussed the contingency with him weeks beforehand and he and his chief engineer, the last of the officers, had opted to leave with the submariners. The problem was that Richard could obtain no support from the largely Russian seamen on board either of the three ships to take them to sea. Already, the Germans had circulated leaflets warning dire reprisals for any person involved with the sabotage of the ships and offering handsome rewards for their handover. Fortunately, Richard managed to find five former Russian army officers willing to assist him with the destruction, although none of them knew their bow from their stern.

Together, they marched on the first ship on their list, the *Oberon*. They were met by a force of armed guards who prevented them from boarding.

'Why not?' Richard protested. 'I have the necessary authorisation.' He was in plain clothes, but proffered a hand-written document he had written earlier in Russian and had signed by Pettifer. In actual fact, Pettifer had no responsibility for the *Oberon* or the other ship the *Elizabeth*, but Richard gambled that if the Russian guards could read, they would still be unaware of the fact. Moreover, he had persuaded the Commissar in charge of the port of the justification of his actions and the Commissar had helpfully stamped the document with an impressive looking seal.

The leader of the guard examined the document carefully, but before he could make a decision either way, Richard snatched it back and pushed past the guard, followed by the army officers. He promptly headed for the quarterdeck and hauled down its Russian flag and replaced it with a union jack handkerchief one of the submariners had presented him the day before. The act caused great mirth amongst the Russian guards, but they still seemed reluctant to allow Richard and his men to take the ship to sea.

'Comrades, this is a British-registered ship, once again flying the British flag in a neutral port. As such, I can no longer permit armed foreigners onboard. Should you wish to continue to guard the ship, please do so from the jetty.' Richard's words seemed to have the desired effect and the Russians shook hands with him warmly before heading over the gangway. Richard lost no time in taking two of the army officers down to the boiler room to begin preparations for sea.

A couple of hours later, there was sufficient steam to set sail. Together with the other three Russians, Richard cast off and headed out to sea. Once in open waters, and after rescuing the union jack handkerchief, he scuttled the *Oberon* before he with his crew rowed back to the jetty in the ship's jolly boat.

The following day was a little more problematic. The *Cameron* was berthed inboard of the *Elizabeth* and again Richard was challenged by an armed guard. Despite his protestations, the NCO in charge was adamant that the *Cameron* would not be sunk.

'But on what grounds?' Richard asked exasperatedly. 'My documents are in order and this is a British ship in a neutral port.'

'Perhaps, comrade, but the cargo is Russian.' Richard checked the manifest and immediately saw the problem. The ship was loaded with torpedoes sent from Britain in support of the Russian war effort. He thought it unlikely that following the Treaty of Brest-Litovsk, this would be of any great loss to the Russians. However, lower down the manifest, he saw the crux of the problem. The ship carried a cargo of clothing and Richard knew from his previous black-market activities the value of trousers.

'Yes, comrade, I now see the problem. Let me arrange with the port commissar to unload the cargo from this ship. In the meantime, I can see no reason why you should object to me taking the *Elizabeth* to sea.' Richard despatched one of the army officers to the port office to make the necessary arrangements, but he wasn't surprised that the Russian NCO seemed unmoved.

'Perhaps whilst we wait, comrade, we might make a deal. You allow me to take the other ship to sea and I will give you and each of your men a pair of trousers.'

Richard's offer broke the impasse and over the next thirty minutes he issued each of the guards with a pair of trousers according to their size. Soon, he was underway in the *Elizabeth*, but the tide had brought in large floes of ice and, consequently, he had to proceed slowly with caution. Just as the ship approached Grohara Light, they were overtaken by a tug. The tug came alongside and

Richard could see twenty armed men on board. Their leader hailed Richard.

'Comrade Captain, I insist you allow my men to take this ship back into harbour.'

'That will not be possible, comrade. This is a British ship and I intend to sink her as soon as I reach open water.'

'No, comrade Captain. Stand by to receive my men.'

'Stop!' Richard bellowed. Still in plain clothes, he pulled his Order of Saint George from his pocket and pinned it to the lapel of his suit before pulling out a tiny pistol from the other pocket. 'I cannot allow you or your men to board this ship. This is a British ship and any firing on it or boarding by force will be an act of piracy. Moreover, I will shoot the first men to step on board.'

'Please, comrade. Do not shoot. I promise we will stay off your ship, but you must let us tow you back into Helsingfors.'

'No,' responded Richard forcefully, despite realising the weakness of a single small-calibre pistol against such a large body of armed men. 'I have authorisation for my actions both from the ship's master as the representative of the owners and from the port commissar. Do you have any papers? I said, do you have any papers?'

'No, comrade, but that is not the point…'

'It is exactly the point. Without papers you are no more than pirates. Now let me be about my business.'

The leader of the armed men was quiet for several minutes whilst he consulted the master of the tug and his men. Finally, he hailed Richard again.

'Comrade, you are in no position to argue. Stand by to accept our tow. Should you resist, I will order my men to shoot.' The armed men raised their rifles in response.

Richard assumed he was beaten, but had one last ploy. 'Hold your fire, comrades. I have already rigged my explosive charges to scuttle this ship. Shoot me or my men and the charges will explode whilst the ship is still in harbour. Do you really want the ship to sink in the narrow channel, shutting in all the other ships in port?' Richard could see the shock on the face of his interlocutor as the words sank in. It was, indeed, true that the charges had been set, but Richard had still to set the fuses. However, Richard was not keen on sacrificing himself or his men when there was still one more ship to scuttle. He decided to offer a compromise.

'Comrade, I have fought side by side with many brave Russian sailors.' He pointed to the cross on his lapel. 'We are not enemies, but my country is still at war with Germany. Return to port and if you can bring back papers cancelling those I already hold, I will return to Helsingfors with you. I will wait ninety minutes for your return or else I will continue with my duty.'

For almost a minute, a stand-off ensued with the Russians' rifles levelled at Richard. He silently prayed to God in case these were to be his last moments on Earth. Then the leader of the Russian armed men issued a crisp order and the rifles were lowered. Without a further word to Richard, he turned and ordered the tug master to return to port. Two hours later, Richard scuttled the *Elizabeth*.

On his return to the jetty, he discovered that only a few of the torpedoes had been unloaded, but the entire cargo of clothing had been looted. There was no sign of any guard and this time he was free to take the third ship to sea unmolested. That evening, the three ships sunk and exhausted by the effort, he planned to spend one last night in Helsingfors before returning to the embassy, but met one of his informants.

'Captain, I beg you not to stay in the city another hour. Can you not hear the German guns?' Richard could, indeed, hear the guns.

'I hear them, Tomac, but surely one more night in Helsingfors will not present a problem. I've had a long day and need a bath and a bed for the night.'

'No, Captain. There isn't time. If you are not on the next train out of the city, you will be trapped here. The Germans are barely five miles away… and there is more. The Germans know of the sinking of the submarines and there is a price on your head!'

Reluctantly, Richard boarded the train and squeezed himself into a compartment full of Russian sailors for the journey back to Petrograd.

*****

'You're absolutely sure of this information, Malenkov?' Dzerzhinsky questioned the man before him. He didn't particularly like the man's morals or his looks, but he had to admit that Malenkov was a good *agent provocateur*. 'It's important that you be sure of your facts.'

'Yes, comrade. I would stake my life on the information,' Malenkov replied. Dressed in an ill-fitting uniform of the Russian Navy, he was short and rotund and a bead of sweat was slowly trickling down from his fat head with thinning hair towards his round spectacles. He wore the red armband of membership of the Centrobalt. Apart from the long nose, he reminded Dzerzhinsky of a toad.

'Believe me, Malenkov. You are, indeed, staking your life on it.' Dzerzhinsky took pleasure in seeing the man blanche. 'Tell me again how you came by this information.'

'I've made it my business to demonstrate my loyalty to the revolution, comrade. As a senior member of the Committee, I have been ruthless in exposing anti-revolutionary fervour. So, when I heard rumours of disaffection amongst our Estonian and Latvian comrades, I naturally investigated.' Dzerzhinsky noted that Malenkov seemed more at ease now.

'Yes, comrade, that's all in your report. I want to know how you came by these leaflets.' Dzerzhinsky picked up a sheaf of dirty and crumpled, poorly printed papers.

'I carefully selected several trusted men in Kronstadt to express disaffection with the Bolshevik cause. In time, they gained the confidence of other sailors of the Baltic Fleet sympathetic to their views. It was then that they learned of a campaign to persuade their Estonian and Latvian comrades to resist any attempts to hand over the Baltic Fleet to the Germans, even to the extent of sinking their own ships. Those papers are evidence of the plot, comrade.'

'So I see, Malenkov. However, I suspect the rumours of German confiscations of land and property, and even the executions in their newly acquired lands may well be true. It's after all, what I would do. I'm more interested in who is behind the propaganda campaign. You believe it to be a British officer? But why?'

'I have no definite proof, comrade, but I believe the man behind the campaign is a Captain Miller of the British Navy. He was in command of the British submarine flotilla until the cowards sank their own submarines and escaped back to England. For some time, I suspected members of my own committee were leaking information to him.'

'The information is of no use to me without proof, Malenkov. Relations with the British are delicate enough as they are at present without me accusing one of their officers of interfering with the revolution. Where is this officer now?'

'I don't know, comrade. I thought he had returned to England with his men, but the dockyard captain in Helsingfors has reported that it was Captain Miller who was behind the sinking of the three English ships there. I can only assume he is in Petrograd, comrade.'

'Very well, comrade Malenkov. The information you have provided will be used to purge the Kronstadt garrison of its anti-revolutionaries, but I cannot act against this Captain Miller until I have more proof of his anti-Soviet activities. But I will order my men to establish his whereabouts. Contact me immediately if he is seen again in Helsingfors or even in Kronstadt. You may go.'

As Malenkov left the room, Dzerzhinsky noted the look of disappointment in Malenkov's face when informed that he needed proof before acting against the British officer. However, he reflected that the information was more useful than he had let on to Malenkov. Interrogation of several now dead anti-revolutionaries had revealed proof that the British were running some form of anti-revolutionary campaign against the current regime, but the *Cheka* had yet to make any connection to the British Embassy. This Captain Miller would need to be found, then watched most carefully and, when the time came, Miller would be exterminated without mercy.

ACKNOWLEDGEMENTS

Initially, I struggled to maintain my flow in writing this book. My mother, Moira, was terminally ill and I was travelling to London every two weeks to see her. Sadly, but mercifully, she died and that, too, interrupted my writing process. I wish to acknowledge her indomitable efforts in my education, without which I would never have been able to follow the career path I did and write my novels. My parents were not well off and, consequently, my mother sometimes took on two part-time jobs to help pay for my school fees and uniforms. Regrettably, she was too ill to read my second novel, but I know she was very proud of my first.

Thank you, too, to a fellow student at the Royal Naval Staff College, Alan Cartwright, who offered me some useful engineering advice on certain aspects of this book. Although overdue, I must thank Rear Admiral Iain Henderson, a former Flag Officer Naval Aviation, for his kind public praise for my previous novel, *The Wings of the Wind*, and my belated thanks, too, to my fellow submariner, John Drummond, for designing the cover art for the paperback version of that book.

Finally, once again, I owe a huge debt of thanks to all those who have been kind enough to leave reviews on-line for my earlier books and to send me feedback by email, Facebook or Twitter. I have paid attention to the feedback and some has influenced how I wrote this latest work. The reviews are the oxygen of publicity to feed the visibility of authors. All too often after finishing a book, it is too easy to forget about it. Please do take the time to keep the reviews coming. Thank you to everyone above.

AUTHOR'S NOTE

In some ways this book was very easy to write as it is based fairly faithfully on actual history. It was inspired by a fantastic biography of Francis Cromer, *Honoured by Strangers*, although my hero has not met with Cromie's tragic end. I highly recommend the book and am indebted to its author, Roy Bainton. Naturally, I have made use of my authorial licence to change the narrative for my novel. Another book I recommend for those wanting to know more of the Royal Navy's forgotten submarine campaign in the Baltic flotilla is *Baltic Assignment* by Michael Wilson. Generally, the events I have described in my novel did take place, although as ever, I might have played around with dates, changed a few names of characters and ships or credited certain actions to different submarines and characters.

It was difficult to research women's working conditions in shipyards, but I did come across a few essays and letters on the subject on Tyneside. Emmeline Pankhurst did visit Russia as an envoy of Lloyd George, although she spent more time in Saint Petersburg than Moscow. The one glaring inaccuracy (that I know of), however, is that Lockhart was already back in Britain when the November Revolution occurred, before his return in January 1918 as Lloyd George's envoy to the Bolsheviks.

Richard Miller may be isolated in Russia, with the *Cheka* on his trail, but the war hasn't finished with him yet. He will return. However, I have taken a break from writing about WW1 and my next novel is about how courage and innovation saved Britain from defeat by German mines during WW2. Publication details will be released on my social media sites:

Website: www.shaunlewis-theauthor.com,
Facebook: shaunlewistheauthor
Twitter: @shaunlewis1805

Printed in Great Britain
by Amazon

58552578R00154